THE BLACK TRILLIUM
SIMON MCNEIL

Brain Lag

Ontario, Canada
http://www.brain-lag.com/

Brain Lag Publishing
Ontario, Canada
http://www.brain-lag.com/

Library and Archives Canada Cataloguing in Publication

McNeil, Simon, 1979-, author
    The black trillium / Simon McNeil.

Issued in print and electronic formats.
ISBN 978-1-928011-04-0 (pbk.).--ISBN 978-1-928011-05-7 (epub).--
ISBN 978-1-928011-06-4 (kindle)

        I. Title.

PS8625.N453B53 2015   C813'.6   C2015-901790-4
                                              C2015-901791-2

Acknowledgements

Writing a novel is unique in artistic pursuits in that there is no other type of art comparable in the time and hours of effort that goes into a novel in which only one person's name ultimately gets attached. But this is a bit of a convenient lie. The truth is that novels are not completed in a vacuum and many people are instrumental to the process.

Thank you to my wonderful wife Yan. Without your support I couldn't have done this. Thank you also to my daughter Hannah. You are the best distraction an author could ask for. Thank you to Catherine Fitzsimmons for taking a risk on a bizarre concept from an unknown author. Thank you to David Blackwood, Charlene Challenger, Patrick Fleming, Sarah Simon and Sara Knauss for helping me to develop my craft. Thank you to Hugh Montgomery for a timely kick in the pants, to Julie Czerneda for teaching me that sometimes a middling short story can be the genesis of an excellent chapter one, and John Scalzi for exactly the right advice at precisely the right time. Thank you to Chris Dakins for always asking for the next page.

Thank you to my mother, Lorraine McNeil, who has always believed in me. And thank you to my father, Charles McNeil. This book wouldn't have happened if not for a conversation we had together in your back yard six years ago.

I love you Dad.

CHAPTER 1

Savannah

SOMETIMES, WHEN THE WALLS of the ancient city press around too much and I feel a yearning for the open spaces, I like to climb up to the highest tower I can find and just sit with my feet dangling over the edge, watching everything below me. The sky seems bluer than it does on the ground, almost as blue as it does in the lands of the red-brown dust that were my home.

I miss home but I can never go back. There is no home to go back to, not anymore. It's all dust, bones and broken dreams now. No crops grow in the lands of endless dust. The rivers are dry. All they produce is refugees and lots of refugees end up in Trana. I don't have to like it. I don't like it. The buildings make the places all too narrow.

When I tell people I hate the tall buildings they look at me strangely. They ask me, "Didn't I see you sitting on the edge of the 390 building just the other day?" I just smile and explain that it's OK being at the top of the buildings. I don't mind it when there is just the sky above and the streets below. I'm not afraid of high places even though I come from the flattest land. It is the narrow places I don't like, the tunnels and the streets.

It's better in the districts a bit farther out from the center. Kensington is nice, though too crowded, the same with Queeneast. I like Blasted Port; it's nothing but open spaces. The problem with Blasted Port is that it's not a good place for a girl to be all on her own with no family. I'd almost rather be out there anyway. The bandits are mostly in it for a profit, and there's no profit in harassing a girl with nothing but the clothes on her back.

I guess if it wasn't for Boyd I'd probably have left Broken Tower by now, would have left behind the skeletons of buildings with their ribbed rebar showing through the crumbling concrete.

But at least I felt like I had a place in Boyd's court, even if it was as unstable as the ancient towers.

I crossed Confederation all on my own. I had to stick a man with a knife once when he tried to force himself on me. These city people all think desert girls are easy prey; we're loose girls they say, we're asking for it. They learn fast that trying to force a desert girl is asking for it. I was hunting scorpions for food while most of the two-penny bandits in Trana were still playing games in their parents' yards.

Boyd respected that. He came from out west too, even farther off, in the lands beyond the mountains and I've always suspected that he thought the same of city folk that I did. Too soft, too weak, too coddled.

Boyd calls me the Scorpion Girl and leaves me right the fuck alone except for when I come to his court. I'm welcome there. He sees to it that I have food if I'm hungry, somewhere to sleep when it's cold. He never tried to force himself on me or nothing either. We have an understanding, a mutual respect, and if somebody needs watching, he knows I'm good at sneaky.

I thought about Boyd, about being a sneaky refugee girl, dependent on his patronage to make my way while the chill of early winter bit into my bones. I hugged a ragged old hide coat closer and hunched my shoulders against the cold.

"LePine's up to something, follow him," Boyd told me the last time I saw him.

He had a good point. LePine, the Under God-damned high minister of Confederation in Trana, was up to something. Boyd was sure of it and if I had read the signs correctly he was probably right. It all came down to Bart MacMillan and his fucking wars. The king of Confederation. It had been his damn wars that drove me to Trana in the first place—they drove the 'Tobans west and the 'Tobans figured they'd return the favour, pushed my people into the Great Desert. And then I'd ended up here, far from home.

Now MacMillan had his eyes on the Southlands and Boyd was sure that LePine wanted to involve Trana. Like it or not, Broken Tower was the closest thing I had to a home. I was damned if I was going to sit idly by doing nothing while Confederation drove me out of this one too.

I was sitting in my favourite spot, looking north at the boundary between Broken Tower and downtown, wrapped in my thoughts as tightly as my winter clothes, when I heard a scrabbling behind me. Nobody ever came up high like this. The scavengers stayed away because they couldn't tear any more rebar out of the walls without risking pulling the ceilings down on their own heads. The smiths and the merchants never had cause to come up this high and nobody bothered living up at the tops of the towers; at least, nobody sane.

Nobody sane except me, that is. I don't think I'm insane after all. I turned to look and said, "Hello, is there anybody there?"

The response I heard couldn't really come from a human throat. The best I could describe it would be as a nasty chuckle, a noise full of mirth and viciousness, a clicking sound that promised pain. I reached into my jerkin and found my knife there. A girl had to be ready for trouble.

"Come out where I can see you," I said and I tried really hard to sound bored, like I wasn't impressed by Mr. Crazy-laugh in the shadows at all. I was scared sick.

Just another one of those clicking little chuckles answered me.

"I don't want to have to go looking for you," I said and I wasn't lying at all.

In the gloom of the building behind me I saw somebody, some thing, moving. It was shaped like a man, naked and hunched over, almost crawling. I knew what that meant.

Trana didn't have the Broken, not like Edmonton did or some of the other towns that survived in the desert. This one had probably slunk here from Cleveland. I couldn't think of any closer nests. I hated and feared the Broken the same as everybody. They were cannibals, freaks; twisted and deformed into something less than human by whatever had been done to them, whatever they had done.

They also rarely travelled alone. I was trapped and facing an unknown number of horrible enemies.

There was no need for pretence any longer. You can't reason with one of the Broken and you can never scare one into submission. I drew my knife and prepared to show them why I was called the Scorpion Girl.

I bit back my fear and tightened my grip on my knife. My hands were shaking so hard I balled them up into fists. My legs felt soft as porridge, quivering from fear, ready to flee. Later, somebody I cared about told me that that shaking feeling was caused by adrenaline. In a fight adrenaline might save your life but it's just as likely to get you killed. The trick is to control it, to let the fear and the anger and the rush of blood throbbing in your ears all ball up into a white-hot knot of speed and focus.

Over the singing of the blood in my ears I could still hear the insect-like clicking of the Broken. I could see it moving in the darkness. The Broken weren't graceful beasts. They could hide in shadow, lurk and surprise, but it wasn't their strength. The strength of the Broken was in savagery.

I took a small step forward. I had to be aggressive. The Broken used fear well. There was something about them that spoke to a primal human terror. They were us at our worst, stripped of reason, compassion and sanity so entirely that they were lower than beasts.

Against them, fear was a weakness. They would exploit that fear, turn it into a weapon that would kill me as surely as their teeth.

In the darkness the thing lurked. I saw a flash of bright green eyes and I knew it would pounce soon. I readied myself to stab the moment it pounced. It stayed in the shadows. I took another step forward. Still it waited. Why was it waiting? What was it waiting for? I checked my lines of sight as much as I could with my peripheral vision. I couldn't take my eyes away from the Broken I'd seen but I'd hate to walk into a trap.

The fear threatened to choke me. I could hardly breathe.

The Broken leapt. It was no better in sunlight than it had been in shadows. Its skin was cracked and oozing. It had scaly growths and claws for hands. Its eyes glowed ever so slightly, a sickening green like algae on a dirty pond. It—he—was naked and aroused by the violence.

I stabbed out with my knife, "fast as a scorpion," I hissed to myself. And of course a scorpion sting has its venom. I couldn't generally get scorpion venom, not this far east, away from the desert. So I coated my knife in rattlesnake venom. The snakes around Trana weren't as venomous as the ones in the dry land, but the venom would still make whoever felt its sting sick. The little knife bit the Broken in his throat. Hot blood sprayed onto my arm, across my face. My nostrils were full of the stink of the beast.

He didn't die immediately. Instead he thrashed, pinned to my knife. I hadn't needed the snake's venom, the blow was fatal. It just took the Broken a moment to realize it.

The Broken's thrashing was no weaker for the wound in his throat. He lashed out again and again and it was all I could do to hold onto my knife. I tried to pull it back but a glancing blow threw me from my feet as I did. I landed unceremoniously as the stricken creature staggered about, clutching at his throat. By happy chance my knife was still in my hand.

I scrambled to my feet and stabbed him again, and again, and again. His clicking turned into weak attempts to scream, the sound frighteningly human as he died but my first thrust had severed his wind pipe and it wasn't loud. Soon he dropped to his knees, his clawed, scaly hands pressed to his throat, trying to hold the blood in. He buckled and his hands fell away as he tried to catch himself before hitting the ground. His palms left a pair of bright scarlet prints on the cracked concrete of the floor. And then he rolled to his side and lay still. As soon as he dropped to his side in an expanding pool of blood I ran for the stairs.

And then I heard the bellows of the rest of the pack.

Thirty-one stories, sixty-two flights of stairs, six hundred and twenty steps: I counted them—it was the only thing that kept me from thinking of the death that awaited and the all-too-human death I'd caused. I had to make it just that far to reach the ground, the street, help. I heard the roars from behind me and before me. I clutched my knife in a white-knuckled grasp and fled downward to freedom.

On the twenty-fifth floor a Broken leapt at me out of the darkness. I didn't see her until it was too late. I would have been a dead girl except that her jump was too powerful.

She threw me against the wall hard enough to knock the wind from my lungs and I felt her hot breath against my face. I squirmed, eyes squeezed shut. I think I screamed. She lost her grip on me and I was free but on the ground below her. I kicked up by instinct, my foot connecting with her scabby gut.

She staggered into the gap at the edge of the stairwell. The years had left the stairs crumbling and unsafe at the best of times. Thrown over the edge, she fell all the way down, occasionally bouncing over an out-cropping of concrete. After the third time that happened she stopped screaming.

I scrambled back to my feet, tears streaming down my cheeks. I wasn't sure whether I was crying from pain, fear or remorse. These things weren't human, they were mindless beasts, driven to feed and to kill and nothing more. It was fear. I was afraid. I cried for myself. These are the stories we tell ourselves. Sometimes we learn to see past them.

With newfound respect for the crumbling edge of the stairs dropping twenty-five stories to my side, I continued my desperate flight. It was dark in the stairs. Farther down the walls were pocked with holes where prospectors had broken through, hunting steel, copper wire, plastic pipe if they were very lucky, but the prospectors didn't like to climb so high even as this.

Twice more as I ran the Broken caught up with me. Twice more my knife flashed and the Broken dropped away screaming and bleeding and the tears stung my eyes worse every time. The stench of blood in my nostrils was making me sick and my head throbbed like a drum with the surge of adrenaline.

I reached the ground level and fled into the street. Despite the cold there were some men in the street below the 390 building, smiths and founders taking a break from the eternal heat of the forge. When they saw me fleeing from the building I don't know what they must have thought. I'm not large, I must have looked not much more than a girl to them, but I was spattered with blood, held a bloody knife in my hands. Tears ran down my cheeks, washing away the blood in streaks.

"Here now," one of the foundrymen said. "What's happening, why are you covered in blood?" He eyed the knife with the nervous glance of a large man who didn't want to make a bad mistake. Of course, he didn't know what action would, in fact, be a mistake.

I dropped to my knees in a bank of fresh snow, soiling it with the filth from my clothes, and the knife fell from my grasp. A crowd was forming around me. There were questions being asked but I couldn't hear them through the pounding of my head. I retched and was violently ill.

The first thing I heard, the first thing that broke through the din in my head, was the same man saying, "Give her some space, she needs air." I supposed he'd decided the best course was to help. Perhaps he recognized me. I was known to the court. People thought me one of Boyd's pets, an exotic reminder of the harsh climes he hailed from before he came east, into soft lands. I'd scoffed at them because I had my pride but in this moment I didn't care what he thought. He wanted to help, that was enough.

I gulped down the air with shuddering breath. After a few tense moments I croaked, "Water, please."

It was only then that I realised how thirsty I truly was. My legs burned, my throat burned, my entire body was aflame with the after-effects of battle. A canteen was placed in my hands by somebody. I don't know who. I drank. The water was bitterly cold and it was flat and it tasted of snow.

I drank half the flask in a draught even though the cold hurt my mouth and throat and then felt I might be sick again, but I held it down. "There now," the founder said. "Take it easy, take your time, but you'll have to tell us what happened in there."

"The Broken," I said. "Have to warn Boyd." It just sort of popped into my head; I had to warn Boyd, had to let him know that the Broken had come into Broken Tower. He'd know what to do, he'd have a plan. I began to chuckle: the Broken in Broken Tower. It seemed fitting somehow but I realized that this was a mad thought.

Half the crowd disappeared. Some probably to look for the Broken; others, the smarter ones, were probably putting as much distance as they could between themselves and the tower. It's what I would have done.

The foundryman led me to a bench of roughly hewn concrete and set me down. It was under the awnings of a forge and the heat from the metalworks radiated out. The warmth was delicious. I hadn't realized how cold I'd been. He asked me to tell him my story and I did. I told him about the attack on the top floor, how I'd fought past three others to make it to freedom. I told him I didn't know how many more there were.

After a while grim-faced men exited the building carrying the gory remains of my escape. Four corpses, three bearing knife wounds, the fourth so twisted from the fall that it hung as limp as a rag doll from the arms of the man that carried it.

I couldn't look. I didn't want to look at the people I'd killed but I forced myself to anyway. Some part of me wanted to remember what I'd done. In death their corpses were undeniably human, despite the claws and the scales. I didn't know what power had twisted them but in that moment I learned an important lesson. The Broken were human. I'd stabbed a man before, and yes, there had been venom on my knife, but that was a little scuffle; a private matter. This was three bodies cut open with my knife, in the cold sunlight and a score of witnesses, in the city where I lived.

I looked up at the ruin I wrought, needing to confront what I'd done. I was horrified and wanted so much to look away, but I couldn't. I was transfixed.

They laid the four bodies out on the ground. I heard the hushed talk: there were no more in there. That they had been the Broken seemed clear enough. Ordinary people didn't have claws, they didn't have patches of tumorous scales. The green glow had faded from their eyes and they just looked milky and diseased instead.

The men knew I wanted to speak to Boyd, and I'd killed. Even though the creatures I'd killed were Broken, this was a matter for him to decide. I heard the decision being made around me. They would take me to Boyd directly. Not unkindly, the folk around led me to his court.

Boyd held court in the shadow of the skeleton of an ancient dome-shaped building, a meeting hall or music hall of the luminaries of a forgotten age. His high throne overlooked a pit, ringed with entrances to the Long Dark but with trees and a pond providing a hint of nature in the bleakness of his little kingdom.

I remember how the light struck the polished steel of the ancient dome behind the throne, a massive heap made from slabs of concrete and hammered steel, sitting atop a raised platform between the dome and the pit that served as his audience chamber. I remember the ice on the square pond in one corner of the pit, new and thin, still mostly black. Strange how a detail like that can stick in the memory.

I also remember that though his chair was in sunlight Dave Boyd sat in shadow. He was bundled in thick furs but the cold didn't seem to touch him. His long hair was tied back at his brow, cascading down his back but it was unkempt. His beard, normally carefully maintained, was scruffy. His blue eyes were all but lost in the shadow of his heavy brow.

He leaned forward in his seat with his chin resting on one hand. When we arrived at his court, my escorts unsure if they were guarding a prisoner or bringing a scout to speak to their leader on important matters, he barely even twitched.

His mind was far away. I suspected it rested in Fredericton.

"Why do you come here covered in blood, Scorpion Girl?" he asked.

The rush of adrenaline past, the sickness of the gore passed, I felt dirty but I was myself again, I was in control again. I glared back at him fiercely. "I come to tell you that I killed four Broken in your domain."

"Please, this is some sort of awful prank, right?" Boyd said.

"Do you know me to pull pranks?" I asked.

Boyd sighed and said in hushed tones, so quiet I could barely hear, "I need no more enemies at my gate." Louder he asked, "You are sure that they were the Broken?"

I tried to answer but I choked on the words. The sight of four twisted corpses arrayed in a row in the snow flashed before my eyes and I felt my legs go weak. I felt the steady hand of the foundryman on my shoulder, supporting me. I glanced at him and tried to let my eyes give him the thanks that could never pass my lips.

"My lord," he said. "They had all the marks of the Broken, plague marks, deformities. The only way I could be surer would be if they were alive and trying to eat people."

Boyd shifted in his seat, agitated enough that he couldn't maintain regal stillness. "There is that. I see no blame here."

I breathed again, hadn't realized I was holding my breath. I realized Boyd's attention was still fixed on me.

"Court is dismissed for the day," he said, not taking his eyes from mine. "Savannah, attend me. We have a private matter to discuss."

I approached the throne as he stepped down. He led me down into the pit below his throne and under the lee of the entrance to the Long Dark.

"Have you learned anything of LePine?" he asked.

"No. I was working on a plan when the Broken..."

"I understand. But leave the Broken to me, I need you to concentrate on LePine."

I frowned.

"Trust me," Boyd said. And I did.

"Alright," I said. "I guess I'll get started."

CHAPTER 2

Savannah

I LEFT BOYD TO deal with the Broken for the moment. He had men and could scour the tunnels of the Long Dark. He was sure the Broken had to have come from there originally. If they'd travelled above ground somebody would have seen them before me. Broken or no, I didn't want to go down there. I hated the tunnels even when they weren't full of monsters.

Broken—of all the things—they sent a shiver down my spine. We'd had a few in the ruins of Edmonton near my hometown. Nobody knew where they'd come from, just another remnant of the dark times of the Collapse. They looked almost human. Their bodies were twisted and deformed but they had two arms, two legs, could walk upright though they often crouched. They were fast, strong and vicious. Cannibals: their favourite food was human flesh.

I couldn't dwell on them. I had other matters. I had a date with Jacques LePine. Boyd was obviously troubled and not just by the Broken at his doorstep. It was easy enough to find LePine. The man was an orderly person, a man of schedules and charts. He had an old wind-up watch on a chain. The thing still worked; it was the most singularly valuable thing I'd ever seen. I'd have stolen it but I was sure I'd be found out. Besides, I didn't have any need for watches. It seemed strange how LePine clung to things like that when the rest of the world counted time by the movement of the sun, the passage of days.

He was tall and narrow with an aquiline nose and pale skin. He wore robes, very much in the fashion of the Fredericton Court. They were made out of cotton imported at great expense and risk out of the Southlands. In deference to the temperature he wore furs over these but he seemed uncomfortable in anything that might smack of outdoor work.

On those rare occasions that he left the garrison at the north-east edge of Trana he travelled with an entourage of four soldiers, big men with sharp eyes. Avoiding their attention would be the key challenge but I'd faced similar challenges in the past. You didn't cross the desert and pass through hundreds of kilometers of displaced 'Toban refugee camps without learning how to sneak.

A few days after I spoke to Boyd I heard that LePine was touring the largest foundry in Broken Tower. I made my way to it, a crumbling limestone monolith, ancient and well preserved. It nestled into the space between the Cathedral of Broken Glass and the Dome at the Square, where Boyd stored finished goods before they were sold or distributed to Confederation.

There was an old clock tower at the front of the building with gaping holes where the clock would have gone. One time a man told me that it was this broken clock tower that gave the district its name. Of course he was an idiot. It was the much larger tower that had fallen into the lake to the south, and all the crumbling towers of the district that gave it the name. This was possibly the least broken tower in the area.

I nestled into the archway of the front door. The heat from the smelters warmed me to the bones after the chill of winter. I peeked around the corner as sneakily as I could manage and saw LePine walking out, his guards flanking him. He was animatedly talking to Myles Bones, the foreman of the foundry.

"But can you increase production?"

Bones shook his head. "Not without training more men and if we bring in more workers we'll just need to sell more goods for food as it is."

"What if I can get you the food?"

"If you can feed the men I can get increased production. You've seen yourself, we have the space. But Boyd ain't going to be happy with you meddling."

"Boyd won't be an issue." LePine glanced around suspiciously. I tried hard to look like another urchin warming herself up in the doorway, not paying any attention to her betters, no sir.

I was glad for the winter cold though. With a hood pulled up tight over my head and bulky hides on I didn't stand out.

"Why don't you join me for a meal and we can talk about the future."

"I would be most obliged to you, sir," Bones bowed low, every inch an ass-kissing slimeball, but LePine seemed to like the flattery. They started out the door. One of the guards gave me the hairy eyeball. I tried really hard to stare into the middle distance, trying to think myself invisible. It must have worked. The guard walked on.

I waited the space of thirty breaths and started after them.

I stayed as far back as I could without losing them. I didn't want to get made.

Unfortunately I couldn't hear what LePine and Bones were talking about. I trudged through the snow in their wake and hoped that they'd save the juicy stuff for their meal.

They ended up at the Blur Street Behemoth. Another stone remnant of the forgotten times, the Behemoth was a combination of pitted aluminum, steel girders and old stone construction. The ancient building had been built and rebuilt a hundred times before the Collapse and hadn't ever been scavenged. It was the palace of a prominent district lord, a man not unlike Boyd. This man was a scholar and much of his palace had been converted into a school for the wealthy and indolent of Kensington, Midtown, and Yorktown.

The school also had one of the best kitchens in the city. I knew, I'd snuck in to steal scraps a few times when I got hungry enough to steal. I guess I shouldn't have been surprised. If I was LePine with more money than brains and I wanted to get a meal walking distance from Broken Tower, this is where I'd go.

I followed them into the echoing expanse of the Behemoth and hoped I could find a corner to lurk in.

The entryway to the Behemoth was mind-blowing. The ceiling soared easily a hundred feet from the lobby floor. It was an arched dome set with gold and blue tiles. Flowers, animals and monsters climbed the cardinal points leading to an inscription on the ceiling spelling out, "That all men may know his works." Nobody survived knew who the mysterious man mentioned was. Some people thought the dedication was religious. Others thought it was a boast of the builder, or of the king who commissioned the building of the Behemoth. Whoever it had been, his name was lost to the Collapse.

I saw LePine and Bones on a balcony near the ceiling. The guards hadn't noticed me but they were watching very carefully. I slunk into the shadow of a stairwell and crept close enough to hear the twang of LePine's east-ocean accent on the other side of a wall. The balcony was empty but for LePine and his men.

"That's what I've been trying to explain to you. Boyd rules only at the pleasure of King Bartholomew, and His Majesty is rarely pleased," LePine said in a voice as oily as his food.

"You know as well as I that there are plenty of rebel sympathizers in Trana. What's to stop Boyd from going rogue?"

I could smell the fatty tang of roasted duck. My stomach rumbled and I realized that it had been a long time since my last meal. I crept closer, the heavenly smell of the roasted duck overwhelming my better sense. I had to see it for myself.

"He wouldn't dare. He'd be crushed like a bug by the royal army."

"So you pull down Boyd, put me in his place..." Bones sounded frightened and uncertain. A good frame of mind for anyone going against Boyd on his own turf from what I could see.

LePine dug into the duck carcass on the table with his fork, tearing off a large strip of the dark flesh and the crisp red skin. "And you make the steel flow into Fredericton like never before. Tear down all those ancient towers if you have to, I don't care as long as the swords and spears are plentiful. We must prepare for war with the Southlands."

"What guarantees do I have that Boyd won't just kill me when I try to take over?"

"The backing of Confederation," LePine said through a mouthful of fatty bird. "I think..."

I didn't hear what Bones thought. A guard patrolling the halls came across me and shouted, "Hey, what are you doing there?"

"Shit," I said. I ran down the stairs. The guard moved to stop me. I kicked out at him as I had the Broken on another set of stairs. The guard was no mindless beast. He had a buckler on his arm and brought it up, bracing with the blow. I bounced off his shield and my foot ached from the blow. Hissing, I dodged to the side and around the guard.

I didn't stop running until I was far south of the Behemoth, in the shelter of ancient trees planted in a huge park at the heart of Trana. I sat down in a bank of snow and took off my boot. My foot was swollen but not broken. I muttered a prayer of thanks to Ostre, the goddess of the hunted, and delicately slipped my boot back on, limping all the way back to Boyd.

When I told him what I had heard he didn't lose his shit. If anything he got calmer, as if he expected the news.

"Tomorrow, summon Myles Bones to answer before the throne, and shut down the foundries until I command otherwise," he said to his councillor Old Smith. I liked Old Smith. A soft man for all the hardness of his muscles, he was bald as a ball. The hair he lacked on his head was made up for by the hair on his big chest, curls of the stuff peeking out over the v-neck of his jerkin as long as some men's head hair and shock-white.

"Are things going to go badly, sir?" Old Smith asked.

"They already are," Boyd said.

Myles Bones proved a fool but Boyd showed mercy. He was stripped of all rank and put to work toiling in the towers as part of a punishment duty. In exchange he revealed everything he knew of LePine's plan. It wasn't much.

LePine didn't get off so easy.

I had a good view when he arrived. I'd climbed up into the branches of a pine tree growing out of a clump of granite that the Ancients had hauled from the distant country in the north long ago.

He must have been surprised when two rough men dragged him bodily from his home because he was still in his bedclothes. But, by the time he arrived, he was merely irate.

"What's the meaning of this, Boyd?"

"I rather suspect you know. I've spoken to Myles Bones."

If LePine was surprised by the news he didn't show it. "So?"

"You can't expect I'll allow you to simply remove me, can you? I am far too accustomed to my place here in Broken Tower."

"His Majesty doesn't care who rules Broken Tower in his name. What matters to him is that the steel flows. There is talk of movement in the south—"

"MacMillan is a fool and everybody knows it," Boyd cut LePine off as he rose from his throne, hand on the pommel of his huge sword. "The Southlanders are never going to invade. They have problems enough of their own. Meanwhile your king demands ever-increasing tithes. How are my smiths and smelters to feed and clothe themselves if the fruits of their labour disappear entirely into the east with no recompense?"

"It's your duty to see to the tithes, otherwise why do we allow you to rule?"

"Does he though?"

Boyd approached LePine. He nodded and his two guards backed away.

"I need to send a message to your king—and to some others."

"If you believe you can convince me to plead for mercy on your behalf you're mistaken."

"No, the message I'm sending with you won't be a plea for mercy." With a single fluid motion Boyd drew his sword and cut across LePine's neck. The cut was clean and took the minister's head from his shoulders entirely. His body dropped bonelessly to the ground, spurting blood into the snow.

Boyd looked down at the corpse in the spreading pool of gore. "It's the other kind of message." He let the heavy sword fall from his hands and he climbed back up to his throne looking like he'd aged a decade in a moment.

"Send the appropriate messages out," he said to Old Smith. "And could somebody please remove that body from my sight?"

I clung to the tree and tried not to be sick. I wasn't sure what had possessed Boyd to kill LePine but I was sure it would have far reaching consequences.

CHAPTER 3

Kieran

WHEN I WAS VERY young there was a plague and my parents died. Things like this were common in Trana, in the Southlands, throughout Confederation, until you reached the Great Desert, where the people were too few for plagues to spread easily. The fact that it was common enough for people to catch plague and die didn't make it any easier being an orphan.

My uncle took me in. He was a pillar of the community, a wealthy merchant and a connected man. Everybody liked uncle Stephen, at least everybody except the Kensington Peacekeeper, Argus Sawchuk.

Sawchuk wasn't exactly a soldier, but he did serve Confederation. He was seen as a necessary evil within Kensington. We were part of Trana and as such under Confederation rule, however unwillingly. A district of merchants, weavers, cobblers and herbalists, Kensington produced little that MacMillan desired for his dreams of conquest (though Sawchuk took a heavy levy of boots each spring) and we were mostly ignored by the lords of Confederation in favour of districts like the steel producing Broken Tower and the farms of the Scar. Sawchuk was the minimal presence that Confederation required of an otherwise unregarded district and for the most part he didn't do anything worse than collect taxes and crack a few skulls if fights got out of hand. Sometimes he'd drag off thieves and murderers to the Confederation garrison, from where they rarely returned. But those were rare occasions in our peaceful district.

He didn't like uncle Stephen. Mostly this was because my uncle was an influential man and vocal in his distaste for Confederation. He also may not have liked uncle Stephen's choice of company and Sawchuk, he latched onto the fact that uncle Stephen lived alone, never married and he cast aspersions on my uncle's manhood.

I didn't know whether uncle Stephen preferred the company of men, nor did I care. Sawchuk was a fool and a less popular man than my uncle by far. Uncle Stephen had an heir, did his duty to the community and was always a fair dealer. Sawchuk was a bully and a servant of the tyrant in the east. Our neighbours cared more about that than about what he might get up to in bed and so, on those rare occasions the two came close to real conflict, my neighbours sided against Sawchuk and opposed his petty power games. I think that rankled the Peacekeeper most of all.

From uncle Stephen I learned how to read, how to do sums. I learned the importance of a man to care for others who didn't have the means to care for themselves. I learned the virtue of honest work, and of giving without thought of return.

Life was good. Perhaps things were hard in the world but they didn't affect me directly and I was satisfied with my life. I rarely considered the people starving at the edges of the great desert or even the refugees of the wars to the east and west. Trana was at peace and Kensington was at the heart of that peace.

When I turned eighteen, uncle Stephen decked out Bellevue Square, the town square of the Kensington district, with paper lanterns and threw a big party for me; I had, after all, entered into adulthood. I'd wiled away the night, dancing with a pixie-like girl named Savannah, which she said was an ancient word for a plain of grass in the days before the Great Desert took them all. She had paint on her copper coloured face and strange tattoos adorned her shoulder like a sleeve of ink; clan markings of the wild folk of the western heartlands. She was savage and lithe and beautiful, dancing to the sound of that drum. We'd ended up lying in the grass under the green-grey trunks of the maples together, the drum throbbing like a third heartbeat in both our chests.

And then I never saw her again. Occasionally I heard a rumour that she was hanging out in Dave Boyd's court in Broken Tower but I didn't bother looking. I mean, it was just a fling after all, and Boyd had a bad reputation. Uncle Stephen certainly didn't like him.

When I was young uncle Stephen taught me a bit of politics.

"Hundreds of years ago, Confederation was a single nation stretching from Breton in the east to the land beyond the Great Desert and the Rocky Mountains in the west to the north as far as north went, where the world was covered in ice." He said this to me, showing me a map from one of his old books. "But the ancient nations were too great to survive the hard times."

I nodded, understanding. Everybody knew that none of the old nations survived long after the seasons changed. Farmland became dust, new diseases spread north, winter brought rain and sometimes choking ice, but never enough and never long enough. And in the seemingly endless summer, people died of thirst and heat stroke. My uncle's books said Confederation had always been a haphazard affair, more of an argument than a nation. Was it any surprise it was sundered?

"It split at the mountains," I said.

Uncle Stephen nodded. "That was the first of the divisions. And then the Southlanders, sensing weakness, invaded."

"But we won the Water War."

"Most people in Confederation have ancestors from both sides; you could easily say we lost as well. The truth is that the Southlanders crumbled from within the same way the northerners did."

I frowned. I didn't like the idea that we hadn't won a glorious victory. It seemed too small and petty that our feared enemy to the south had fallen to inner strife rather than the strength of northern arms and will.

"The Southlanders held Trana for fifty years after the Water War but they realized they could not hold it, not with their own nation crumbling, and they left."

"Was that how Confederation started?"

This time it was uncle Stephen who frowned. "Not at first. At first there were just the city-states." He pointed to each on the map in turn. "Ni-pegg, Salt Mary, Trana, Quebec and Fredericton. Each of these five cities commanded the land around it independent of the others. And then the MacMillan clan seized Fredericton and everything changed."

"Why did they lay siege to Quebec?"

Uncle Stephen went silent and refused to answer. His hand wandered to his heart where I knew he was marked with a single black flower with three symmetrical petals. Any talk of the Black Trillium was met with stony silence—though I had heard rumours of rebels who fought under that banner.

Not every rumour of rebellion involved mysterious societies though. Dave Boyd had, himself, engaged in rebellion, killing High Minister LePine and sending his head back to Fredericton in a box. Though I suspected my uncle of rebel sympathies, this news didn't seem to make him any more inclined to like Boyd, nor inclined to discuss the reasons for his enmity. Still, Kensington was abuzz with talk of what this would mean for Trana. People were afraid.

A while after the rumour started, I was standing in the awning of a shop around the corner from uncle Stephen's house, drinking hot spiced cider to ward off the chill and arguing with my friend Teddy Li. "I say we should rebuff MacMillan's men when they come. Trana is too valuable to put to the torch. This could be our chance for independence."

"I'm sure hotheads in Quebec City said the same thing in the time of MacMillan's father," Teddy said. He spat on the ground.

"Right, and I suppose you think we should just give Boyd over," I said.

"Don't really think it's our choice. Kensington has no power over Broken Tower," Teddy said.

"We're all Trana," I said.

"You might as well say we're all Confederation."

"Fuck Confederation," I said, the bravado of a truly rebellious deed performed in the district almost next-door sparking a fire in my belly.

"That sounds dangerously close to traitor talk," said Sawchuk. The bastard must have snuck up on us when we were arguing.

Teddy took one look at Sawchuk and took off down the street, stammering out an excuse about having errands to run. I turned and faced him.

"There's no law against talking," I said. Sawchuk had an angular face and a big bristly beard, black flecked with grey. He had a truncheon in his hand and was tapping it impatiently against his thigh. He looked like he wanted a fight.

"There's a law against inciting rebellion," Sawchuk said.

"You really think old Teddy Li and I are going to kick off a rebellion?" I asked.

"I'd put nothing past the protégé of Fairy Steve." Sawchuck said and he popped his knuckles.

I ignored the insult. I was long past caring what he had to say about my uncle anyway.

"Everybody thinks MacMillan mad, pushing all the people his father conquered to supply a defence we'll never need against an enemy who will never attack. The gods only know we'd be better off with nearly anybody else ruling us," I said, "but I'm not taking up any arms. In fact you're the only one carrying a weapon."

Sawchuk raised his truncheon. I'd gone too far and I was sure I was going to catch a thrashing at his hands. I prepared to defend myself though even I didn't know whether that meant fighting back or running away.

As I tensed myself a ragged man, his hair matted, almost dreadlocks, reached out and grabbed the truncheon. He was wearing mud spattered, trail worn clothes, and his face was almost as rough as his clothes. He had a big, hook nose and dark, black eyes, but his skin was pale.

His beard was big and tangled—it even had bits of straw in it. I noticed, almost as an after-thought, that he wore a sword at his hip. Few people did in Kensington. We were, after all, a civilized district.

"Is it a worthy thing to beat an unarmed young lad?" When he spoke, his voice was full of gravel, and his accent was clearly French. I didn't speak much of the language, so I was happy he spoke in English.

It was strange, the ragged man seemed to be holding Sawchuk's truncheon almost delicately, and yet clearly Sawchuk, a big and powerful man used to fighting, couldn't make it budge in the slightest.

"The little bastard insulted me, he's lucky if I let him off with a beating. I'd be within my rights to call him out for a duel." He strained against the ragged man, trying to free his truncheon.

"Yes, to duel a young man just out of childhood for the insult of calling you a thug. I can see how that would work well for your reputation, Peacekeeper," the stranger said gently.

"Perhaps I'd be better served venting my spleen on you," Sawchuk said. He lashed out at the stranger with a kick that could knock down stout doors. The odd man sidestepped the kick as if he'd seen it from a mile away and thrust out the fingers of his free hand almost delicately, striking Sawchuk on the hip. The peacekeeper's supporting leg buckled and he fell in the street.

"What did you do to me?"

"Discouraged further violence, be thankful that's all I did."

I boggled at somebody treating Sawchuk so cavalierly and I could see him struggling to stand.

"You'll pay for that."

"Somehow, I doubt it," the stranger said. He kicked Sawchuk in the face and the big man collapsed unconscious.

"How did you—" I asked, but the stranger cut me off.

"We should get off the street before he comes to, young Master Benton," he said curtly.

"How do you know me?" I asked.

"I am a friend of your uncle. Please take me to him," he said.

I was concerned that he knew my name, but my uncle had many odd acquaintances and it wouldn't be the first time a stranger asked me to lead him to my uncle's home. He'd beaten Sawchuk into unconsciousness though. That would have repercussions. I said nothing and looked at him suspiciously.

"Please," the stranger said.

I shrugged my shoulders and led him home. What else could I do? Take him to the peacekeeper?

My home was a crumbling old brick building at the heart of Kensington that barely kept the wind out. It was just two long, narrow rooms, one atop the other, divided into several damp little store rooms and cellars and a tiny basement with a ceiling so low I had to crouch.

We had a walled garden in the back of the building, crumbling cinderblocks brightly painted, and a canopy of ancient trees creating a private space. The garden had little plots of flowers in the summer, though it was fallow now and was otherwise covered in a wooden deck. A stone fireplace burned, taking the edge off the winter chill back there.

Uncle Stephen liked to while away the hours there when not engaged in business, and he was there, sitting close to the fireplace, ignoring the chill, when I brought the stranger back. The stranger greeted him, "Stephen, it is good to see you again."

"Jean," uncle Stephen said, honestly surprised. "I'm sorry, if I'd known you were coming..." He stood up and embraced the ragged man warmly.

The stranger, Jean I presumed, returned his embrace. "It is nothing, nothing, I've been wandering in the Southlands. I just returned back and heard about what happened in Broken Tower."

Uncle Stephen's face fell and his countenance looked dark. "Yes, that."

"We should talk," he said.

"Kieran, please leave us for a while."

"Oh," I pleaded. "Can't I stay? I'm a man now. Whatever it is, you know I'll help."

"For now, please." He said please, but when that finality crept into my uncle's voice there was no argument. I frowned and left them to talk in private.

Later that day I was tending the fire in the kitchen hearth. Uncle Stephen came back in from his deck. His lips were almost blue from the cold but whatever he'd been speaking to his friend about had been clearly more important than his comfort.

"Kieran, I've spoken to Jean. He told me what happened, with Sawchuk."

"You aren't mad, are you?"

"No, I understand."

"Well good, because I didn't mean to attract his attention, it's just..."

"He suspects me. And not entirely without reason; surely you have suspected."

I gave my uncle a skeptical look.

"You know the stories about the fall of Quebec and the freedom fighters who opposed MacMillan's father."

"The Black Trillium," I said.

"And I'm sure you have heard that some of them survived. Well..." He paused and he looked at me steadily. "Jean and I both fight for the Black Trillium. We have since we were young. In Jean's case he was at the fall of Quebec."

The fall of Quebec. It was one of those moments of infamy you heard about in hushed rumour, almost legend already, though not yet in the distant past. That Mr. Chamblais might have actually been there was shocking. I sat still for a moment, trying to control my surprise and awe before I spoke.

"And now something has happened."

"In Broken Tower. The lordling there killed a Confederation minister as an offering to us, seeking allegiance. We turned him down. We weren't ready to free Trana and he's forced our hand. Things are going to be very hard in the next year. War is coming to Trana. So you have a choice to make."

"A choice..." I could hardly believe what he was telling me. It made sense. My uncle's strange friends, his opposition to Confederation, Sawchuk's suspicions, all these things fit the pattern of a rebel in hiding.

"Yes, you can fight with us. If you do you will have to do... terrible things. War is always terrible. But you can. Or Jean can bring you to safety somewhere nearby."

"What about you?"

"I have to stay here. It's my home. I'll fight to defend it."

"So will I," I said.

"Be careful Kieran, I never wanted to draw you into a war."

"No. But if I start running now, when will I stop?"

"If you are sure," he said.

And I was.

"Yes," I said, and I looked up at uncle Stephen burning with fierce pride.

"So why were you fighting with Argus Sawchuk?"

"I was talking with Teddy Li about the situation, you know, down in Broken Tower and he came around, accused me of treason."

"The situation is fragile, we must be careful not to alert the wrong people clashing with lumps like Sawchuk."

The stranger slipped into the room then and said, "The situation is beyond fragile. It is devolving and there will be war soon."

Uncle Stephen seemed to deflate a little, his shoulders sagging. He took a deep breath. "I know that, Jean. But I'd prefer it didn't start on my doorstep."

"The truth is that we must deal with Sawchuk."

I had a fantasy of drumming the bully out of Kensington, tarring him and feathering him, anything to see him gone.

"Let's go now!"

"You'll stay put today." Uncle Stephen sounded firm.

"But..."

"No, your uncle is right. Sawchuk won't readily forget you were the reason he was beaten today. He'll be on the lookout for you as soon as he recovers and the chances are good he won't be alone. You stay put, for today. Tomorrow we will see to your education."

"Yes, sir," I said. "I understand." I thought calling him sir would be appropriately respectful, but he just chuckled at me.

"Mr. Chamblais will suffice," he said.

"If you don't mind me asking, Mr. Chamblais, what do you mean you'll see to my education? I already know my numbers and letters."

"There is much a rebel must know beyond reading and writing. I don't suppose you know how to handle a sword."

I'd never thought of it that way. I'd played at swords with my friends when I was a kid but Kensington was a peaceful place. I hadn't ever learned to fight.

"But first you must be initiated."

"Initiated," I said. "Some sort of ceremony?"

"Something like that."

The rest of the day passed slowly. I stayed inside while uncle Stephen and Mr. Chamblais "dealt with the Sawchuk problem" and the weather was miserable in any case. I felt almost resentful, like I wasn't getting to join a romantic brotherhood of freedom fighters, but was instead being made a prisoner in my own home by a strange raggedy man.

I went to sleep reluctantly, my head buzzing with thoughts of heroism and rebellion, excited and terrified about what lay before me.

CHAPTER 4

Kyle

THERE HAD BEEN RUMOURS that the Black Trillium survived the destruction of Quebec City, but few people believed them. I suspect nobody wanted to believe them. They were, after all, our greatest foe. The Salters bent their knees to our might, the 'Tobans had fled before us, Quebec was a burnt ruin returned to the wilderness.

But if the Black Trillium had risen again in Trana...

"The Black Trillium murdered your grandfather," my father said. He'd been drinking and he had that look in his eye when the crown felt too heavy and he remembered all the blood that he'd waded through to secure it.

"None of those assassins survived the night. That was the end of them—the Three Brothers fell with Quebec and the Black Trillium died murdering the rightful king."

I'd believed my father despite the reports that came out of Trana of the Black Trillium active once more and stirring up dissent. And despite the rumours in court that perhaps my father had helped my grandfather on his way to the grave. And then Oswald LePine came to me, tears in his wild, wrathful eyes. "My father is dead." The anger did little for his pale complexion, his thin face. His big nose was red and he looked more a child than a man, but he had always been a good friend to me.

"What?" was all I could think to say.

"If you would only pay attention to the business at court," Oswald said. It was fair enough. Since Sophie and I had hooked up I'd had little time for the business of court.

It wasn't just the sex—though she was amazing in bed.

Sophie knew things. I knew that more than a few of the courtiers, including my idiot brothers, thought she was a witch. Still, between her skill with a sword and her knowledge of the sciences, she seemed more like a legend from before the Great Collapse, or from the stories of the fabled Wizard in Green, than somebody of our time.

Fair though Oswald's criticism had been, I wouldn't normally have stood for such a thing, except his father had just died.

"Oswald, we're friends, tell me what happened. I'll help."

"Dave Boyd," Oswald said. "He did it, he killed my father."

"Who?"

"Boyd, he's the district ruler who commands Trana's steel trade." Oswald spat the words like they were poison in his mouth.

"Have you spoken to my father about this?" I did not command the army.

"Your father refuses to dispatch an army while the southern threat remains so immediate."

Of course he did. My father thought of little but the southern threat. They were the only ones to have ever beaten him. After Quebec fell, and Salt Mary, he'd looked south. It was the only campaign I ever rode out with him on and I had been very young.

The Southlanders were not well unified but the little nations called the Eastern Counties, stretching along the ocean from Bangor in the north to Charleston to the south, had been fighting in constant little internecine skirmishes since the days of the Collapse.

We met their army at Bangor, on our own doorstep compared to the vast distance to Salt Mary or Trana. Their cavalry was light, armed with long spears and fearless in the face of our heavier troops.

Our forces were routed. My father, mad with battle-rage, had refused to sound the retreat. In the end I had to, or face capture, death and the end of Confederation. His generals said I'd made the right call, that the day was lost. He'd never forgiven me.

The Southlanders never came for retribution but still he waited, day after day, year after year. Courtiers whispered and found themselves exiled. His grasp on the army remained strong. And I was forgotten, the coward son. My brothers had his ear now, not me.

"I'll speak to him," I said, though I dreaded the conversation.

I marched to the throne room dressed in my best armour and carrying my precious sword in the sheath at my hip and swung open the doors. I hoped that a warlike appearance would help Father take me seriously.

High up on the steel throne my father stared down. The twin bands of yellow gold and grey steel fronted with the blue gem that was the crown of

Confederation seemed heavy on his brow.

My brothers, Adam and Seth, were arguing in depth: some piece of minutiae about hunting rights in the border regions with the Southlands. My father looked bored. I didn't blame him for that. Adam gestured wildly, his gesticulation bird-like and nervous as he insisted his friends were rightfully entitled to hunt in the Saint Croix valley. Seth, barrel-chested and boar-like, said that the lands were promised to his cronies following the failed excursion in exchange for keeping watch against the southern advance.

My father was unlikely to care which set of unimportant hangers-on got to shoot for deer there so long as they kept their eyes pointed south. When he looked up, his bored expression faded, replaced with a wrathful, penetrating gaze.

"Oh, it's you."

"Father, I come to ask for a force to put down Dave Boyd's rebellion and to punish him for the death of your High Minister, Jacques LePine," I said as confidently as I could.

My father scoffed. My brothers goggled at me, furious that I would interrupt them. Good. I didn't like either one of them.

"If I need my soldiers to practice retreating it doesn't have to be all the way from Trana."

I ignored the slight. I should have expected it. "The men are strong. They can manage the walk, you know they can. We've fought in the snow before."

"No," my father said.

"Do you truly intend to let rebellion in Trana go unpunished? What would the commanders think?"

I let that barb settle. If the commanders of his army abandoned him, my father was finished. They'd stayed the course with him as they had with his father before him largely because they were loyal men but even so, I knew there was some dissatisfaction.

"Father, there are more important matters to discuss," Adam said. "The Saint Croix Valley issue—"

"So help me, Adam, I will call you out," I snarled and my hand fell to my sword.

"Stop this idiocy," my father said, but I could see the hint of concern on his face.

"Give me a thousand men. That isn't even a third of the army. With them I can bring Boyd to heel quickly. Trana is close enough I could be back before the Southlanders could trouble you."

"You failed when last you commanded troops." The old argument, the old slight.

"I have never been given the chance to prove differently since then," I said.

"Who would you bring?" my father asked.

"Colonel Antonelli and his cavalry. They can move faster than any other force I could muster."

"And the fact that Antonelli is your crony..." My father sounded disappointed, but he always did; more to the point, he was backing away from his previous response of a simple 'no.' As for calling him my crony, that was hardly fair. Colonel Marc Antonelli was my closest friend. He had been my whole life. Even though he and Oswald barely got along, I'd still trust nobody more to help me on this mission.

"Certainly Marc is somebody I can trust," I said.

"Fine then, but you have four months only," my father said. "I expect you back within that time. I will need my armies ready should the Southlanders attack come summer."

"Four months to ride to Trana, bring Boyd to justice and ride back again?" I asked.

"Yes, and not a day more," my father said.

"I hear and obey, father." I couldn't suppress my smile even as I crossed my left arm across my chest and bowed my head in a formal salute to my father.

"Comport yourself well, my son," my father said. "This will be your only chance to correct your past mistakes."

I looked up from my bow and glanced at my brothers. They were both carefully guarding their expressions; the toads.

"I understand, father."

"You may go."

Bowing, I left my father's presence.

My bodyguard, the mute giant Brutus Cloven, fell in behind me as I left the chamber from where he'd been waiting in the anteroom. He was milk-pale, entirely hairless and his eyes were pink. The giant looked freakish but he was a comforting presence too. He'd been with my family as long as I could remember, stolid and silent, a worn marble statue of loyalty.

Brutus never spoke a word but his pink eyes never missed a threat, and he'd saved my life on many occasions.

"We ride out tomorrow at dawn," I said to Brutus. "Round up your best guards to accompany us. We'll have enough trouble in Trana, if the rumours of the Black Trillium prove true."

Brutus saluted and left to follow my orders. He looked more nervous than usual, as if marching on Trana was somehow particularly unsettling to him. Or perhaps he simply didn't like travel.

There was one other person I needed to speak to before sending for Marc and planning the campaign. It gave me shivers just to think it. At long last I would be planning a campaign.

I walked to her suite, one of the most lavish set of rooms in the entire iron palace. They had been mine once. Even a disgraced son of the king could expect good lodgings.

I opened the door and she was there, brushing her long black hair. Her huge green eyes fixed on mine from her mirror, a real glass one, not bronze. That mirror alone cost as much as the arms and horses for a dozen knights, but it was just the least of the marvels in her room.

And if I could I would have given her more.

"Sophie," I said. "We leave in the morning, for Trana."

"But I haven't finished searching Fredericton for it."

Ah yes, the manual, the book of sublime martial skill that she hunted.

"If there were any swordsman with the skill you say the manual contains in Fredericton, we'd have found him by now," I said.

Sophie frowned, her big red lips beautiful even in a scowl. "I suppose you are right."

"Trana is the largest city in Confederation, there are fifty-thousand people there. Perhaps somebody will have heard tidings of the manual." I knew how much the manual meant to her. It was seeking it that led her to Fredericton to begin with. All she knew is that it was somewhere in Confederation. Or at least that is all she would tell me.

There were many things about her past that Sophie kept even from me.

She smiled. "Yes, perhaps Trana would be a good place to seek the manual."

"And when you find it?"

"I will be eternally grateful," Sophie said and she turned, looking at me in the flesh rather than the glass of her mirror.

"When we return," I said. "I will make you my queen."

"Yes," Sophie said, "when we have the manual, I think I would enjoy being queen."

"I have much to do," I said. "Be ready to ride at dawn."

Sophie nodded, and I went to find Marc. It was time to prepare to march on Trana.

CHAPTER 5

Kieran

THE HOUSE WAS EMPTY when I awoke in the cold blackness before the dawn. I got up, boiled water and washed my face. I heated up a pot with the remnants of yesterday's barley gruel and ate a quiet breakfast, wondering what the day would bring.

As I was washing up, my uncle returned, carrying a bundle of black cloth under one arm. He banged some snow from his coat and said, "It's time."

We left the house and Mr. Chamblais joined us on the step. The three of us walked together out of our home, out of Kensington and into the wide street that formed one half of the crossroads called Chi-town.

"We will be leading you to one of our secret places," Mr. Chamblais said. "When we arrive you will be inducted. Answer all questions truthfully and when you are commanded to perform a task, obey without hesitation."

I looked questioningly at uncle Stephen and he just nodded his head.

"Listen to Mr. Chamblais. This is a serious business we are in and your life will depend on what happens today. If you can't do it... you'll have to turn back now and we'll figure out... something."

"No. I'm ready." I bit back a rising tide of apprehension. It was war. I knew what that meant.

Back in the time of the Ancients a raised curb had been placed down the center of the street. The paving stones within the curb were different from those without and there were two ruts where once metal rails had run. Nobody knew what those rails had been for; that secret was lost to the ages and the rails had long since been pulled out and melted down for their steel. But we remembered the rails because of the ruts where they had been, the empty holes standing testament to what had once filled them.

My uncle and Mr. Chamblais led me into that central street.

We walked north, passing out of Chi-town. Foot traffic had cleared a path through the snow here but the ground was wet and cold water wicked up into my boots. Once, other metal rails had crossed the road we were walking, running east across almost the whole length of Trana.

There was a fog in the air that lent an additional chill to the morning. When we crossed north of the cross-street the atmosphere changed, becoming threatening all at once. The shadow of the university loomed before us, troubling and silent.

Uncle Stephen told me that, in his youth, the ancient complex had been a happy place. That changed the night of the fire. Since then the university had become a haunted ghost-town. Slowly, the blocks around it had emptied as few people dared live in the oppressive shadow of the empty halls and alleys.

Sometimes people tried to re-colonize the university. They always vanished. Even Confederation soldiers avoided it. I looked to uncle Stephen and he nodded his head. We were going to continue in the shadow of the horrible place.

North of the cross street was an ancient building of dark brick covered in the brown vines of fallow ivy. Its copper roof had mostly rotted away and its windows gaped empty but nobody had torn it down. It marked a boundary few would violate willingly. We passed to the left of the building, the far side from the university itself and when we got around my uncle unbundled the package of cloth—three long black cloaks with deep cowls. He gave one to Mr. Chamblais and another to me before tying the third around his own neck, lifting the hood so that it hid his face in shadow. I followed suit.

Covered in these dark cloaks we slipped into the silence north of the ruin.

Other men drifted out of the empty buildings to the west and joined our group, one by one. None of them paid any heed to the looming forms of the crumbling buildings over our right shoulders. We walked for a kilometer or so when we came to a place where the road dipped into the ground. Two more men in cloaks waited for us there, each holding torches. They turned silently and led our procession under the ground.

After some time, possibly a minute but probably much longer, we came into a room with beige and yellow tile still clinging to the walls. There were pillars of concrete, one of them half-clad in forest green tiles that looked almost black in the torchlight. There was a circle chalked on the floor. The circle was marked by three candles set at equal distances along the circumference from each other. Further lines drawn between the candles formed a three-leafed shape that, if you squinted right, could just possibly be a trillium flower.

My honour guard led me to the center of this circle. Nine of them retreated to the edges of the circle. The tenth, I do not know who it was, stayed standing, facing me silently. He drew his sword with a hiss of steel on steel. It gleamed dully in the torchlight. It was scratched and nicked, a working sword and not a decoration on some fat merchant's wall.

In the flicker of torchlight and candle light I could not see the faces of any of the men in the hoods. I do not know who spoke. It was not my uncle. That is all I am sure of. "Who stands before the Black Trillium?"

"My name is Kieran Benton," I replied. I hoped I said the right thing. My fear was mounting by the moment. This had all suddenly become dangerously serious.

"Why do you come before us?" asked a second voice.

I decided that this was not the time for a smart-ass remark. "To join the Black Trillium."

"Do you pledge your life and honour to freeing the people from tyranny?" a third voice asked me from somewhere behind me. This one might have been my uncle. He sounded familiar.

"Yes," I said. I couldn't exactly back out now.

"Prove yourself," said the man in front of me. This I knew for sure to be Mr. Chamblais. He raised the sword in his hand. I stared defiantly at him, refusing to flinch, refusing to give him the satisfaction of seeing the terror I felt in my eyes.

He reversed the sword and put it in my hands. "Go downstairs. There is a servant of tyrants chained below. Bring me his head."

They expected me to kill somebody? It was that moment when the truth finally sank home—this was no game. This was a deadly serious and terribly real decision I was making. If I joined the Black Trillium it was to kill tyrants, to kill their servants. This is what it meant to be a rebel. It wasn't tweaking the noses of idiots with clubs and running away before they hit me.

I took the sword and I walked toward the staircase, down to the lower level of the Long Dark. One of the torch-bearers put his torch in my free hand. I walked into the pit and found a man bound there on his knees.

Argus Sawchuk, the feared peacekeeper of Kensington, wielder of truncheons, tormentor of young men with romantic notions of rebellion. He was not so fearsome anymore. His rocky face was a network of bruises. He looked like a corpse already in the torchlight.

He looked up at me and he spat at my feet. "I always knew you were a bad seed," he said.

I didn't like Sawchuk. Nobody really did, he was not a good man. But I didn't want to kill him. He was the servant of a hated tyrant but the sky was wide and MacMillan far away.

At least he had been far away. With LePine dead he would be coming here. He would be coming, and men like Sawchuk would be poisoned daggers in the backs of those who would be free.

But he hadn't done any of those things. I couldn't kill a man for what I suspected he would do.

But if I didn't kill him... I didn't know what would happen. I doubted it would be pleasant. His death was my initiation, my test, my proof that I would serve the Black Trillium, that if I must kill, I would.

I froze, dropping the torch on the ground. It guttered but didn't go out. It sent crazed shadows dancing along the walls. A part of me wanted to drop the sword too, but I didn't.

"Don't just stand there, traitor," Sawchuck snarled. "Kill me or set me free."

I would like to say I rationalized it. I want to say I didn't do it out of petty spite for the many little hurts he'd imposed upon me. The truth is, I don't know. I don't remember thinking at all in that moment.

The sword fell like thunder.

By all the gods, why was there so much blood?

CHAPTER 6

Kyle

I FOUND MARC ALREADY preparing. He was not a tall man, but stout, broad at the shoulders with big hands. His beard was thick and black, his eyes just as dark.

Marc's father, Pierre Antonelli, had overcome much to gain the trust of my father in the confused months following the death of my grandfather. He had been a member of the Black Trillium. But when Quebec City fell and he wanted to sue for peace, his fellows wanted only revenge.

It was thanks to the warning of Pierre Antonelli that the assassins were caught. He even put on the black hood and executed his former friends himself.

Even so, Marc's father never advanced as far in my father's army as he should have. There were too many courtiers who feared the loyalty of a man already a traitor once over. He died, a lieutenant only, at my father's side, fighting at the walls of Salt Mary, when Marc was just a boy.

He died saving my father's life, and his dying wish was that my father would care for his son.

My father honoured that wish.

Marc, for his part, never showed any outward signs of the grudge I was sure he felt that his father had been passed over. I think it still hurt him though. Certainly he was not fond of Oswald's father who had spoken out against his own in council. My father had ultimately disregarded his warnings—Pierre Antonelli was too great an asset on the battlefield to throw away easily, a prodigal fighter. Marc and Oswald nearly came to blows many times in our youth and I had to intervene to stop Marc from hurting my weaker friend but we'd remained close nonetheless.

"So," he said. "We finally get to go on campaign together."

"I know," I said. "Exciting, isn't it?"

He scoffed and looked down at his brightly polished helmet. "I'll be happy enough if we can do this all with minimal excitement."

I decided not to beat around the bush. Marc had to know. "Look Marc," I said. "I think we're going to be facing the Black Trillium in Trana."

Marc gave me a skeptical look. "The Trillium died when my father..."

"Some of them may have survived. There are reports from Trana. They are confused, but the signs suggest..."

"I hope they're there." His eyes flashed with unaccustomed anger.

"Are you going to be alright with this?"

"I'll kill every one of them."

"I know your father was loyal."

"Damn it, Kyle." Marc turned his back on me. "It's not just about that. I see the way people look at me. Oswald..."

"This isn't about Oswald."

"Isn't it? It's his father we're going to avenge." I could see in the set of his shoulders how tense Marc was and I tried to appease him.

"Look, I'm sorry."

"No. It's alright. But my family has lived under the shadow of those bandits long enough. Like I said, I hope we do see the Black Trillium there. I'll kill every last one that I find."

He left my chambers without another word.

In the morning we rode. The road from Fredericton to Trana was a cold one in midwinter. My men grumbled about the chill, made all the worse by their steel armour. I tried to keep my spirits high and encourage them to proceed through the chill likewise. There would be warmth enough in Trana by the time we arrived. I worried about Oswald. He hardly spoke those first days on the road. He just sat on his horse brooding and silent.

I'd wanted him to stay behind. He wasn't a warrior and I feared he'd do something rash. But it was his father whose head came to us in a box and he wanted to see his revenge in person. I felt I had no choice but to bring him.

Still the days drew by and the silences grew longer. I glanced at him and the anger on his face frightened me. I'd never known Oswald to feel anything so passionately. I wondered what it would feel like if it had been my father who had been killed and not his. But that wasn't the reality. My father sat on his throne, eyes turned south for the slightest hint of war and Oswald's was dead, murdered in the west.

The Allagash River had few fords and we had to detour as far north as Fort Kent to find a stable crossing. The town had been part of the Southlands before the Water War. It had changed hands between the eastern states that eventually became Confederation and the Southlanders a dozen times since, only firmly entering Confederation in the time of my grandfather. Many locals still chafed at their status as citizens of Confederation and our army got dark glances as we passed along the main road of the town.

Brutus stared around, his expression alert, always on guard for threats against my person, but his apprehension was unfounded and we made it through the town unmolested. Eventually we achieved the southern shore of the St. Lawrence River. Quebec City was a ruin but the bridge survived. The river never froze, even in the depths of winter, and there would be few ways to get our army across safely. Ice floes had been known to sink boats and I had few engineers in my company. My father held them back.

So the bridge was our best way across. Now it was fortified and guarded by soldiers of Confederation, ever watchful for threats approaching Fredericton from the west. I sent Marc ahead to advise the captain of the bridge that my force would be crossing.

"I don't like this place," Sophie said, staring at the burnt ruins of the Chateau Frontenac. She hugged herself in the folds of her soft mink furs and shivered against the cold.

The red brick walls still rose jaggedly against the crumbling skyline of the ruined city but the roofs had collapsed and the windows stood empty, black and vacant as the eye sockets of a skull. Black scorch marks marred the brick across the building. It was a shell of the glory of the city in the past.

"My family was from here," Oswald said. "Of course we joined with Confederation long before the siege." He looked pointedly at Marc who was returning from his conversation with the bridge captain and was just out of earshot.

"Marc's father proved himself a thousand times," I said, not eager to open up this old wound.

It frustrated me to no end that Marc and Oswald weren't better friends. I would have liked nothing more than to heal the rift between them as both was capable in his own way—but I doubted I ever would. They were just too different from each other. In childhood, I was the tie that bound them. As men, the friendship of youth was cracking and it bothered me. Marc and Oswald had been closer than my actual brothers to me growing up. It pained me that they increasingly didn't seem to enjoy each other's company.

"I showed the captain your father's edict. He'll let us pass without trouble."

"Of course," I said.

"Do you want to go into the city and pay respect to the war monument?"

"I'd rather press on," Oswald said. "My father's death must be answered for."

"It hardly would take more than a day and it might be wise to seek the blessings of the gods," Marc said.

"Superstition." Sophie scorned religion and she knew Marc had a devout streak.

"Good common sense."

I held up my hand, calming the debate. "We'll press on. I'm sure that the gods will understand. We are operating under a tight schedule and have important matters to see to."

"If you say so." Marc sounded unsure.

I glanced around. Oswald and Sophie seemed satisfied with my decision. Marc seemed less so. Brutus looked odd. He stared at the ruins of Quebec City and I could swear I saw a tear in his eye.

It must have just been the wind. I'd never known the brute to express emotions at all, let alone something so vulnerable. Brutus was a hard man, simple but hard.

We turned our backs on the ruins of Quebec City and rode southwest across the snows to Trana and destiny.

CHAPTER 7

Kieran

I STAGGERED NUMBLY OUT of the lower tunnel, dragging the blood-stained sword behind me. The men in the cloaks, the faceless men, were all still there. Only one had lowered his hood: uncle Stephen. I dropped the sword and sank to my knees. He came to me, helped me up and met my gaze with sad, serious eyes.

"It's never easy the first time. But you must be fully committed. We have to know that. There's no room for doubt."

"I know," I said, though I didn't feel it in my heart. In fact, in that moment I felt nothing but sick—with myself for killing the man, with my uncle for being part of this, with the world in which rebels must exist, in which men must kill to save others.

I felt unclean. He said it had been a clean death; that Sawchuk felt no pain, as if that made it better somehow.

I hated myself; I thought I might even hate my uncle a little bit.

It didn't matter. I was bound in bonds of blood and oath and murder to the Black Trillium. There was no turning back.

They moved toward me, surrounding me in a wall of black robes. I dropped my sword on the ground and they were upon me. The men ripped my blood-stained shirt from me, leaving me bare-chested in the gloom of the torchlight. Two men held my arms as they came to me with black ink and with needles: a black flower, three petals, two pointing upward and one pointing down, over my heart marked me as theirs. I let them mark me unresisting. Everything seemed distant. I'd killed a man in the dark and in cold blood. I'd earned the mark, I thought bitterly. I deserved to be marked, branded. I was Black Trillium.

I had a secret I could never share but with them.

I would never betray the Trillium. I was theirs, body and soul. I had killed, and I knew that every soul in the room with me had also killed. No matter what other secrets were shared, this secret, this knowledge of death, would hold power over all.

As I was given my tattoo there was some pain, I guess, but I didn't feel it. The turmoil I felt in my heart was much greater than the pain I felt above it.

As the final touches were made to my tattoo the hands let me go. The hoods were lifted back and I saw ten faces, men I knew, merchants and elders and, yes, rough vagabonds—Mr. Chamblais and two more like him.

"Welcome, Brother," he said to me. He was the first to take my hand. He smiled warmly, welcomingly, proudly. He was my elder in every way, twice my age at least, of a different background, a different place, but now I was his brother. I became his brother the moment I took up a sword and signed my name in enemy blood.

The others crowded around to shake my hand, to clap my back, to welcome me into the fold, but my mind wasn't there. My mind was with a bloody sword lying forgotten on the ground.

They brought me a cloak with a hood. The cloak was black and the hood was long. It would cover my face. When I was about on business of the Trillium I would wear the cloak. It masked our identities. It let us lead our secret lives.

It felt good. With the cloak on nobody could see my face—nobody could look into my eyes and see a murderer.

The day went on from there. There were passwords to learn, stories to be told. They had made me one of theirs, now it mattered that I understand who they were. Aside from a few leaders, any member of the Trillium only ever knew about ten more, generally the one who spoke for him when he was inducted and three times three more. Three was an important number for the Black Trillium. They said that three had special power. Three times three was especially powerful and so that was how our numbers were organized. An added advantage was that no one man could destroy everybody. No one man knew every member of the Black Trillium.

To coordinate we had a secret language: passwords and casual statements which, when said in the right order, carried occult significance. The number three and flowers factored heavily into these passwords. Flowers for the dead, three for the power it brought.

Afterward we ate a meal together down in the torchlit gloom of the Long Dark. As we ate, uncle Stephen and Mr. Chamblais spoke to me.

"When we held Quebec City against MacMillan we were betrayed from within," Mr. Chamblais said to me between mouthfuls of rich chowder made from the little striped mussels that were so abundant along the shores. "When we exacted revenge against the Conqueror, we were betrayed a second time. Almost all of us died in one hot night of knives and blood. Ever since then we have moved in the shadows."

"Who was the traitor?"

Mr. Chamblais grimaced. "You could say he was my brother—an oath brother anyhow. But he was seduced by the lure of power and prestige in the Conqueror's court. He thought our cause was lost and so he sold us out."

"And that's why Quebec City fell?" I asked.

"It was," Mr. Chamblais said. "I am one of only five people to survive the siege, and what came after."

"An oath brother. Do you mean like the Three Brothers?" For a moment I forgot the guilt, forgot the stench of blood and puke in the pit, and marvelled at the idea that, perhaps, there was a man in the room who had walked with legends. Tales of the Three Brothers were popular in Trana. They had roamed the north between Quebec City and Salt Mary rallying the people against the advance of MacMillan in the days before the fall. They'd disappeared after the collapse of Quebec City; the stories said they died defending the walls.

Mr. Chamblais just chuckled. "You shouldn't believe every story you hear." I was disappointed.

"How can we win a war if we don't fight?" I asked. The Three Brothers had symbolized fighting against the Fredericton tyrant for me. I felt as if their falseness weakened their symbolism in some fundamental way. At that moment, with blood fresh on my hands and ink fresh over my heart I desperately needed symbols to cling to: three petals on a flower, three rebels defiant, a tyrant with three sons to kill.

"We do fight, we just fight from shadows, and not on the field. Our weapons are fear, confusion and guile, not horses and armies," Mr. Chamblais said, his gravelly voice lilting slightly. He took another sip of his chowder and fell quiet.

"I don't know that I can hate them," I said. "They are people too."

"Don't hate them," uncle Stephen said. "Hatred leads only to bitterness and not to victory. Don't hate them, just don't pity them either. They take the steel and the grain of the poor, the workers and builders and farmers. They are parasites. You don't hate a leech for being a leech, but you salt it nonetheless."

I said nothing. I felt I had much more to think about than I had before this all began. I had become a rebel and discovered that the romantic notions I'd held were an illusion.

I think uncle Stephen saw the conflict writ large behind my eyes. "It is enough to know that we kill them because they would happily kill us first if they had the chance."

"What happens when we win, when we've killed the last of the MacMillans and torn down the walls of Fredericton?" I asked.

"When we win the people will be free," uncle Stephen said, as if it were a self-evident truth.

I fell silently upon my meal, concentrating on the lake-flavours of the mussels and the broth that they floated in. I loved the idea of freedom. But I was troubled—would we tear down the MacMillan regime and replace it with nothing at all? I banished the thought. The fight in front of us was more important than whatever came afterward. We finished our meal in solitude, each man trapped in his own thoughts.

"You will have to begin your training tomorrow," Mr. Chamblais said. "I will teach you."

I glanced questioningly at my uncle.

"We told you that we fight from the shadows; that fear is our weapon. We don't inspire fear in our enemies just by being secretive. Every member of the Black Trillium must be, at the very least, the equal of a dozen knights of Confederation. They are trained to be expert soldiers. You will be trained to be an expert soldier."

If uncle Stephen had said this to me yesterday I would have punched the air in joy. Everybody grew up hearing stories of the Three Brothers of Quebec City (even if they were just a story for children), of the Wizard in Green, and all those other master warriors who could accomplish nearly impossible feats.

Now, with blood-stained hands and an ink-stained heart I wasn't quite so certain. How many of those legendary warriors had blood on their hands? I was willing to wager, more than a few.

"Mr. Chamblais is the best of us all," uncle Stephen said. "It's an honour that he agreed to train you."

I said nothing.

"You should thank him, Kieran," he said.

"No," Mr. Chamblais said, and I felt a surge of relief. "Let Monsieur Benton thank me after the first time what I teach him saves his life. Then, he will appreciate the gravity of the gift I offer him much better."

I almost wanted to thank him for letting me off the hook, but the ominous tones in his voice portended that he wasn't.

CHAPTER 8

Savannah

THAT WINTER IN TRANA was a harsh season. Food was scarce. The crops hadn't been good in the summer before and, even before the death of LePine, shipments of food from Fredericton had been reduced on account of the "war" effort.

After he died, the garrison cut us off. Boyd dealt with the few Confederation men in Broken Tower quickly and ruthlessly enough to secure the district against any internal coup and the garrison couldn't hope to take Broken Tower by force of arms without reinforcements from the east. They did the only thing they could to retaliate and stopped distributing the food that was stockpiled there.

We shivered our way through the cold months at the end of the year with empty bellies and cold fears about what would happen when Fredericton came to make us answer for what we'd done.

Broken Tower isn't the richest district of Trana. It doesn't have the best moorage—that's all down in Blasted Port. It doesn't have rich shops like Kensington or bountiful crops and beautiful parks like Queeneast and the Scar. Back before the Great Collapse, Broken Tower had been the middle of it all. They say that the money people all lived in the giant glass towers making money and trading money and taking everybody else's money. They say that the music halls always had lavish shows and the restaurants served food from all over the world, cooked by the best chefs from Europa.

But now all Broken Tower is good for is scavenging rebar and smithing tools. It is a good enough living and, the gods know, Broken Tower steel is in high enough demand, but a district can't prosper on one market alone and no man can eat steel and concrete. Without its biggest patron and without any friends in the other districts it was hard for Boyd to feed his people and I could see it wearing on him.

We got the first reports of cannibalism just before the start of spring, when food was at its scarcest. I was mooching around court like usual. After my involvement with LePine I think Boyd felt some obligation to see to my needs at least a little. It wasn't a happy place—but it was better than starving.

"Could it be the Broken?" Boyd asked Old Smith who had just recounted the terrible scene.

"I doubt it, the Broken aren't... well, I hesitate to say, but they aren't generally the types to cook their prey."

"Ah," Boyd said. "We have to do something about the food situation before things get any worse. Can I afford to disburse any more of my personal stores?"

"Your private granary is nearly empty, sir. You've been sharing it with the court already to keep us up and moving and it was never meant to feed the whole district."

"Could we appeal to the other districts?"

"We could, but the garrison has cut off supplies to them too."

"So go to the farmers in Queeneast or the Scar. Surely they can spare a few pigs, goats, anything."

"Already have. They've got food aplenty, but taxes of their own to pay to the king and their leaders don't want to be held culpable when MacMillan comes."

"Approach the Trillium again."

"Are you sure that's wise?"

"No."

I'd heard talk around Broken Tower about the Black Trillium before but I'd always discounted it and here Boyd was talking about trying to use them to get supplies.

"They will probably want concessions."

"I won't surrender my throne. The gods know I fought hard enough to earn it."

I was sent to mend fences with the other districts, try to win us some food. Boyd said I'd have to earn my keep again. I'd not been useful since I'd trailed LePine.

"I'm not a diplomat," I said. "What do I know about asking for food?"

"You ever been a beggar?"

"No."

"I find that hard to believe, Scorpion Girl."

"Never had to beg. Stole a bit I guess. I think it might be better for you to send Old Smith."

"She has a point," the old councillor agreed. "I'm well liked among the districts. Send me."

Boyd sighed. "Fine, yes, go."

I turned to leave.

"Not you, Savannah."

"What?" I was getting tired of this. Perhaps I was also a little bit snippy from an empty belly.

"Have you heard any rumours about the Broken? They may not have been responsible for this latest horror but I hardly want to be fighting them and Confederation at the same time."

"Haven't seen them since the start of winter," I said. "Maybe they all got cold and left."

"I doubt it. Can you patrol the Long Dark, try to find them?"

I didn't like that idea. I hated the tunnels. "Must I?"

"You were right, you were not as well suited to negotiate with the other districts for food. But you are very well suited to stalk unseen through the parts of the city nobody else goes to."

"I don't like the tunnels."

"You've had more experience with the Broken than most people. I'd at least expect you to be able to get back alive with a report." It was a fair point. I hated the tunnels but it'd get me out of the cold at the very least. I opened my mouth to speak, to say yes, I would but I didn't have time; a runner came charging into the clearing shouting, "Report!"

Boyd sighed heavily. "What is it now?"

The runner was panting so heavily it took him a moment to collect his breath but he managed in time to wheeze out, "An army out of Fredericton, a thousand men on horseback sighted to the east. Lord, Kyle MacMillan himself is at the head of the column."

"So my doom comes," Boyd murmured. I sat down on a cold block of concrete at the foot of his throne and wondered if I might be better off just bailing.

CHAPTER 9

Kieran

As WINTER MOVED INEXORABLY toward spring, the rhythms of the sword slowly worked their way into my soul. For nearly two months I bore the mark of the Trillium upon my heart. For nearly two months I lived under the twin burdens of the weight of my murder and the anxiety of knowing that, out there somewhere, the armies of MacMillan massed, preparing to visit destruction upon Trana.

Mr. Chamblais and uncle Stephen had decided, the day after my initiation, that the first priority was to train me in the ways of combat. When MacMillan came upon us every man in the Trillium must know how to fight.

To that end my days were dominated by a simple rhythm. I would rise, eat, go into the yard and I would train. It was cold spending so much of the winter out of doors but I worked so hard the chill barely touched me. My mentors seemed to think it was best I learn how to fight in the harshest of conditions so that I would be able to do so if need ever arose.

For the first half of the day I would be under Mr. Chamblais' care. He taught me the way of the sword. For the second half of the day uncle Stephen would teach me to box and to wrestle. He was shockingly talented at both. I was surprised that I'd never known. I'd never seen him fight, never seen him so much as raise his voice to another person, let alone his hand.

I enjoyed the pugilism sessions with my uncle more than sword training with Mr. Chamblais. Uncle Stephen encouraged me to hit him and oh, did I ever want to do that. I suppose I was still feeling some guilt over the death of Sawchuk, and some anger at my uncle for failing to prepare me for the precipitous moment.

Though he was a harsh master and I didn't much care for him, I had to respect Mr. Chamblais. His skill with a sword was a wonder to behold and he seemed sincere in his efforts to pass those skills onto me.

He told me I was a natural. He said he'd never seen a man take to the sword as quickly. I thought he was trying to win me over, because he also drove me very hard. I think I felt more wrath toward him than to my uncle. He put the sword in my hand, after all.

I tried to remain polite. I'd have been a fool to be rude to a man like him. But he had to have seen the anger in my eyes, and the disgust I felt for myself.

If he did he said nothing. If it weren't so obvious to me I'd have thought he knew nothing of how I felt.

In fact he was a surprisingly kind man, for a rebel and a killer. He was a harsh teacher, and pushed me hard, but he did not spare his praise when I performed well.

I studied dutifully under him. The routine let me escape from the guilt that plagued me for the killing. When I had, in earlier days, dreamed of the lives of heroic rebels, the notion of being a sword-swinging hero had attracted me more than everything else.

The stories didn't mention the blood.

There were other lessons, beside those of sword and fist. I didn't know how many people were actually in the Black Trillium. We were a very secret society and I only knew the ten men who had inducted me.

I did know that there were influential men in half the districts of Trana who had the black flower over their hearts. I knew that we had, with deft subtlety, taken control of much of the city.

I wondered at the fact that MacMillan had allowed this to happen.

"MacMillan doesn't know," uncle Stephen said, when I brought it up over lunch one day.

"How is that possible?" I drank some water. I had a long afternoon of wrestling practice to look forward to. I wanted to drink as much water as I could comfortably hold.

"A man dies apparently of an accident. Another man is disgraced in some petty scandal. Someone else assumes his influence, one of ours. He doesn't declare himself Trillium after all. He'll pay lip service to the tyrant. We only move openly in districts that are fully under our sway. Elsewhere we are a rumour in the night."

"Do the other leaders know?" I asked.

"Some of the district leaders suspect. Dave Boyd, for instance," uncle Stephen said.

"But he isn't one of ours, is he?" I asked.

"No." Uncle Stephen frowned and sipped at some peppermint tea, his favourite thing to drink in the summer. "He arrived in Trana about half a decade ago, and quickly rose to power over Broken Tower. The last lord there was a bandit, and worse, so Boyd was accepted as a lesser evil. He has survived mostly because neither we nor our enemies in Fredericton are particularly concerned to replace him. Until recently he remained largely neutral. His actions of late are perplexing."

We finished our meal and rested for half an hour. With lunch pleasantly digesting, we returned to the work of moulding me into a warrior.

Word got around that my uncle had his eye on me, taking a more active role in the community. Sawchuck was missing, probably run off back to Fredericton and nobody particularly missed him.

Or so the story went.

Somebody had to keep the peace in Kensington and Uncle put my name forward.

He was well liked in the district. His cloth was of good quality, his prices fair, he always paid his debts and had a pot of peppermint tea on for anybody who stopped by. People listened to him, and I was a fit young man.

If I felt a pang of guilt and disgust, if I felt ghoulish for having taken the place of the man my own hands had killed, I kept it to myself. I was serving the rebellion by filling this role, not robbing the corpse of my victim. I just had to keep telling myself that.

Still, it was uncomfortable for me. The most uncomfortable moment of taking over Sawchuck's duties had been when I had to walk into the garrison and announce that I had been chosen as the new peacekeeper in the Kensington district.

Confederation garrison was a huge place; it loomed on the north-eastern edge of the city hulking like a giant replica of a barn but made of brick and steel rather than wood. They say it predated the Great Collapse.

The ceiling was much higher than any man could reach and the ground below had been partitioned into dozens of tiny alcoves and aisles by little stalls with walls barely as high as a man was tall. A single hammer rang in the tiny forge around the back.

There weren't many soldiers there. Once, in the time of the Conquerer, there had been a few hundred soldiers stationed here but, over time, Bart MacMillan had pulled them out, drawn them back to his fortress in Fredericton. Trana didn't cause trouble. "Trana the Good" they called us and we were known for our peaceful bearing.

He didn't fear rebellion from us. What he feared was the idea that those horse-riding savages in Newark might decide to ride north instead of south someday. With rumours of the wars ending in the Southlands he'd been even more afraid of this and now there was a mere token force in Tana, a hundred infantrymen armed with spears and uniforms of stiff oiled leather.

The captain of the garrison, Captain Harris, was a jowly man with an expansive belly peeking up from behind a big wood desk. He was one of those strange men who felt an urge to shave—perhaps his beard was patchy and embarrassing—but the strains of a hard winter were telling on him and he had at least three days of stubble across his weak, flabby chin.

He also had an exceedingly intelligent look in his piggy little eyes.

"You're the new peacekeeper for Kensington?" It was a question but he made it sound like a bored statement.

"Yes, sir," I said.

"You know what to do?" Again his question came out without any actual sort of questioning in the tone.

I nodded. "Break up fights, make sure drunk idiots sleep it off. Send any serious troublemakers, killers and thieves and such here."

Captain Harris narrowed his eyes. "You escort serious troublemakers here. And keep an eye out for rebels. Everybody knows that bastard in Broken Tower has gone rebel. They could be anywhere."

"Why don't you move in and take him?" I asked.

"That's 'why don't you take him, Captain,' " Harris snarled, then shrugged. "I'll let that slide this time. Why don't I take him? Because I'm not a damn idiot is why. Boyd'd take my head off if I tried to pull him out of there. Besides, Kyle MacMillan himself is riding here with a thousand men and horses to deal with Boyd. He'll get his."

"I'm sure Lord MacMillan will be able to sort it out, Captain," I said, desperately hoping I kept the sarcasm out of my voice.

Apparently I did because he changed the subject. "What happened to Sawchuck anyway?"

"Couldn't say, sir." Was I sweating, was I nervous? I didn't like the appraising look on the captain's face. Could he see my guilt with his piggy eyes?

"No." It was a flat sound, neither soft nor loud, it was the sort of 'no' that somebody used to being obeyed would say. "You can say, you can tell me—at the very least—what the rumours are in Kensington. Surely a bright young man like you listens to rumours."

I tried hard to keep the fear off my face and said, "The rumours say that he went back to Fredericton."

"Do they?" Captain Harris leaned back in his chair. "Interesting since he was a local boy."

"That's what they say, sir."

"Keep your ears open," Captain Harris said. "If you hear anything else about Sawchuck's disappearance you let me know. He's not the first sturdy peacekeeper we've had to suddenly disappear back to Fredericton." His voice dripped with sarcasm. He knew. But if he knew I'd be a dead man. No, he suspected, suspected everything, but he knew nothing.

"Yes, sir," I said and saluted. I swear I didn't breathe again until I left the garrison far in my shadow.

That day was past though and I'd had no more dealings with the soldiers at the garrison. They depended on the peacekeepers to do their job. I, for my part, didn't have to bring anyone to the garrison for being 'serious troublemakers.' I certainly didn't bring Captain Harris any rebels. I'd have had to turn myself over with them, after all.

I didn't get much sleep that winter. My days were spent training combat, my nights in my peacekeeping duties—and that gave me a perfect chance to put my new-minted pugilistic skills into practice. I had to show restraint—I didn't want to seriously hurt anybody—but people still drank, fights still broke out and as peacekeeper it still fell to me to end fights before they got out of hand.

About six weeks after I was initiated Mr. Chamblais came to me at the usual time and said, "Today I teach you something special."

He took me into the yard and I was surprised that uncle Stephen was not there. He usually kept an eye on our practice sessions.

"I've told you before that you are a natural. You've taken to what I've taught you so well I'd swear you had practiced the sword your whole life. You are the first pupil I've found worthy of my greatest secret." He drew his sword. "When I was young, I travelled very far. One time I found myself in a distant place, far to the south."

"Oh?"

"Those were dark times. I'd barely escaped the sack of Quebec City and I had no friends." He began practicing a series of strange movements with his sword.

"While I was there," he said between strokes, "I met an old hermit who lived in the back of beyond. I performed some services for him and in exchange he taught me this." He demonstrated some more of the strange moves.

"What is it?" I asked.

"The Triumvirate sword art—or part of it at least," Mr. Chamblais replied. "The sword art has two forms within it; there was a third but it is lost to time. This is the Form of Limitless Cunning. The other is the Form of Limitless Aggression. Of that one I have heard rumours but I have never seen it."

He stopped for a second and looked at me seriously. "Only a talented swordsman can make use of the Triumvirate sword art. A lesser man wouldn't have the speed or the skill necessary to use it."

"I can't be ready then," I said. I was green, untested.

"Normally I'd agree," Mr. Chamblais said. "But with you... I think maybe you are more ready than you think. You are a natural with the sword. Maybe at first you won't be able to use it to its full potential but, in time, you can master it."

I thanked him for his gift and began to learn.

It was a Form of Limitless Cunning, the name was well earned. Every movement was deceptive. Every strike a feint and every feint a blow; the sword art was built to be unpredictable, under-handed, as insidious as kudzu and as deadly as a wrathful bear.

From that day on my sword practice was dominated by the Triumvirate sword art. From that day on I saw uncle Stephen only after lunch. Mr. Chamblais had forbidden him to watch.

My life had fallen into a groove. I'd almost set aside the guilt I felt over Sawchuck. And then Kyle MacMillan's army marched into the Scar—one thousand cavalrymen, just as Captain Harris had predicted, just as I had reported.

"You know what we must do," Mr. Chamblais said.

"The garrison has to burn. They can't have a fortress ready-made for their army," uncle Stephen said.

Mr. Chamblais nodded solemnly. "*Oui.* It is time for the Black Trillium to be revealed to the world once more."

CHAPTER 10

Kyle

SPRING'S FIRST BLOOMS OPENED on the day we came upon Trana in the Scar, a few kilometers east of the garrison. The Scar was mostly farmland and parkland. The houses built here had crumbled quickly in the confused time after the Collapse, but the people remained to till the land. Closer to the center of Trana, the concrete of the city resisted even the ravages of centuries. But the only building in our field was a fetid stable of modern construction with a roof of rotting thatch, which we hastily converted to a gaol.

"This is the greatest city of Confederation?" Sophie asked.

"Look at it," I said. "It goes on forever."

"If I wanted to look at miles of farms and a few ruins in the distance I could have gone to any number of cities. Where are all the people? Where are the sword masters or librarians who might have my book?"

"We're only on the edge here," I said. "The city's got to be nearly fifty kilometers across. There will surely be more people closer to the center."

Sophie scowled.

The farms were impressive. They were still fallow, they'd been recently planted, but eventually they would grow to become rows upon rows of corn, as orderly as an army. My men led their horses carefully along the narrow roads that ran through the fields.

This corn fed the tables at Fredericton, fed our armies. The people in the Scar fed so much of Confederation.

I turned to Marc. "Let it be known that any man whose horse tramples these crops will be executed."

"Crops?" Marc asked.

"Well, where the crops will grow."

"You sure that's wise?"

"I wouldn't expect any soldier in my army would be fool enough to let his horse destroy the food that will feed my father's summer campaigns."

"I'll relay the order," Marc said. "But accidents happen."

"It's just a simple matter of avoiding trampling the crops. It's not the science of the Ancients," I said.

Marc saluted and pulled away to spread the command.

We rested in the Scar, near the corn fields. It was simply too late to carry on all the way to the garrison. We had more men than would comfortably fit anyway. I had half a mind to stay here for the time being.

Later we rested but I couldn't sleep. My head buzzed with thoughts as I lay awake, staring at the ceiling of the command tent. Sophie slept, curled beside me. She'd pinned one of my arms to my side and I wasn't particularly comfortable but I didn't want to disturb her. I lay there for hours, too anxious, too excited to sleep. I was here.

Time passed and Sophie rolled in her sleep. Freed, I slipped from my field bed and out of my tent into a cool, silver night. The moon was hidden beneath a late-night overcast, creating a diffuse silver glow in the early hours before the dawn.

Out there somewhere Dave Boyd was likely as awake as I. But while I was awake with nervous energy he would stare into the dark of night and wonder if he would ever see another. My army had the population of every man, woman and child in Broken Tower. He was powerless against me. I grinned into the night, counting the terrors I would visit upon Boyd before I turned him over to Oswald to dispose of.

A commotion, the flickering of torches held by running men and shouts of alarm at the western edge of the camp broke my reverie. I reached down to my belt to draw my sword but I had no belt, no sword, just the loose cotton trousers I'd worn to bed.

"Damn," I swore and took off at a run to the source of the commotion. A commander doesn't relinquish his duty even when he sets his sword aside for the day.

When I arrived at the westernmost watch-post into my camp I found a tight cluster of men. They were surrounding a boy, hardly fourteen, who was kneeling on the ground. He clearly hadn't struggled, he didn't look the sort, but one of my men had struck him a blow above the eye and blood trickled down his face.

Good, we wanted to discourage visitors in the night.

"What's the meaning of this?" I asked quietly. Nobody spoke; there was no need to be loud. I had always found it put people off their game when a man was startlingly quiet and calm when shouting and wrath were expected.

"He says he's a messenger, sir," said one of the watchmen, a sergeant named Messier who Marc had flagged as one to watch for potential promotion, "but I think he's a filthy spy."

"That is 'My Lord,' Messier, I appreciate your concern for my well-being but don't forget your place," I said. "Leave us. I want to speak to our little spy alone."

"But, My Lord, what if he's an assassin?" Messier protested.

"I'm sure I can deal with one little boy," I said with a little moue of a smile. The guards all laughed. And it was good because it was a sincere laugh, not the nervous chuckle of an underling laughing at an overling's weak attempt at a joke.

One by one the sentries returned to their posts.

"So, messenger, give me your message," I said as I watched Messier dawdle away with an occasional backward glance.

"Begging your pardon, My Lord, it's in my pocket."

He was trembling as he reached his hand into his jerkin. An assassin, yes, this boy who couldn't even deliver a letter without shaking was a fearsome assassin. No knife came out from his breast pocket. Instead there was a letter sealed with the circle-and-spike mark of Broken Tower.

"A letter from Boyd?" I was honestly surprised. I hadn't expected to hear from Boyd before I came for his head.

"My Lord."

I tore open the seal and began to open the envelope. The messenger boy sat there, stinking and looking stupid. I looked impatiently over the edge of the half-opened envelope and said, "You may go."

He stood and fled east as fast as his legs could carry him.

I opened the envelope and read the terse letter.

The letter read:

All Hail Lord Kyle MacMillan,

Your humble servant Dave Boyd, lord of the district of Broken Tower, master of the King's forges in Trana, bids you welcome and hospitality within his domain. I understand you have just reason to be cross with me for recent unfortunate events.

All can be explained. I am not your true enemy. But I know who is.

Dutifully Yours,
David Boyd I

In the margin, beside where he wrote that he knew the identity of my true enemy, there was a little mark. At first, in the flickering light of the torches, I mistook it for an ink blot. But as I scanned it a second time I realized it was something much more ominous. A flower with three petals, one pointing downward, two pointing up, traced entirely in black ink.

The Black Trillium.

"Men!" I roared, and was satisfied to see that several guards, including Sergeant Messier, who mustn't have gone far, rushed into the clearing less than a minute after my shout. They'd waited just in earshot in case I needed help. It was almost sweet.

"Awaken Lord LePine, and my generals. Tell them that their master orders them to attend him at the command tent at once," I commanded.

The guards saluted and rushed off with barely a barked, "My Lord."

I returned quickly to my tent and roused Sophie.

"What is it, love?" she asked, the residue of sleep making her words soft in her mouth.

"Read this," I said, thrusting the letter into her hands.

She frowned at the paper but as she read the brief note I could see the fatigue fall from her. "Surely it can't be some sort of a trick."

"A foolish one if it is." I paced the tent, frustrated. "He has to know that even if he hadn't delivered Lord LePine's head in a box of Trana steel our witnesses would be proof enough that he killed LePine himself."

"Then why?" Sophie asked.

"To confuse us, to throw us off balance," I suggested.

"If that were the case it seems to have worked. And yet..." She trailed off softly.

"Yes?" I wondered what she had seen that I'd missed.

Sophie frowned in concentration, pacing herself through the thought, being careful and considering the angles. "He didn't say he wasn't the one who killed Lord LePine; merely that he knew who your true enemy was."

"The Trillium," I snarled.

"So it would seem," Sophie agreed. "There is nothing for it. We'll have to take Boyd alive."

CHAPTER 11

Savannah

I KNEW THAT BOYD had something up his sleeve to deal with the MacMillan army camping in the Scar. I also knew he was a cagey bastard and was playing the hand close to his chest. I figured I'd find out in time what it was and, if I didn't, I could always run again. I wasn't an easy one to catch when I didn't want to be.

Still, I was divided. Part of me wanted to stay and see how it would all play out. If Boyd were so sure he was a dead man he'd have high-tailed it out of here by now. After all, who would stick around just waiting to die when he could run? I know I would have run, for damn sure. No, if he was staying it was because he had some way out of this mess.

But whatever it was, he wasn't telling and he didn't seem to be in the mood for answering questions either. He just sat up there on that brutally glorious throne of his and brooded.

Night fell and finally he called for paper and a quill.

He scratched out a hasty letter and sealed it with his personal mark. "Take this to MacMillan," he said to the boy who had brought him the paper. With a terrified nod the boy left.

And then Boyd cleaned his sword.

He sat around doing nothing for a day when he could have been halfway through 'Sauga by now and then he sent one letter to the guy coming to kill him and then... this.

It boggled the mind.

Old Smith had finally had enough. "Begging your pardon, sir, but shouldn't we be seeing to our defences?"

"Tell everybody to allow MacMillan and his men to pass to the court unmolested," Boyd replied.

"Are we setting a trap, sir?" Old Smith asked.

"No." Boyd's response was flat. If I could assign any emotion to it I'd almost say it was bored.

Old Smith looked like he was about to speak but Boyd waved him away. He walked out of the court looking put out. I could tell how worried he was about the situation but there was nothing he could do—nothing any of us could do but wait.

Nobody slept that night but a few people passed around a bottle and one of the merchants produced some ganja bought on a trip into the Southlands where it grew. The strange thing is that the whole night Boyd never left his damn throne, not the whole damn night. He just sat there looking grim.

And then dawn came and we heard the brassy roar of the trumpets. I climbed up into the tree in the pit, where I'd perched when Boyd killed LePine, my usual place in his court, out of sight but all-seeing.

Kyle MacMillan had arrived.

He arrived with a hundred men, armoured and on horseback. They approached the square in uniform rows and halted between the remains of two ancient and crumbling towers across the street. MacMillan approached from the head of the force with four lieutenants. Together they rode to the far edge of the pit that marked Boyd's court.

As they did that the other soldiers moved around the edges of the square, probably planning to hem everybody into the square. It was a futile gesture. Everybody who lived in Trana knew that Broken Tower and the other central districts were honeycombed with the tunnels of the Long Dark. If we had to flee it would be into places no sane outsider would venture, certainly not on horseback.

MacMillan was tall and bright eyed. His hair was blond, his beard was neat and he was every inch the royal son of a royal family. The lady at his right was so beautiful that she made my fists itch. I could tell just by looking at her that she was a bitch.

MacMillan dismounted gracefully and, with stern glances around him, strode to the edge of the pit. "You claim you can explain why you killed Jacques LePine."

Okay, so that's what the letter had been about then. Not what I'd expected, but I figured, at the very least, I was in for a show.

Boyd nodded his head. "I can," he said gravely.

"Well?" MacMillan snapped.

"Your father does not rule here," Boyd said.

MacMillan spat on the ground. He didn't look happy with that answer. "My father rules everywhere in Confederation."

"He claims all of Confederation, but Trana has been falling to the Black Trillium while he sits idle," Boyd said softly. The wave of shock that ran through the crowd was not soft though. It smashed like storm-waves under the first full moon of the early spring.

It was odd though, how MacMillan and his companions reacted. Or, rather, how they didn't react. They'd been expecting him to say that.

The short, stout one in the heavy armour just grunted and didn't react much.

The small one with the snake-like look to him; the one who, at second glance, looked like Jacques LePine only two decades younger and a head taller didn't seem to care. He was too busy directing his hatred at Boyd. I don't know if he even noticed the words.

The big albino didn't respond at all, he stood there, watching with his hand resting on the head of one of his big axes.

MacMillan and his bitch, they both smirked as if they'd got the answer they'd expected, the answer they'd wanted.

The bastards knew before they arrived here that Boyd would bring up the Black Trillium. What was more, they were happy that he'd said it.

What the hell was going on?

"Are you telling me you serve the Trillium?" MacMillan asked.

Boyd shook his head. "Don't be absurd. They despise me. They're anarchists and patriots and I am a foreigner turned lord."

I thought about that for a moment, and I had to admit I agreed with Boyd. He could be a bit of a bastard sometimes, but I wasn't sure I trusted somebody who promised no rulers. That usually just became rule of the strong—and that was no different from what we had now. Just more confused.

"Do you claim that they forced you to kill a minister of Confederation?" MacMillan gestured theatrically as he spoke.

"I do not claim that." Boyd scowled from under his heavy brow. Yeah, Boyd noticed too.

"So explain to me why I should spare you," MacMillan said, his words as sharp as my little knife. I don't think anybody missed the cruelty in his voice that time.

"If you spare me I will lead you to the Black Trillium." This sent as many reverberations through the crowd of onlookers as when he first brought up the legendary band of rebels. It was one thing to acknowledge that the Black Trillium even existed, to claim to be able to lead the MacMillans to them... He was inviting a war on Trana. It wasn't that anybody liked the rebels. You'd see a black hood and a mask slinking through the shadows with a big sword sometimes and you'd keep out of the way. That was generally enough, but the order was never inviting—and there was no guarantee they planned anything better for Confederation than MacMillan had delivered. I didn't fancy becoming an enemy of that lot if Boyd started a war with them.

"I think you had best explain yourself plainly," MacMillan said.

"It is simple. I discovered the extent that the Trillium rules Trana almost a year ago. I entreated them to ally and they told me to set aside my throne and surrender all claim to rulership over Broken Tower. I refused to do so and they refused any further discussion.

"I killed LePine because his plan to supplant me would have strengthened the Black Trillium ultimately, and to bring you here." Boyd scoffed, a sound half gallows humour and half bitter pain. I could tell he was running at least a little bit of a con. I just wasn't quite sure how. MacMillan didn't even know Boyd. I don't think he realized he was getting strung along.

"Why didn't you just report this to my father?" MacMillan asked.

Boyd leapt up from his throne and bellowed, "I tried." A cruel grin spread on his face. "But apparently, this was the only way you would listen to me."

"You weren't entirely ignored," the bitch said. "Kyle, where do you think the rumours you heard originated anyway?"

MacMillan grunted and looked uncomfortable. "You can lead me to their lairs?" He seemed feral, hungry as he watched Boyd, a morsel of venison dangling before a wolf.

"I can lead you to their leaders. I have... ways of finding them," Boyd said darkly.

"And in exchange?" MacMillan asked carefully.

"When you have routed them out I will be your father's minister over the entirety of Trana," Boyd said. I had to give the man credit, he had balls.

"I cannot speak for my father," Macmillan said. He was stroking his beard as if in thought but I could see the artifice there; he'd already made up his mind.

"If you return with the heads of the leaders of the Black Trillium tied to your saddle he won't deny me that," Boyd said.

"Fine, it's a deal," MacMillan said, and waved his hand as if in defeat.

And that should have been that. I'd have sworn that should have been the end of it then. But it wasn't, because the snake-like man with hatred in his eyes shouted, "I will not have this!"

"Oswald," MacMillan said. "Please, we were over this last night. See the bigger picture here."

"He was my father Kyle, you can't ask me to set aside my grief in the name of expediency."

MacMillan turned to face the other, taking his eyes off of Boyd. I glanced around and saw Boyd's men and MacMillan's glancing around anxiously, wondering if violence had been averted or if greater violence was to come.

"This is for Confederation." MacMillan crossed the distance to the snake named Oswald. "It's bigger than any one of us." ·

"Your father wasn't the one whose head was chopped off and sent to you in a box. If he were..." I didn't think Oswald was likely to see reason. He had a personal stake in the matter after all.

"My father?" MacMillan scoffed a little.

"Kyle, heed Oswald," said the stout cavalryman, breaking his silence suddenly. "We came here to bring Boyd to justice. Remember our mission."

"I will thank you not to second-guess me, Marc. This is more important than even Oswald's grief. Our old enemy resurfaces here. We can crush them once and for all."

"Do you think I don't want to see the Trillium crushed? To finally expunge the mark on my family's name?"

"Your family may be willing to shrug off a personal matter like this for politics," Oswald said. "But I have rights as a noble of Confederation. And I intend to exercise them. Even a MacMillan can't overlook that."

"Don't do this, Oswald," MacMillan almost whispered. I could barely hear him.

"I would really rather not," Oswald said.

"He'll kill you. I've seen his sort before." MacMillan glanced at Boyd who pretended not to have heard, but who watched the two captains nonetheless.

"You think I don't know that?" Oswald shivered and glanced at Boyd. "But if you won't secure justice for my family, I'd rather die and take my vengeance."

"That's not vengeance, it's just suicide." I could see the pain in MacMillan's eyes. I'd never seen Boyd fight, but he carried his giant sword as if it was nothing, and he moved like somebody who could handle himself. He was covered in scars, and many of them looked sufficient to have been mortal wounds. On the other hand, this friend of MacMillan's looked soft, with supple arms as thin as saplings and a chest like a coat rack. He looked like he'd never seen a day of hard work in his life, let alone a real battle.

"If we fight, and he dies, I have my vengeance. If we fight and I die I have to believe you'll honor my dying wish and cut his head off for me. Offer it as a sacrifice to my father."

"Don't do this, Oswald," MacMillan said.

"No, I've decided." Oswald drew his narrow sword. Its hilt was covered in gilt and it looked more like a long needle than a sword. It wasn't a battlefield weapon. "I will face you, David Boyd—a duel. No quarter asked or given."

"Oswald LePine?" Boyd asked, standing and adjusting his sword.

"That is I," the thin man said.

"Are you sure, boy? I have no desire to kill more of your family. What happened to your father... it was necessary."

"So is this."

He looked to MacMillan. "I greeted you in peace and would prefer us to resolve our issues peaceably. I understand the gravity of what I ask, but I would prefer not to have this man's blood on my hands."

MacMillan looked away. "Then die on his sword and spare us this farce." He called out to his men, "Secure the exits, nobody leaves the court until this matter is decided."

His soldiers moved to try and block off the streets leading away from the courtyard. They didn't descend into the pit before Boyd's throne though. I knew there were ways into the Long Dark down there. I tried hard not to look, though I noticed some of Boyd's more loyal followers edging to put themselves between MacMillan's men and these secret ways.

"Today is not my day to die," Boyd said. "I'm very sorry Lord LePine, but I must besmirch your honor. Please forgive me." It seemed an odd thing to say, and it confused MacMillan and his friends as much as me. It was a momentary confusion, but enough.

Boyd jumped from his throne. He crossed clear over the pit, forty feet across, drawing his sword in mid-air. He landed gently in front of Oswald and cut downward, shattering the nobleman's sword with a single blow.

A second stroke with the flat of his blade rendered Oswald senseless. Boyd grab him by the back of the neck and jumped backward, returning to his throne, where he held the young man dangling senselessly over the pit.

This sent a rumble of shock through the crowd. Boyd's skill was nearly superhuman.

"This duel is madness. Let my men leave the square freely, and we can talk about the future. You know I could snap your friend's neck. I have not. He will live—and I will hold his life as a peace bond until we settle these matters."

The woman who travelled with MacMillan, the one with the western dress and madness in her eyes, pointed at Boyd and asked, "Where did you learn that lightness skill?"

"I know who you are," Boyd said.

"Is it Kite-Stepping? Did you learn it from him? Did he give you the Triumvirate sword art too?" She was working herself into a lather. Her hand had fallen to the hilt of her sword.

"We can discuss this peaceably," Boyd said, carefully, and gestured with a nod to the still unconscious form of her companion.

"Let me test your skills," she said.

"Sophie, is now really the time?" MacMillan asked, but she ignored him.

She jumped across the pit without first dismounting, rocketing off the back of her horse, and then drifting down like a feather to land on the ledge near Boyd, sword in hand. She attacked, and Boyd responded, parrying her sword strikes with the armoured form of her friend, who he used as a shield.

MacMillan called for order, and his men moved to respond. Boyd's own men tried to make it to the stage to support their lord, and the square fell into a low-level melee as the soldiers and workers of the two sides grappled with each other, each unsure if they were battling, watching a duel or attempting to intervene.

"Draw your sword and fight me properly," Sophie snarled. Boyd shook his head and backed up, deflecting her sword strokes with her limp friend. She sneered in frustration as she withdrew a dozen killing blows for fear of wounding Oswald.

They fought back and forth across the ledge, she attacking, he defending. Neither gaining the advantage, after some forty or fifty exchanges, Oswald began to slowly come to.

Confused and half-conscious, he could tell he was being moved about roughly and began to struggle. This, finally was too much to retain the stalemate between Sophie and Boyd. She withdrew one of her thrusts a hair too slowly and scored a gash across Oswald's cheek. A thin spray of blood sparkled in the winter air. He screamed and thrashed violently, shaking loose of Boyd's grip and falling into the pit below, where he landed in a clatter.

Sophie grinned and doubled her attack. Boyd had no choice but to draw his sword.

A forceful wind seemed to blow between the two of them when their blades first met. Sophie's attacks were nimble and clever, full of deception and changes, but the raw power that Boyd displayed was enough to counter her cunning at each turn. They fought another dozen or so exchanges, while around them the fighting in the courtyard became increasingly intense.

Eventually Boyd found a slight opening and kicked Sophie, sending her tumbling into the pit with Oswald.

She landed gently and prepared to jump back up when Oswald came up to her and put his hand on her shoulder. He whispered in her ear and she nodded.

"That was the Triumvirate sword art," she said to Boyd.

Boyd nodded. I couldn't believe what I was seeing. Of course I'd heard the name, the Triumvirate sword art was the art of the Wizard in Green. The man was a campfire legend. The stories said he'd tamed the Broken of Edmonton. He'd also founded a kingdom with the knowledge of the Ancients, was eight feet tall, couldn't be killed by mortal men and had lived through the cataclysm and the five hundred years since. Every swordsman with even a hint of skill liked to claim he was using the Wizard's lost sword art. And every one of them was full of shit.

"Come down here and face me with it where dirty tricks can't help you," she said.

"Happy to oblige." Boyd jumped into the pit.

He engaged Sophie again for a dozen exchanges, parrying left and feinting right, until she had him turned around with his back to Oswald. That's when Oswald struck, drawing a dagger from his boot and lunging to plunge it into Boyd's calf.

"Look out," I shouted.

Boyd acted on instinct, knocking back Sophie with a powerful blow from his sword and then reversing the movement, thrusting behind him.

His sword hit Oswald's armor directly and punched through the plate as if it wasn't even there. Blood gushed out of Oswald's mouth and the dagger fell from his hands.

"Oswald!" MacMillan shouted.

"I didn't mean that to happen," Boyd muttered.

MacMillan pushed his way through the scuffling crowds and to the lip of the pit. He jumped down and landed well, if without the poise Sophie and Boyd had shown.

"Take him alive," Sophie said.

"We'll see," Kyle said, and they attacked together.

He fought like she did, a bit clumsier than her, a bit more powerful. It was clear that she was his instructor and not the other way around.

"Teach me your half and we'll let you live," Sophie said cryptically.

"Not going to happen. Your father..."

Sophie didn't let him finish, instead she redoubled her attack with increasing ferocity, screaming in berserk fury. Even so, for a fleeting second, I almost thought Boyd might be able to beat the two of them together. By all the gods, could the man fight! His attacks burned through any defence. Parries were next to useless against him, the power and weight behind his blows was simply immense.

MacMillan and his woman could only jump out of the way of those massive strikes. Simply put, Boyd was one of the greatest warriors to have lived in a very long time.

But facing a vicious attack from two directions he was slowly pushed back, and at the edge of the pool he stumbled, and the bitch ran six inches of steel into his gut. I'd seen gut stabs. You could survive them, if you got to a doctor in time, but usually they just made sure you died slow. He grabbed onto her and tried to avoid slipping. She twisted the sword ever so slightly in response.

"I'll never give it to you," he wheezed.

"You'll die if you don't," the bitch said, and the strangest thing is that MacMillan said absolutely nothing as he watched his best lead on the Black Trillium bleed to death. He would let Boyd die if she wanted it. I shivered. MacMillan might have been beautiful but there was a madness about him and his companion that terrified me.

It wasn't fair that a man like Boyd would die like that. He'd sheltered me and gave me a reminder of home when I'd felt lost. I felt indebted to him. I leapt out of my tree and into the pit. I didn't have Boyd's eerie grace nor MacMillan's power. I landed hard and tried to absorb the shock in my knees but it hurt. I stumbled and almost fell. MacMillan saw me and reached for his sword but I wasn't moving toward him. His companion was struggling with Boyd's weight but at that moment, he let go of her and fell into the pond. The big old fish scattered around him and the water flew through the air as the pool darkened with his blood.

I scooped up Boyd from where he'd fallen and I ran. The killer woman cut at me with her sword but she must have been off balance and the edge of her sword barely scratched my shoulder, sending a hot shiver of pain through me but not enough to slow me down.

Nobody stopped me, nobody expected me. MacMillan's hundred men couldn't easily bring their horses down into the pit, and even if they could have, they were busy containing the crowd of Boyd's supporters trying to escape in every direction above. I half-carried him (by all the gods was he heavy) into the shade of the overhang that ringed the pit, and from there, down into the Long Dark with the sounds of pursuit ringing in my ears.

CHAPTER 12

Kyle

IT TOOK LESS THAN a minute for everything to go to hell. They say that no plan survives the first engagement with the enemy but I couldn't shake the feeling that I hadn't even got there yet.

Boyd would have thrown his lot in with me. But he had the missing piece of the Triumvirate sword art manual, and Sophie would kill to possess it; truth be told I would too, though maybe not quite as impulsively as she had. Damn the woman. She took a cut at the girl who rescued Boyd but she'd been unbalanced and her blade barely nicked the girl's shoulder. She kept running.

Sophie screamed with rage and dashed headlong into the tunnel without even a torch.

I grabbed a nearby soldier and shouted over the din, "Get a torch and follow Sophie into the tunnel. Make sure she doesn't fall into an ambush. And ask her, politely, to return to me."

She wouldn't like that. I'd sworn an oath to her to help her recover the lost pages of the Triumvirate sword art, to complete her knowledge of that most sublime of all fighting styles, in exchange for her teaching what she knew of it to me. I needed the sword art too. With the complete art, I could claim additional legitimacy in court, appear a stronger successor to my father, destroy my brothers.

Boyd had the art, and it was the real deal, of that much I was sure. I didn't know how he came to possess it. That secret was likely tied into the secrets of Sophie's own past, secrets she did not share. But we didn't know the lay of the land here. Running headlong into tunnels right now, when Boyd's supporters were running every which way, was a good way to get stabbed in the dark.

And no sword master was good enough to be immune to a sneak attack on unfamiliar ground.

The square began to calm. Most of Boyd's people had gotten away. My soldiers were ill suited on horseback to deal with the alleys and tunnels around here. Sophie returned with the soldier I'd sent to fetch her. He had a bloody nose but seemed otherwise unharmed.

"What are you thinking?" she snarled. "He's getting away!"

"He's bleeding heavily. He won't get far, and I doubt the girl will be able to carry him long. And it's safer for us to do this properly, not rush off half-cocked. There could be an ambush."

"But if he has the manual..." She was nearly in a frenzy; I could see it in her eyes. I loved the woman, damn me but I did. She was the strongest person I'd ever met and I wanted to please her. But she'd probably killed my only route to the Black Trillium.

OK, so she'd managed to avenge Oswald and I appreciated that. He'd been an idiot to insist on a duel, but even so I couldn't let his death just stand; I couldn't do nothing. But I wished she would have done so after I had the Black Trillium in my grasp.

Why had he demanded a duel? OK, stupid question, I knew exactly why he demanded a duel. I'd sold him out. I'd promised him revenge, brought him to the feet of his father's killer and I was about to let the man walk.

"What if he hides it?" Sophie interrupted my thoughts again.

"And what if he was taught it?" I snapped back at her. It was a valid question. We both suspected that the other half of the manual was out here somewhere but there was no reason to believe that Dave Boyd had the actual book. He could have been taught.

"If he was taught it he will tell us the name of his master before he dies," Sophie snarled. "That manual is mine by right."

"We will find it, my love." I smiled at Sophie as I said it even though I had no happy thoughts left after this cock-up.

"We won't find it standing out here in this court full of baffled idiots." Sophie was looking around with a hungry gaze I knew all too well. "You." She pointed at an old man whose richer clothes hinted that he was probably close to Boyd's favour. He was bald, or rather all his hair seemed to have migrated to his chest, where curly and white hairs peeked above the neck of his jerkin. "Come here."

The man walked nervously toward her. I didn't blame him. "We suspect he's one of Boyd's inner circle," Marc whispered. He'd been handling the containment of the square. "Please try to keep him breathing so we can question him more generally."

I nodded. I didn't need to mention that when Sophie was in a rage, a wise man walked softly around her. "That girl took Boyd underground. Are there any hiding places down there that she'd be likely to use?"

"Begging your pardon ma'am, but that tunnel leads down into the Long Dark; they could be anywhere," the old man said.

"What is the Long Dark?" I asked, not unkindly. Sophie would not enjoy being thwarted. If I seemed like I was on the old man's side he might be more forthcoming than if I let my love do all the work.

"Tunnels, My Lord, miles and miles of the things; the Long Dark stretches to the four quarters of Trana from the Scar in the east to 'Tobico in the west and from the lake to Willow-Dell in the north."

Sophie roared in wrath and sheathed her sword in the old man's breast. The blow missed the heart, deliberately I'm sure. He made a sad sound as he collapsed in the street.

I glanced at Marc and saw contained fury in his face. This was precisely what he'd wanted to avoid. I looked at the man, slowly dying on the ground. No doctor would be able to heal him. I took out a knife, knelt and cut his throat, let him die quickly. "Was that entirely necessary?" I asked. "He was trying to help us."

"They don't respect us, don't respect you. They need to fear you," Sophie said softly, and a hint of softness in her eyes that, while certainly not tears, showed me that she regretted what she'd had to do; she thought it was necessary. I didn't agree, the death of this old man did not serve us, but I knew her heart was in the right place.

"Come, let's go down into this Long Dark, but let's do it properly, with soldiers at our backs and torches."

Sophie nodded. I turned to look for Marc but he'd departed my side. He was kneeling over Oswald's inert body. In life he'd hated Oswald, and yet he, first of all of us, had thought to see to Oswald in death. I felt terrible to have disregarded a friend and companion so, even one as misguided as Oswald had been at the end. If only he hadn't made it an honour matter. He knew my father would never allow me to stand in the way of a formal call for a duel.

It was an ancient and gentlemanly way to resolve conflict with origins that far-predated Confederation. Once, a duel prevented two armies from going to war; now that all armies were my father's I was beginning to doubt the tradition.

Still, tradition it was and I would have been marked dishonourable if I had refused to allow the duel, misguided and stupidly fatal though it had proven to be. "Marc," I said. "Could you please organize some men to see to Oswald's body? I want him given a funeral as befits a lord of the realm. Have a pyre built on the lake. At sunset we will see to his disposition."

Marc nodded mutely. I looked around for Brutus. He'd disappeared in the chaos of the fight. It wasn't like him—he was usually at my side. Perhaps he'd seen some threat I'd missed. I found him watching over the prisoners, standing between Sophie and anyone else that might earn her displeasure. "Brutus, you will accompany us into this Long Dark. Choose ten brave men and give them torches."

Brutus grunted. It was the closest he ever got to speech. He used simple sign language to speak to his troop of elite guards, men chosen for sharp eyes and strong backs, not for brains. Not that Brutus was likely to choose somebody for a quality he severely lacked.

Five minutes later we descended a staircase into a land of shattered marble and granite, once polished until it gleamed but left in horrible disrepair by the ravages of time.

The torchlight illuminated a concourse and empty alcoves that would have been shops and food vendors.

The trail of blood on the ground was clear, black in the torchlight, and we moved quickly. We followed the trail deeper into the Long Dark, following tunnel after tunnel across the length of the city. I thought the tunnels would never end. And they didn't.

Somewhere, down in the dark, we came to a hall where the tile was coarser, the naked concrete scored with age but sturdy, as if this tunnel had been built to accommodate the passage of wagons heavily laden with steel rather than people. There was a stair and this led deeper into the earth. Below was a long, low tunnel. Pillars in the center were made of pure steel a full two feet to a side. Such riches! I had never believed such a place still existed and yet nobody had harvested this bounty. Were these the bones of the earth itself?

Nobody spoke in this tomb. Each side of the wide tunnel had a raised platform about three feet above the floor of the center. Garbage and debris had accumulated in the center of the floor but the path along the edge was clear.

Four narrow tunnels stretched out of the chamber, two going north and two going south.

We followed the trail to one of the northern tunnel mouths but there it went cold. There was a pool of blood on the ground, like our quarry had stopped there. It was fresh, still warm, and they couldn't be far.

But after the pool the blood just... stopped. We searched, and there were doors and tunnels in the area going in half a dozen different directions, a thousand places to hide.

We looked in all of them. But we couldn't find the trail again; there was no further trail of blood.

We had lost our quarry. They had disappeared somewhere in these tunnels in the bowels of the earth.

Dejected, we turned back.

"I can't believe you lost him," Sophie snapped.

"We don't know how far those tunnels go. There were too many turns, too many secret ways."

"He has the Triumvirate sword art."

"We will find him. We won't leave without him, alive or dead."

"We'd best not."

I said no more as we returned, wrapped up in my thoughts.

The rest of the day passed seeing to Oswald's funeral. As the sun dipped low, we pushed the boat with his pyre raised upon it out into the lake and set it ablaze. It was a funeral befitting a hero.

I felt a wrenching in my gut like he didn't deserve it, like he had spoiled my ambition and that of my love with his death. I swallowed the feeling; it was unworthy.

As the boat burned to the water I turned my face away and returned to the seat of Boyd's court. As I arrived, a soldier rushed to me shouting, "Report!"

"What now," I murmured to the world in general. I really didn't expect good news. It was good that I didn't. The news wasn't good.

"My Lord," said the soldier. It was Sergeant Messier again. "I went to the local garrison to connect with the troops your father left behind and get the lay of the land. And, My Lord, they're all dead. The whole garrison is dead."

CHAPTER 13

Kieran

WE WAITED UNTIL NIGHTFALL. Darkness would level our forces. That's what Mr. Chamblais said. There were one hundred men in the garrison. There were only twenty of us, two cells.

In order to preserve our secrecy we met wearing our dark cloaks and long hoods. We covered our faces with masks and put plain, dark clothes on beneath our capes. It was stifling in the heat of the day. Though spring was young, it was already hot under our robes. They'd seemed a blessing in January, but March evenings were usually warm. Uncle Stephen used to speak of a time with cool springs but I thought he might have been having me on. Regardless, even after dark it was too warm to be comfortable in the stifling layers of our disguise.

The second cell arrived dragging a wagon laid high with barrels. They exchanged the necessary signs and counter-signs with us and together we set out north to the Steel Avenue, brooding at the northern boundary of Trana: the street of the garrison, the street where I would prove myself in battle for the first time.

I was sick.

Sick with excitement, sick with fear, sick with disgust; partly disgust I felt over the feelings of excitement and fear that threatened to overwhelm me. My sword pressed against my leg, a reassuring weight. I was no master; I knew that much after my short months of practice with Mr. Chamblais, but with my rudimentary understanding of the Triumvirate sword art I was reasonably confident I could handle the men in the garrison, assuming I didn't freeze up of course.

In the hoods and masks and darkness I couldn't see any faces but I thought I knew which man was my uncle. We didn't speak as we walked along the wagon but we exchanged an eye-less glance under our hoods and he clapped me on the shoulder.

If only I could silence the misgivings I felt.

I'd killed Sawchuk, and that death alone still haunted me. I'd killed him in a manner that wasn't entirely in cold blood. Until Mr. Chamblais put the sword in my hands I had no way of knowing that I would be asked to kill.

Even so the guilt had torn at me for two months.

Now I was going with a team of men to kill not one man, but a hundred.

I didn't like Captain Harris. I hadn't had the time to get to know any of the other troops at the garrison well enough to dislike them. But could I bring myself to kill a man just because he was a servant of my enemy? A man I didn't like?

Of course I could—I'd done so once before.

But would I?

Now there was the question.

"What's in the wagon anyway?" a voice asked. I didn't recognize him.

"A surprise for the Fredericton boys," said another unfamiliar voice from the other side of the wagon. "I dug an old book from a ruin in London when I was down that way. It was still clear enough to read a little. Most of it was over my head, but this stuff, I figured this stuff out."

"What's it do?"

"It doesn't like fire much."

I decided not to add any questions of my own. The man with the surprise didn't seem inclined to share any more.

We arrived at the garrison in the darkest hours of the night, must have been right around midnight. I remember the moon was half bright and half dark and I felt like I was the moon, a stain covering the shining half of a man with best intentions.

The garrison loomed hulking against the skyline. No other building for miles had the size, the mass of it. It was a brutal testament to the glory of the time before the Great Collapse and to the ambition of the tyrants of Fredericton.

There were torches lit at the doorway and two guards standing duty. They looked sleepy and didn't notice us slinking through the darkness.

We slipped away from the wagon. Eliminating the sentries was the most delicate part of this operation and so the duties fell to Mr. Chamblais and to the leader of the other cell.

As they slipped through the night I could hardly follow their movements, even though I knew precisely where to look. A half-sleeping guard would never see them, and the sentries never did.

Mr. Chamblais came from the left; his counterpart from the other cell came from the right. With two simultaneous blows they took the heads off of the sentries. I recognised the form of the stroke Mr. Chamblais used; it was the opening gesture to the Triumvirate sword art, called 'Sheathing the Drawn Blade in the Flesh.' I noted that I recognized the motion with horrified fascination and set to work unloading the mysterious barrels that did not like fire from the wagon.

They were terribly heavy and it took some time to place them in the lee of every buttress on the garrison. I wondered what they would do. I supposed I would find out.

By the time we'd finished, half of the barrels were unloaded from the wagon. The other half would be placed inside after we'd dealt with the remaining men.

We crept into the garrison. Inside was a wide stair. Two of the separated metal stairs that the Ancients made move with arcane powers sat on each side, with a wider tile stair running up the center. The little stalls within worked to our advantage, cutting off any direct line of sight.

The guards in the garrison were hardly crack troops. Captain Harris had a certain animal cunning but they were in general those slovenly troops unimportant enough not to have been called back to Fredericton when MacMillan first began mustering his troops a year ago.

Most of them were asleep in their beds when we came in. The eight other soldiers who had drawn the short straw for over-night watch had all settled down in one of the little stalls to gamble. We could hear their shouts of glee and groans of anguish as we entered the building, silent as spectres.

Moving on soft-soled feet, ten of us slipped toward the glowing lights of the occupied stalls while the other ten went farther into the building. We crept around the corner but we hardly needed stealth. The guards were preoccupied with their games.

I felt my hand creeping closer to my blade and was disturbed by the sensation. I didn't want to be anxious for the kill. I wanted to be reluctant, to hesitate.

I saw a man, I believe it was my uncle, thumb the hilt of his sword from its sheath a mere finger-breadth. Violence was in the air. I felt like I would vomit.

We crept as close as we dared. It was the moment to strike.

It was my first battle and I remember it with perfect clarity but, in my memory, it is a series of tableaus, not a fluid event.

I remember Mr. Chamblais and the anonymous leader of the other troop, the two most experienced warriors in our two cells, leaping over the walls of the stall, vaulting from standing eight feet into the air with silent grace and swords held at the ready.

I remember a shout of surprise stifled quickly and the sound of the card table shattering as a body smashed into it, blood pooling on cheap paper cards.

The sword was in my hand and I began with 'Sheathing the Drawn Blade in the Flesh,' flicking the sword out of the scabbard and into a perfect horizontal cut with a single motion. It proved as effective in my hands as it had been when my tutor had performed it, and the first cut of my simple arming sword took the hand of a shocked sentry as he struggled to draw his blade. The second stance, 'Eagle Returns to the Nest' looped around to take the sentry a second time, digging into his throat and there my blade wedged stuck.

I cursed, but I'd been taught how to handle such a situation. Swords could be recovered at leisure by victors. I let it go and dropped, avoiding the hasty attack of another sentry as I withdrew the hold-out dagger from my boot.

Uncle Stephen took the guard who attacked me, running him through from behind with a workman-like thrust that was not from the syllabus Mr. Chamblais had taught me.

I looked around for my next enemy but they were all already dead. From the depths of the building we heard the sounds of guards awakening, cries of confusion. The enemy was aware of us, and there were ninety of them, only twenty of us.

I recovered my sword and returned to the fray.

It turned out that far fewer than ninety sentries were alive to face us. The other ten men had cut down thirty in their sleep, or at least before they had the chance to arise from their cots.

The remaining sixty men were up and were armed. They'd formed a bleary-eyed circle around Captain Harris. It didn't help them much. When only thirty remained Harris called for surrender and the men laid down their swords. Our prisoners outnumbered us but they were in our power.

"Go find some rope or some chains," said Mr. Chamblais to me. "At least until we decide what to do with them."

I saluted. My sword was slick with the blood of the fallen and I didn't much feel like talking anyway, or hanging around the site of the carnage. So I went looking for something to bind our prisoners. I hoped we would spare them. I couldn't countenance killing men who had surrendered, even in war.

And then I went down the steps into the cellar of the garrison and, in that moment, all thoughts of mercy, every self-doubt I'd felt since killing Sawchuk, vanished.

I had expected cells. I'd expected prisoners. I hadn't expected what I found. There were ten prisoners in the cellar. The "real troublemakers" that Harris had wanted me to bring into the garrison apparently included three women, three children and one person who was so badly damaged I could not determine their gender. To this day the charnel house beneath the garrison is the starkest memory I have.

Five of the ten prisoners were dead already. They had been brutalized. The room stank of blood and piss, vomit and worse things. The dead hung from hooks or from manacles attached to the walls. No attempt had been made to give them dignity in death. Considering the state of the survivors I didn't know what dignity they could be given.

The survivors were worse. All but one had their eyes put out. Different methods had been used for each. This one had burns on her cheeks. Another had gouges from a knife. He was sobbing quietly. He was the only one making any noise. If they hadn't been moving I'd have mistaken the lot of them for corpses. The silence was oppressive. The last, who still had his eyes, had it worst. He'd been cut a hundred times in a hundred places. Some of the cuts were shallow, others deep. Strips of skin had been cut from his flesh. He wouldn't live long. He stared at me with his shocking white eyes and opened his mouth to speak but he had no tongue and no teeth. Blood oozed from the wounds in his mouth. I thought I recognized him. He might have been an old drunk from Kensington with a fondness for bar brawls but I wasn't sure. He was just too damaged. His eyes begged me to put him from his misery.

I granted them all the mercy of the blade. My little dagger put an end to the suffering of five tortured souls. And then I was sick. The stench was so powerful that I couldn't have contained the sick, even if I'd been hardened to the terrible things I saw.

I collected the blood-slick manacles off the walls, easing the corpses to the ground and slathering my robes in filth. Later I would burn them. I carried the bloody chains back to the floor above, where the prisoners, the scum who tortured children until death was a blessing, awaited judgement.

I dropped the manacles in a heap and threw back my hood. I lowered my mask and I stalked up to Captain Harris, an avenging angel.

"You know me," I said.

"Traitor," Harris said.

"No." I had no interest in talking with him, in arguing. Instead, with the same dagger that had given mercy to his victims below, I cut his throat.

It was better than he deserved.

I led Mr. Chamblais and the other cell leader below to show them what I had found. After that we all agreed—there would be no sparing the prisoners. Nothing could forgive them for the terror below.

We hauled the cots down and laid them in a heap. We bound our prisoners with chains and led them below, piled over them with the corpses of their dead comrades and doused them all with pitch. They struggled and screamed at first.

I put my dagger through the gut of a couple and that quieted them. My fury was a living thing. The other men deferred to me even though they shouldn't have. They let me have this vengeance. I struck the spark. I set the fire to light.

The screams as the guards burned were muffled by the bodies of their fallen allies. Before the blaze got too great we took the log books Captain Harris had written out—interrogations of the trouble makers. All ten had been brought by Peacekeepers to the garrison for crimes ranging from petty theft to treason. All had proclaimed their innocence. All had confessed by the end.

Behind the building we buried the ten poor souls. It was a defiant act. The Under-God claimed the bodies of those buried in the earth. He could make them rise and seek revenge. I was unafraid. I'd given revenge to the dead, they would not rise. I wrote on each grave, "Rest well for you have been avenged," just to be sure.

The fire grew inside. We were nearly a mile away when it reached the barrels, the ones that did not like fire, the ones he found in a pre-Collapse book. The wind of the detonation made my cloaks billow about me even from there. I didn't look at it.

CHAPTER 14

Savannah

WE WERE SLIPPING DOWN into darkness, but while my darkness was one of fear, a claustrophobic desire to leave the dead roads of the Long Dark, for Boyd it was the darkness of the grave. "I have to stop now," he gasped.

I wasn't surprised. There was too much blood. It was sticky, pressing my clothes against my skin, making them cling to me as if held on by a thousand scarlet fingers. I had too much blood on me; the blood of the day's misadventures was everywhere. I was sure it was all I'd ever smell again and it sickened me.

We were in one of the lower galleries of the Long Dark. Not the lowest but certainly getting down there. We'd passed out of the King Gallery and into one of the narrow, dingy tunnels where rusted metal still clung to some walls, too degraded to be of any use to scavengers.

We had no light.

I was blind and Boyd mustn't have been any better, both of us stumbling along in the dark under the ground. It didn't matter. This stretch of the Long Dark was one of the straight tunnels. They were well charted, safe, or at least as safe as the tunnels ever got. I supposed that wasn't much now that the Broken were here. Regardless, the Ancients had built the tunnels to last.

This was cold comfort to me. By all the gods, did I yearn for the open sky, for clear spaces. I offered up a prayer to the sky mother; I might have been better off offering my prayers to the Under-God whose name people didn't speak, but we weren't that desperate yet.

The world had collapsed to four senses and they clashed discordantly upon each other in the absence of the unifying fifth. The stench and stick of blood, the drip of distant water and the ragged sucking sound of Boyd's laboured breathing, the tang of salt in my mouth from my own sweat—a cacophony of sensation in the dark.

Why was he so heavy? I wanted to drop him but I knew I couldn't.

"I can't go any further, not as I am." He was hoarse, the big man's big voice left ragged with pain.

"I couldn't let them kill you like that," I said.

"I hardly expected to live," Boyd said and it nearly broke my heart.

"I'll make a bandage for you," I said.

"Out of what exactly? Your shirt?" He laughed painfully.

"No, your shirt," I said sharply, but there was no malice in it. We needed to move. If I didn't stop the bleeding I'd be carrying a corpse. If it had come to it I'd have made a bandage for him from my shirt. It wasn't like he could see anything untoward down here in the absolute darkness of the tunnels.

But another thought occurred, more pressing even than the need to doctor Boyd: if I didn't stop the bleeding we'd lead any pursuers right to us and I knew for a fact that I did not want to face Kyle MacMillan or his woman in a fight. They frightened me. I could handle myself but they were something else. Boyd had abilities beyond my comprehension and they'd beaten him when push came to shove.

I tore his jerkin free and began shredding it into strips. I thought I could hear scuffling sounds in the distance. Pursuers probably; I'd have to work quickly.

Boyd gasped in pain as I tied the bandage onto him. I feared the wound was a mortal one.

"Why'd you do it?" I asked.

"Why'd I try to make a deal with MacMillan?" he asked and his voice sounded sluggish. That was worrying too. If he lost consciousness here we were fucked.

"Yeah." It wasn't exactly witty repartee but all I needed was to keep him talking. What I said to do the job hardly mattered.

"I'm stuck between two sides. MacMillan just wants my metal. He doesn't care about my people. The Trillium don't care about my metal but they'd take my workers from me. I needed to get one of them on my good side, didn't really care which one." It took him a long time to finish speaking but he finished in time. The silence was ominous. His breathing sounded shallow in the dark.

"Seems like you picked your side when you killed LePine." It was true, it really seemed like he intended to throw his lot in with the Black Trillium, but then he'd offered to sell them out to MacMillan.

"Yeah, I fucked that up. When I found out LePine was going to replace me... I needed friends somewhere. I thought maybe the Black Trillium would ally with me. But I think I'd served under MacMillan dutifully for too long. So I tried to back up, get on-side with the son when he came."

"Fucked up is right," I muttered.

"It looked like it would have worked but..." It was perfectly obvious what 'but' he was referring to. He'd refused to give that horrible woman what she wanted: the secret of his sword art. It was strange, though. Their techniques had been so similar.

"I think I can move again," he said, cutting off any further discussion of what had happened in the court of Broken Tower. We continued a scant few yards up the tunnel when a glimmer of eyesight returned, the flicker of distant torches. Our pursuers were nearly upon us. I helped carry Boyd up a small flight of steps and through a service door. I closed the door behind us, carefully easing it on rusty hinges. It creaked and I was terrified we'd be heard. I held my breath and pressed my ear against the door in the total blackness of the stairwell but I didn't hear sounds of pursuit.

Slowly, inching our way across the floor by degrees, we discovered we were in a stairwell leading up. We climbed it and came to another door. It was locked but I didn't want to be trapped in the tunnels. I set Boyd against a wall and borrowed his sword. It was so heavy, how could anybody use such a heavy sword?

Perhaps it was just that my arms were tired. If I hadn't been so sticky with blood I'd have been sticky with sweat.

Using the sword as a lever I managed to break the rusted lock on the door. It swung open, creaking so loudly it was almost a shriek. Again I stopped, listening for shouts of discovery or maybe for the clicking of monsters in the dark. Silence was all I heard and sunlight filtered through to us; diffuse but almost blindingly bright after the absolute black of the lower tunnels.

I knew where we were now—the upper tunnels of the Long Dark, the Twilight Shops.

Shops no longer of course, these tunnels were unsafe, some of the most heavily scavenged parts of the city, an endless hive of tunnels and rooms all lit in the half-light glow of occasional skylights and of pits from the street levels. Sometimes bandits holed up down here. I'd spent my first winter in Trana here too. I was glad for my knife that winter.

We walked a ways in the half-light. A red marble floor and red marble walls paid homage to lost glory. We came into a chamber that had once been roofed in glass at street level, the Chamber of the Grand Skylight. The marble floors here were littered with drifts of half-rotted leaves. It was a famous place within the Twilight Shops, a wonder of the Long Dark, but it didn't have a good reputation. Bandits roamed these empty halls.

Boyd was getting heavier by the minute. I looked at him and his face was white. His bandage was soaked through with blood, it looked like a bright red sash on a dandy's feast-day dress.

"Set me down here," Boyd said.

He was so heavy that though I didn't want to comply, I did.

"I need to rest for a while," he said.

"I shouldn't have carried you off. You need a doctor."

"No, you did the right thing. Whether I live or die won't be in their hands. I've lost a lot of blood and I won't lie. It's not good. But still, there are some things that matter more. It is out of her reach." Boyd reached into his pocket and produced a small book. It was only a few inches across and it was missing the front cover. I looked at the exposed first page and noticed it had writing, and diagrams of a swordsman. "Take this, keep it safe. Bring it to Saul Shatterfield, bring him back for me. I'll try to hold on until he comes."

"No, I should stay with you, protect you."

"I can look after myself." He grinned through blood-limned teeth. "It's just a little gut-stab. Remember, show the manual to nobody but Saul Shatterfield."

"You give it to him when you are stronger." I tried to refuse the manual but Boyd forced it into my hands. "

"Just do it. Protecting the manual matters more than protecting me does now." With a heavy heart I took the book from his hands and slipped it into a pocket of my jacket. I heard a scuffling behind me and turned to look, Boyd's heavy sword in my hands. I expected to see Kyle MacMillan, his woman, an army of their soldiers. I hadn't expected to see the crouching and emaciated shapes of a pack of the Broken.

Not for the last time, I wondered where they were coming from. I supposed I'd die never knowing. I felt a hand on my shoulder and almost jumped out of my skin. I spun, blade at the ready, but it was Boyd. He was ashen faced but standing.

"Take my sword and run. I have enough life left to spend it on your safety."

"Why?" I asked.

"Because you tried to do the same." He grimaced and he was much more terrible than the crouching, leering creatures, waiting to leap.

"Remember to take the manual to Saul Shatterfield," Dave Boyd said to me and then he charged the Broken and I fled.

I heard animal screaming, the sounds of violence and what might have been a great man, terribly used, roaring his last defiance.

And then I heard nothing more and I fled through the Twilight Shops, heavy sword dragging behind me and tears stinging my eyes.

CHAPTER 15

Kyle

"SEND ONE OF YOUR men to deal with the damn garrison. We have to find Boyd. We have to get the manual," Sophie said, not for the first time in the last hour. She was still bitter that we'd lost Boyd and that girl; they were beyond our reach, at least for now.

It's not that I didn't want the manual. But mastery of an ancient and arcane sword technique could wait until I'd resolved matters of more pressing concern, like a hundred of my men dead, the men with the best knowledge of the lay of the land at that, and a fortress burnt to the ground before I could occupy it.

These were serious problems and, though I loved Sophie, her monomaniacal devotion to discovering the source of Boyd's prowess was grating on my nerves. I breathed in and out mindfully three times before saying, "We will recover your manual before we leave this city, I promise you that much. But for now, we need to see to the garrison."

"Surely your colonel could handle the situation at the garrison." Surely he could. I didn't want to tell Sophie what I feared—that Marc would be too rich a target for the Black Trillium to pass up. I didn't want to lose two of my friends in one day and his family had a history with the Trillium. The idea that there might be Black Trillium members alive who remembered the Antonelli name, who had reason to want to exact vengeance on anybody with that name, was an idea at the forefront of my mind.

"I want Marc to stay back at camp," I said rather than speaking my mind plainly.

"Ah." Sophie drew out the sound, as if coming to a slow realization. "You don't trust him."

"I never said that," I protested. In fact, quite the opposite, I feared for his safety. Then again, he'd been very upset ever since Oswald died. I hadn't heard him say a word since the funeral in fact.

"Traitor's blood," Sophie said gently. "It will out."

But that wasn't fair. Marc had always been the picture of loyalty. Truth be told, his father had never given my father the slightest cause to doubt his loyalty. And he was watched carefully.

The fact was, Marc had already risen higher in the ranks of Confederation than his father ever had. Surely he'd appreciate that.

No, it wasn't fair to question Marc's loyalty.

"It's not a matter of trust," I said. "I trust Brutus but I wouldn't send him to investigate a scene of a battle several hours old."

"Well..." She didn't need to finish that thought. Brutus was big and he was strong but he wasn't a towering bastion of intelligence. He followed orders well enough as long as they didn't require more than a grunt from him.

Brutus was standing as close to me as Sophie but he didn't seem to notice that we were speaking of him, deaf to our criticism of him.

"Not that I'm saying that Brutus and Marc are the same as each other," I said, trying to pass the comment off as a brush-off.

"Of course not," Sophie agreed with a snicker. It seemed that I'd succeeded in distracting her, at least for the moment, from the matter of Dave Boyd's sword skills. She was in a better mood. I wasn't though. Oswald, damn his eyes, why'd he have to go and get himself killed?

A duel, of all the stupid things...

I banished the thought. I had other matters to contend with.

Marc was all too happy to leave Broken Tower and return to our camp in the Scar. Brutus accompanied me and Sophie along with a dozen of our best men to the site of our garrison.

The place was marked on my father's maps as 'Pacific Garrison.' It seemed an odd name for a building, miles from the closest lake and closer by far to the Atlantic than the far Pacific. Sophie, whose home had been on the Pacific Ocean before she came east, said so too. "It looks nothing like our architecture. Why did your father name it so?"

"Father didn't name it. The building had the word Pacific hanging from it in my grandfather's time. It was a crumbling ruin then. He rebuilt it, used it as a fortress during his campaign to pacify Trana. The name stuck."

Sophie shrugged. It was still the most I'd heard her say of her home in many months.

I knew little of her past. She came from the Duchy of Seattle, a mysterious nation far to the west of the Western Heartlands. She dressed, and acted, like a noble, though she never mentioned her family name. I was sure she came from a ruling family of that far duchy.

I suspected more. She called the Fredericton court "primitive" the first time she'd seen it and behaved more regally than any of my father's erstwhile wives—certainly more regal than my own mother, the daughter of a local fishing magnate who supported my grandfather's campaigns up and down the St. Lawrence with ships, supplies, and steel.

You heard stories of the Duke of Seattle, that he was a wizard, or a master of pre-Collapse machines. Some stories even said he was the Wizard in Green.

But I also knew that Sophie hated to speak of whatever royal blood she came from. More than that she hated her father, whoever he was, and would fly into a rage if asked about him. I had no intention of doing so.

When we arrived at Pacific Garrison all that was left of the place was its foundations. The bricks were blackened with flame. Buttresses lay smashed. Some force had carefully laid waste to this fortress.

The destruction was a magnificent testament to brutality. It was so purely terrible to behold that it was almost a form of beauty.

I sent my men ahead, keeping only Sophie and Brutus at my side. They returned, reporting nobody alive within the fortress. They all looked a little sick.

It takes quite a lot to leave hardened soldiers looking sick. I wondered what terrors lay before me in the ruin of the garrison but I followed them. A single door frame remained standing at the front of the building, standing against all odds, though the wall that once held it was mere rubble, barely half the height of the frame at the highest.

Carved into the door frame was the mark of the Black Trillium. The motif decorated the door a dozen times or more, each carved by a different hand: the signatures of those who had committed this crime.

Inside the ruin was nothing but ash and shattered brick. The metal roof of the building was blasted and warped, as if devil hammer-blows had torn it apart from within.

"Black powder," Sophie said off-handedly. "Or some other explosive. Probably black powder, even you primitives could make the stuff, although you'd need an awful lot, and a fire, to accomplish this sort of damage."

"What?" I didn't fully understand what Sophie meant, though as always, it frustrated me to be called a 'primitive.'

"Before the Great Collapse we had ways of creating forces far more powerful than any hammer blow, fire hotter than the greatest forge," Sophie said with longing. "Few remember how to make even the least of these. If your enemies have this secret it is important you do too. I will show you how to make it."

"Why have you never done so before?" I asked. With power like this we could destroy our enemies and spread Confederation into the distant south and west to the edge of the great desert or beyond.

"A mere parlour trick at best—at worst an indiscriminate weapon." Sophie sneered. "The skill of the sword masters is far greater than this."

I wasn't sure whether I believed Sophie. I wasn't sure I wanted to. The idea of a destructive force so sublime that even this devastation was a 'mere parlour trick' didn't strike me as a good thing. But I said nothing.

Brutus grunted and pointed deeper into the ruin. I followed his gaze and saw a heap of rubble, piled nearly flush with the top of a pit, probably leading into what had once been the basement of the garrison. But on second glance I didn't think it was rubble. No, it wasn't rubble at all. It was a massacre.

I walked to the edge of the mound of the dead stupefied with horror and disgust. A hundred burnt corpses, twisted by heat out of any natural human shape lay massed before me.

Chains bound their hands and feet together here and there. Some of the bodies were contorted into forms that suggested they were still alive when they were set aflame. Others showed signs of having been killed before being burnt, shattered skulls and broken bones, though perhaps that was just because of the heat.

But, no, this was even more horrible than if all of my father's loyal men had been burnt alive. The living and the dead had been cremated together.

A single one of my dozen crack troops had the temerity to accompany Sophie and Brutus and I, and he didn't look well. He didn't look at the heap. Not if he could avoid it. I wouldn't have wanted to either but I found it hard to look away. Even Sophie, who I'd never known to blanch at the sight of blood, looked disgusted. Brutus, simple Brutus, simply sighed sadly and, not unexpectedly, said nothing at all.

"My Lord, there is more," the soldier told me.

"Show me," I said, breaking my gaze from the charnel heap.

What he showed me was a row of ten simple graves behind the ruin of the garrison. Graves, not even pyres! Who buried their dead in this day and age?

Somebody who wanted the dead spirits to rise, that was who. I may not have subscribed to the superstition that buried corpses would arise as restless shades, but still...

On each headstone a single hand had scrawled, 'Rest well, for you have been avenged.' But what could possibly have been done to ten sorry souls to warrant this madness? Whoever had buried them here, the Black Trillium surely, wanted to let us know that a terrible vengeance would come. That was why they didn't burn the corpses properly. It was a message, but I didn't know the reason behind it.

I dropped to my knees, unable to countenance what I had seen, before ten silent graves and I wept for the cruelty that would cut short a hundred lives in the name of revenge.

I would have liked to think I would never sink to that level. But in that time, in that place, part of the pain I felt was the realization that I would, in a heartbeat, cut down a thousand Black Trillium assassins, ten thousand. I would wade in their blood, and still it would not be vengeance enough to repay them for what they had done in this place.

CHAPTER 16

Savannah

BY THE TIME I stopped running I was lost. I couldn't hear the Broken any more. Frankly, I didn't care if I could. I was exhausted, exhausted emotionally, physically, spiritually. The great-sword of Dave Boyd was all but falling from my hands and I couldn't put one foot in front of the other.

I hated it down there in the gloom of the Twilight Shops. The walls pressed in on me. I felt like I was struggling to breathe. Then again, maybe that had nothing to do with my dislike for confined spaces. Maybe I was struggling to breathe because I was so exhausted.

The Twilight Shops were full of chairs. Plastic—the stuff didn't rot, it couldn't be worked and nobody in his right mind would come down into the Long Dark for a chair when wood chairs were easily made.

Before I'd fled into the east, into the land of concrete canyons and plastic chairs in abandoned tunnels, I remembered a warm cottage near a river. My mother had a rocking chair of wood and woven reeds. When I was sad she'd hold me on her lap and rock back and forth until I calmed.

But the only comfort there was in the Twilight Shops was the cold kind: a place to sit when too tired to carry on. I collapsed in the chair with the sword across my knees and pulled out the little book Boyd had given me, flipping through it.

I can read a little. It isn't like I'd do it for fun, but when I was coming east that had come in handy for me as often as my little knife. It's amazing how many folks at the edge of the desert would give a hot meal and a place out of the night wind in exchange for reading a letter, writing a letter for them to send to somebody in the next time.

I knew my letters, and I knew a bit about swords and knives. The sharp end goes in the other guy. But the manual, if that's what it really was, didn't make any sense.

There were diagrams, but they were just crude drawings of little men holding swords. They were, in fact, worse than useless. You didn't fight by standing still. Everybody knew that, you kept moving. So how could static drawings, postures or stances, be of any use?

Besides the diagrams all that the manual offered was a series of little poems. The first one, for instance, said:

In a den where no foes may go
Fox unseen, it moves to and fro

But what the hell was that supposed to mean? What did some stupid little rhyme about foxes have to do with swordplay? I flipped through the pages looking for some sort of a glossary, but there wasn't any.

I did note, though, that the pages were numbered, the numbers ranging from 41 to 80. It was the second half of a book. I wondered what happened to the first half. My mind was wandering. I was tired. The little book nearly fell from my hands in my fatigue and so I decided the wise course of action would be to put it away.

Moments later my head fell against my chest and I was asleep.

I awoke to the clatter of Boyd's sword, my sword I suppose, since Boyd was probably long dead, banging against the cracked tiles of the floor. I screamed a little at the sudden noise and the suffocating dark. But I quickly realized what I'd heard. The Twilight Shops were pitch dark. It must have been night outside.

The Long Dark was easier when it was truly dark. I could imagine myself in a room of any size. The blackness didn't have to be the pressing black of a narrow space, it could be the empty black of the sky at night in the desert.

I told myself that anyway but it rang hollow. The desert glowed silver in the moonlight. It was only ever this black when you stared too long into a campfire and then turned to look away from the fire too quickly, before your eyes had a chance to adjust.

A whole night of fire-blindness but without the comfort of a fire was not a pleasant night. Still, I didn't like the idea of trying to find my way out of the Long Dark without any way to make a light.

I picked up the great-sword. It was still far too heavy for me to imagine using, even with both my hands, but it was reassuring to have the massive blade across my knees even so, and I sat in silence, watching guard against the dark.

It must have been an hour later when I saw the flicker of a flame. It started as the dimmest hint of light. At first I wondered if morning was dawning, but as it approached I realized the glow was too localized. In time I recognized it as a single candle flame and I scrambled to hide behind a heap of rubble.

The man holding the candle was old and bent. His face was craggy and looked like granite in the flickering shadows of the candle and his dirty grey hair was long and stringy, held away from his face with a leather thong. He was dressed in old, worn buckskins.

His eyes were as dark as mine, in fact, he looked enough like me that he could have been my grandfather, if the truth be told, though my family had lived in the west and were all dead anyway.

He was muttering quietly to himself as he came, so quietly that I didn't even realize he was speaking until he was nearly upon me. He stopped in front of my hiding place and I heard what he was saying under his breath, "I told him, I told him no, you can't do it, you can't treat them like dogs but no, he'd never listen. Little spider, little rat, come to Saul, it's nearly dinnertime."

He was giggling to himself and would twitch a little sometimes, though I could see no reason why. Surely this couldn't be a coincidence. Saul, it wasn't a common name. Boyd asked me to find Saul Shatterfield, to deliver the manual to him.

Could it be that easy? The man didn't look in his right mind though. Was a mad man living off spiders and rats in the Long Dark truly the great master Boyd believed could protect the manual from MacMillan and the Queen Bitch?

It had to be a mistake, a coincidence, but I had to know. I stood. "Saul Shatterfield?"

The twitchy old man jumped so suddenly that he nearly dropped his candle. "No, Saul Shatterfield doesn't live here." He refused to look at me while he spoke, and immediately turned to leave me alone in the dark.

"Wait!" I shouted.

"No, no, nonononono, there isn't anybody down in the dark places, just little spider, little rat. Nobody comes into the dark places. It's just in my head, but you thought you could trick me. But you can't." He waved a finger above his head but didn't turn to face me.

"Please, I'm all alone."

"Yes, all alone, old Saul is all alone down in the dark. Nobody comes into the dark places," he said, muttering under his breath.

He'd called himself Saul again. The guy was mad as a sun-burnt dog but, whether he was Saul Shatterfield or not, he had a light. He could get me out. That is, he could if I could convince him I was real.

"Dave Boyd sent me." That got his attention. He stopped and turned to look at me through big, black, crazed eyes.

"Dave Boyd is here?" he asked.

I swallowed back the dryness in my throat and said, "I'm sorry, but he didn't make it."

Old Saul's eyes fixed on the great-sword still resting in my grip. "That's Dave's sword. He brought it here from his master. Where did you get that sword?" His posture shifted slightly and, for a reason I couldn't quite put a finger on, I found myself suddenly quite afraid of Old Saul.

"He gave it to me just before he died," I said. I felt the throb of misery in my heart at the fresh wound, newly re-opened.

Old Saul took a shuffling step toward me. "It wasn't yours to take."

"He was dying, we were attacked by the Broken. He gave it to me in case he wasn't able to hold them back," I said in a shaky voice. A pit of terror opened in my gut and threatened to drown me. The moody and insane man before me was more horrifying with each step he took toward me.

"The Broken, yes. But who broke them? That is what really matters. You young things know so little."

"Look," I said, "if you want the sword..."

"Not my sword!" Old Saul said. "Never mine. It belonged to Dave's master. Don't try and involve me with him!" He made a warding gesture. It seemed defensive enough, but there was something about him, the way he held his body, an aura almost, that made me sure that Old Saul, whether he was Saul Shatterfield or not, was a much more dangerous man than Kyle MacMillan would ever be.

"He asked me to find you. He wanted me to give you something." I hoped to appeal to his humanity. I was terrified that he would do something terrible to me down here and I suspected that, for all my speed and all my vicious courage, if he wanted to do something terrible to me something terrible would happen. But it seemed to work. As I spoke the menace faded from his posture. I set down the sword, slowly, cautiously, and withdrew the little book from my pocket.

"He asked me to give you this, to keep it safe." I held the book before me with both hands.

Old Saul crept forward slowly and peered at the manual. When he realized what I had in my hands his eyes went wide and he snarled, "Keep that book away from me. It's evil!" He turned on his heel and ran.

I was dumbfounded. Why would he react like that?

Regardless, in the madness of the situation, I could think of only one reasonable response. I put the manual away, lifted the heavy great-sword off the ground once more and chased after Saul, shouting, "Wait!"

CHAPTER 17

Kyle

I RETURNED TO OUR camp in the Scar feeling wrath in my very bones. Brutus rode to my left, the picture of stolid stoicism. Sophie, riding to my right, spoke gently to me of vengeance. The cynic in me couldn't help but chuckle when she said, very matter-of-factly, "And, of course, vengeance will be much easier to obtain once the entirety of the Triumvirate sword art is in our hands. Don't assume I don't want revenge as deeply as you."

"Did you though? They weren't your men."

She gave me an angry look and said nothing. Her back was rigid with coiled rage.

"Sorry," I said gently. "The whole situation here is just absurd."

"There is nothing absurd about obtaining the sword art."

I sighed heavily. Her behaviour had been weighing on my mind all day—she was getting obsessive over the damn manual. "Why does this manual matter so much all of a sudden?"

"You know I stayed in the east only because I heard the second half of it was here."

"I thought you stayed in the east for me." I knew Sophie loved me. I also knew how important the damn book was to her, though I wasn't really sure why. It bothered me that she might care more for the book than for me.

She snorted angrily but made no retort. For once I was just as glad for her silence.

We arrived back at the camp and I went immediately to my tent to sleep. Sophie slipped in with me but she was still acting with icy chill. I just ignored her. If she wanted to be petulant about her sword art she could be so.

When the next morning passed in icy silence I'd had enough. It was hard enough planning the order of the camp without one of my captains, the one person who I'd expected to be able to confide in acting like a spoiled child. I waited until we were alone in the command tent. I sat down, my elbow resting on my desk, with a map of Trana spread out on it. I tried to affect a stern expression and said to Sophie, "Sit down. We need to talk."

"I'd rather not."

"Sit down or so help me I'll send you back to Fredericton."

"You wouldn't. You couldn't."

"Try me." I tried to put my father's flinty determination behind my words. "Sit down."

She sat.

I tried to soften my tone. "Explain to me why the Triumvirate sword art is so important to you."

"Isn't it enough to know that it is the pinnacle of sword techniques?" Sophie sounded cold, as distant and implacable and cold as the mountains that divided the lands of Confederation and the great desert from the Duchy of Seattle. She must have been furious that I'd threatened her, more furious that I'd succeeded. "Whoever masters that art will be an unbeatable warrior." It was the same excuse. It pained me that I knew it to be an excuse.

"Being an unbeatable warrior is a worthy goal. But we have armies to fight for us if needs be and I know perfectly well you are willing to use an army to achieve your goals." I was certain Sophie had some other reason for seeking the damn manual. I hadn't the faintest clue what but I suspected it was high time I correct that particular deficiency in my understanding, before it came back to bite me.

"You know there are two halves to the Triumvirate sword art," Sophie said. "The parts that aren't lost anyway. The first one, the one I taught you, is called the Form of Limitless Cunning. The half Dave Boyd displayed is the lost half, the Form of Limitless Aggression."

"Yes, I know that." And I did know. This wasn't news—that there were two halves to the sword art was no mystery.

"The Form of Limitless Cunning is common enough, in a way," Sophie said bitterly. This was new. I'd never heard of another using it. "My father taught it to a few of his students. And they taught it to others."

The idea that others had our masterful sword art frightened me. Still, it wasn't entirely surprising. The Triumvirate sword art was valuable, but a coin had no worth if it was never spent. As an art, it existed only as a tradition of instruction. But, beyond this, Sophie was finally opening up about her father. She'd never done this before. She hated the man, refused to talk about him. I wanted to know. I wanted her to let me in. And if he was truly as masterful as she said, there was every possibility he'd be a threat to me. It underscored my need to know more.

"Alright, so Boyd's half is rarer, is that it?" I asked, avoiding mentioning her father, but she surprised me.

"It was my birthright!" I'd never heard Sophie raise her voice like that. Her words were sharp as daggers and I felt so much pain beneath it. "It was my birthright and he traded it but wouldn't teach me."

"Why?" I made my words gentle, and held her hand in mine.

She pulled away. "He didn't want his precious little flower of a daughter studying to be a warrior so he kept it from me. I snuck into his study in the night and stole the manual. I practiced it and practiced it and, in time, I managed to master the first half of the book."

I said nothing but I took her hand again. This time she didn't pull away.

"Some ragged vagabond from out of the east came to my father's court. My father treated him like royalty, opened up our coffers to him, offered him gifts, clothes, weapons, knowledge. The vagabond had something to do with ending the wars in the south. My father cared about that once."

"And it keeps my father up at night. A unified Southlands might make a push north. It's why he's kept his armies so close to Fredericton."

"My father's aims may not have aligned perfectly with yours. But Seattle is far away. Why do you think I came to Fredericton to begin with?"

"To look for the manual."

"I was also looking for the manual. But let me tell my story at my own pace. My father wanted to give the vagabond his manual as well. He found the manual gone. When he learned what I'd done he tore the manual in half. The half I learned he kept. The other half he sent east to be hidden in the farthest reaches of the world.

"For months I was his prisoner there, but he wouldn't stay mad at his little flower, not forever. I left as soon as he let down his guard." I felt my heart soften. I'd had problems enough with an uncaring father, one who passed over his most worthy child and squandered his gifts, his love, on by-blows. I could understand her wrath, and I could accommodate it.

I reached out and took her hand. "A pact," I said. "Before we leave this city we will find your manual and we will extinguish the Black Trillium, but we must both promise not to sacrifice one objective to hasten the other."

"A pact," she agreed. She smiled warmly and snuggled closely. Her big green eyes blazed with passion, the fey wrath that was her default expression blending with something softer, warmer.

I took her hand. I instructed the duty officer to take care of the daily logistics and I took Sophie back to our private tent. We were fumbling at our drawstrings as soon as the flap of the tent fell back into place, beyond words, beyond wrath or the shared memory of pain.

Clothes stripped away, I marvelled at her beauty, pale milk skin, high breasts and luminous green eyes. With almost feral strength she pushed me down and climbed onto me, and we kissed again, more passionately, tongue seeking tongue, the heat of our breath mingling.

Field cots in my father's army were not for the soft. Ours was particularly luxurious and yet even it amounted to a down-filled pad thrown onto the canvas floor of the command tent. The tent was pitched on a flat field of concrete in the middle of a cluster of corn farms. Even through the floor and the cot I could feel the cracks and edges of the pavement digging into my back as Sophie rode high above my hips, grinding against me and digging into my chest with her nails.

The sex was angry and primal and a cathartic defiance of death grasping for life. It was just what both of us needed. I felt pain and pleasure in equal measures and knew I was alive more clearly than I ever did.

I almost roared in pleasure. We stayed together, forgetting the cares of the world, the impending deadline before which I had to deal with the Black Trillium, the manual, forgetting everything for the entire day. Eventually we fell asleep in each other's arms, slick with sweat, exhausted and satisfied. We slept straight through to the following morning. We were unafraid; Marc was a capable commander and had an eye for logistics. The camp could run fine in our absence under his steady hand.

And so it was with some distress that I discovered after dressing that the camp was in a state of disarray. Many of the troops were milling about, confused, others were leading horses back to camp from several directions. The tether lines had been cut. The guards were thick near my tent and looked suspiciously alert under the watchful gaze of Brutus, who had his heavy twin axes in his hands and his arms crossed across his chest.

I elbowed my way through the guard with Brutus following at my heels, and tracked down my newly promoted officer, Lieutenant Messier. "What the fuck is going on?"

"My Lord, the Black Trillium attacked us in the night. They cut our horses loose and set fire to our grain stores."

"And nobody bothered waking me up?" I was not amused.

"In all the confusion, My Lord, we all thought Colonel Antonelli would do it." Messier sounded nervous. I stared at him, exasperated, and waited for the other shoe to drop.

"But we can't find Colonel Antonelli anywhere."

"Well, who posted the guards around my tent then?" I didn't want to have to play guessing games with the man but he was newly promoted and probably didn't expect to deal with shit like this so soon after getting his new stripes.

"Your bodyguard rounded up some of the best men and formed a defensive pattern around your tent, but they wouldn't let anybody go inside. I think they were afraid that there might be a traitor in the camp, Lord." Yes, Messier did have a brain in his head, however harried he might seem. If Black Trillium forces got far enough past our sentries to cut loose our horses and burn our grain there was a very good chance that there was a traitor in our midst.

Somebody would have had to lead them past our night-sentries. That was a very serious matter and one that I would have to address. And I'd also have to address Marc's disappearance. But there was a more pressing matter. "How much of our grain survived?"

"We have enough to see us through today, My Lord," Messier said nervously. That meant they'd burned damn near the lot of it. No fodder for our horses, no food for our troops. The Black Trillium had dealt us a terrible blow while I slept.

And, in order to deal with it, I would have to do something equally terrible. "Command the farmers to harvest their crops. Every ear of corn, every grain of wheat, every carrot and every spud is to go directly to our army."

"But the peasants will starve," Messier said. And he was right. This would be a terrible burden on the peasantry.

"Tell them to ask the Black Trillium for their suppers." I said. After all, if the Trillium hadn't burnt my stores I'd never have made such a desperate play. The time for rest was over.

"Assemble the best scouts you have," I said to Messier. "I need Colonel Antonelli back and I need to know where the lairs of the Black Trillium are so that we can destroy them all."

CHAPTER 18

Kieran

I CLASPED THE LEDGER to my chest; it was a talisman, a life-line to my humanity. Burning those men was a terrible thing. I had to own that—it was my decision, not Mr. Chamblais, not uncle Stephen's. I had made a choice to have the prisoners bound, to force them into the bonfire, to burn them alive and screaming, surrounded with the remains of their fallen friends. And I'd done it for ten souls and for the secrets in this ledger.

There were other names. There were dates. There were supposed "crimes."

Occasionally somebody was set free. Beside each "innocent" notation in the ledger there was a note—the bribe the person had paid to be released. The soldiers at that garrison hadn't been humane; it would have been a stretch to call them human. They'd happily tortured children to death for the crime of stealing a fish, a loaf of bread, and they'd let Dorian Smythe, the worst of the Blasted Port bandits, a known murderer and a thief a hundred times over, go free for "five casks of ale and a whole roasted boar."

What I'd done had been cruel. But the fire I'd set was the cleansing fire of righteous fury made manifest.

I remembered watching as the other men carved our mark into the door frame of the garrison, signing the destruction, letting our enemies know the Black Trillium was alive and would fight for Trana. I didn't carve a flower into the door frame. I'd left marks enough on the ten graves.

We met the day after the raid on the garrison in the Long Dark, entering again through the tunnel in the shadow of the university, which remained ominous and terrible even with my new-found strength of purpose. We were hooded and masked; after all, our two cells may have worked together but it was still crucial that we not know each other's faces.

Holding torches, carrying swords now clean of blood once more, we descended into the tunnels. We stood in a circle all looking inward at a ring of black cloaks, faceless black hoods and hands holding torches.

Mr. Chamblaiss' voice echoed out through the chamber. "My friends, last night we struck a heavy blow against the tyrant in Fredericton. We destroyed his fortress and executed a hundred of his men. We avenged the innocents who were slaughtered in ways so cruel they verged on inhuman.

"But know this: A greater task remains. Kyle MacMillan, eldest son of the tyrant himself, remains with a thousand men and horses camped in the Scar. They will be hunting us."

There was a scuffling sound from outside the ring. Mr. Chamblais fell silent and as one we drew our swords. A bizarre clicking came from out of the darkness.

We began to fall, wordlessly, into a defensive formation, to prepare a retreat. Still, it struck me as odd that somebody would sneak into our meeting and then spoil the element of surprise. We expected soldiers. We did not get what we expected.

A pack of men and women, I don't know what else to call them. They were human, that much I could tell, but they acted like beasts. They had faces marked with pocks of disease, lank, filthy hair either tangled with dirt or greasy with filth, and they were naked. Many sported deformities, blotchy skin, twisted features, one had an extra finger, another had a talon but made of human flesh for a hand. Their eyes glowed with a horrid greenish light.

They crouched and shuffled into the light of the torches and their glowing eyes reflected a deadness of the soul.

You heard stories. People who lived in the wastes, stripped of reason and dignity. They were called the Broken and they were cannibals and worse.

But the closest the Broken ever came to Trana was the ruin at Cleveland. They never crossed the lake or the river and they never crossed the Great Desert. I'd never seen one, never expected to see one, and yet, what else could they be?

Whatever they were they had no fear. They didn't care that we were armed and they were not. They threw themselves at us with beastly abandon. The third motion of the Triumvirate sword art was called 'Washing the Impure Coil.'

Stories told that one of the Wizard in Green's earliest adventures had involved doing battle with the Broken in Edmonton—the things had held the people of the city prisoner and fed on their children. He, at the age of sixteen, had destroyed their nest.

'Washing the Impure Coil' was the technique he created to deal with the

Broken threat. You stepped backward with one leg, slid the other forward, lunging without advancing or retreating in truth and thrust the blade far ahead of you, seeking vital points.

I needed use only this technique as I battled the Broken, keeping them at bay, cutting them down with thrust after thrust. I felled a dozen of the beasts before Mr. Chamblais called for a general retreat. The Broken kept boiling out of the lower gallery of the Long Dark, an endless stream of stinking, screaming horror.

They fell like wheat but they were as plentiful as wheat too and my sword arm was getting heavy. I thrust at one of the Broken, but I missed my mark and it jumped on me, dragging me to the ground.

The stench of its breath was almost palpable. I remember there was something black and tarry around its mouth, and I didn't want to know what it had been eating.

Uncle Stephen pulled it off of me with a chop of his own stout sword. He cut the creature's hand off, but it just wheeled, biting my uncle on the forearm, tearing off a strip of flesh with its teeth. He snarled in pain and, gripping his sword tighter, stabbed the creature once, twice, three times.

It fell.

I clambered to my feet and we managed a retreat. We fell out of the tunnels in an orderly fashion. The Broken seemed intimidated by the brightness of the sun and did not follow. We scattered as soon as we fled. Uncle Stephen, Mr. Chamblais and I returned to Kensington, now even more of a stronghold for us than Harbord, and saw to our condition there. The other men took to their own hiding places in Harbord or elsewhere.

Of the three of us only uncle Stephen was injured. He was still standing, but he'd lost a lot of blood. It seemed the Broken nicked a vein and it was nearly as bad as if he'd opened his own wrist. He washed his wound and I helped him dress it. It would leave a terrible scar but at least we were safe.

That night we met in uncle Stephen's yard. The three of us were joined by Andrew Hess, who Mr. Chamblais introduced as his contact in the Harbord cell.

"Most of our men got out safely," he said. "Bryson Baker took a wound to the throat. He died on the way back. We'll see to his dependents."

"I'm sorry for your loss," uncle Stephen said.

"Those things... they were the Broken, weren't they?" I asked.

Mr. Chamblais nodded gravely. "I've seen them before, in Cleveland."

"But there's never been a nest of them in Trana," uncle Stephen said. "Where did they come from?"

"Perhaps the Southlanders have finally dealt with Cleveland, now that the war in the Southlands is over, maybe they are refugees." Mr. Chamblais didn't seem to like the idea much but he still voiced it. He wasn't the only one wondering if the Southlanders had driven the remnants of Cleveland here. Trana saw many refugees. We generally welcomed them with open arms and had profited greatly from doing so. People with the luck, strength and will to escape the horrors in other lands, to make their way to a new place and to start a new life were valuable.

The Broken, not so much.

"We must make sure the people know. And we will have to begin posting a watch on all entrances to the Long Dark," Hess said.

"There's a thousand entrances to the Long Dark, maybe more, how could we ever watch them all?" uncle Stephen asked.

"The people all know the local entryways, even if only to avoid the Long Dark. The Trillium will not be the guards. The people will guard the entryways since it is their homes at risk."

"If you are sure. You live closer to it than we do," uncle Stephen said, though I heard a hint of skepticism in his voice. I decided to hold my tongue. I felt out of my depth.

"Trana people look out for each other," Mr. Chamblais said. He looked at uncle Stephen. "I believe you were the one who told me that once upon a time."

"I suppose I did." He smiled weakly.

Our meeting dissolved soon afterward and we went to bed. The next morning, I rose early to the sound of Mr. Chamblais shouting in alarm. I came to their chambers to find uncle Stephen still in bed. His complexion was pale, his breathing laboured and he was hot to the touch.

"His wound is festering. He needs a doctor," Mr. Chamblais said.

"I know where one is."

"Go quickly."

A doctor had opened up shop in Kensington earlier this year, a strange man by the name of Fletter-Daish. I'd never needed his services, however, many people in the community swore he was a miracle worker like out of one of the old stories. His home was only two short blocks from our own. A shingle out front bore his name, the word Doctor and a hand-painted symbol of a staff entwined with snakes.

I sprinted out into the wan light of dawn, ran up to the doctor's door and pounded on the knocker as forcefully as I could. I waited a minute and nobody came. I knocked again, waited. The seconds passed slowly by.

I was about to start shouting when the door creaked open by the slightest degree. An ancient face peered through the crack in the door at me through heavily lidded eyes and said, "It's terribly early to be disturbing an old man."

"It's my uncle! He's sick," I said in a panic.

"Alright." Doctor Fletter-Daish sighed. "Just a minute."

I waited on his doorstep for a tense minute that felt like an age. The doctor returned, bag in hand, and said, "Now how about you take me to see your uncle?"

I led the way as quickly as the old man could follow. Though his home was a mere two blocks from ours, I still fretted the entire way, my own stomach in knots.

I'd lost enough people to disease for one lifetime.

I led him up the stairs to our second-story room. Uncle Stephen was in bed still, sweating and breathing heavily. Mr. Chamblais was at his side. He'd taken the dressings off the wound and he was washing it. He looked ashen.

"Oh dear," the doctor muttered. "Go fetch me more boiled water. Be quick about it."

I nodded and ran from the room, to the sound of the doctor and my mentor speaking in hushed voices.

When I returned, he washed my uncle's wound again and then poured a powder into the boiled water. It dissolved, turning the water a yellowish brown colour. He made uncle Stephen drink it slowly. He took his pulse, examined the wound and re-dressed it in clean cotton cloth, imported, no doubt at great cost, from the south.

After a while my uncle's breathing calmed and he slipped into a gentle sleep. Then the doctor spoke to me at last.

"I fear your uncle's illness may be beyond my skill to treat," he said. I was about to speak, to protest, to beg him to save Uncle's life, but he continued. "I can make him comfortable and buy him some time but I'm afraid I will be fighting a losing battle. I haven't any experience with the Broken. I don't even know if this is a disease or some sort of venom."

"But you're a doctor—aren't there tests you could do? Symptoms you could look for?"

"There likely are tests and certainly the symptoms your uncle is suffering tell us something. The problem is that I don't know what.

"I can treat the symptoms; but many toxins stay in the body, and even if I can sustain your uncle, without knowing how to treat the toxin, I doubt I can do more than prolong his life.

"I will do what I can, of course. The fever can be lessened and I can give him medicine that will prevent the inflammation from putting pressure on his brain or heart. But without a true expert in the Broken, I fear his chances over the long run."

"So I'll find one," I said.

"I know of one man who understands the Broken, truly understands them. He might have the knowledge necessary to treat your uncle." he said. "He lives somewhere down in the Long Dark under Trana. He's a genius, an adventurer who spent his whole life studying the Broken, their lives and habitats. If anybody can treat the poison of their bites it would be him. Seek out this man. Seek out Saul Shatterfield."

CHAPTER 19

Kyle

COLLECTING ALL THE GRAIN from the farmers in the Scar proved troublesome. First of all, it was mostly grain held back from the past year. There were few crops ready this early in the spring. Without that grain, people would starve and the new harvest might be endangered. A few dozen of them tried to resist and, ultimately, my men had to take steps. Fortunately, it took only a couple of public executions for rebellion before the peasants grudgingly acquiesced to the inevitable and handed over their reserves. I regretted those. I didn't want to be seen as the sort of man who publicly beheaded farmers, but I couldn't allow them to think it was safe to challenge my authority.

I tried to console myself that these people had allowed the Black Trillium to infiltrate their communities. They'd done nothing to stop the rebels from destroying my food, the food of my men.

Brutus didn't look particularly happy. He might have been dumb as a stone but I'd seen him at times being a gentle soul. I even found him playing with a stray dog once a few years back, an idiot grin plastered across his all but mute face.

Funny to think the same day I'd seen him cleave the top of a man's head off with his twin axes, like a hungry man clipping the top off a hard-boiled egg. I suppose life is built of contradictions.

"Buck up," I said. "The peasants will go into Trana seeking food, they'll put pressure on the Trillium but they won't starve." Hopefully my assessment was right—it was all I could come up with to assuage my own conscience.

Brutus grunted noncommittally and looked away.

Sophie approached from the command tent where she'd been briefing

Lieutenant Messier and the other junior officers about setting up a search for Marc. He was either a traitor or a prisoner of the Black Trillium. As such, it was crucial that he was returned to camp unharmed. We had the manpower for an extensive search. Unfortunately, the Scar was the biggest district of Trana at over a hundred and seventy square kilometres, and there were countless valleys, gulches and hills within the district—not to mention extensive ruins remaining from the old city with all the pits, concrete basements and crumbled buildings that went along with them.

Hopefully the Black Trillium was holding him in the Scar. If they had taken him into the inner districts of Trana, where the ruins were much more extensive and the buildings not harvested for salvage much better preserved, we would never find him.

It was worrying me. I had promised Sophie we would find that damn manual. I'd promised myself to find the Black Trillium, to bring them to justice. But how would I find either in a city made almost entirely of bolt-holes? How could anybody possibly find anyone in a city the size of Trana?

It boggled the mind and discouraged me. I decided the best course of action was not to worry too much about it.

"What's wrong with Brutus?" Sophie asked as she arrived.

"He isn't too happy about what we had to do to the peasants."

"You have to take a firm hand with them." Sophie had an aristocrat's view. Furthermore she had a rather isolated one. Although she was reluctant to speak of her past, I'd gathered the court at Seattle was insulated from the masses by some sort of wizardry, or possibly some mechanical devilry from the time before the Collapse.

Even in light of her recent revelation about the sword art, she still didn't want to open up about that part of her life.

"A firm hand is all well and good, right up until all the peasants rise up and cause a revolt that distracts us from our true goals." I didn't think the farmers could pose a credible threat to my army. A thousand knights with spears and horses were more than a match for a thousand farmers with pitch forks and hoes.

Still, a thousand knights chasing peasants across the district would be vulnerable to further attacks by the Black Trillium. They were a more credible threat, especially as I had no clue of their numbers beyond great enough to eliminate a garrison of a hundred men and level the building in a single night.

That must have been dwelling on Sophie's mind as well. "I've sent a dozen men to scavenge for the materials necessary to make black powder. If your enemies think that they can defeat us by destroying a few buildings I intend to show them that we are likewise capable."

"Thank you." I smiled at her. "I was thinking about that."

"You have a lot on your mind. Do you want me to handle leading the search for Antonelli?"

"No, I owe Marc at least that much—that I personally head up the search," I said.

"And what if it turns out he really is a traitor?" Sophie asked gently. She knew I wasn't comfortable thinking that way about my friend.

"No, not Marc," I said, but there was a sinking feeling in my gut, like maybe I should be willing to consider the possibility. Marc had been my closest companion since my childhood, and had advanced because of it. I still hated to think that he might harbour a grudge for how his father was treated by mine, that he might be anything other than my closest friend.

But now with the grain silo destroyed, horses scattered and Marc missing, I had to consider it.

"But what if he is?" Sophie said.

"If he is I'll execute him myself, and make sure the deed is done as painlessly as possible."

Sophie embraced me, resting her head against my chest. "You will make a good king, better than your father. He is such a fool."

I spoke in a hushed voice. "If I can return with Trana under control once more and the heads of the Black Trillum dangling from my saddle I can sway the senior generals. Then I won't have to strive against my younger brothers just to get what should be mine by right, to inherit Confederation."

"Why even wait? The generals would follow you. And when we have the whole of the manual in our power you will need not fear your father's personal strength." Sophie nearly purred it. After all, it was another very good reason to take possession of the Form of Limitless Aggression, to complete the Triumvirate sword art.

I agreed, but I wasn't comfortable talking openly about overthrowing my father. I changed the subject. "So tell me about the attack on our camp. What have you managed to figure out?"

"The horses were cut loose first," Sophie said. "There were two guards watching the hitching lines. They were both killed quietly and efficiently—decapitation." I grimaced. I didn't like the idea that somebody could chop the heads off my men on a whim from within my camp.

"After that, whoever it was moved halfway across the camp to the grain silos. They didn't alert any of the inner sentries in the process, or at least none are missing. They set fire to the silo and then left. There were four guards posted at the silo. All four were also found dead."

"Any others dead or missing?" I hoped the answer was no. Six men were enough to lose in a manner such as this but, beyond that, a nagging sense of something else wrong, something I was missing, assailed me but it was too fleeting and I couldn't quite pin down what it was.

"None." Sophie shook her head and her big green eyes gazed into mine with signs of concern that mirrored what I felt in my heart. "But consider this: none of the camp guards were disturbed, none of the outer watchmen."

"So the Black Trillium had helpers within the camp."

"Helpers with influence, a high ranking traitor. Somebody with a past tied to the enemy."

"Can we account for the activities of the sergeants last night?" In a way I hoped we couldn't.

Sophie shook her head and spoke slowly, choosing her words carefully.

"Not entirely. Most of the sergeants were asleep in their tents when the attack happened. If one slipped away it would be hard to prove. But honestly, do you believe a sergeant could have the necessary pull to accomplish this madness? You know there is only one man who could have done this: the one who fled."

"I can't believe this of Marc. Not him."

"And his father was Black Trillium. So he saw which side his bread was buttered on at Quebec City. Perhaps they've been looking for a chance for vengeance all along." Sophie's words terrified me because they made sense, they really made sense.

But I didn't like the implication of that.

"Either way, we can't do anything until we find Marc," I said. "Have we made any progress there?"

"We're setting up a search pattern; concentric circles starting from the camp and extending in all directions from there. I've got two hundred men assigned to the search."

"Can we spare so many? What of our missions?"

"The sooner we can recover Antonelli, the sooner we can get back to our true business here." She didn't bother mentioning which of our missions she personally saw as our true business. I thought I could guess.

"Very well." I turned to the tethering lines. "We'll lead the search personally. Whether captured friend or treasonous foe, the recovery of Marc Antonelli must be our primary goal. Let's find him quickly."

CHAPTER 20

Savannah

I CHASED OLD SAUL through the darkness of the Twilight Shops. In part I think I wanted to stay close to another person. I was usually fine with solitude but, after what happened to Dave Boyd, I didn't much feel like being alone. And then there was the matter of Boyd's last instructions to me.

Old Saul seemed to be totally cracked but he also had light, maybe even somewhere safe to stay until daylight. Even without Boyd's request I might have followed him. Knowing that Boyd wanted me to take the book to Saul Shatterfield (who I suspected this man of being) left me even more determined to follow him. But why had Old Saul acted so strangely when I tried to give him the book?

What was it about this book that frightened him so much?

I don't know how long I chased him. It felt like an hour. My lungs burned with the effort and my legs were sending daggers of pain into me. I needed rest, needed real sleep, not half-sleep propped in a chair with a sword over my knees.

Fortunately, Old Saul eventually stopped running in a vast chamber in the Twilight Shops. I think I recognized it. High above, higher than any space I'd ever seen, steel girders still remained, arching impossibly over the chamber. Scavengers hadn't taken much of the steel; the arches were only able to support themselves without gaps. If you took away one piece of steel the whole arch would collapse and take you deep into the pit beneath the earth along with it. Nobody could survive a fall like that, so they left this steel alone.

This was the Cathedral of Broken Glass, a haunted mausoleum to what had once been. Stories said that it had been a shopping place once, one right at the heart of Trana. Now it marked the northern edge of Broken Tower and the eastern edge too, for that matter. It had been a place of worship for a while but nobody felt comfortable coming here.

The steel arches were too terrifying a roof to look at. You could imagine them falling on you at any moment.

Like almost all the places in the Twilight Shops, the Cathedral of Broken Glass was full of little alcoves that had once been shops. I found Saul crouching in one of the smaller of these alcoves. It was a mess, a sure sign of a disturbed mind. The walls were covered in writing. I glanced at them but I couldn't make out any of the words. They looked like nonsense, or maybe some other language, possibly more than one other language. Some of the words were made with letters I recognized, though I couldn't make out all of them.

Other words were made with the odd, complicated and squiggly letters that were common in Chi-Town, Kensington and a few other districts. Those I couldn't read at all.

Strange though the walls were, the rest of the room was even stranger. There were stacks of boxes everywhere. Most of the boxes had little holes in them. One of the boxes at the top of the stack didn't have a lid on it. I saw... things... in the box, and felt a surge of sudden, unsure disgust. I peered into the gloom of the stall, stared at the box. As I watched, a centipede wriggled out of the box.

With blinding speed, Old Saul snatched the creature up and put it in his mouth, chewing loudly and apparently enjoying the disgusting thing with gusto. I've seen some messed up things in my past. Sometimes, when I was desperate, I'd even eaten meat that I didn't know the source of. Possibly rat, possibly gopher or raccoon or one of the dozen other little pest animals that people hunted for food and fur.

But live bugs?

Yuck.

Old Saul was avoiding me again. I looked at what he was doing and found that, his snack over, he was writing something in a blank corner of one wall, down near the floor, with a stick of crude charcoal. He was muttering to himself as he wrote. "No, no Shatterfield. Saul Shatterfield is gone and won't come back." He chuckled manically. "Nobody can find him because he's gone. No Shatterfield, not any more, just Old Saul."

"Saul?" I was divided. I wasn't certain I wanted to spend time around this lunatic. He had clearly filthy personal habits. I mean, seriously, eating live bugs? But I felt a pang of pity for him. He wasn't a well man. And yet Dave Boyd had told me only he could protect the manual.

It seemed like he was Saul Shatterfield, regardless of what he was muttering about Shatterfield being gone. Why was this manual safest with a crazy old man living in the Twilight Shops?

"Go away, you aren't real," Saul snarled. "People who aren't real aren't allowed in my house. Didn't you see the sign?" He waved vaguely at a piece of foreign writing near the entryway. It looked mostly like gentle curves and dots. I didn't recognize the script from any language I'd ever encountered.

"I can't read that."

Saul chuckled again. "That's funny." He looked at me with his crazed, dark eyes dangerously intense. "You are a figment of my imagination and you can't even read simple Arabic."

I seemed to recall Arabic being a language from before the Collapse. "Are you a scholar?"

"No!" Old Saul said with evident distress. "Not a scholar. No books, see, no books, just rats and spiders, scorpions and centipedes. Tasty snacks, try some. They're good for you."

"Thanks but no," I said cautiously. "Look, I need to talk to you. It's about Dave Boyd."

"Boyd's gone, all gone, lost to the evil book. I told him not to read it but nobody listens to Old Saul."

"Boyd is gone," I said, and felt a renewed pang of pain, "because he was murdered by Kyle MacMillan and pulled down by the Broken."

"The Broken? No, Defiled." Old Saul's eyes became momentarily astute. "Don't be silly, no Defiled in the Long Dark. That's why I chose here. No Defiled, safe. Yes, just me and my bugs. No books, just bugs, tasty bugs, good bugs, have some."

I ignored his second invitation.

"Please, you have to help me. I don't know where else to turn with this." I took a few steps toward him. He shuffled his feet, pressing himself into the corner and turning his back to me, but he didn't run. I was in his den. This was where he ran to. I thought I understood this much about him at least.

"Old Saul can't help anybody."

I decided to try a different tack. "Evil people want the evil book."

"No, no, that would be bad. If evil people get the evil book they'll just use it to do evil things. We can't have that."

"So will you protect it?" I hoped I was getting through to him.

"No, no, it's evil, won't touch it, it isn't safe."

Damn.

I sat down on a clean space of floor and tried hard not to think about what was producing the rustling noises in the box next to my shoulder. Old Saul started rocking back and forth, banging his head gently against the wall. "It doesn't add up, doesn't add up, the numbers aren't right."

His shoulders shook like he was sobbing under his breath. I'd never seen somebody so... broken.

I wanted to help him. I told him so.

He just laughed. "No helping Old Saul. Old Saul is beyond all help. No, he's gone, gone and he's not coming back. Nobody can fix it."

I tried something, I figured it would either get through to him or it would lead to an awkward situation and me running as fast as my legs could carry me from this strangely spry old man. "I'm not an ordinary girl. Dave Boyd called me a scorpion girl."

He stopped sobbing and turned around again, looking at me inquisitively. "A scorpion, eh? But what sort?" he asked curiously.

I hadn't the first clue how to respond. A scorpion was a scorpion, right?

"They're all the same, aren't they?"

"No, some are big, vicious, useless. Others, are small, deadly. You don't strike me as entirely useless. Perhaps you are one of the little ones. The Leiurus maybe. Boyd was right to send you to me, little Leiurus."

"My name is Savannah."

"Scorpions don't have names. But I'll call you Leiurus, yes, Leiurus is a perfectly suitable name for a scorpion girl." He stood and walked over to me, peering intently at me. I decided the best course of action would be to remain perfectly still. I was winning over this nutcase but he was still crazy, and I suspected dangerous.

Eventually he nodded, in evident satisfaction.

"So," I said. "Can you protect Boyd's manual?"

"I told you, little Leiurus, I can't touch it. The book is evil." He paused in thought for a moment. "But good and evil don't matter to a scorpion. You're such wonderfully simple creatures when it comes to moral conundrums. I'll tell you what. You hold onto the evil book and I'll teach you how to protect it yourself."

I didn't see much likelihood of a better offer, but I needed to specify something. "As long as I don't have to eat any bugs."

"Oh no, I can understand you don't want to eat bugs, that would be like a human eating a monkey or an ape, they might be relatives of yours. No, little Leiurus, I've got something better for you. I've got all this rat and if somebody doesn't help me finish it off it's going to spoil."

CHAPTER 21

Kyle

TWO MONTHS OF SEARCHING, and nothing. Not the barest hint of where Marc might be. My men scoured the Scar. Every basement, every pit, every valley and every hill; they searched everywhere. And then, on a gloomy, overcast summer morning, when the air was thick with heat and water from the lake and stank of rotting fish and human sweat, Lieutenant Messier reported to the command tent.

He was standing in the doorway, bright and efficient and alert even though the shine was far from worn off the morning. He'd taken well to his field promotions in the months since the attack. He may not have been the warrior that Marc had been but he had a logistical mind and I'd come to rely on him to handle the day-to-day operations of the camp.

He had a letter in his hand. It was sealed with a blood-red drop of wax. I recognized the mark. It was a letter from my father.

"Lord, a messenger arrived a few minutes ago." He extended the letter to me, like a talisman.

I suspected I knew what the letter was. I was late. I should have arrived home, long since. Instead I had sent no word, had not contacted my father. He must be expecting me. Nevertheless, I took the ominous letter from Messier and tore it open. After reading it I said, "Thank you, Messier. Please bring the messenger here directly."

"Yes, My Lord." Messier saluted and turned to leave.

"And Messier," I added to his retreating back.

Messier stopped, listening for his commands.

"See to it he doesn't talk to anybody on the way in." I was interested to see how Messier handled that instruction.

"Yes, Lord."

Good.

I glanced back at the letter. I'd not liked what it had to say the first time. I liked it less the second.

My Son,

I have been waiting to hear word from you; your mission was simple, execute Dave Boyd, chastise his followers and return. I expected you back weeks ago.

And yet, spring is nearly over and you have not reported back. Furthermore you still have my thousand men and my thousand horses. I have need of those men.

Return to Fredericton now. You have failed me again. Your mission is over.

Bartholomew MacMillan I, son of the Conqueror, Great King of all Confederation

This would not do.

Sophie stepped into the command tent. "What's troubling you?"

I showed her the letter in mute anger. She took the page and read it, her face inscrutable.

"We expected your father would do this. But there is little he can do to you. It isn't like he is likely to come here with another thousand men to collect you, he is too fearful of an attack from the Southlanders."

"I know." But I still felt uneasy. I was not ready to confront my father. I longed to prove myself his equal, a worthy heir. Just like he had to Grandfather, at least, if the stories I heard told around camp were to be believed.

How did one prove himself worthy heir to a conqueror? He did it through conquest, or by conquering the one he would succeed. I knew Sophie wanted me to take what was mine from my father. She'd said as much to me several times since we'd come to Trana. But I still didn't know if I could.

Regardless, the time was not right. I needed a victory to win the support of the troops. If I moved against the old man it would be my head on a spike.

The flap to the command tent opened and Lieutenant Messier entered, escorting a messenger, still dusty from the road west.

"Thank you for coming." I smiled brightly at the messenger.

"Thank you, sir," the messenger replied just a hint too crisply, as if he resented having been dragged here. Also, he called me 'Sir,' rather than 'Lord,' as was my due as son of the king and heir apparent.

Messier didn't like that. I could see his disapproval for the laconic way of the messenger writ large across his face.

"Was it a long trip from Fredericton?" I asked.

"I didn't come all the way from Fredericton, sir. A messenger bird arrived at the Kingston garrison, I sent it on to Trana but it returned with the message still unread. I hastened here in person when that happened."

"Tell me, did you read the message my lord father sent before you delivered it?" It was a reasonable enough question. I had already decided what was to come—that decision had been made the second Messier had shown me the letter. Still I felt a need to keep up appearances.

"No, sir."

"And did you speak to anybody about your mission?" I smiled serenely at him.

"No, sir, the mission was supposed to remain secret, sir."

"Very good." I gestured for him to leave. "You may go. There is no return message."

"Sir," the messenger barked. He turned to leave and, as soon as his back was to me, I drew my dagger from my boot and threw it. The dagger buried itself to the hilt in the messenger's neck and he fell to the ground, twitching wordlessly in a growing pool of his own dark, red blood.

I burned the letter. "Lieutenant Messier, there was no messenger from my father this morning. There was a prisoner, a member of the Black Trillium. You brought him to me for interrogation and, alas, he died while trying to escape."

"I understand, Lord," Messier said.

"Very good; now please dispose of the body. Every prisoner should get a proper cremation after all." I smiled at Messier. He saluted crisply and dragged the body out.

"There will be consequences," I said to Sophie.

"You will overcome them," she said.

"You know, the hills are dangerous this time of year; so many bandits about. Who knows how many messages might go astray?" I grinned at her, held her hand.

"What does it matter? I say you tell your father you killed his messenger, destroyed his message. What will he do? You can overthrow him."

I kept my peace. I scarcely dared even think such things.

Soon after, we discovered a good omen that disregarding my father's wishes was the right course of action. It was less than a day later that we finally found Marc in the filthy tattered rags of his once-splendid clothes in a pit on the north-west edge of the Scar. The walls were concrete and sheer and there was no way out. This bestial city seemed pocked with these hollowed-out holes where buildings had once stood.

His beard was long and unkempt, his hair filthy. I found him myself, while patrolling and, when he saw me, he screamed for joy and raved, half mad from loneliness and exposure. Mostly he begged to be freed from the pit.

I wondered if this was a false smile. This could all be a display for my benefit. He could have grown out his beard, found a site in our path when he was ready to return, to make it seem like he was held prisoner.

After all, there were no guards watching him, no stock of food.

No, he couldn't have been there long. He'd have died of starvation and thirst by now if he had been.

But, then again, he was an old friend. Perhaps I owed him the benefit of the doubt.

Well, as Sophie was wont to say, I could always spare him now, kill him later. I could not do the reverse. "OK, I'm lowering a rope down to you," I called back.

Marc scrambled up the rope and embraced me warmly. If he was a traitor he was a good actor. But I'm sure his father's friends had thought the same in Quebec City.

I returned the embrace and grinned at my friend. I only hoped he didn't see the steel in my eyes.

We returned to camp and I assembled my lieutenants together at the command tent. Brutus watched the door. He was frowning at Marc. It seemed he shared the suspicions that Sophie harboured and that I, as much as I hated to admit it, now entertained.

Lieutenant Messier was also there, and, of course, Sophie was at my side.

"So, Marc," I said kindly. "What can you tell me about the night you went missing?"

Marc began his story in a husky voice. He claimed the two months exposed to the elements had harmed his health. "I had just finished my rounds and was returning to my tent when I heard a noise from the horse lines. I went to investigate and I saw a single man dressed all in black cutting the horses free. I tried to sneak close to him, to apprehend him. He must have heard me though, because he turned and stared at me."

"Who was it?" I asked.

"I don't know. He was wearing a mask. When he saw me, he must have got scared because he ran. He was very fast and I lost him in the dark. I was on my way to raise the hue and cry when he struck me a blow on the back of the head. At least I think it was him.

"I woke up bound and gagged. I struggled. I tried to free myself but he had me trussed like a suckling pig. All I could do was glare at him. If wrath could strike a man dead... Eventually the saboteur came to me and moved me to the pit. I think he expected me to die there. Perhaps he was too much of a coward to do me in himself. It took me a day to free myself. By the time I severed my restraints I was half mad with thirst. There was a muddy puddle in one corner of the pit. I drank deeply.

"For the next, I don't even know how long, I languished in the pit subsisting off rainwater and grubs. I tried to climb free but the walls were too high and too sheer. I tried to dig a path out but every time I made a handhold it just caved in. Once I nearly brained myself with a rock the size of a cow's skull. After that I gave up. I stopped even calling for help. I resigned myself to end my days in the pit, scrounging in the dirt until winter claimed me." He shivered. "The truth is, only my wrath kept me alive. I will see my captor found and hanged."

"So you are saying that everything that happened that night was the work of a single man." I was sure he could hear the tone of disbelief in my voice.

"It seems to strain credibility," Sophie said. She was looking at Marc with the eye of a merchant watching a scale.

"On my word of honour." Marc said. His sincerity was either true or he was putting on a damn good act. It was such a shame his story was so weak.

"My Lord, I know you are close to this man, but this sounds like a fabricated story. Please consider the safety of your men," Messier said.

Marc stared at Messier. "Who is this person?" His voice was sour with bitterness and hatred.

"Never mind him. About the man who apprehended you, you're certain you don't know who it was?"

"I only ever saw him that one night. He wore a black mask and plain black clothes. I don't know; somebody tall..." He trailed off. "I'm telling you the truth. I swear it!"

"Every liar swears he's telling the truth," Sophie said.

"And many serpents learn to whisper honeyed words in the dark." Marc's eyes flashed and he glared at Sophie, gripped the arms of his chair as if to rise and strike her.

"Enough of that!" I stepped between Marc and Sophie and glared at Marc. He settled. I'd never known Marc to be a master actor. His voice had the ring of truth. And yet, I didn't know what I dreaded most—the idea that Marc might be a traitor or the idea that somebody else was and I had no idea who.

CHAPTER 22

Kieran

MY LAST HOPE WAS Saul Shatterfield. And my search took me deep into the Long Dark. I hadn't gone in blind, still it'd done me no good and in two months of searching I was reduced to walking darkened tunnels. As I searched one abandoned place after the next, I thought back to when I started my search. Doctor Fletter-Daish had told me to find Shatterfield in the dark, but I didn't know where to start. So I sought out Mr. Chamblais instead.

I found him sitting in Uncle's yard, staring off into space. A mug of hot water sat in his hands, forgotten. He had never been a jocular man, but since my uncle fell in he'd become increasingly dark, distant.

It was a harsh reminder for me that I was not the only one who cared for uncle Stephen, who would be hurt if he died.

As I entered the yard, he poured a second cup of water and invited me to sit. Wordlessly I joined my mentor.

"How is your uncle?" His lilting, gravelly voice had a grave tone to it.

"Dr. Fletter-Daish can do nothing," I said flatly. I couldn't afford to let my emotions show now. I still had too much to do.

"*Merd!*" Mr. Chamblais rarely swore.

"He told me I should seek out Saul Shatterfield, said he was some sort of master, a specialist in the Broken. But I don't know how to find the man."

Mr. Chamblais lowered his chin and looked up at me from under a heavy brow. "*Oui*, Old Saul is special. But I don't know if he will help you."

Hope, panic and a dozen other emotions threatened to overwhelm me. I counted my breaths, waiting for the clarity of calmness before asking, "So you know him?"

"I know Shatterfield, mostly by reputation of course. His Stone Hands are a respected style."

"I'm sorry, is he a warrior?" I hadn't expected that.

"He is, after a fashion. Mostly he is a madman, but I suppose he remains both a brilliant doctor and a dangerous fighter; perhaps more dangerous than if he were sane, as he is so hard to predict." Mr. Chamblais said all of this in a gentle, slightly sad voice.

I pursed my lips. My fear was that if Shatterfield was some old madman living in the Long Dark he wouldn't be of much help, even if I could find him.

I sipped at my water and was silent for a long moment. After a while I asked, "But could he help?"

"I don't know. I suppose so. His legends are as confused and contradicting as the Wizard in Green." He chuckled bitterly. "Or my own. And I'm no help. But the rumours of Shatterfield say he was a man of learning."

"Do you know where to find him?"

"I don't. But perhaps one of the apothecaries about town would know more. Other than that, try somewhere dark. He's always liked bugs, enclosed spaces. He'd likely be at home in the Long Dark."

"Where the Broken are."

Mr. Chamblais nodded, sipped at his water and looked at the sky.

"It sounds like you know him a bit better than just having heard his reputation."

"I met him once. This was about ten years ago. I was attacked by a gang of bandits down in the Long Dark. He was sleeping in the tunnels and I all but tripped over him. He helped me fight off the bandits, but then he fled. I told you, he is mad."

"What do you mean mad?"

"Mad, crazy, not right in the head; I'm no doctor, boy. I don't know. But Saul Shatterfield is off."

"I don't remember you visiting ten years ago."

"You were perhaps nine years old."

I exhaled slowly. "The Long Dark is a lot of space to cover." I stood to go.

"Perhaps you should consider more of a plan than just wandering dark tunnels." Mr. Chamblais fixed me with a steady gaze. His red-rimmed eyes hinted at tears but his voice was steady.

"What do you suggest, sir?"

"Ask around with the herbalists in town. Perhaps one will have word of Shatterfield's haunts."

"Thank you."

"And make sure to make time each day for your training."

"But I already know the sword art—I can practice anywhere."

"Don't go rushing out of your training so quickly," Mr. Chamblais said sternly. "I still have more to teach you."

I blushed with embarrassment. "Of course, sir, sorry."

He waved away my apology. "We're all distracted. You are a natural at the fighting arts but you lack experience and your technique needs much work." Mr. Chamblais stood, facing me. "While you search for Shatterfield I will begin instructing you in the Nerve-Shocking Fingers. It is a technique of my own first master, and since he is dead, and taught no others, it is a secret of the Black Trillium, my secret in fact. I know you are hastening to begin your search but humour an old man his ways of coping with pain. Let me give you this gift."

"Please, show me."

With lightning speed he lashed out at me with two fingers, striking me on the shoulder. I felt my arm go dead and fall uselessly to my side. He struck again and my other arm became as useless as the first. A third blow, halfway between my chin and my navel, caused my legs to become numb. I fell, though Mr. Chamblais caught me.

I'd felt no pain but he'd rendered me entirely helpless. "What did you do to me?" I asked, trying hard to keep the fear and hurt out of my voice.

"I have stunned your nerves, rendering you paralyzed. The effect will wear off in a few hours. Or I can release it like this."

Mr. Chamblais struck me in a few specific points on my back and vigour returned to my limbs in a flush of pins and needles that quickly faded. "These strikes are the first three movements of the seventy-two techniques of the Nerve-Shocking Fingers. Heed them well. I will give you a mnemonic to help you remember."

We practiced the form until Mr. Chamblais was sure I had it memorized. It was hard. When I practiced on him I could only apply the technique one time in four. Furthermore, Mr. Chamblais knew subtle counters to the Nerve-Shocking Fingers that allowed him to escape from the paralysis they caused.

When he was confident I'd remember the techniques he said to me, "Go now, find Saul Shatterfield, perhaps he can save your uncle."

I left, but I wasn't at all sure that I wasn't leaving on a fool's errand.

And it had proven to be. For two months, I talked up apothecaries and herbalists. When that failed, I sifted through ruins, explored darkened tunnels, always seeking signs of Saul Shatterfield, constantly watchful for the Broken or for soldiers of MacMillan. I found nothing.

I rarely came above ground except to train, but when I did the news wasn't good. Trana was flooded with refugees from the Scar. MacMillan had apparently confiscated grain reserves and blamed the Black Trillium for his actions. He said raiders from the society torched his grain stores. His army needed to eat. The city elders, from Three Forks to Queenwest, were grumbling about the extra mouths to feed. Mr. Chamblais, for his part, was mystified. He said the Black Trillium had executed no raids against MacMillan's camp.

People were worried that it would be a hard winter, the refugees being the ones who grew most of the city's grain. If they didn't return to their farms soon, Trana would starve.

I set aside concerns over food. The winter was still far off and though the price of food was rising, people in Kensington hadn't begun rationing just yet.

Spring passed in futility and summer was all but upon the city in an early muggy swelter. Lake smells cast a reek across the southern half of the city; the scent carried through the tunnels of the Long Dark and I was more than a little bit concerned about falling ill myself. I felt half out of my life. Many days I didn't even make it home from my searches through the tunnels of the city, instead camping in the dark, or taking shelter in an unclaimed ruin. It was a hard two months. My feet blistered, my legs ached.

And then, one day, I was exploring a section of the tunnels known as Rosedale. It was called such because, as was the way of the Ancients, this section of the tunnel had been marked with signs on the tiles that proclaimed the place to be Rosedale. Some of the chamber names in the Long Dark seemed to be tied to names of nearby streets. Others, like Rosedale, seemed more obscure, though certainly there were roses there.

This was one of the things that marked Rosedale as a strange part of the Long Dark—the chamber was roofless, open to the sky, with tunnels at each end leading back under the earth. In the time after the Great Collapse, somebody, a gardener with a literal turn of mind, perhaps, had planted rose bushes in the lower region of the chamber and they now grew thick. The blooms were blood red and looked thirsty in the early summer heat.

I'd been walking all day through dark tunnels and the summer sun was wonderful on my skin. I decided to stop a while on the platform beside the rose bushes and practice my sword forms.

I stretched and drew my arming sword, running through the movements of the Triumvirate sword art, first slowly and then more quickly.

I was halfway through my third iteration when I heard a voice saying, "That is a very interesting sword form. I wonder where you learned it."

I turned to look and saw a singularly strange man leaning against the wall at the mouth of the southern tunnel. The man was older, though I couldn't say by how much. He had ash-brown hair fading to grey at the temples and a very precisely groomed beard. His eyes were bright green and his build was sturdy. Though sturdy, he was also very tall. He looked powerfully built under his strange garments.

And his clothing was certainly very strange. He wore robes—hardly fashionable clothing in Confederation, though I heard tell that some of the southmen liked to dress that way. His robes were a very rich green, the colour of fresh summer leaves, but were traced with lines of copper.

He wore a belt of tooled leather clasped in gold and from his belt hung a sword, the most beautiful sword I'd ever seen; it was hard to believe such a blade could have been forged by human hands. It was a large sword, and long, but what drew my eye was the hilt. The sword had an intricate and flowing form of metal creating a near basket around the hilt. All parts, pommel, branches, contre-guard and quillon were traced in copper, silver and gold and were studded with emeralds. I'd never seen so much finery in one place. Paintings of Bart MacMillan didn't have so many jewels as were on this one sword. All in all he looked the spitting image of the Wizard in Green, stepped out of the fireside stories and into flesh.

His voice had an odd accent, rounded syllables that reminded me of that elf-girl Savannah. Perhaps he was from across the desert like her.

"Um," I said.

He chuckled, it was a crystalline sort of laugh. "I am sorry, I suppose that was a very personal question considering we just met. But, tell me, what is a single swordsman doing alone in these forgotten tunnels?"

"I seek somebody," I said. I didn't quite know what to make of the stranger.

"You have found somebody." Oh great, a cryptic stranger, what luck.

"I seek a doctor." I didn't like his smirk.

"Some have suggested I have a little crude skill in medicine," he said, his voice still bubbling like a mountain stream, the smug smile still there. I really didn't like the smirk.

"Are you Saul Shatterfield?" I mean, he might have been. Nobody had told me what Shatterfield looked like.

"Oh, you mean the bug man." He scoffed. "No, but I saw him recently."

I felt a surge of triumph rising through me. He'd seen Shatterfield. I wanted to jump and shout. However, the man was exceedingly strange so I restrained my excited impulse, gulped and levelly said, "If you would be so kind as to direct me..."

"Nothing is free." He grinned as he spoke. "If you want directions you must give me something."

"What could I possibly have that could interest you, sir?" I was actually sort of curious what this strange man would ask for.

"Experience."

"I'm sorry, but I don't follow." This guy was really getting on my nerves.

"I am new to this land. I don't know how you Canadians fight." Now there was a word I didn't hear too often—Canadian. I mean, everybody knew that in the time before the Collapse, the land of Confederation had been named Canada. But the name was as dead as the rest of the past.

"Indulge me with a gentlemanly duel, to first blood. Win, or lose, I'll point you to the bug man." He glanced at his fingernails, buffed them against his shirt. The gall of this man!

"I don't want to hurt you," I said cautiously. "I've killed men before, the Broken too."

"I doubt you will." The nerve!

"Very well then. To first blood." I drew my sword. The plain, functional arming sword seemed crude next to the piece of sharp-art the man wore at his side.

"To make it more interesting, if you beat me, I'll give you my sword."

I saluted him. I was tired of the game-playing.

He returned the salute. It was the same salute—the Triumvirate salute! But the Triumvirate sword art was rare; it had to just be coincidence.

I attacked.

I must admit I let my frustration with his arrogance get the better of me. I didn't ease into the attack, instead launching a lethal offensive. I didn't want to kill him, but I figured I could at least discourage him from being so rude.

He moved so quickly I could barely even track it and parried my sword. The parry seemed gentle, almost bored, but the power of it nearly tore the sword from my fingers. I staggered and felt an itching at the base of my neck. I jumped forward and spun, parrying his sword, though just barely. It had been only one pass and already I was breathing heavily. My opponent just looked at me with subtle disappointment.

"Surely you can do better than that," he said. "Again."

I attacked again with a more subtle and devious approach, but again he was prepared. It was all I could do to stop myself from falling, and again he stopped short of drawing my blood and ending the duel.

"You've won," I said.

"I have not drawn your blood."

I lowered my sword.

"Raise your weapon or the first blood drawn will come from your heart," he snapped and his entire posture seemed electric.

I fought back the urge to cringe in terror before this madman and did what he told me.

"I'll end this when you tell me this: who taught you this fighting art?"

"My master is Jean Chamblais."

"That'd be one of Arroyo's pupils, probably," he muttered. "I can never keep them straight."

I didn't recognize the name.

"Alright," he said. "One last pass. Give me your best, though. I'll know if it isn't, and I'll punish you."

I nodded grimly and attacked with everything I could. He avoided it all without parrying.

"Not good, not good," he muttered and with a flick of his finger he sent my sword flying out of my hand.

I felt a searing pain in my wrist but his huge backsword was already flying straight for my throat. I dove to the ground and felt rose thorns snag on my clothes. His sword changed direction and came at me edge-first from above. But it left me the slightest of openings.

I struck out with the Nerve-Shocking Fingers. My first blow took him by surprise and paralyzed his off arm. I saw it fall, I had the opening I needed to shock the nerves of his sword arm.

And then he made the subtle counters I'd seen Mr. Chamblais use to escape from nerve-shock. Only where Mr. Chamblais could escape in ten seconds, he managed it in less than one! But only Mr. Chamblais knew the Nerve-Shocking Fingers, aside from me that was. Who was this man? I had little time to ponder these questions, because as I stumbled in surprise he caught my fingers. His grip was like iron. With the small finger of his left hand he scratched the back of my hand, drawing a small bead of blood.

"Apparently, that isn't the only rare art your master taught you," he said with an oddly gentle tone. "You are most certainly from Arroyo's lineage. After all, those tricks weren't taught to him by me."

"What?"

"But I forget, Arroyo is probably twenty years into the grave by now. Your master may not have mentioned him.

"Needless to say, your master was student to one of my students. This makes you a great-grand student of my style and thus equivalent to one of my students yourself.

"Now is the part where you bow to me, as befitting the master of your school."

"What?"

"Are you stupid, boy? Bow."

"Wait, no, I don't know you. I don't go bending knee to strangers."

"I suppose I'll have to provide you with some proof then." He seemed mildly disappointed. I felt my knees go soft with fright, but I didn't give in.

"Watch carefully, perhaps you'll learn something."

He took a few steps back from me and began going through the movements of the Triumvirate sword art.

I had thought Mr. Chamblais to be a master of the techniques. But he was as novice as I was next to this strange man. Every movement was perfect. And the speed and power he brought to the art was shocking. As his sword drifted through the postures of the sword art a wind howled through the tunnel. Tight young petals were ripped from the roses and the air was quickly full of a curtain of red, following the pattern of the sword. I watched, dumbfounded.

He finished with a flourish and sheathed his sword.

"And now, bow to your great-grandmaster."

I dropped to my knees, head bent in supplication. He walked over to me on soundless feet and touched the back of my head.

"That will do," he said.

"But how is it possible? Mr. Chamblais is near forty and you're saying you taught his master?"

"Yes, I forgot how short lived you lot could be," the Wizard in Green muttered. "Young man, I am ninety-five years old."

He hardly looked fifty. Perhaps he was a madman. If he was, he was a madman with incredible skill. Still, he didn't seem mad. His posture, manner, dress and word choice spoke of a man fully in possession of his faculties, and a man of erudition at that.

I was well educated by the standards of Trana. Uncle Stephen taught me to read when I was a young child, and I had some facility in mathematics, in logic and philosophy and yet, I got a feeling that, to his eyes, I was nothing but a crude bumpkin.

"I will take you at your word then." I bowed hesitantly.

"That would be wise." I didn't note any hint of gloating in his voice. He sounded almost bored. "And I am going to do you a favour. I will teach you two things about the Triumvirate sword art that you did not know. In exchange, I ask for one piece of information only."

"Thank you." It felt wrong—it felt almost smarmy—but what else could I say? The Wizard in Green didn't seem to see my response as out of place.

"Good. Now, first, my question." His green eyes fixed intensely on my own as he spoke. "An errant girl of mine fled my home some time ago. I had reason to believe she was in Fredericton but when I got there I found she'd already left. I was told she had come here." He produced a piece of paper. It was strange. The one side of the stiff paper was white and ordinary—though of incredible fine quality. The other side glistened like the surface of a clear, still pool in the sunlight. And there was a drawing on it.

At least I say it was a drawing because I don't know how else to describe it.

The image was strikingly lifelike. It was almost like looking into a mirror except instead of my reflection it was somebody else's.

"Have you seen this girl?" The girl in the picture was tall, like him, had green eyes, like his, and long, straight, dark hair. Her eyes were intense and her face sullen. She was coldly beautiful but not comely.

"I am sorry, but I have not." I didn't want to lose out on the chance to learn something of my sword art from the master, so I added, "But if she is with the Fredericton people she'll be at the military camp in the Scar."

The Wizard in Green frowned. "Yes, it would be like her to plant herself somewhere heavily guarded. Thank you, young man; what is your name anyway?"

"Kieran Benton." The silence hung after my words, pregnant with anticipation.

"Very well, Kieran. I believe I made certain promises to you. First, the location of Saul Shatterfied. He has a home which he shares with a caretaker in a building roughly two kilometers from here due south down that tunnel. Be careful. His mind is unstable and he isn't fond of visitors."

My heart jumped in elation. Finally I knew where to go.

"Thank you so much!" I said as I turned to go down the tunnel.

"Not so fast," the man said. "I made another promise to you. I promised to teach you two secrets of the Triumvirate sword art. This is important. Your skill is sub-standard and I'm almost ashamed to have somebody so untalented in my lineage. Still, I like you and so killing you isn't ideal. The only other option is to make you better. A few hours with my instruction may equal a year of diligent practice, and I'd be offended if you refused my offer."

"I don't want to offend you, sir," I said, "but I'm on a crucial mission and a life hangs in the balance."

"But you had time to practice in the sunshine and enjoy the warm air? No. You can spare a few hours."

I hesitated, glanced at the strange wanderer, down the black aperture of the tunnel. The truth was uncle Stephen was very much the same as he'd been the day before and the day before that. I had spent two months searching. I could spend a few hours more.

I nodded my head.

"Very well," he said. "You've grasped the basics of the technique well. And that's a good foundation. But the Form of Limitless Cunning has 27 stances and 729 changes. Your master has only taught you 27 of these.

"I'll be fair, you do well enough not always walking through from beginning to end and back again, but your changes between the stances are abrupt and obviously improvised except for where you learned them within the form.

"And your inner cultivation is entirely lacking. There's nothing we can do about that today, though. Let me show you the changes..."

He began demonstrating transitions from one technique to the next. Though the Form of Limitless Cunning had a simple enough basis, it was clear watching him practice these changes why the art had a reputation for subtlety and deception.

After he showed me the changes he began drilling me. We practiced until the afternoon began to grow golden and the sun dipped toward the horizon. By the time we finished, under his expert hand, I'd learned nearly a quarter of the transitions.

"That's good for one day," he said. "Some day, perhaps, our paths will cross again and I'll give you a second lesson. In the meantime, you've performed adequately.

"But, before you go, I promised you a second secret. You know less than half of the sword art."

"Yes, I know that. My master said he didn't know the form of Limitless Aggression." I tried hard to sound deferential. It was hard work being this polite to the stranger. Still, he was trying to help me, and he didn't need to.

"Ah, but did you know that the Form of Limitless Aggression is here, in this city?"

"No, I did not." My, but that was an interesting tidbit of information.

"When I sent the Form of Limitless Aggression away from my home, I knew of only one man I would trust to hold it. I did not know, at that time, that he had fallen into madness. I sent it into the care of Saul Shatterfield."

It seemed just a little pat. Why would Saul Shatterfield have the book? The Wizard in Green had given me more questions than answers, had given me new-found skill with my sword, yes, but also a whole new set of problems.

The doctor I sought was mad. The doctor I sought held half of the Triumvirate sword art. The doctor I sought was the only man the strange master in green robes would trust. I wanted to ask why this was so. I wanted to refuse to believe.

The Wizard in Green saw the confusion in my eyes, the questions unasked, and he said, "It is enough for you to know that once, Saul Shatterfield was a great scholar, one of a handful I would dare call friend. Moreover, he was a man of peace who I could trust not to take up a great martial secret, and he was a man of not inconsiderable martial prowess himself."

"They say he's an expert on the Broken and on poisons. My uncle was poisoned by a Broken. I only hope Saul can save him."

"Strange. I've never heard of the Broken using poison before. I will tell you this: your sources were correct—there is nobody in the world more expert in poisons than Saul Shatterfield. In his prime, only his brother was his equal in medicine of any sort and he fell to darkness long ago.

"You may go now. But heed this warning: be careful when you go there. Shatterfield is not a sane man, and he doesn't react well to new people. His caretaker, a young woman, seems a little odd, but sane. It might be wise to approach her alone first. Regardless, do not mention me. I excused myself without paying my respects to either and would hate to seem rude."

"Thank you. You may have saved the life of somebody who matters dearly to me." He'd pointed me on the right track, I could feel it. This had been a most auspicious meeting.

"I hope we meet again, Kieran Benton, disciple of the third generation of the Triumvirate sword art."

"Until we meet again, sir," I said and bowed again, before turning away from the strange man and walking alone into the shadows of the Long Dark once more.

CHAPTER 23

Savannah

OVER THE TWO MONTHS after I met Old Saul, I learned that he rarely slept. He assumed I was likewise inclined and so thought nothing of waking me up in the middle of the night for this training session or that. He told me that I would have to learn Kite-Stepping and Stone Hands, esoteric skills he believed I needed in order to defend the book. Sometimes this involved activities I understood: lessons in fighting, physical conditioning, all that stuff. Other times the training took stranger forms. I was often sent to catch centipedes in those first early weeks. When I asked why, no explanation was forthcoming.

Centipedes like dark places. They also move with blinding speed and bite ferociously when caught. The growing warmth of the days drew them out in ever increasing numbers. Even so, Old Saul made it very clear that I was to bring back the vile things unharmed. Each time he sent me on one of these 'training' missions he'd instruct me to come back with one more. By the end of the first week he already had almost thirty of the disgusting creatures, crawling around in a little box he called my "trophy case."

During the day, after a breakfast which, if I was lucky, contained no traces of rat whatsoever, he would teach me the series of arcane gestures and mnemonics that made up the Stone Hands. The way Old Saul explained it, the use of these gestures helped direct vitality to my hands, making them more able to be weapons.

He demonstrated the end result of this skill quite dramatically one day by ripping exposed rebar out of concrete down in the lower chamber of the Long Dark with his bare hands. Needless to say I was impressed, though when I tried, all that happened was that I stubbed my fingers, leaving the rebar unmolested.

As far as Kite-Stepping, it involved the ability I'd seen first when Boyd fought with MacMillan. Except Saul was far more talented. With a seemingly effortless motion he could leap vast distances, move with blinding speed. The first day he taught me this skill, he took me to a section of the cathedral that had once been a hub of the shopping area. Terraced concrete balconies surrounded an open space so that one could see the fourth floor from the bottom. He could ascend to the top tier with a graceful jump.

No matter how hard I tried I couldn't even get my fingers over the ledge of the lowest balcony. Old Saul laughed, not unkindly, and told me I just needed more practice.

Old Saul would work me until I was ready to drop and then he'd give me water and send me out for food that I could stomach. I offered to cook for him too but he made a face and said, "Pigs and cows and vegetables? Eurgh, those aren't proper food for a man to eat."

Saul seemed happier with raw spiders and insects.

When I went out I looked for Boyd. I wanted to give him some sort of funeral. I went to the place where we'd parted but I found no sign of him there—I left a knife and some fruits as an offering to him in the afterlife, and figured that was the best I'd ever get.

Even so, I searched. But the search was fruitless. Wherever the Broken had taken him, it was well hidden.

A strange thing also began to happen as I studied with Saul. Though he could not stand to look at it, when Old Saul wasn't around (off hunting bugs or on some other strange, mad errand) I would read the manual given to me by Dave Boyd.

I discovered that, after receiving an education in martial mnemonics while practicing Old Saul's skill, I could more easily understand the metaphor the manual was couched in. I was beginning to understand the manual. Armed with that new understanding, I took up Boyd's sword and began to practice the Art of Limitless Aggression.

I found that it worked well together with the strength training of the Stone Hands. I wondered if Dave Boyd had made the same discovery and felt a pang of grief. That was my life for almost two months, training, shopping, hunting crawling things in dark places and talking with a madman. The more time I spent with Old Saul, the more comfortable he became with my presence. He was still never normal but he was at least more at ease.

It was supper time in early summer and we had just finished practice for the day. I was telling Old Saul about life back home, saying, "And then, when the sun was right, the mountains would change colour from red to a brilliant pinkish orange, as if they had all been dipped in red gold. On those days it almost seemed like the crops would be good and life would be easy and Confederation was nothing but a distant bad dream."

"Everything is a dream." Saul was popping spiders into his mouth and crunching them noisily as he spoke. "That is why everything is broken up. In dreams memories don't run in straight lines. We remember the future, forget the past. Yes, forget, it's best to forget—even blood mountains, little Leiurus."

"It hurts." I stared into our little cooking fire and tried to find some clarity. I didn't want to dwell in my pain. "You know, the feeling that your home is gone.

"But I wouldn't change that. I don't want to lose it. I am who I am because of the things that I survived. They made me stronger even though they hurt."

"No." Saul tilted his head to one side and frowned the way he did when he didn't want to think about something but found himself doing so anyway, prodding at the thought like a tongue going after a bad tooth. "Better to forget. So much darkness and pain and defiled souls."

I remembered hearing Old Saul talking about the Broken that way shortly after we met, defiled, he'd suggested somebody had done the breaking. This was the first time I'd heard Saul mention the creatures since. He had taught me how to avoid the Broken and he did the same, drawing away any time one came near but never mentioning them.

"What history do you have with the Broken?" I asked. I probably shouldn't have.

Saul dropped his bowl on the ground where it landed with a wooden thunk and curled in upon himself, crouching in a near-fetal pose. "Nothing. I don't know anything about the Broken. No such thing as the Broken, only dark dreams. Don't ask me, I don't know."

I didn't believe him. He knew something even if he didn't want to say.

"They are a danger to Trana. They could make us into another Cleveland," I said to him slowly and carefully.

"No, no nonononono. We can't have that, no, Cleveland is a terrible place. I don't ever want to go there again."

Nobody went to Cleveland. Wait, correction, nobody sane went to Cleveland. So, maybe Old Saul had been there.

"If you can help me figure out where the Broken are coming from, why they came to Trana so suddenly, maybe we can stop that from happening."

"I can't remember." His face was a mask of pain. "The Broken, I know the name, faces. I remember Cleveland, I've been there. But the details, the little things, names, events, why I was there, it's all just a black hole. No, nononono, I can't go back there. Not now, not even in my head. Don't make me."

I said nothing more and stared into the fire but all I saw was darkness.

When things went wrong the source was unexpected. I'd just started paying attention to the writing on the walls, his "diary in the walls," as he sometimes called it, and I wasn't ready for it to all fall apart. I'd ignored the words for most of the time that I'd been with Old Saul. They didn't strike me as being particularly important. They were a symptom of poor Old Saul's madness and, as I became used to his mental state, I tended to ignore the fact that he'd decorated his little alcove with words in half a dozen languages.

I'd taken over the alcove next to his as soon as I decided to stay down in the dark with him so I only ever even saw the writing when I came to visit Old Saul in his room, delivering live centipedes or eating with him, although, I've already said enough on the topic of meals with Old Saul.

The two of us were both, in our way, very private people. I think that's why we got on so well. I had gotten used to being on my own when I came east as a kid. I didn't want much to do with the 'Tobans after what they did to my home. The Salt Mary folks were distant: trappers, miners and fishermen with no interest in outsiders. By the time I got to Trana I was used to being alone with my thoughts, and what's more, I found I preferred it that way, usually.

Old Saul talked a lot but mostly just to himself. I couldn't honestly say whether he'd been a people-person in the past but I knew that, as he was, he was terrified by the prospect of other people in his space.

I suspect, underneath his crazy "little Leiurus" talk the reason he was able to tolerate me in his space was because I was quiet and private and didn't impose myself upon him. But because I didn't impose myself it was a long time before I began to suspect that the writing on his walls was anything other than the scrawls of a tortured mind.

While I studied the Stone Hands and Kite-Stepping, Old Saul had, out of necessity, taught me something of his strange medicines. A person, if she was very lucky, could manage some skill in these powerful arts but true mastery was elusive. Old Saul had long ago devised recipes that helped the body recover quickly from the extreme conditioning his arts required and that helped strengthen the recipient. He taught me some of these recipes, along with an understanding of the body and its ways sufficient to understand how the medicine worked, and what to do if something went wrong.

Many of the ingredients came from the same crawling things he delighted in eating. I suspect that may have been the original source of his fascination. Other ingredients included moulds, fungi and the excretions of creatures that lived far from the light.

When I hurt myself training he would feed me these bitter draughts and, the next day, I'd awake healed and feeling stronger than ever.

On the day that everything fell apart I discovered the recipe for one of these medicinal draughts on his wall. And then I realized what the wall was. Scrawled around me, in six tongues or more, was one of the greatest medicinal manuals in the world. I was saddened that I could read so little of it but I immediately began reading, studying.

I wanted to take notes. I wanted a record of the medicines. Down in the dark I only had one source of paper. Dave Boyd's manual. I grabbed a stick of charcoal and began hastily scribbling in the margins of the manual, copying out every line I could read, including some that I could not understand.

With the basic knowledge of anatomy and herbology Old Saul gave me, I could make sense of some of the recipes and of some of the instructions, tests for poisons, to determine if somebody suffered from plague. There were remedies to treat infection, potions to hasten healing, elixirs to prolong life and poisons that would take life away in moments.

With these few notes alone I suddenly had access to more medical knowledge than almost anybody I'd ever met.

A few entries appeared to be French, which I could not speak. A few others were in some other language still, one with some similarities to English but with strange, guttural words.

And then I found the most tantalizing recipe of all. It was labeled 'Five Venoms toxin' and the first ingredient was 'Venenum Leiurus.' Two other ingredients were written in plain enough language, 'Centipede Carcass' and 'Phallus Impudicus.' I wasn't sure what the last one was exactly, although I knew the word 'phallus' and could make a few wild guesses.

I suspected whatever an 'Impudicus' was would probably object to losing its phallus but I supposed the centipedes wouldn't really like being part of a soup either.

I copied the whole recipe into the margins of Dave's manual as carefully as possible. I was perplexed, the recipe was like nothing I'd ever seen before.

I finished scribbling and went to find Old Saul. I was beginning to make progress on his two martial arts, and I was finding I really enjoyed them. I could make the first balcony with a jump now, and if I couldn't pull the rebar from the walls yet, I at least didn't hurt my fingers anymore. Saul was poking about the Cathedral of Broken Glass and seemed unusually agitated.

"What's wrong?" I asked.

"Not safe," he said. "Somebody was here."

I saw no signs of intrusion and told Saul so as gently as possible.

"No." He was getting more agitated. "Not see, not smell. I feel it, in my teeth, somebody was here. Somebody was watching us."

"Do you know who?" I was worried now. I'd learned that sometimes Saul's strange feelings were worth paying attention to. He certainly knew how to avoid the Broken well enough, though he never explained how.

"Green man," Saul said. "I can't see him, he's in the empty places." The only green man I could think of was the Wizard in Green but he was just a legend. Saul was an educated man, I didn't doubt he'd heard the stories, but this was a new form of his madness.

"Why can't you see the green man?" I hoped to get something more out of Saul, to see if I could figure out what he meant, whether he was just being crazy Old Saul or if we were in some sort of danger.

"No, no, nononono, I owe Green Man a debt but I can't pay him back. How can I pay him back?" Saul began pacing, waving his arms agitatedly as he spoke. "I don't remember what I owe him. I made him a promise but I don't know the promise, the promise is in the dark place, how could I know? No, nonononono, I can't go there. Can't remember. It must not be restored."

I'd long since figured out that there were things in his past, things he wouldn't talk about, couldn't talk about. There were things in his past I don't know he fully remembered. Perhaps he was too afraid to remember.

For the rest of the day Old Saul acted afraid. He was on edge, flinching and twitching at every noise. Shortly before mid-day he started complaining about a stench. I couldn't smell anything. I mean, yeah, we were down in the Long Dark, there were plenty of things down here that smelled pretty awful, but I was used to those smells. Saul was too. At least he'd never complained about them before.

But he kept on complaining about the stink. He kept complaining it was getting worse, coming closer, and I still couldn't smell anything.

At sunset we had a visitor, and the visitor was the one who ruined our arrangement. The first I heard of him was the sound of his boots ringing on the tiles in the Long Dark. He came from the north, through the tunnels of the lower galleries.

The sight of him was a shock—a memory of simpler days. I'd slept with Kieran Benton on his birthday a year ago. Everybody who passed through Kensington knew him. He was the luckiest little orphan boy in the world. His uncle was the richest man in the district, one of the wealthiest merchants in Trana.

When I'd last seen him, Kieran had been tall and slight of build, with pale skin (too much time indoors) and sparkling blue eyes that came alive with mischief. He had a reputation for being a bit of a ladies man. I should have known better, but I was lonely and it had been dark and he was kind and well-spoken and terribly handsome.

I'd left the next day and hadn't been back to Kensington much since. I wasn't avoiding him. I just felt like sticking around Broken Tower.

He'd changed.

He had a beard now. Not really full but coming in nicely. He was darker. It seemed like he'd spent long hours in the sun, and his build had filled out, he was thick with muscle and wore a sword on his hip. His blue eyes were intense and held hidden depths.

The lucky little orphan boy had grown up, and I wasn't sure that he hadn't grown into somebody a little bit terrifying.

He scared the hell out of Old Saul, that's for sure. As soon as he strolled into view, wearing the gloom of the Twilight Shops like a cloak, afraid of nothing, not bothering to employ stealth though he was alone and there were Broken down here and maybe bandits besides, Old Saul roared in terror and took off like a shot, Kite-Stepping to the top tier and fleeing.

As he fled I heard him shout something strange. "I won't go back to him, not ever!" My teacher, my friend, had fled before this boy from my past as if fleeing the spectre of death himself and so I chased him. I ran as fast as I could, but his Kite-Stepping was better than mine and he glided from platform to platform like a feather on the wind. I couldn't keep up. Still I ran and Kieran, trapped on the ground below, followed. He shouted to me to stop while Saul disappeared into the darkness beyond. I stumbled and slowed. I gave up. I returned to the ground and faced Kieran, hoping to break him on the rocks of my anger. How dare he disrupt my life? How dare he break in and frighten my friend?

"Savannah?" he asked. "Is that you?"

"Who'd you think it was?" I bit off the words.

"Was that Saul Shatterfield?" He sounded worried.

"Yes, and you scared him away, you idiot!"

Kieran stared at me like there was something wrong with me. As if my anger was misplaced. His face was a map of wounded sadness and despair that I didn't understand. The silence between us grew heavy for a few seconds. "We have to find him, right away," Kieran said, breaking the tension. I wasn't sure I trusted this stranger that I had once known well enough to even want to help him. What had happened to the flirtatious boy I once knew? Did he see me in the same skewed way? Most important of all, would Old Saul be alright? Would he come back?

I suddenly realized that this last question was the one that I dreaded the most. I feared almost as much what that might mean.

CHAPTER 24

Kyle

IN THEORY, MARC WAS a rescued prisoner, a friend and ally who should be returned to his station and to duty. But I still had a problem: the nagging fear that he'd arranged the whole thing—that he was a mole of the Black Trillium.

We'd kept him confined to the medical tents on the basis that he would need time to recover from his ordeal but he was growing restless.

Sophie and I were reviewing maps of the city when he finally stormed in wearing a uniform that now hung off his bones, betraying the wasting he'd suffered in his confinement.

"I can't stand this idleness any longer. Please let me return to my post." His eyes were wild, haunted and feral.

Sophie and I each looked at him coldly. "Marc, please come in, no I'm not busy at all," I said and Marc looked wounded. I looked away, slightly ashamed at myself for greeting him with sarcasm.

"I'm sorry, Kyle, but why are we just sitting here? Every day the Black Trillium whispers in the ears of the locals, every day supplies get dearer. Soon we won't have sufficient supplies to bring the army home and still we sit. Still we do nothing. And I just sit in my hospital bed, watching troops doze in the sun."

I didn't want to tell Marc the truth, in case he was a spy. We hadn't been idle all this time. Instead we'd been gathering every old map we could so that we could come to understand the Long Dark, its twists and turns, its hiding places. Somewhere out there was Dave Boyd's manual, and it hadn't even been a day after we recovered Marc before Sophie demanded we resume our search for it.

Sophie broke the silence saying, "Surely you don't expect to be privy to everything we have been working. Yes, the Black Trillium has its whisperers, but so do we. And there are plans we had to lay if we are to accomplish our goal."

"And which goal is that? Avenging Oswald and his father? Or that gods-damned book?"

Sophie's hand wandered to the hilt of her sword.

"Marc," I said, standing and inserting myself between the two. "Go back to the hospital tent. We'll see to returning you to duty soon, I promise, but for now get some rest." I beckoned to Brutus, standing silent sentry by the entrance to our tent. He grunted and escorted Marc out.

"Marc is right though, that we've been idle too long. We've learned all we can from maps. We should return to the field, and the search," Sophie said.

Sighing, I looked up at her. She sat imperiously, slumped in a folding camp chair. Her sharp green eyes bored into me with the unspoken demand in them, that I do what she wished. "Yes, but I will not endanger our forces. Brutus and Marc stay behind, and Messier too, he'll have to command in our absence."

"A good choice; you can't trust Marc and Brutus is far too limited." One could almost mistake her approval for love, but then, I'd just given her what she wanted. I wondered if Sophie loved me the way I did her. It was a wrong thought. Of course she did.

We set out with five men the next day. We rode into the city by way of Queeneast and Blasted Port. We had nothing to fear from the petty bandits of the empty, ruined lands around the port. As we rode I had the terribly unsettling feeling of being watched. I glanced over at Sophie and she was scanning the bushes that grew up around the road in Blasted Port. Her big, green eyes were filled with nervous suspicion.

A green shadow darted across the road and Sophie looked panicked.

"What is it?" I asked her.

"Don't ask, ride," she hissed and whipped her horse into a frenzy, fleeing the green shadow. I shrugged and followed. I didn't see how a flicker of green in the bushes could frighten her. It was probably just a lone bandit who had decided not to test his luck.

Still I didn't want to spend the day following after Sophie because of letting her get too far ahead. I whipped my horse and led my men on, out of the desolation of Blasted Port and into the much more urban ruins of Broken Tower.

Without Dave Boyd at the helm the ruins seemed somehow more menacing. Say what you would of the man, his firm hand kept Broken Tower from slipping into the decay and disorder of the district next door.

Perhaps that would change now, though I rather doubted it would be long before some bold man took command of the district, to keep the steel flowing—

if not for the poisonous presence of the Black Trillium in the streets, one might have already. Broken Tower was paved in gravel and sand, the by-products of the steel industry, and the crunching of the little stones under the shoes of our horses was the only noise we could hear. This had become an ominous place, and in this jungle of twisted steel and crumbling concrete, fear of the green shadow in the bushes seemed almost reasonable.

Who knew what lurked in the ruins?

We came, at last, to the entrance to the Long Dark that we'd last used when we pursued Boyd and the refugee girl. The horses would go no farther. We tied them to a hitch of hammered rebar and descended into the dark.

The darkness under the earth felt heavy like a blanket of lead. This was not the dark of a moonless night. This was primordial blackness, not merely a dimness of light but a sucking vacuum that drew light into it like a voracious and bloated beast, devouring, empty, always hungry and gnawing.

The trail of blood was long gone. The dried stains long since faded into the general fetid condition of the King chamber. I snapped my fingers and one of my torch-bearers came forward with a treasure, a map of the main tunnels in the Long Dark.

The tunnel system under Trana was much too sprawling to ever fully map. The entire city was littered with the damn hollow spaces under the earth. It was a wonder the place didn't all just collapse into a big sink-hole. I suppose the scavengers knew well enough not to harvest the steel bones that kept these empty spaces inflated.

Our map indicated that a section of tunnels called "The Twilight Shops" ran parallel to this tunnel for a kilometer or more. This system of tunnels was quite sprawling and had more hiding spaces than usual. It was also one of the few parts of the Long Dark that wasn't in endless darkness. The Twilight Shops being called thus was because of the fact that they seemed cloaked in the twilight hours from sunrise until sunset.

The Twilight Shops were purported to house a complex of thieves' warrens. I wasn't concerned by that but it struck me that they'd be a good place for an injured swordsman to go to ground. We struck out for the nearest entrance.

A door hung slightly ajar. Inside the tunnel revealed a staircase of slotted metal. At the top of the stair was a double door. Our time with the maps proved valuable to us. Though there were many points of exit from this central tunnel, there were few places as labyrinthine as the area called the Twilight Shops. A person trying to lose followers would likely have taken this route. There had been a lock on the door once but it was long since forced. At least somebody had taken this path before. We walked in the twilight of the shops and found the name was good. The light was enough to make it so that the torches weren't necessary but still dim, and the hallways filled with a hundred vague shadows.

In a room open to the sky, drifts of leaves covering the red marble floor, we found signs of a fight—old blood stains on the floor, scattered debris and a single severed arm, worm-eaten and oozing, nearly covered by one of the drifts. By some fluke of chance this gory reminder of the battle had failed to be carried away by scavengers, though it was in an advanced state of decay.

We went to examine the ghastly object.

"This was severed with a sword-blow," Sophie said. I had to agree, upon inspection it looked that way. The cut was far too clean to have been some other method of dismemberment.

"Spread out and search the area, look for anything suspicious." My command seemed almost comic. What could possibly be suspicious about a rotting arm in a drift of leaves?

My men saluted and left, searching in various directions while Sophie and I scanned the room for more indications of whether this battle pointed toward our quarry. We found nothing, but before long one of the other men reported back, "Lord, we found a door not far from here, it is locked from the other side and it was smeared with something; dried blood, I think."

"Seems suspicious," Sophie agreed.

"Show me," I commanded.

And it was how my man reported it. All seven of us gathered there. The door was locked and smeared in the brownish stain of some noxious substance—mud perhaps though I suspected dried blood—an X crossed it, caked thick as if to make it more lasting.

"Force it open," I commanded to my men. They struggled with the door, which was barricaded from the outside, but we'd come prepared for such obstacles and some time with crowbars and bolt cutters allowed them to force the door open a crack.

Inside was a filthy nest. Crouched in the ruins of the nest was a single man. Pale and frail, he had dark rings under his eyes and his beard was matted. In his hand was a small dagger, and not the greatsword he'd wielded against us. The man was Dave Boyd.

"Would you look at that?" he said. "I actually survived long enough to fall into the hands of my enemies." He sounded tired, resigned to his fate. He set down his blade. Sophie reached for her sword but I stayed her hand before she did something foolish.

"Give us the manual and we'll see to it you receive medical care, wealth, your office restored."

Boyd scoffed at me. "The manual is gone, I destroyed it."

"You know what was written in it." It wasn't a question.

"I won't teach you, I'd die from torture before I'd reveal those secrets to her." Boyd pointed at Sophie.

"How do you know my father?" Sophie demanded. "How do you know me? Are you a spy?"

"You stabbed me, woman, I won't soon forget that," Boyd snarled.

"You will tell me!"

Boyd sighed. "You saw me before in the Palace of the Lord of the Forbidden Isle, Duke of Seattle and the California Protectorate. I visited your father. Once he thought me the best hope for lasting peace in the south." He scoffed again. I felt stunned. All this time I'd known that Sophie came from a distant land, that she bore herself with royal bearing, but Seattle? The place was a rumour, a myth.

"The vagabond. You've changed." I'd never before seen as much fear and jealousy in Sophie's eyes as I did in that moment and I wished I understood what had passed between them before. In the stunned silence you could have heard a pin drop. Instead we heard an ominous clicking.

"What was that?" one of my men asked.

"My neighbourhood is terrible." Boyd was almost laughing. "And you are about to meet the neighbours."

CHAPTER 25

Kieran

WHEN I FIRST SAW Savannah in the Cathedral of Broken Glass with the old madman I'd thought my eyes were deceiving me. I remembered her as a fierce refugee from out of the distant west. She'd been savage and a little dangerous and then she'd vanished.

I'd heard she had taken up with Dave Boyd but, even before I'd joined the Black Trillium, I'd known there was bad blood between Boyd and my uncle. There was little trade between Kensington and Broken Tower at the best of times.

Now there was a haunted and perceptive look in her eyes. She wasn't a savage refugee. There was fear there, but it wasn't the fear of insecurity. It was the fear of somebody who had a home and loves to lose.

And she was with Saul Shatterfield. The stories I'd heard hadn't exaggerated his state. He was filthy and ragged. I didn't think I liked the chances that he'd be a dependable doctor. I thought of uncle Stephen lying sick at home, dying of the venom of a Broken bite and I felt bitter rage at the world for letting me get so close and then taking it all away again. I'd tried to chase after Shatterfield, just as Savannah had, but I'd never seen a person move like him before. He seemed almost able to fly as he bounced around the platforms of the ancient building. Even Savannah, who evidently had some of his skill, couldn't match his pace and he was gone.

I wondered if I was being punished for my cruelty.

For a moment, after I asked Savannah to help me find her friend, she paused, her face fell into sadness and she seemed lost in thought. Her eyes were bright and it looked almost like she was crying. "You chased him out of his home, you bastard, who knows where he'll go?"

I didn't know where she got off saying things like that. I snapped back at her, "How was I to know he'd run? I needed his help, I came here for help."

"Yeah, well look what you've done."

"It's my uncle, he's very ill. Only Saul Shatterfield can save him."

"Oh," she said. I could see the understanding in her eyes. She'd heard the urgency in my voice, felt the edges of my pain.

"Please," I said, "help me find him."

She seemed to think about it for a brief while, fighting with herself over how to reply. She nodded briskly. "Fine. But we'll have to move fast. With his Kite-Stepping skill he could be literally anywhere."

I guessed she was talking about the ability he had to jump twenty feet into the air from a standing start. It was a wonder, of course. But after all the strangeness I'd seen in the last year I was numbed to these sorts of surprises. When the Broken crawled from the dark places of the earth, remnants of the Three Brothers took on apprentices and the Wizard in Green appeared out of legend on a secret quest, what was one more miracle?

I nodded. The Wizard in Green had said that Shatterfield was a powerful warrior in his own right. And he was a madman. I felt a pang of unease at that thought.

"He'll probably not go up though," Savannah said. "He feels safer in dark places where he can hide."

"The lower galleries?" I couldn't think of a darker place.

"He goes there for medicinal supplies," Savannah said. "I wouldn't be surprised if he headed that way."

"Let's go."

She put her hands on her hips. "You are in no position to be telling me where to go in my own home."

"You live with this madman?"

"Somebody has to look after him." She spat on the floor in disgust.

"I'm sorry, I didn't realize. I thought you hated it down here," I said.

"I used to." She said no more, and I didn't press her. Her tone of voice was too final. Quickly we went down into the darkness.

There was no light in the lower galleries so I lit a torch. The acrid smell of pitch had become familiar to me after two months but the passage wasn't. After so long searching the Long Dark you'd have thought I'd know about a passage as large as this one.

"How did your uncle fall ill?"

"He was bitten by a Broken."

She stopped abruptly in her tracks. "What?"

I guessed I'd have to give her some details. "We were down in the Long Dark, scavenging." I knew Savannah had been with Boyd at one point, and I couldn't be sure of her loyalties; it wasn't like I could say that we were down in the Long Dark plotting rebellion. "And we were attacked by a swarm of the Broken. We escaped but one of them bit uncle Stephen. He became deathly ill the next day."

"And so you sought out Old Saul."

"The best doctor in the city told me to seek out Saul Shatterfield. He told me only Shatterfield could cure my uncle. Hey, how do you know about the Broken anyway?" She hadn't seemed surprised that I'd faced them.

"I fought them once," she said, but she wouldn't elaborate. We fell into silence again as we continued to walk through the Long Dark, searching for some sign of Shatterfield. After a short time we came to a door. Savannah stopped and said, "I met Old Saul not far from here. He's a creature of habit. He may have passed this way."

"If you think so," I said and waited for her to lead the way.

We entered the passageway. There was a steel staircase there. We climbed it. At the top there was a double door. It was also hanging open.

"These doors should have been closed. Not many people come down into these tunnels," Savannah said. "Maybe it means Saul has been this way."

We stepped out into the late-evening gloom of the Twilight Shops.

And then the screaming started.

CHAPTER 26

Savannah

I WASN'T SURPRISED WHEN I heard the screams. This was Broken territory. Old Saul must have been terrified if he came this way. I was apprehensive to come here myself. I only came this way when I was looking for Boyd and, even then, not often. But the screams were human and they were angry. There would be violence and it might be possible that Kieran and I could make a difference.

The screams came from down the hall that Boyd and I had fled along. Kieran already had his sword in hand. The way he held it was strangely familiar, though I dismissed it at first. I didn't know that many swordsmen.

Then again, when had Kieran become a swordsman?

We took off at a sprint. He had a head start on me, disturbingly ready for violence, but I was faster. Kite-Stepping had given me a reserve of speed few could match.

Drawing my own sword, Dave Boyd's sword, I dashed past Kieran, long drifting strides carrying me ten feet to a bound. Seeing me drift past him I swear I heard him grunt in frustration and he ducked his head, charging head-long after me.

When we got to the room with the open ceiling and the red marble floor, the room where Boyd made his last stand so that I could escape with the manual, we found a grisly memento. A single severed arm lay on the floor, the leaves around it disturbed. By the tumorous growths and claws on it I'd hazard it was off one of the Broken, though I couldn't be sure as it was mostly rotted.

The hand curled slightly and the index finger seemed to point, tell-tale, down a side hall I had not explored. The blade I'd left for Boyd, and the offerings were long gone. I guess I shouldn't have been surprised. There were plenty of animals down here.

Another scream issued, it was coming from the tunnel the finger pointed down. As Kieran arrived in the room I dashed off, Kite-Stepping toward the sounds of the scream, ready for whatever I faced, praying the one screaming was not Old Saul.

I found a crowd of the Broken. The brutes were clustered around an open doorway, the ones in the rear pushing and struggling to pass the ones in front. A small knot of people fought against the crowd of the Broken. MacMillan and his teacher, Sophie.

I was half-tempted to turn around then and there. But then I saw who they were defending. Dave Boyd; he wasn't well, but he was alive!

The bottom of my stomach dropped out. I'd abandoned him! I had looked for him so many times, but it didn't matter. I left him struggling to live and had run away. All this time I'd dallied with Old Saul while Boyd suffered in secret.

He had the little dagger I'd left behind. At least I'd given him that much.

I was overcome with shock, joy, guilt and sadness and the tip of my sword wavered. In that second I was almost lost. The Broken saw me and my weapon was not at the ready. They would have fallen upon me and, strong though my Kite-Stepping was, skillful though I'd become at Stone Hands and at the Form of Limitless Aggression, I was unprepared. I should have died in that moment.

But in the timeless seconds it took for the Broken to realize I was behind them, for ten of the wretches to peel off from attacking MacMillan and his companion and turn their eyes to me, Kieran arrived.

He fought exactly like MacMillan did. They could have had the same teacher, their styles were so similar. That sent a chill down my spine. What if Kieran had become a servant of MacMillan and his ilk? His family had wealth, status. It wasn't impossible they had connections to Fredericton.

One thing was certain: Kieran was good. Peppering the Broken with rapid-fire thrusts and sneaky cuts, he put down three before they even realized he was there. In the fourth his sword jammed against bone and was momentarily stuck. I saw him preparing to strike the fifth Broken with a bare-handed blow.

I steeled myself; I wouldn't be able to do much for Boyd or anybody if I let the battle overwhelm me. I brought my sword to bear and, with the blade sailing in a powerful arc, threw back the horde of the Broken.

Kieran got his sword free and lunged under the arc of my sword, dispatching a wounded Broken with another wily thrust.

It was odd. Our styles seemed to complement each other.

The same could not be said entirely of MacMillan and his companions, who were fighting back-to-back. He'd brought soldiers with him, and the woman who'd wounded Boyd. Some of the soldiers had fallen before we arrived, caught in the initial press of the Broken. The two remaining had pulled into a loose phalanx and were trying to shield MacMillan and Sophie.

When she saw me fighting the Broken she broke ranks. One of the soldiers tried to provide her with cover and he was pulled down under a pile of Broken, who leapt at the opening with rabid intensity. He cut down two before he was dragged under, screaming. She ignored the soldier's death and cut a swath through the Broken directly toward me. There was murder in her eyes though I didn't understand why.

As she approached, Kieran thrust two fingers into the gut of an oncoming Broken and the creature fell to the ground, clawing at the floor with its arms but with legs turned useless. I'd never seen a strike like that. Nor, it seemed, had anybody from MacMillan's party. The Broken sensed a change in momentum and pressed harder. Devoid of her guard, the woman retreated back to MacMillan's side and gave up her attempt to face me.

But the tide was turning. The five of us were more than a match for the screaming, clicking, slobbering crowd of wretches. They fell to our blades. And eventually Kieran and I faced MacMillan and his companion across a field of the dead.

"You have something of mine."

Dave Boyd laughed. It was a painful sound. He was not a well man; the two months had not been kind to him. "That's my Scorpion Girl." He sounded proud. "Found Old Saul I see."

I nodded to him, but I kept my attention on her. I knew a nutter when I saw one and she was mad like a rabid dog.

Unfortunately, Kieran didn't seem much better. He was all but growling at MacMillan and he gripped the hilt of his sword so tight that his knuckles were white. "I know your face MacMillan, and hers."

"Then you have me at a disadvantage," Kyle MacMillan said. "I don't have the first clue who the hell you are. Though I'd surely like to meet your teacher."

"I am your death," Kieran said.

Seriously, who says something like that? I supposed that there was unfinished business between them, and that Kieran was young enough to believe his words threatening.

"Stolen arts and stolen airs," MacMillan's companion snarled. "I will take him myself."

"He called me out personally, Sophie," MacMillan said to his companion though he didn't take his eyes off Kieran. "I will face him personally. Well boy, I am right here."

"Could you both please stop waving your dicks around long enough to see some reason?" Boyd asked, his pain and frustration burning through his words.

Kieran glared wrathfully at Boyd.

Kyle snorted. "Yes, I do have more important matters to attend to, such as apprehending you."

MacMillan's psychotic companion seemed to have accepted MacMillan's desire to deal with Kieran. Not that this was a good thing necessarily. She was stalking toward me with murder in her eyes.

She raised her sword and I jumped away from her, drifting down the hallway. Back-drifting was dangerous, but not as dangerous as a psycho with a sword.

"Sophie," Boyd said. "If you ever want to live to flee your father another day you might want to listen to me too." Yeah, things were getting surreal. Was there a circular I was left out of?

"You won't distract me from my prize with idle threats. Kyle, kill Boyd. We don't need him if we can take her instead."

"Boyd's right," Kieran said. "I've met your father myself. He's here, and he's looking for you."

"Liar." But she paused, the certainty draining from her.

"There's a hell of a lot more Broken where those came from. The entire region is thick with them," Boyd said, his voice husky with pain. "That's why I boarded myself in to begin with."

"So? The Broken die like anybody else," MacMillan snarled. I could tell he wanted a shot at Kieran. I could tell Kieran reciprocated though he'd become taciturn.

"So if you kill the boy, try to take Savannah or I prisoner, do you fucking think you'll be able to escape from fifty more of those things?"

Punctuating Boyd's claim, we all heard the chittering sound of Broken mandibles from down the hallway, but coming closer.

Kyle looked down the hallway, and I could see him calculating his odds.

"Sir, perhaps it would be prudent for us to retreat," the last of his surviving guards said.

"Yes. We can deal with other matters on the surface," Kyle said. "A temporary truce then, until we've got out of this pit?"

The Broken sounded again, closer this time. I stepped a few feet closer. All of a sudden the two bastards with swords didn't seem as threatening as the empty hallway to my back. "I'm willing to play nice as long as you keep your bitch on a short leash."

The woman snarled at me, her expression equal parts hauteur and feral wrath, and her grip shifted on her sword.

"Sophie, now is not the time," Kyle said. There was a moment of trembling stillness. And then she nodded and let her blade fall to her side.

Had I been a little bit less mature I might have stuck my tongue out at her but, honestly, I was basically running my mouth on auto-pilot by that point. I was out of my depth and I knew it.

"Those creatures are probably thirty seconds away, lad. Come with us or escape alone, but I intend to leave now," Boyd said.

We all held our breath.

"Fine," Kieran said. "Until we all get out of this alive and no further."

From down the hall I heard the shuffle of footsteps. "Good," I said. "Now, let's get the hell out of this pit."

CHAPTER 27

Kyle

THE STRANGER WITH THE angry eyes wanted to kill me and I was damned if I even knew who he was. But he was a killer, true enough. Somebody had taught him the Triumvirate sword art, and what was that thing he'd done with his fingers? I'd never seen somebody paralyzed with a poke before.

He worried me. I was confident that Sophie and I could take him though. He wasn't as practiced with the sword as I was, I could tell.

The western girl who was with him took a few steps towards us. I recognized her from before, she'd been the one who'd stolen Boyd from us, and it seemed as if she was his student. She fought with his style and she could move with lightness like Sophie and Boyd could. I wished Sophie would teach me that trick.

The girl seemed frightened, poised between running and attacking. And she kept glancing at Boyd as if trying to convince herself he was real. But she was honoring our truce.

"How the hell did you manage to survive?" she asked Boyd.

"I've taken a few hits in my day," he answered.

"Through the gut? With a sword?"

"Occasionally. But hush now. We'll talk later. The Broken are attracted to noise."

Of course, if she kept talking Sophie might just kill her before the Broken ever got the chance—she hated being called a bitch. I could feel the heat coming off her face even though her back was to me.

I saw shapes moving in the darkness. Boyd did too.

"Savannah, could you and your friend help me up? I'm afraid I'm rather at the end of my rope," he asked the tattooed girl. Honestly I didn't understand why the westerners did things like that.

Boyd stood up. He wasn't moving well, that much was plain. He'd suffered for his voluntary imprisonment. There were dark rings around his eyes, dead looking things that they were.

This was the man who had forced us here. He was either our greatest ally or our greatest enemy and I still didn't know which. I was honestly getting beyond the point of caring. I just wanted to take Boyd and be gone.

"Don't try anything stupid," I said to the wounded man.

"Wasn't planning to."

The western girl flushed, at least I think she did, it was difficult to tell with the darkness of her skin. Regardless she answered Boyd, "I was just holding it for you."

"I think your need is greater than mine," he said to her. She nodded her head and we fell into our uncomfortable march.

I did not trust this interloper who had so recently declared his intention to kill me. It was clear that the western girl trusted Sophie no more. Sophie immediately took the lead.

"Watch our rear Kyle, I don't want to take a sword in the back."

The stranger pushed past me and, hand on his sword, said, "When I come for your ilk it won't be from behind." They stared at each other for a brief second before each looked away, content to ignore each other until we got clear of danger. Boyd was hardly in a position to fight, despite his little dagger, and all any of us could agree on was that he should be escorted out of this place, preferably alive (at least I hoped Sophie still wanted him alive). Sergeant Pelle took his arm and helped carry him, surrounded by us.

I fell in the back next to the westerner.

"I would consider it in your favour to know your names," I said. "So I know what to shout should we come under attack."

"Savannah," said the westerner. Her friend said nothing, gritted his jaw.

"You aren't inspiring trust in me."

He said nothing, became even tenser. "Don't be an asshole, Kieran," Savannah said. He glanced back at her angrily but she said nothing more.

"My name is Lord Kyle MacMillan, crown prince of Confederation, but I think you already knew that. My companion is Sophie, and this gentleman is Sergeant Pelle," I said.

Nobody said anything more.

For a time I thought we might actually make it to the surface without incident. Of course, the shortest path was closed to us, but there were a thousand ways out of the Long Dark, especially out of the Twilight Shops, which had once tied into the lower levels of many of the towers of Trana. For a time I thought we wouldn't have to fight, that the only foes we needed to fear were the ones that walked at our side.

I was wrong.

Before we'd made it even halfway to the nearest exit, the closest unobstructed stair to the surface, the Broken boiled out of the dark places.

I'd fought their kind before. Retreating from the rout at Bangor we'd taken shelter in a crumbling old ruin and it'd been infested with the Broken. Even though our army had outnumbered the freaks three to one they still attacked to the last.

I have to say that my enemies, my companions, comported themselves well. They would have been more than a match for all but the best of my soldiers. It was clear that both were green warriors but it was equally clear that each had masterful instructors.

As I watched Kieran casually run through a Broken with 'The Rising Hawk' I marvelled that others knew the Triumvirate sword art. I resolved to speak with Sophie about the supposed exclusivity of the skill when we made it to the surface.

The last of the Broken fell under Savannah's blade and I was sure we had attained the surface. In my rush I nearly didn't notice the masked man who jumped from the shadows of the gate. He was a slight man. He wore a heavy set of robes in the southern style and a demonic mask, painted red with a leering face, forked tongue lolling from a black gash of a mouth.

With a narrow sword he cut down Sergeant Pelle, who fell, clutching his throat and unable to scream. We'd hardly had time to even move. I felt a pang in my stomach. None of the men I'd brought with me here had survived our excursion into the dark. I resolved that his death would not be in vain.

The masked interloper jumped out from the middle of our group and landed in front of us, sword at the ready. His voice was high and reedy. It seemed affected, like he was trying to mask the true tone of his voice. "You may have killed my pets, but that doesn't mean I will let you off."

I didn't have the patience for this. "Go to hell," I said as I cut out at him with 'The Back-Handed Compliment.'

His counter was entirely unfamiliar to me. The simple truth is that it shouldn't have worked. It was the most awkward and clumsy parry I'd ever seen. And yet when my sword clashed against his it stuck in place. I could not wrap my blade around his to cut him along the side of the head. Furthermore I could not withdraw my sword. The western girl attacked the masked man and he parried her with the same clumsy counter, dragging my blade reluctantly with his, and just as with me, her sword was trapped, pinned to the sword of the man in the mask as if by magnetism.

Her friend lashed out with his unarmed attack, the one using two fingers of his off-hand. The man in the demon mask tried to parry his attack but could not manoeuvre his own blade effectively enough to do so while the girl and I both struggled against him. The finger blow struck him on the sword arm and, as suddenly as it had begun, the bizarre magnetism that trapped my sword ended.

The man in the mask recoiled and fled, using the same sort of strange bounding leap that Savannah had used in the fight below. We chose not to give chase.

We stepped into the dim light of night-time Trana. After the dark of the underground it seemed bright, though it was only moon light and distant torches.

I turned to look and, in the black of the tunnel behind us, there were no signs of life. Corpses of fallen Broken lay in silent testament to our bloody escape from the underworld. I smiled and readied my sword.

"We have achieved the surface. For that I thank you and may spare your lives. Now be good and lay down your swords." I wasn't about to let these three dangerous foes escape, notwithstanding the interest Sophie had in the skills of Boyd and his protégé.

"No, we don't need both of them. Kill the boy, kill the girl. We'll keep Boyd for ourselves. He's clearly the master."

"Now is not the time, Sophie."

She moved toward the western girl with murder in her expression.

"I'd rather just be going if it's all the same to you," Savannah said. She was watching Sophie stalk closer and coiling in on herself, preparing to leap perhaps.

Sophie saw what she intended and used her head, putting her sword to Boyd's throat. "Fine. So we spare the girl and kill Boyd instead."

"Let him go," Savannah snapped.

"Lay down your sword and you have my word he won't be harmed," I said, giving Sophie a stern look. She stared back at me blankly.

It would have worked had her friend not chosen that moment to attack. I'd give the youth this much, he was a vicious bastard. He went for me, not Sophie, and his sword would have found my throat had I been even an instant slower. As it was, I barely parried in time.

Savannah decided to throw in on the side of her companion, since battle was engaged anyway and Sophie was struggling with Boyd, who was trying with the last of his strength to delay her. I found myself fighting off two skillful fighters alone... and losing.

They were both using the Triumvirate sword art but it was different from when Sophie and I would use our arts together. While Kieran used the same techniques I knew myself, Savannah used the Form of Limitless Aggression. The two fighting together managed to be far more effective than either was alone.

I would have died. But Sophie saved my life, jumping into the fray, helping me to separate my two assailants. Having done so we regained the upper hand; even so the fight flowed furiously between the four of us. And then, as fast as the fight had begun, it ended.

Savannah saw her chance and jumped, her leap nearly as impossible as that of the masked attacker.

Kieran didn't wait for us to kill him. Instead he fell into a backward roll and, as he rose, threw a handful of concrete grit and gravel in my face. I wiped my eyes but he was already running away.

Dave Boyd was limping in the opposite direction. Dave Boyd, who knew the Form of Limitless Aggression.

I knew who Sophie would prefer to chase. I gave up on Kieran for the moment.

I put my sword to Boyd's throat at the same moment as Sophie.

"Don't think of trying to run," I said, my mood black, the wrath seeping like oil into my words. I glanced at Sophie, and the ecstatic look in her eyes gave me chills.

CHAPTER 28

Kieran

SAVANNAH BAILED, DRIFTING AWAY using the unnatural leaps she favoured. I'd have paused to wonder about that if I didn't have more pressing concerns, chiefly that I was now facing Kyle MacMillan and the woman who I was now nearly certain was the Wizard in Green's daughter. So I didn't pause to wonder. I ran and I didn't stop running for quite some time.

Eventually I found myself in the shadow of the Dome at the Square. The dome, raised on a platform, sat nestled between two curved towers. These towers were not as high as the ones surrounding them and had long since been stripped of enough steel to make them unsafe—more the skeletons of buildings than buildings in truth—but the dome remained in good condition, used for the storage of finished goods from the forges of Broken Tower. The entire structure was at the northern edge of a large concrete square. A squalid pool sat at the southern end and the crumbling remnants of a ramp leading up to the dome encircled to the east.

From a raised portion of those remnants Savannah drifted down, nearly giving me a heart attack in the process. "By the Under-God's balls," I cursed.

Savannah's landing from ten feet up was so gentle she didn't even stir up the dust and she seemed almost casual. Her dark, almond shaped eyes betrayed that she felt far from casual though, and she still had the huge sword of Dave Boyd in her hands.

She must have been stronger than she looked—the greatsword of Dave Boyd had a blade nearly four feet long. Savannah wasn't the tallest person I'd ever seen. Later I saw that she generally carried it slung across her back. She had to. She'd have tripped over the thing if she'd carried it at her hip. Even so the sword nearly dragged along the ground.

"Put that away," she said, glancing at my sword, which was pointed at her. She didn't seem amused.

I sheathed the blade. I trusted my ability to defend myself if she took advantage. Still I didn't want to seem too deferential, I was very angry with her for leaving me alone with Boyd and his companion. "Now how about you do the same?"

She lowered the tip of her sword until it touched the cracked flagstones.

"You abandoned me to those two."

"You got away," she said dismissively, as if that made it alright.

"No thanks to you." I spat on the ground and she looked at me coolly.

"Who do you think I am? Your mother?"

My eyes narrowed. "My mother is dead."

Her expression softened. "Well, then we have something in common."

I did not feel like talking about my feelings with her. "It's not safe out here. Those two Confederation psychos might catch up with us any moment."

She glanced nervously down the street. "Yeah, come with me. I know a place."

What the hell, it wasn't my neighbourhood. Maybe she knew a place at that. She led me north and into a door in the base of the east tower overlooking the dome. Her hiding place did not inspire me with confidence. The towers of the dome were not sound or safe. As I saw the denuded walls, rebar and copper wire stripped out of concrete and plaster, leaving haphazard track-marks of decay; crumbled heaps of rubble piled in the corners, I bit my lip, choked back the comments about buildings one good sneeze away from collapse, and looked furtively at the sagging ceiling.

We passed through a cavernous room filled with the rotting remains of plastic-sealed wood furniture. From the room we went into a hallway decorated with the rusted fixtures of long-scavenged pipes and corroded aluminum chains, not even worth scavenging.

Savannah led me deeper into the building and down a staircase, eventually slipping into an alcove beneath the stairs, quiet and dark.

"We should be safe here. Nobody ever comes down here."

"No shit," I muttered. "They'd probably be too worried about the ceiling falling in on them."

Savannah shot me a frustrated look. "Why do you want to kill Kyle MacMillan?"

I couldn't just tell her 'because I'm a member of the Black Trillium' so I settled on saying, "Because his father is a tyrant and Trana should be free."

"Never pegged you for a patriot." Her voice seemed inquisitive and there was a penetrative look in her eyes. She was trying to read me.

I tried to keep my expression carefully blank. "We all grow up eventually."

"You won't get Saul involved in any foolish rebellion. He's a frightened old man, no matter how powerful he might happen to be." She was fishing, hoping to get me to give something away.

"I told you, my uncle is sick. I didn't even know Shatterfield was a warrior." That might have been a lie but there was honesty in the sentiment. I had warriors aplenty to call upon. I needed medicine.

"I don't want to be a rebel either. I'm no patriot." It wasn't fear in her voice. If anything it was obstinacy, stubborn pride.

"Nobody asked that of you."

"You were upset that I left you alone to fight MacMillan." Was that a hint of sadness in her voice? I wasn't sure. Perhaps she regretted what she'd done. I had conflicted emotions about Savannah. She was a beautiful woman but I'd been with a fair number of beautiful women. I didn't usually feel all flustered when I ran into them months later.

I brushed aside the feelings. They confused and frustrated me and I wanted a clear head. "Your sword skills, they are like the Triumvirate sword art but... different."

One of her narrow eyebrows lifted. I'd piqued her curiosity. "You mean your sword style? Where'd you learn it?"

"I was taught it." A vague answer, sure, but I didn't want to reveal my connection to Mr. Chamblais.

"I learned it from a book."

"Did Saul give it to you?" I asked, remembering just in time that she didn't like using his last name.

"No, he hated the thing, said it was evil. I got the book from Dave Boyd." Now that was unexpected. How in the world had Boyd got the manual? The Wizard in Green thought Shatterfield had it.

"How did he get it?"

"Look, do you expect me to tell you my whole life story?" She sounded irritated so I backed off a little.

"That explains why our sword play worked so well together," I said, glancing down at the floor.

"What?"

"I fought better with you at my side than I've ever fought before," I said, still looking down. I hoped she wouldn't notice I was blushing in the dark.

"It was the first time I'd actually fought, using a sword."

"You were very good. Where did you learn to jump like that? Was it Shatterfield?" I glanced back up into her eyes and was sure she was blushing now too.

"Do you think we're safe?"

"I don't know," I said honestly.

"Maybe we should just stay down here then, for a little while." I could almost hear her embarrassment, it was like we were both kids again.

"It is probably for the best," I said, trying for stoic and missing.

She nodded and shifted, hugging her knees to her chest. It was going to be a long night.

CHAPTER 29

Savannah

IT WAS DARK UNDER the stairs and I should have felt safe. As sinister as Kieran had seemed at first he didn't frighten me. And yet, I wasn't comfortable, I felt small and frightened and lonely.

We sat for a time in silence. When I'd been with Old Saul the silence had been comfortable. This was not the same sort of silence and I did not feel comfortable at all. In the gloom of the stairs in the night I found my thoughts turning back to the flight from the Broken, to the fight at the exit. I'd run.

That hadn't been right.

I shouldn't have done that. Perhaps I'd spent too long away from the world. I'd started running when I carried Dave Boyd away from Kyle MacMillan and Sophie the Bitch. In a way I'd never stopped. All that time in the Cathedral of Broken Glass with Old Saul I'd told myself I was learning how to fight, but as much as I loved the old man, almost like a father, that wasn't the lesson he taught me. He'd taught me to do just what he had been doing for who-knew how long and for who-knew what reason. He'd taught me to run away.

He hadn't meant to. Whatever it was that had hurt Old Saul had left him terrified of everything. Running was all he had left.

I wasn't going to end up like him, broken and running for ever and ever.

The sun was rising outside and the shadows under the stairs had gone from nearly black as pitch to a mere over-all gloom. There were plenty of cracks in the building through which the morning sun could shine.

The Confederation hadn't come for us, and I was through with running. "Why did you take up a sword?"

Kieran was only half awake and I suspected that this would be the best time to get something out of him about his own past, about how the care-free boy with the easy smile and a clever way with words had become a grim and skillful warrior. "I didn't have a choice, did I?"

Now that was an interesting non-answer. "I guess I didn't really have a choice either." And that was true. I'd had to learn how to fight. Otherwise I'd have fallen to Confederation and the bitch would have the manual.

"Why did Dave Boyd give you the manual? I thought Saul had it." He was waking up quickly. If I wanted to find out what he'd been through I'd have to give a little too.

"I don't know anything about Saul having it. Boyd wanted me to protect it."

"I'm not sure I trust Boyd."

I smiled. "I'm not sure I trust you, Kieran Benton. You turn up spouting rebel phrases and using the same sword techniques as MacMillan and that woman... Sophie."

"I met a man, I think he was related to her, maybe her father." Kieran was peering off into space, as if recollecting a vivid memory. "He said the manual had been his once, he said he sent it to Old Saul."

"Boyd seemed to know Sophie, her father. Maybe he is the one who sent the manual to Saul. Anyway, Saul hated it. Boyd probably figured it was better to hold onto it than to leave it with Saul, in his state."

"Would you show me?" Kieran asked.

"Only if you show me yours," I joked and poked Kieran with my thumb. He grinned and waggled his eyebrows. Perhaps there was a bit of the boy remaining in the man. It was nice to see him smile—nice to know he was still able to smile.

We left the little den under the stairs in higher spirit than we'd entered and emerged blinking into morning light in the square. It was nearly empty. Ever since Boyd had disappeared people had been keeping their heads down.

"I guess here is as good as any place," Kieran said with a fleeting smile.

"Yeah."

"We shouldn't dawdle too long. We still need to find Shatterfield."

"It's not safe underground. Old Saul is resourceful. He'll turn up eventually."

Kieran sighed. "I hope so."

All I could was smile weakly. "OK, show me what you can do with a sword."

And he began. The Form of Limitless Cunning seemed familiar. It had elements in it that were the same as elements of my sword form. However, where my form forced through obstacles, slapped aside swords, ploughed through defences, his would whip, snake and sneak. In my mind I could see how the two forms should go together to make a cohesive whole, but there was something missing, some key element that would allow the two styles to merge into a whole that was absent from the manual and not evident in his style.

He finished with a final cut, thrusting subversively up from a low guard and grinned at me. His face was flushed and there was sweat beading his brow. He seemed proud. I suspected he hadn't had many opportunities to show off before. It seemed strange though. He had a flair for the flamboyant. I'd have thought him hot to show it off to anybody with two tits and a pulse. "Your turn," he said.

"Alright." I drew the big sword off my back and set it at the ready position and then I began.

I felt awkward at first. I'd only ever practiced this sword art in private, in dark places where nobody could see. When I'd used it against the Broken it had been a matter of life and death and I'd had no time for thought.

Now I was displaying it, proudly, and to an appreciative audience. Kieran watched me with a look part lazy enjoyment, part bright enthusiasm and perhaps just the slightest bit carnal hunger. It felt good to be watched.

My palms felt slippery against the hilt of the sword as I moved through the form, warming up, finding my pace, getting to the point where I lost myself in the movement of the great blade.

The sword sang in the air and sunlight gleamed on the steel of the blade. I felt my cares fade from me and forgot, if just for a moment, the Broken, Confederation, and the loss of my mentor. I was the sword dancing.

As I finished, the sword felt heavy in my hands.

"That was beautiful," Kieran said, and I knew he was being sincere, there was no hint of dissembling in his tone. "But there was something missing from it."

"You saw it too."

"Yeah." Kieran leaned on the hilt of his sheathed blade, lively brow knotted in concentration. "But I don't know what it might be."

"I am not sure either." And I wasn't sure, but I suspected. I knew that the page numbers in my manual started exactly two higher than halfway through. Having seen Kieran's form I knew that the Form of Limitless Cunning was the same length as the Form of Limitless Aggression, twenty-seven postures.

It seemed to me that maybe what was missing was some key, some concept, through which the two forms could be used as one.

I explained this to Kieran.

"You said Dave Boyd gave you the manual, right?" Kieran knew this, he was going somewhere with his question.

"Yeah." I left the word hanging there, waiting for him to continue.

"So if MacMillan has Boyd he could, in theory, get the Form of Limitless Aggression from him." Kieran had a point, but I didn't think Boyd so weak.

"He'd die first," I said.

"You have never seen a Confederation torture chamber." The smile disappeared from his face, a dark cloud passed before his eyes.

"We have to rescue him. He's severely hurt. I don't even know how he survived."

"MacMillan has a thousand soldiers."

"I never said it would be easy." It would probably be suicide.

"It's more important that we find the missing piece first," Kieran said. That was cold. He was telling me that MacMillan would probably torture Boyd to get the Form of Limitless Aggression from him but rather than rescue Boyd he wanted to go chasing after a piece of paper. What had happened to him?

"The Kieran Benton I know wouldn't say something like that." I thought I was right.

"I hate the thought too." Kieran lowered his head and sighed. "But they won't be able to do any lasting harm to Boyd, not if they want him to teach them the Form of Limitless Aggression."

"The two forms are equally matched."

"But much stronger used together. I fought much better with you at my side."

"No, if we're right, if there is a missing page, only Boyd will know where to find it. We should rescue him."

"But what if Saul has it?"

I was about to speak when I saw a single, hunched form approaching us at a run from across the western edge of the square. He was a wizened old man, looked a little bit like Old Saul actually, and he was shouting for Kieran.

When Kieran saw the old man running up he looked very worried. "That's the doctor who is caring for my uncle. But how did he know where to find me? And why is he here?"

The doctor approached and, wheezing from exertion, said, "Young Master Benton, I'm glad I found you. It's your uncle. He's slipped into a coma. I don't know how much longer he's going to last."

CHAPTER 30

Kyle

WE DECIDED IT WOULD be better to escort Boyd back to camp than to go chasing off after Kieran and Savannah. It was a hard choice but neither of us wanted to risk losing Boyd again. The ride home was miserable. It is never a happy thing to be riding home leading four empty horses, with a fifth being ridden not by the proud warrior who rode out upon it but by a prisoner instead.

We didn't speak much as we rode through the night back to the Scar. We also couldn't help but feel like we were being watched by somebody. "I don't like this," Sophie said to me.

"Nor I." At least we had Boyd. That meant that the loss of our men wasn't a complete loss. He might not have the manual any more but he knew the sword art. If we could compel him to teach us the manual might not be necessary.

I glanced at Sophie and smiled weakly at her. She met my gaze but she didn't return the smile. I didn't blame her. I felt so angry over the loss of my men.

They never stood a chance.

Dave Boyd was laughing at us when the Broken began to crowd into the doorway, laughing though our deaths would surely mean his own. My five men all died quickly and they didn't die well. They were dragged under, one by one, by the sub-human creatures that didn't know fear, didn't care about pain and would keep coming until they were disabled or killed.

Legend said that the Broken were made from people, made as weapons. I could believe those legends.

Watching the Broken, wounds gaping in their flesh where my men's swords had struck them, as they clawed and bit and buried the men in a frenzy of rage and hunger was enough to make me sick.

But I had no such luxury.

Sophie and I fought. We fought and every sneaky trick of the Triumvirate sword art came to our aid to stay alive for just one more minute.

And then Kieran and Savannah arrived, and they killed the Broken using our sword arts, using both halves of the ultimate whole. And when they'd destroyed all of the Broken, when those two... nobodies... had saved our lives, that smug bastard had said he had come to kill me.

But there were more Broken coming, and Boyd had been right, we wouldn't survive without them.

"You might as well just kill me and get it over with." Boyd broke my reverie.

"What makes you think I intend to kill you? I thought you did it all just to warn us about the Black Trillium." My voice dripped with sarcasm.

"I won't give you the sword art."

Sophie tugged on the lariat we'd slipped around Boyd's neck. If he ran, it would be easy enough to choke him to death. She didn't keep the pressure on for more than just a second. Even so, the thick-necked man coughed.

"You'll give it to us," I said.

Boyd laughed hoarsely. "What makes you think you can compel me? Hell, what makes you think you can even hold me once I've recovered enough to teach you?"

"We'll make sure you live a good, long time, but you needn't really recover to instruct us," Sophie purred. Oh yes, we would make sure Boyd lived a long time. If it was needed we could hurt him until he craved death, until he willingly gave us all his secrets just so that we would end his miserable life a second sooner. Yes, we could do that.

But not yet. We'd try the easy way first.

"Do you children really believe you can torture me into revealing this secret? You're amateurs playing at power."

"We overthrew you, reduced you to lurking in a stinking pit, too wounded to even escape until we came back for you. Who's playing at power?" I met Boyd's gaze and it was unwavering.

He just laughed again. "We'll see how well you fare once I've recovered."

Sophie pulled his noose fully taut. His hand snaked up and he began straining to slide his fingers around the rope. "Let's just kill him and leave him in a ditch here," she said. "His student has the manual. We can find her, take it from her."

Boyd's face was bright red, and every sinew in his body showed on his skin. Ever so slowly his fingers closed around the rope. A tiny noise escaped him, a hiss of breath and the noose stretched and snapped. The pop of the rope splitting echoed around us. Sophie recoiled and her horse reared. She struggled to stay on as Boyd slumped forward in his saddle, rubbing at a vivid purple welt around his throat.

His voice was a hoarse death rattle. "No, you aren't killing me today. Here is what will happen. You will fetch me a doctor and see to it that I'm healed. You'll do so because I'm the only hope you have to survive when her father comes to collect her.

"And anyway, you won't find Savannah. She's one of the most resourceful people in the whole of Trana and I'd guess she has some friends. I never taught her Kite-Stepping. Truth is I never taught her anything, so I'd guess she's found some other mentor. And if I'm not off my guess, the boy she was with was Black Trillium. He has the look about him—and he hated you."

Sophie brought her horse under control. "Don't listen to him," she hissed.

"No. We'll make Boyd comfortable. No killing. Damn it, Sophie, but we *have* the sword art right here. And perhaps we can convince Boyd to share it freely if we show him some kindness. We aren't monsters. As for the matter of your father, we'll discuss that later. It's high time you tell me some truth about yourself." I spat on the ground.

Sophie said nothing though her face was nearly as red as Boyd's. Boyd leaned against the neck of his horse and laughed raggedly. "Yeah, I'm sure you'll convince me." And then his eyes closed and, with the last of his strength sapped, he fell into unconsciousness.

We arrived back at camp and I passed the unconscious Boyd over to Lieutenant Messier. "Send out some men. I want you to scour the city for the best doctor so we can get him on his feet and healthy again as soon as possible. But be careful. He's the strongest man I've ever seen. Post a triple guard on him at least and make sure he's securely bound when he awakes."

Messier saluted and left, leading Boyd's horse with the unconscious warrior still prone on its back.

Sophie and I went to bed.

In my sleep I was pursued by shadows, faceless enemies who taunted me and cut at me with subtle knives. Every time I turned to fight back the shadows faded and struck again from the other direction; always at my back, always out of sight, out of reach, insubstantial.

I collapsed, exhausted even in my dreams, and the shadows closed around me, pushing me into an oblivion more complete than any sleep.

I awoke sweating in the bright light of mid-day, and there was a man in my tent.

He was a large man, dressed in dark blue, and his face was masked. In one hand he held an axe. In the other he held two swords—mine and Sophie's.

Our eyes met and I saw a flat, reptilian cruelty in his. This man intended to kill me. I scrambled out of bed. I was naked, unarmoured and unarmed.

The man said nothing, made no noise, he just attacked.

The axe whistled in the air and as it sped for my throat I couldn't help but marvel at the craftsmanship. It was a beautiful axe, well made. Whoever sent this man to kill me was wealthy. I wondered if it was the Black Trillium or my father.

I suspected the former, though, sadly, I could not be sure.

I sprang out of the way but my feet got tangled in my sheets. I stumbled over my cot on the floor, accidentally kicking Sophie as I struggled to stay upright. It was all that saved her life. Her eyes snapped open just as the assassin, having missed me with his first blow, brought the axe downward, to plant it in her. She rolled out of the way, screaming defiance, and the blow barely grazed her, tearing a strip of flesh from the meatiest part of her arm but missing a killing blow.

Sophie's screams alerted my guards. Brutus rushed into the room, his own axes, the ones that had been a gift from my father, at the ready.

There was a moment of understanding between the two hulking, silent killers and then my bodyguard attacked and was out-matched. The masked assassin caught Brutus's two axes on the haft of his own. Blades locked together, he brought his knee up, connecting with Brutus's groin. A second kick threw Brutus backward, crashing into two other guards on their way through the door and bowling them over.

Sophie was on her feet by then, prepared to fight and showing no concern for her modesty. The dark red of her blood trickling down the pale white flesh of her arm was terrible to behold and her green eyes showed nothing but murderous wrath.

It was then that I realized that Sophie had not taught me everything she knew of the fighting arts. Her bare-hand fighting was peerless. With a first brutal strike she knocked the assassin's chin back. While he was reeling from the blow she drove an elbow into his stomach, stomped on his foot and kneed him in his face, as it descended.

I'd never seen anybody move that fast before. And she would have won, I'm sure she would have won, but then she went for her sword.

It gave the assassin the slimmest of moments to react. His axe bit into her side right above the hip. It bit deeply and Sophie collapsed.

"No!" I screamed, or thought I screamed, and I flew into a rage. I resolved in the barest fraction of a second to die at her side. I saw Sophie lying bonelessly on the ground, a growing pool of blood like a halo around her. I saw Brutus scrambling to regain his feet, a look of frustrated, impotent rage on his face, I saw it all and it seemed to be standing still. I raced toward the killer, preparing to end my own life for revenge.

I saw the axe rise up in slow motion, pulled free from my lover, and I knew I was a dead man.

And then I was showered in a spray of gore.

The brown eyes of the assassin were full of surprise. The axe fell from his hands as he stared down at the whip-thin point of metal protruding from the left side of his chest. He coughed and blood dribbled from his mouth.

"It wasn't..." he started to say, but he never finished his pained words. He slid off the sword and fell on top of my lover.

Standing over both forms was a man in green robes. The robes, traced with copper and gold, were nearly the same colour as his eyes, as Sophie's eyes. He had Sophie's eyes. The man looked every inch the Wizard in Green.

Time returned to normal.

The Wizard in Green threw me a packet of white powder.

"Rub that in the wound and then dress it in clean bandages if you want to live," said the Wizard in Green in a voice that was horribly familiar. It was as if Sophie's own voice were that of a man. "I will return for her when she has recovered."

"But the wound, no medicine will suffice."

"This one will. Or I will end you," he said and I saw tears in his eyes, and the same madness that sometimes haunted hers. Boyd had promised me only he could save me if Sophie's father came for her. In that moment I feared he may have overestimated his capabilities.

And then the man was gone, vanishing as suddenly and as miraculously as he had come.

I looked at Sophie, white skin stained red, barely conscious but trying to scrabble along the ground toward me, away from the Wizard in Green, and I looked at the packet in my hand.

I didn't have long if I wanted to save her. I tore open the packet and set to work.

CHAPTER 31

Kieran

I FELT THE WORLD fall out from underneath me. It didn't matter if Dave Boyd faced torture. I didn't care if Confederation got their hands on the Form of Limitless Aggression. My uncle was on death's door and I needed to do something. I ran.

Savannah followed. My flat-out sprint seeming to be a casual stroll for her. I'd have to learn how she did that sometime, but not at this moment. Now there was only family, the responsibility I felt to my only kin.

I vaulted over a chunk of concrete at the edge of the square and hoofed it full-speed along Queen. The jagged teeth of the spires at the heart of the city began to fade into the distance as the district of Broken Tower drifted south and we continued west. Soon the buildings around us were three-story brick buildings, rebuilt countless times since the Great Collapse but ancient in form, and in good repair.

I spared a look out of the corner of my eye as I reached the wider part of Queen that delineated the three-quarter point in the journey from the Dome at the Square to Chi-Town. Savannah was matching my pace. She was frowning, not the frown of somebody who had just got bad news but rather the frown of somebody deep in serious thought.

"Maybe I can help your uncle."

I stopped running, hands on my knees to catch my breath. "What?"

"I learned a little medicine from Old Saul. Maybe I can help."

"You learned his medicine?"

"A little—he doesn't hide it; wrote prescriptions and instructions across his walls. I can read a little. I thought it might come in handy sometime."

"If you can save him..." I couldn't finish. I looked away.

We started running again.

When I started this fool's errand two months ago I thought I'd return eventually triumphant, the hero. Instead, each night, I returned to this deathwatch: a painful and unending stasis. The colourful paint flecking the bricks of my home seemed faded; perhaps it was only that the joy in my heart was faded.

Drenched in sweat and reeking of despair and exhaustion, I walked into the shade of my home. Mr. Chamblais was sitting with uncle Stephen. My uncle's eyes were closed and his breathing was short. I approached the bed and grabbed his hand. It felt like it had just come out of an oven.

Mr. Chamblais looked up at Savannah. "Who is this girl?" he asked.

"She's the student of Saul Shatterfield," I replied.

"You found him?"

I closed my eyes, not wanting to drown the hope I could hear in his voice. "Yes, and I lost him. But I know Savannah. She thinks she can help."

Savannah came to my side. She touched a hand to my uncle's forehead, tested his pulse, looked at the fresh scar where he'd been bitten.

"This is wrong," she said. "If he's suffering from an infected bite why did the wound heal so well?"

Mr. Chamblais and I both shrugged our shoulders. Neither of us were doctors. Savannah pulled out a ragged book, and Mr. Chamblais' eyes opened wide. The little book wasn't much to look at, torn in half along the spine, front page stained with dirt and with blood and who-knew what else, but it was a swordplay manual, and I'd seen enough of those to recognize it as depicting Savannah's style, the one that fit so neatly with my own.

I looked over Savannah's shoulder. She wasn't reading the martial form but rather bits of text penciled in by some other hand in charcoal in the margins.

The letters were smudged and the shaping of them suggested limited formal education but what they said—it was a medical manual, of that much I am sure, but I couldn't make heads or tails of most of it. Savannah thumbed through it for a while and eventually said, "I uh, I think I need to take some blood. Are there medical tools here? A doctor was caring for him."

"Perhaps in the kitchen, I don't know for sure," Mr. Chamblais said.

I ran to the kitchen and began to search. I looked for anything unfamiliar, anything that might be medical supplies.

Near the stove I found a metal bowl with a white strip of cloth draped over it. I lifted the cloth and found tools: needles and little knives, a few herbs, some bandages. I brought them back. "Are these what you need?"

"I think so," Savannah said.

"You... have practised medicine before?" Mr. Chamblais said anxiously.

"Not as such." Savannah sounded unnerved. "But I know how to do this, in theory."

"This is the best you can do?" Mr. Chamblais asked.

"Yes, I'm the best he could do," Savannah snapped. "And I'm a little bit terrified, but I'm trying to help here. Frankly things can't get much worse. So you have two choices: let me try to help, or do nothing and watch this man die."

"I'm sorry," Mr. Chamblais said quietly. "Please, do what you can."

Savannah pricked Uncle's finger with a needle and pressed a little bit of blood onto two pieces of paper. "Get me the following things," she said and started listing off various medicinal ingredients. I knew what most of them were. Those that I didn't recognize I asked her to go over.

"I don't know," she said. "Look: It's medicine. It's not that different from baking, right? You follow the instructions and if you do everything right you end up with a good result."

Many of the ingredients were poisons. Snake's gall, dried centipede, scorpion venom and nightshade. I asked her why she needed poison. "I have to run some tests on his blood. Some of these poisons are for those tests. The others are powerful medicines, if used correctly. At least, as far as I'm aware."

There was an herbalist in the neighborhood. I hadn't gone to him when my uncle fell ill. He wasn't a doctor; just a man who knew how to capture plants and animals that he might sell later. Usually we went to him for simple remedies, or for spices for cooking.

"Haven't seen you in, oh, must be forever, Kieran," he said with a smile as I came in the door. When he saw my face his own fell.

"I'm terribly sorry. I need some help. I need the herbs on this list. I'll pay whatever you wish." I handed him the paper.

He looked it over. "I have most of these," he said. "But this is no ordinary medicine. Some of the things here, you could seriously hurt somebody with this. How'd you get this?"

"My uncle is nearly dead. A friend believes she can help him but she needs these."

"If your friend uses these ingredients wrong she might kill your uncle, even if he was in good health. Are you certain you trust her?"

"She studied medicine with Saul Shatterfield," I said. I mean she had, a little, and at this point she was the only hope we had. I needed to get the herbalist moving.

"Saul Shatterfield is still alive? I thought he died years ago, back when that fire swept through the university." The herbalist began preparing my order, pulling powders and dried plants from little wooden drawers, measuring them carefully and wrapping each in a little square of cloth.

I didn't know anything about a fire at the university. I told the herbalist this.

"There was a time when you could walk around in the university district. A beautiful place it was too. All that changed, oh, must have been nearly forty years ago, when the fire swept through the inner buildings. It's been a ghost town ever since."

"What does that have to do with Shatterfield?" I asked, intrigued.

"He was a scholar there, a doctor and an adventurer. He vanished after the fire." The herbalist measured out another of the ingredients and went back for another.

"He's alive, and he's insane. But he has a student and her mind is sound. She's trying to help my uncle."

"Saul Shatterfield alive, hah, will wonders never cease." The herbalist handed me my pack of medicine. "Hope your uncle gets better."

"You and me both," I said as sprinted out the door.

As soon as I put them in her hands Savannah set to work. The next few hours were tense. Savannah worked, grinding powders, mixing chemicals and Uncle lay there, breathing short, shallow breaths and through it all Dr. Fletter-Daish didn't come back.

Where was he?

Unable to stand the tension any further I left, went searching for the doctor. I back-tracked to Broken Tower, to the Dome at the Square, but I saw no sign of him. I asked people on the street and at first I heard nothing. And then I stepped into the shop of the same herbalist I'd visited earlier today.

"Back again, Kieran? How's your uncle? Do you need more medicine?"

"Actually, I'm looking for Dr. Fletter-Daish," I said. "Have you seen him?"

"Yeah, I saw the doctor. One of my best customers. He stopped in to replenish his stocks and when he left he ran into some soldiers out front." He rambled to a halt.

"Soldiers?" I tried to keep the panic out of my voice.

"Looked to be Confederation to me," he said and spat.

"Is the doctor alright?" I no longer even bothered trying to keep the fear from my voice.

"Looked OK the last time I saw him, he went with the soldiers willingly enough. I'd say they seemed downright appreciative." He nodded his head vigorously and smiled helpfully.

"Thank you," I said, trying hard not to sound dejected. I could only guess why the Confederation would need a good doctor.

I walked back to my home as the sun began to set.

Savannah was sitting in the front room with Mr. Chamblais. Neither looked happy.

"My uncle... is he?"

"He's alive," Savannah said gravely. "And free of illness." Strange. He certainly was sick. Savannah saw the puzzled expression on my face and continued, "I don't know how to treat him, don't know if he'll pull through, though I did my best.

"Kieran, your uncle has been poisoned, and I don't think it was any natural venom that did it."

CHAPTER 32

Savannah

KIERAN COULDN'T HANDLE THE tension and I couldn't concentrate very well with him pacing around so I sent him out to look for that old doctor, Fletter-Daish. I completed a few tests I'd found referenced on Old Saul's walls and I suddenly felt a pang of worry. There was something wrong with this situation— Doctor Fletter-Daish had overlooked obvious things. And yet he supposedly had a sterling reputation. It was clear that Kieran was involved in one rebel group or another; I half wondered if the doctor might be a Confederation spy. After all, the condition of Kieran's uncle was certainly creating a distraction for a few rebels.

Then again, I was new to the whole medicine thing, hadn't ever had a patient before. It was possible I'd just screwed up somewhere. I took some fresh blood from Kieran's uncle and tried again, got the same result.

Tried a third sample. Again the same.

There was no indication of infection at the site of the wound or through Stephen's system. A disease contracted through a bite should have had some visible signs at the wound. Even venom should have left an indicator at the point of entry. This seemed like something else. I knew a thing or two about poison before I even came to Trana and this seemed like deliberate and methodical poisoning, the sort of poisoning that happens over time. Kieran's uncle hadn't been poisoned once. He'd been fed poison regularly to keep him in this precarious state. I brought Mr. Chamblais in and showed him what I'd found.

He wasn't a doctor any more than I was, but when I explained to him what I was seeing in the tests, when I explained how the test was supposed to work, he had to agree with me.

When Kieran returned I told him the truth—his uncle had been poisoned.

Kieran sat down. "How is that even possible?"

"I don't know," I said. "The Broken don't even use weapons, let alone poisons, and they're basically people, right? They don't have venomous bites. Besides, I'm almost certain that the poison used on your uncle was plant-based."

"But uncle Stephen fell ill from the bite."

I shrugged. "I don't think that's possible." The truth was that I was very disturbed. The Broken were behaving wrong: using poison, sneaking undetected around Trana. It was if they were being controlled. And there had been that man in the demon mask. "I think somebody is using the Broken."

"That's preposterous," Mr. Chamblais said. "You can't control the Broken, they have no ability to reason."

I shrugged. "Unless one of you has been poisoning him, or unless you want to blame that doctor you found. Honestly, the only right thing he did was send you to find Old Saul."

"Stephen has been my... friend for thirty years!" Mr. Chamblais was getting pissed. Fine, I didn't really like the guy. There was something a bit off-putting about him. I could see where Kieran had got his new intensity from.

"Neither of us would ever want to hurt my uncle," Kieran said gently, levelly, playing the peace-maker. "But what do you mean, about Doctor Fletter-Daish screwing up? He came highly recommended."

"So you sought him out?" If it was the doctor who poisoned Kieran's uncle things would be much easier.

"Well, yes. He's been around the neighborhood for a while now and when uncle Stephen fell ill... I mean, he lives around the corner. Of course I went to him." Kieran spoke quietly and his voice was grave. He took all of this very seriously. Good, this was a serious topic. Somebody was trying to murder his uncle. I was glad he was taking the time to think things through rather than losing his cool like his teacher, or whatever Mr. Chamblais was.

"Old Saul is an expert in certain fields of medicine," I said. "Particularly in medicines, and poisons, derived from the excretions of animals and fungi.

"He kept notes on several, how to make them and their effects—your uncle's case closely resembles one from his notes; a particulary insidious combination of poison mushroom and centipede carcass. A large dose is almost immediately fatal. But if a small dose is administered every so often it builds up slowly in the body. The victim wastes away and eventually... they die." I didn't tell him the one other thing Old Saul had written about it on his wall. This poison was an ancient process. Old Saul's scrawls had been unclear, he changed languages several times, but he mentioned this poison in the same breath as the vile sorcery that created the Broken.

"So we're back to square one," Kieran said bitterly. He had his elbows on his knees and was grasping at his long, black hair with both hands. "We need to find Old Saul."

"Yes, and unless that doctor of yours gets back soon we need to find him today. Your uncle won't last longer than that." I tried to be kind. Kieran was handling this whole situation well but it was a lot to deal with. Somebody was using weapons from before the Collapse to kill his uncle. That was not a problem most people had to deal with.

"We won't be seeing him any time soon." Darkness was creeping into his tone. He'd found out something awful, I could just tell. "He went somewhere to the east with Confederation soldiers."

I supposed there could be a reason for that. Dave Boyd would need a good doctor. And if he was a spy...

Mr. Chamblais didn't handle the news well though. "What?"

"He'd stopped by Otis's medicine shop on his way back here when some soldiers came up to him. I was talking to Otis while he prepared the herbs and he says they spoke for a short while and then the doctor went with them."

Mr. Chamblais glanced furtively at me, looked away, then glanced at me again. "Could I please have some privacy with my student?"

There are few ways to pique a girl's curiosity more than to act as suspiciously as that. I wondered what he wanted to say to Kieran that I couldn't hear. "I'll go check on your uncle." I tried to sound oblivious.

And I did check on him. He was the same. I had done all I could to make him comfortable but I had to be honest with myself, I was no doctor. I wasn't even an herbalist. I was just somebody who'd copied the half-mad medical theories of a great doctor into the margins of a sword manual. I couldn't save him. It was an awful feeling, it felt like helplessness.

After seeing quickly to Kieran's uncle I snuck back down on feet used to the silence of the Long Dark and hid just out of sight.

"The doctor had care over him throughout. There was no avoiding him seeing the mark. If he recognizes it we could all be in grave jeopardy." Mr. Chamblais was speaking in hushed tones but he sounded like he wanted to shout.

"I know." Kieran didn't sound happy either, though neither of them seemed angry at the other. Kieran hated Kyle MacMillan, wanted to kill him. What was there between this Kensington boy and Confederation?

"We might have to consider the possibility that your home isn't safe any longer."

"But why would the doctor tell? I mean, do we even know that he saw?"

"Of course he saw. He looked after your uncle for two months while you searched and I... I tried to hold things together—your uncle was instrumental to many allegiances here. These people aren't naturally trusting souls. Between Confederation spies spreading lies about the Black Trillium destroying crops in the Scar and your uncle's illness it's been hard enough just to keep the order from dissolving."

And there you had it. Kieran was working with the Black Trillium. I had to admit, I wasn't surprised. There weren't that many rebel groups in Trana.

"Savannah is friends with Dave Boyd. The doctor will almost certainly be with him. She wants to mount a rescue."

"That would be a good opportunity to see to the doctor. When you have found Shatterfield go with her, help her rescue Boyd. Bring the doctor back too, or silence him if necessary." Cold. The doctor had been keeping Kieran's uncle alive, if barely. I had run across a few secret societies in the past. Mostly they were either rebels, religious cults or both. Mr. Chamblais sounded more business-like than average.

"I understand. But I hope I can bring him back alive." Kieran sounded determined, hard. I knew in that moment that as much as he might prefer to bring back this doctor alive, he would kill the old man if he had to.

"Do your duty to the *Fleur Noir*. We are all that stands between the people and the tyrant in Fredericton with all his excesses. I will continue holding the alliance together here."

"I understand," Kieran said gravely.

Kieran was a member of the Black Trillium. I tried to process that. Hell, everybody had secrets and I guess I was a rebel and all with Kyle MacMillan and Sophie chasing me for the secrets I had in my head. If Kieran didn't trust me enough yet to tell me this one I wasn't going to give him a hard time over it. Not yet anyway.

I crept back up the stairs and then made sure to make plenty of noise coming back down again. Kieran and Mr. Chamblais were not talking anymore when I got down.

"Alright," I said, "if you're ready I think we should go find Old Saul, before it's too late."

CHAPTER 33

Kyle

TIME STOOD STILL. THE world was red and white, a smear of gore on pale skin.

The little packet in my hands, paper I thought, seemed like such a little thing against which to balance a life. But you heard rumours about the Wizard in Green. He was a magician, an immortal. He was a master of the ancient machines from before the Collapse or of some magic that came after. He was a deadly warrior and a healer, a ruler and an explorer.

He was a legend.

But there were his eyes. The same eyes that looked at me pleadingly from Sophie's blood-smeared face, wild and savage.

I couldn't tell if she was conscious anymore. Her eyes had glazed over and her breathing was weak. I wanted to scream, wanted to rage. I knelt at her side and spoke soothingly to her. "I'm here. It'll be alright." I really hoped I wasn't lying to sooth the dying.

The floor of the tent was smeared with blood, it was pooling, it wouldn't soak through the canvas floor fast enough. It was dark, a red that was almost black. I'd seen blood before. I'd never expected to be terrified with the sight of it.

The powder: I had to rub it in the wound.

I poured the powder into the gash in her side, sparing only a little for the cut on her arm. It started doing... something... but I was in too much shock to pay much attention. I had finished the easy part.

The second part, that was much harder.

There was something sickeningly penetrative about pressing my fingers into the axe gash in Sophie's side, a perversity that left me weak in the knees. I was glad I was already kneeling but, as the cupric tang of blood filled my nose, played across my tongue, as the harsh breaths of my dying love filled my ears, her life blood spattered across the floor of the tent, as I felt the warm moistness of her bowels beneath my fingers, I didn't just want to collapse to my knees, I wanted to vomit.

It took as much of my strength of will not to empty the contents of my stomach on the spot as it did to keep my fingers massaging the bizarre medicine into the wound.

I felt the flow of blood around my fingers slow and then all but stop and I knew the medicine was working.

"Get me bandages, go now!" I shouted at Brutus who was standing above me, dumbly staring at the gore, at the horrible sight of two lovers bathing in blood. He left at a run.

I went to work on Sophie's arm.

It took much less time, it should have been easier, it was just a surface cut, I didn't have to put my hands inside her. But it wasn't any easier. My tolerance for gore long since reached, I would have felt sick at the sight of a paper cut.

I finished my ghastly work, staggered away from Sophie, out of the tent, and was promptly sick on the ground out front. I was still heaving, gasping for breath, when Brutus returned with bandages.

I staggered to my feet, I wasn't even aware that I was still naked. I wiped the vomit from my mouth and smeared fresh blood across my face. The renewed scent of copper from the blood nearly caused me to convulse into heaving again even though there was nothing left to sick up.

I sucked back a lungful of hot summer air and, reeling like a drunkard, returned to the tent. Brutus, with a look I could only call regret, was gently dressing the wound in Sophie's side. She still didn't look well but for the first time since the assassin struck her I believed she might still live.

I collapsed onto my cot, the sheets were already soiled with blood anyway, and rested my head in my hands. I was sitting like that when, five minutes later, Lieutenant Messier burst into the tent with an old man in tow.

The old man had white hair, a large nose, and a ruddy complexion. A wrinkled face concealed beetle-black eyes that showed sharp intellect. He was wearing the rich robes of a successful doctor and was carrying an herbalist bag.

"Help her," Messier said.

The doctor glanced once at Sophie and said, "Of course, immediately. But perhaps somewhere with fewer corpses."

"Messier, take him away. I want to know who he was as soon as possible.

Whoever sent him will be punished," I rasped.

Messier saluted. "Brutus, help me with this." The giant paused for a second, seeming reluctant, and clearly upset, but he nodded and the two carried away the body of the would-be assassin.

The doctor said nothing more, inspecting the bandages, the wounds and the blood on the floor. After a while he said, "She has lost a terrible amount of blood but, it's strange, she's barely bleeding now." He saw the paper packet lying in the pool of blood on the floor of the tent. "Where did you come across this?" There was a hungry look in his eyes.

"That is none of your concern." I tried for imperious but my throat was raw from vomit and my mood black with despair. The doctor nodded deferentially but I thought I saw a flash of defiance in his eyes.

I stood and left the tent, wandering naked through the camp, to the creek it backed onto. I splashed into the cold water and methodically began washing the gore off my body, out of my beard, out of my hair. It was everywhere. Even after I washed and washed and washed I could still taste the tang in my mouth.

Messier was standing by the edge of the creek. "How long have you been there?" I asked.

"I followed you, My Lord. You shouldn't be alone. There might be other assassins in the camp."

"Where is Brutus?" Brutus was never far away. He was always ready to protect me. Brutus had failed.

"Watching over the mistress." All business, that was Messier. Always dependable, always business-like.

"Good... Is she going to be OK?" The chill of the water was bringing me back into myself again. I could ask the difficult questions.

"Doctor Fletter-Daish says that she should survive. She lost a terrible amount of blood but her heart is young and strong." Her heart was strong. Mine ached with disgust and fear and pain.

"Is he a good doctor?" It seemed a reasonable question.

"You told me to find the best."

Had I? When had I?

He saw the look of confusion on my face. "For Boyd."

"Right, Dave Boyd." I splashed water across my face again and felt another surge of lucidity in the cold.

"My Lord, I think we should arrest Colonel Antonelli." He looked grave.

"Come again?" I still wasn't tracking right.

"My Lord, there was just an attempt on your life, it was very nearly a successful one, and everybody knows Colonel Antonelli is the traitor." If he was talking this way, things were bad. A good commander listened when his officers spoke about what everybody in camp knew.

"Colonel Antonelli is an old friend." I didn't want to acknowledge the suspicions I felt.

"But My Lord, may I speak plainly?"

"Please do."

"My Lord, he's from a Black Trillium family." And there it was.

"Increase the watch on Colonel Antonelli but do not act against him." I had feared this moment. The troops were beginning to develop the same doubts of Marc that Sophie and I had privately harboured.

"My Lord." Messier saluted.

"Now, go get me some trousers." I was getting cold sitting naked in a creek.

"Yes, My Lord." He fled.

I dressed and saw to it that Sophie was ensconced in the hospital tent. Brutus had a quadruple guard posted around the tent. He might have failed but he was taking the matter seriously. Not for the first time, I wondered how the mute bodyguard managed to muster troops so fast. Sign language probably.

Doctor Fletter-Daish was sitting beside Sophie's bed. He looked grim but I suspected he always looked grim. "She will live," he said.

"Good," I said. "She is very important to me."

"That medicine you got, it saved her life. It was pre-Collapse, wasn't it? If I knew where you came by it..." He wanted the medicine. But I had no more left, and taking the magic or science or whatever it was they used from the Wizard in Green was a fool's game.

"A powder that stops bleeding and speeds healing would be a powerful tool for whoever had it. Sadly I have no more."

The doctor nodded. "I won't ask how you came by it."

I nodded. I just felt so tired. Sophie woke up four hours later and asked for water. The doctor served her a medicinal broth designed to help stimulate the blood. She complained it tasted bitter.

I stayed by her side for hours, until I heard shouting from outside. I slipped out of the tent and took a sword from one of the bodyguards. As I followed the noise so did four of the guards follow me.

There was a fight in the mess tent.

Lieutenant Messier and Marc were fighting. Each was dressed in full armour and each had his sword drawn.

Messier fought like a soldier, a veteran of many campaigns. He was strong, tough, simple. His style was no master style but it was clean and efficient. He was no match for Marc. My old friend was a master swordsman of the Hapsman school, the same school that my father and grandfather had both practiced.

Messier attempted a downward angling cut and Marc slapped the blade contemptuously aside. Just as I reached the front ranks of soldiers watching the fight Marc drove the tip of his sword up, stabbing nine inches of steel into the soft part of Messier's jaw and killing him instantly.

Messier fell twitching and bleeding to the ground, silent in death, Marc's sword still jammed in his head.

"I know he's been spreading rumours about me," Marc said. "He's been angling to replace me ever since I came back. You want your traitor? He's right there on the floor. He's the one who tried to kill Sophie, I'd stake my life on it."

"I think you already have." I looked around to the other soldiers in the tent. "Arrest Mr. Antonelli. The charges are murder, insubordination and treason."

CHAPTER 34

Kieran

"I THINK THE BEST thing to do would be to head back to the Cathedral of Broken Glass," Savannah said as we left home. "Old Saul is a creature of habit. He ran when you frightened him, but when he believes the danger is past he'll come back.

"He has too much invested in the place. His writings, his pets; yes, I'm sure he'll come back."

We walked out of Kensington and headed toward downtown, cutting across Chi-Town rather than going back through Broken Tower. If you never penetrated Chi-Town farther than the big streets along the edges of the district you'd never suspect that the entire district was full of beautiful, ancient, crumbling, and hastily repaired houses. Many of the merchants whose shops were in Kensington lived in Chi-Town.

The edges of the district, with their strange picture-words on faded plastic signs, yellowed with age, and crumbling shop-fronts lent a seedy sort of feel to the area that kept away many outsiders. Penetrate a block in though, and it was a district of fragrant gardens and stately homes.

You could almost believe, on a hot day in the summer, when the scent of violets and roses hung heavy in the air, that you were in a time before the Great Collapse, a time of comfort and beauty.

Candles and oil lamps in the windows were a testament to the activity happening even after the sun had gone to bed. People went to bed late in this district. I glanced at Savannah and saw her shoulders sag in relaxation. The atmosphere of this place affected her too. It would have been easy to forget that we were on a mission of vital importance. It would have been so easy to be the flirting young man I had been again, walking hand in hand with a pretty girl on a warm summer night when the heat made clothes seem like a bad idea and wine and beer flowed freely.

It hadn't really been so long since that had been my life: one season. In one short season I'd gone from being the spoiled nephew of a wealthy merchant to a rebel with secrets, responsibilities and no time for love.

Savannah met my gaze. I'd hardly realized I'd been looking at her.

She smiled, blushed. Her cheeks got so pink when she blushed. "We should hurry."

"Yes, we should." I felt a pang of guilt. My uncle. He would die if we didn't do something soon and I was thinking about a girl.

We increased our pace to a light jog.

As we left Chi-town and came into downtown the buildings changed. We were into the ruins of huge concrete buildings with few windows. These were less well preserved. Bricks were easy to make and so old brick houses were rebuilt, one crumbling brick at a time. A large concrete building, rebar lining the walls, copper wire thick throughout, was nothing more than a heap of easily extracted resources.

These buildings had once been monolithic, a network of hospitals, but now they were empty, crumbling shells; the broken teeth of a ravaged skyline.

We passed by the hulking, ruined testaments to the past and came quickly to the Cathedral of Broken Glass. I kept my eyes down and tried not to let my gaze wander to the broken glory of the city or to Savannah.

We stopped at the northern end of the Cathedral and Savannah said, "I'll go in alone. Old Saul is more likely to trust us if it's me he speaks to. You frighten him."

"I'll wait here then," I said. Savannah nodded and turned on her heel, slipping into the broken building and down into the earth.

I had to face facts. I had feelings for her.

I had remembered her fondly enough, sure. I'd been with her on one of the most glorious nights of my life last year. But meeting her again, seeing the person she'd become in the year since, thoughtful, loyal, compassionate, catalyzed that fondness into something more.

But how did I tell her? At least how did I do so without seeming like a love-struck kid or, alternatively, a horny little bastard trying to get into her pants again?

Now wasn't the time for such thoughts. I had duties to fulfill. I could afford to wait.

Savannah returned with Old Saul in tow. He walked up to me, his wrinkled old face scowling and oddly familiar somehow and sniffed me. "I don't trust him, little Leiurus. He smells like trouble." I didn't mention that he could use a bath and all.

"It's OK. Kieran is my friend." She was trying very hard to soothe the old guy. I tried to look friendly and non-threatening. I'd forgot how hard it was to look non-threatening when carrying a sword.

"If you say so. But keep between the two of us, he smells wrong."

I sniffed absently at my own clothes. I didn't really smell like anything except sweat. "If it makes you feel safer, I have no problem with Savannah walking between us. But, please, come quickly. My uncle is very ill and needs your help."

Our walk back home was awkward. Old Saul kept sneaking suspicious glances at me. He was just about the most paranoid person I'd ever seen. I had trouble believing that this broken shell of an old man was the greatest medical mind in all of Trana.

Still, things really didn't get bad until we got back home and, after preparing Mr. Chamblais who considerately left the house so as to avoid spooking the mad old man, led him to my uncle's bedside.

He looked at Savannah's notes and his skin went ashen. "No, nononononononono, you never said it was *that* poison." His hands were shaking so badly he could hardly have read the paper.

"I could be wrong," Savannah said. "I didn't want to worry you until I was sure."

Old Saul was backing slowly away from Uncle's bed, his hands still shaking, fingers nearly tearing the paper in their white-knuckled grip. "It can't be. It can't. All gone, burned up. No, nonononononono, can't be. Don't make me say it."

I thought back to what Otis had said about a fire at the university, how he thought Saul Shatterfield had died there. Suddenly the shadow of the forsaken district seemed oppressive, even from blocks away.

"Please, sir," I said gently, "you have to help, my uncle's life hangs in the balance."

Old Saul shook his head and sank into a corner of the room, hands hiding his eyes. "The poison here, it can't be. It's all gone, burned up. Can't be. No. Nobody knows, I never told a soul. Shatterfield knew, no Shatterfield, just Old Saul. All burned up."

Savannah crouched next to Old Saul, she took his hands in hers and looked into his eyes with a gentle sadness. She could have been a dutiful granddaughter, kneeling before her grandfather in his time of distress.

"It's OK," Savannah said. "Nobody needs Shatterfield. Just Old Saul. Old Saul wrote about the poison. Old Saul can help." She squeezed his hand.

"The cure is lost, burned up." Old Saul sobbed. He had tears running down his cheeks.

"You can find it again. I believe in you."

Savannah might have believed in the old man, who swallowed his sadness and nodded his head weakly. But I was afraid that uncle Stephen was a dead man.

CHAPTER 35

Savannah

I COULD TELL THAT Kieran was disheartened. He'd spent two months searching for Old Saul and risked his life on at least two occasions in the process. He was hoping for a miracle. All he'd got was a broken old man.

Still, everybody believed that this broken old man had once been the very best doctor in Trana and that he remained a leading expert on poisons and their antidotes.

He sniffled, nodded and squeezed my hands. The look in his eyes was terrified but I knew that there was determination there, steel in the expression. He would do his best. All we could do was trust him.

In the short time I'd known him, gods, it felt like a lifetime, Old Saul had never once given me reason not to trust him. I smiled at him and I could see that my smile eased him. I gave his hands one last squeeze and went to Kieran.

"Trust him. If anybody can save your uncle it's Old Saul."

Kieran's dark brows knitted in pained thought and he gave a curt nod. "Let me know if he wakes up." If, not when. He was in pain and knowing that hurt me. I felt a kinship for him. Not just because he was an orphan, not just because he was a rebel, not even because he was another kid who had to grow up too fast.

Kieran was somebody who felt things deeply and I couldn't help but be moved. The strength of his feelings caused me to feel. I remembered his eyes on me as we'd walked through Chi-Town and a chill passed through me.

He felt deeply, and I was moved in kind.

But then, hadn't I known that? Why had I left Kensington for Broken Tower last summer? Was I afraid that if I'd stayed I'd become just another caged bird?

No, that was silly. I hadn't left because of him. I liked the open sky at the tops of the towers, no towers in Kensington, just low brick buildings under ancient trees.

When he left the room, leaving me alone with Old Saul and the comatose Stephen I felt a little pang of relief and that was followed immediately by a pang of shame at that relief. It wasn't Kieran's fault I was on edge. I was on the run again, not from the 'Tobans now but from Confederation, the same people who'd driven the 'Tobans into the land of my birth.

That had to be it.

"That boy carries a flame for you." Old Saul's words broke the silence like a stone falling into a pond. I glanced at his face and I saw a hint of something there, some calmness or certainty that had been missing before, as if going about this work was helping to ease the pain that had broken him.

"Are you alright, Saul?"

He breathed deeply and let out a shuddering sigh. "Old Saul never is. But in this place, it's better. Quiet. To help, to heal, these things make it easier. At least for now."

I felt tears in my eyes and forced them back. I would not break down into tears, not now. "That's nice," I managed.

"What do you think you'll do about the boy?"

"It's not the right time to be thinking about things like that."

I glanced at Old Saul and he was watching me patiently. "Fire burns sometimes. Sometimes it makes things clean. Time doesn't matter to it." It was crazy. Old Saul said crazy things all the time. There wasn't profundity in what he said, right?

Old Saul returned his attention to Kieran's uncle, taking his pulse, looking into his throat, his eyes. It was as if we hadn't just been speaking of love, life and death moments ago.

Crazy.

I left the room, went downstairs, making sure to make some noise in case the two rebels were having secret talks again.

Things were plenty complicated already.

Kieran and Mr. Chamblais were standing close together when I came down the stairs. They had been talking though I hadn't heard what they'd said. "Ah, Savannah," Mr. Chamblais said brightly. "We want to repay you for your help. Kieran has told me about how you helped him to escape from the Broken in the Long Dark, how you helped him to find Old Saul." Now that was interesting. He hadn't called him Saul Shatterfield. Kieran must have told him I didn't like that. And he was making an effort. What else had Kieran told this man about me? Who was Mr. Chambais to Kieran anyway?

"Yeah?" I figured I knew what was coming.

"Kieran also told me that Confederation took captive a friend of yours."

Yeah, I was right.

"Dave Boyd. Yeah, we're friends."

"Tomorrow he will go with you to this Confederation camp and take him back." At least this made it clear why he was being so nice. He hadn't guessed I'd overheard what he'd told Kieran, how he wanted Kieran to rescue or kill Fletter-Daish. So now he wants to be my best friend? I bit my lip to stop myself from blurting out that he was a hypocrite and a liar.

"I don't have any sort of a plan. I haven't ever seen the camp."

"Then it is fortunate that I have friends who have seen it."

"I know who you are."

"What?"

"Savannah, what are you saying?" Kieran asked, stepping almost imperceptibly between me and Mr. Chamblais.

I glanced at Kieran, looked away, feeling a flush of shame in my face. I liked him, I hoped what I had to say wouldn't end up hurting him, but I needed to air this before we made plans. "I know. You're with the Black Trillium. You have no love for Dave Boyd, or for me. Stop trying to act like you're my friend."

"That is a dangerous accusation to level," Mr. Chamblais said, and his posture changed, shoulders rising, brow furrowing.

"Come on, I've shown goodwill, brought you the only person who could possibly save Kieran's uncle. I could have easily fled from Kieran and gone to the Confederation, bargained for Boyd's safety. I didn't. I don't trust anarchists and I don't trust people who say they want to free a place from foreign influence since I'm not originally from around here myself. But even so I decided you lot were probably better than the alternative and I've thrown in with you."

I hadn't noticed I was walking closer to Mr. Chamblais as we talked. By the time I finished we were nearly nose to nose, staring each other down. He looked away, a hint of glowering shame in his eyes.

"We're not like all that," Mr. Chamblais said. "We don't want to drive out newcomers, we just want Trana to be free."

"And what happens the day after that? Who makes sure food gets to the poor? Who organizes militias and sends them to die to protect your freedom? You can't just tear down a state and replace it with nothing." I tried to ease back as I said this. I hesitated even to ask, but I needed to know before I went any further.

Mr. Chamblais just looked away. I looked at Kieran and he was pensive, staring at his feet and saying nothing.

"What else did you hear?" Mr. Chamblais was the first to cut through the tense silence.

"Enough. And I know you'll have Kieran kill that doctor if he must. I think he shouldn't—I suspect the doctor was the one poisoning Stephen, though I don't know why. You might want to ask him."

"What do you mean, Savannah?" Kieran asked. He put his hand on my shoulder and tried to draw me away from Mr. Chamblais.

I shook him off half-heartedly. "There are three options: one—the doctor with the best reputation in the city of Trana has less skill than me at medicine, two—he knew what was wrong with Stephen and did nothing, or three—for whatever reason it was the doctor who was behind the poisoning. What do you think is more likely?"

"No, you're right. And I am ashamed," Mr. Chamblais said. "I should have thought. No, I should have acted!" He turned away, pressed his hands on the top of a nearby table of reclaimed wood, lovingly oiled before but now showing signs of inattention. "I have sat here for too long. I have waited for too long. I should come too. And if the time comes to deal with Doctor Fletter-Daish, however he should be dealt with, it should be me who does it."

"Assuming I want your help, assuming I can trust you."

"Savannah, do you trust me?" Kieran asked. And that was a good question. Did I? He'd been at my side when we'd fought the Broken in the Long Dark, and I got the sense that if he went to rescue Boyd I could trust him not to abandon me. I said nothing for a long time and he stared at me with sad eyes, waiting for me to speak.

"Yeah, I guess."

"I trust Mr. Chamblais implicitly."

"Fine," I said, almost choking on the word.

"The camp is most of a day's gentle ride from here and it will be a perilous operation. I suspect we could all use a good night's rest before we leave. And so tonight we rest, tomorrow morning we ride," Kieran said.

I decided not to mention that I'd never been on a horse before. I met Kieran's gaze. He was afraid and he was determined, but when I looked into his eyes I saw an ember of lust and of a warmth more comforting than lust there.

I looked away first.

It wasn't much later that we sat down to a meal of awkward pauses and furtive glances. "You should both understand the danger we will be putting ourselves in tomorrow," Mr. Chamblais said, his French accent seeming thicker. "There are three of us, one thousand of them."

"We do understand, sir," Kieran said. He could be polite when he needed to be but with this strange, shaggy old French rebel he was particularly deferential. It was something to remember about him.

"It is good that you do. There is a good chance that tomorrow may very well be our last day. We want to maximize the chance that this will not be the case. Think on that." His fork scraped against his plate as he cut another bite of his pork chop.

I said nothing but I couldn't help but think: this was serious, I was really going to do this, to spit in the eye of an army for one man.

I must have been as crazy as Old Saul. Then again, I'd promised myself no more running. Perhaps this was my way of making good on that promise. Respect for bravery and distaste for dishonour were the things that had got me into this mess in the first place. Perhaps I was discovering my own courage, my own honour.

Even if he had his own reasons for helping, Kieran was an honourable man, brave too. And Mr. Chamblais as well. Their rebellion may not have been mine but I found I couldn't help but respect these men. They were walking, eyes open, into the pit for the good of a cause.

We had very little conversation after that. We went immediately to bed.

Kieran's home was simply two long rooms, one atop the other, with a basement warren of little rooms with low ceilings. Kieran, Mr. Chamblais and Old Saul all remained on the upper floor to sleep, leaving me alone on the lower floor.

I stretched out on a couch and tried to sleep but sleep wouldn't come. Instead I lay awake for hours, staring at the ceiling.

Some time around midnight, I heard the sound of footsteps on the stairs. I watched as Kieran crept down the stairs (trying not to wake me) and went out into the yard behind the house. On an impulse I rose and followed him out.

He was standing in the center of the courtyard, with its high fences and ancient tree boughs, staring up at the cloudless night sky. There were a million stars and the moon was fat and bright.

There was no sound. No light but starlight and moonlight. In his white bedclothes Kieran shone in the moonlight, his long black hair spilling over his shoulders like a piece of the night sky brought to earth.

"It all started here," he said. He must have heard me. I wasn't trying to make noise but I wasn't trying to hide myself either. I honestly didn't know what I was doing there besides the fact that I couldn't sleep.

"It's a beautiful place." What else could I say? I didn't know what he was talking about.

He just scoffed and I thought this might be my last night.

I stepped before him and put my head on his chest. I breathed deep. He smelled of sweat, fresh hemp cloth and cooking scents.

"Savannah?" His voice was worried. He didn't want to do the wrong thing here. I didn't know if I was doing the right thing or not but I knew now how I wanted to spend what might be my last night.

"Don't say anything. Just let this moment be..." I trailed off and looked up, my body pressed against his hardness. His bright eyes shone in the moonlight and then he kissed me.

His lips were soft, his beard carefully trimmed and groomed even if it was still a little sparse, being only a year old. He was a practiced kisser. I was under no illusions that he had been celibate in the last year. Even a year ago the boy he was had been a tender and warm kisser.

His arm wrapped around me and his hand rested against the back of my neck. I tugged at the draw-string on his light hemp bed-shirt and it came loose. A light down of black hair stood out against the whiteness of the bulge of his chest.

Over his heart he had a tattoo, a single three-petaled flower done in black. I didn't realize that easterners wore tattoos. I thought that was something only we did back home, in the west that I'd lost.

I didn't have time to ponder this though, he was already pulling off my shirt. My own family-marks revealed across my right shoulder as the hint of a cool night breeze brought goose bumps to my bare chest.

We lay down on the wood deck of the yard, under the stars, and kissed, caressed, explored, undressed. I felt hot, and not from the night air, which was deliciously cool. His skin almost burned against mine.

The moon gave an ethereal glow to everything and his blue eyes looked silver in the ghost-light. His hands against my breasts, across my hips, in other places, sent shivers of anticipation up my spine. And then, when I felt nearly consumed by fire, by desire, we joined, two souls become one in that moment, struggling towards life, spitting in the face of death.

CHAPTER 36

Kyle

I WENT WITH THE guards as they carried Marc to the gaol. In part I felt like I had some duty to do so—to him—as if his past friendship somehow mattered enough to at least walk him as far as his prison.

As the guards threw Marc into the cell he said, "You're making a horrible mistake."

"My mistake was bringing you, trusting you. I should have known that you'd turn back to the Black Trillium."

He glowered back at me and his eyes were piercing, his sunken cheeks lending them extra intensity. "I've never been a traitor. You let petty rumours circulate against me; while I was imprisoned and suffering you listened to poisonous whispers. We've been friends since childhood! Have I ever betrayed you?"

"That only makes your treason all the more painful, Marc. Now shut your mouth before you regret it." I turned to leave him alone in the dark of his cell.

"Kyle, it's all her doing. She doesn't want anybody to have your ear but her."

I didn't let him say anything more. I wheeled around and hit him in the face. Hit him hard enough he fell over, blood dripping from his busted lip.

I dropped my knees onto his chest and felt a rib give way, snapping under the force of the blow and I punched and punched and punched until his face was swollen and bruised almost beyond recognition. The guards stood by watching in case he tried to resist. He didn't.

I'll give Marc this: he was a tough bastard. He was still conscious. The look he gave me, from the one eye not swollen entirely shut, was pained but it was the emotional pain that he felt, not the beating.

I staggered to my feet, reeling with rage and adrenaline, and I spat in his bloody face. "You can rot here until I decide what to do with you." And I lurched out of his cell for the last time.

"You should wrap your knuckles if you intend to fight," Marc had said to me on my seventeenth birthday. "Otherwise you'll break your hands on your opponent's head."

It was a tradition in the MacMillan household. No boy could be considered a man until he had succeeded in battle. Back in the time before my grandfather, Fredericton had been a weak county surrounded by other weak counties, far from the centers of power to the south and east. Battle had been necessary just to survive.

My grandfather changed all that and proved himself in the process. His first act as Count Fredericton had been to conquer Halifax, have the count and his family hanged and declare the founding of Confederation.

He'd been fifteen at the time.

When my father came of age the war against the Salt Mary folks and the 'Tobans was still far from won. He'd personally led the siege of Thunder Bay, he had been the first over the black stone walls. He'd stood on McKellar Island, his famous sword, 'Foedrinker,' stained red with the blood of a hundred fierce Salt Mary warriors. He'd been a month over sixteen.

I had been born in a time of peace. My grandfather, now passed, had conquered the east. My father had pushed the 'Tobans into the west, made Confederation the single greatest nation in the known world.

He had his eyes set on the Southlanders, but he hadn't yet planned the disastrous expedition that forever poisoned me in his eyes. Instead my battle was in a ring, against a single man, boxing, kicking and wrestling rather than the glorious victories of my ancestors.

I felt ashamed.

But Marc had been at my side, encouraging me to protect my hands, to wrap them with strips of cotton.

My enemy was a slave, a captured 'Toban. When I snapped his neck I was declared a man by my father who grinned and boasted of my martial prowess. But I felt reduced. One slave, unarmed and alone was a hollow victory beside the thrill of conquest.

Marc understood that. He'd drunk with me that night and when I raged and roared at the unfairness of the world he'd agreed with me, supported me, been a friend in a time of pain.

I hadn't wrapped my hands. Now my knuckles were split and bloodied, his blood and mine merging together in the cuts. In some places it was the mark of oath brothers, though Confederation did not subscribe to those savage practices.

Marc was more a brother to me than either of those slick little bastards that came forth from my father's loins. Marc had betrayed me.

There was no punishment I could conceive that would suffice to vent my fury. I staggered out into the night, blood dripping from my swollen knuckles, and roared at the inconstant moon that glowed bloated and corpselike in the sky.

I wanted a drink. But there was nobody to drink with. Oswald was dead, Messier dead too, Sophie lay in her sick-bed, Marc had betrayed me, Brutus was a mute. Anybody who knew me, anybody who could relate to me was taken from me. I was alone, I was enraged, I was drunk on fury and despair even without liquor.

I sat down on the ground and stared at the blackness of the ground at night. The uncaring stars shone on my head but I didn't see them. I saw only the blackness within me.

I rose and reeled to the tent where we were keeping Dave Boyd. I hadn't wanted him in the same tent as my Sophie. There was bad blood between them. Still it remained to be seen whether he was prisoner or guest, enemy or ally, so he wasn't being kept in the gaol. He was being kept near the center of camp under heavy guard.

I walked into his tent and he was awake, reading a book. I pulled out my wine-flask, full of the potent grain liquor the Southlanders in Newark brewed and tossed it to him.

"Drink with me," I said.

"You won't get me drunk enough to teach you the sword art—" he began.

"To hell with the fucking sword art. Drink with me."

He shrugged, took a swig, passed the flask back to me. The liquor burned as I poured it down my throat. The burn helped. It distracted me from the fire in my heart, behind my eyes, the fire that burnt away reason and made me want to kill indiscriminately just so that somebody else would feel the pain I felt.

I passed the bottle back to him. "He tried to kill her."

He took a draught, longer this time, not the hesitant first pull. "What?"

"My best friend tried to take Sophie from me." I took back the flask. "How do you know her?" I passed him the flask.

He pulled at the flask. "I couldn't say."

I took the flask. "You are in my power. I could have you strangled in your sleep. Will you deny me even this?"

He took the flask, drank more heavily. "There are some people I fear more than you. The worst thing you can do is kill me."

"Her father has come and gone. He saved her life. But he said he'd be back to take her from me."

"Then if your life matters to you, say goodbye to her," Boyd said. "Her father isn't exactly an evil man. But he is entirely without mercy. If you try to resist, if you try to help her resist him..."

"She matters to me. I love her."

"She doesn't love you." I guess the liquor was doing the trick because I let that slide, I didn't leap on him and beat him as senseless as I'd beaten Marc.

"You don't know that."

"I know her."

"Not like I do."

Boyd scoffed but held his tongue. That was probably wise, even feeling the mellowing effect of the liquor I would have had to give him a beating if he'd said something clever. I decided to change the topic. "I hate this city."

"You can't rule the city. It's hard enough ruling just one weak district."

"Sometimes I think it would be best to burn the whole place to the ground, do to Trana what my grandfather did to Quebec City."

"You can't burn steel and concrete," Boyd said, missing the point.

"With enough black powder..." If I hadn't been drinking I wouldn't have let that slip. Sophie had helped me produce the stuff after what happened at the garrison. I had about ten pounds of the powder and my men were scouring Trana for more saltpeter even as I spoke.

Boyd gave me a penetrating look. "Black powder is a powerful tool. But there are some things best left in the past."

So this strange man knew Sophie from the past and knew about black powder. My curiosity was piqued even further. The night was getting old though and I was tired. I was thinking about parting company with Boyd when I heard a runner shouting for a report. He was one of my father's personal guard.

"Shit," I muttered.

"Prince Kyle, your Lord Father has arrived. He commands you present yourself before him. Immediately."

I tried hard to look sober as I processed this. My father was here and I was drunk as a skunk, my love was recovering from grave injuries, my mission objective was sitting comfortably in a tent until I figured out what to do with him, Oswald LePine was dead and Marc Antonelli was in the gaol on charges of treason. I thought about running away. But in the end I couldn't do that. I went to face my father.

CHAPTER 37

Kieran

WE LAY SPENT, A tangle of arms and legs, in the silver moonlight. The night was still not too hot but we were both sticky with sweat. We smelled of sex. Savannah was dozing with her head on my chest. I still didn't feel much like sleeping but at least I didn't feel the mad tension anymore.

I had felt like my mind was going to fly apart. Uncle, the madness of Old Saul, the renewed pangs I'd felt for Savannah, my hate of Confederation, my own (muted) unease with my place in the Black Trillium. I was a mass of conflicting emotions, competing drives.

But under the stars, with her tattooed arm draped lazily across my chest, the soft sound of her sleeping breath in my ear, I felt truly tranquil for the first time in months.

> In peace there's nothing so becomes a man
> As modest stillness and humility:
> But when the blast of war blows in our ears,
> Then imitate the action of the tiger

Uncle Stephen had a large library, ten books carefully copied by a deft scribe, illuminated and glorious. When he'd taught me my letters I'd read this line in one of them, a most difficult book, and I couldn't help but remember it in that moment.

I was going to war. Tomorrow I would be walking into hell, and yet I did not want to be a tiger. I did not want to be ferocious. I wanted nothing more than modest stillness.

Lying on the hard deck, with the moon as my lamp, pale white light on Savannah's copper skin, I felt that moment of tranquility. This was my time of peace, for tomorrow I would be at war. Tomorrow I would be a tiger.

Tonight was very nearly tomorrow.

I dozed into a deep sleep, untroubled by dreams, unworried to be discovered lying haphazardly naked with this elfin woman.

I awoke when Mr. Chamblais threw a heap of stiff leather garments at me. I looked around and Savannah was already strapping the leathers over her clothes.

"Get these on," Mr. Chamblais said. "They aren't as good as steel plate but they'll protect you better than nothing, and you can move quietly in them."

If he had seen Savannah and I together he had the good grace not to mention it. We dressed in awkward silence. Mr. Chamblais left after a few minutes to see to our horses. Alone again. "When we get back," I said to Savannah, "we should talk."

"Don't think you can hitch me up like a tame horse." Her eyes flashed threateningly.

"Wouldn't dream of it." But I knew that I wanted more than just another fling. There was something between the two of us and I knew Savannah felt it too.

"Good." She fumbled with the leather helmet. Her hair was long and it was tangled. Her time with Saul Shatterfield hadn't left her particularly well groomed. Eventually she managed to get it onto her head, though her hair stuck out around the bottom like black straw.

I suppressed a chuckle, but she saw it in my face and flashed me a wide-eyed stare, challenging me to laugh.

Happily I had an easier time with my helmet. I think she'd have laughed me to death if I'd had any problems.

The armour was stiff and a little bit uncomfortable. I could tell it bothered Savannah too, but it was the first time I'd ever worn the stuff and I guessed it was the same for her.

We traipsed out front and found Mr. Chamblais holding the reins to three horses and smirking widely. He was wearing a dark green cloak, and two more were tossed over the saddles of two horses. "Green cloaks for hiding in bushes in daylight," he said.

I wondered back to a man in emerald green. It was a different shade, but still...

And then we set out. It was a long hot ride. Early summer was always hot in Trana and there had been very little rain. In our heavy leathers it was miserably hot, and with the lake so nearby, humid too.

We rode along Queen Street until we'd reached the eastern edge of downtown, the Street of Gods. Then we turned north, riding past ancient stone cathedrals, cathedrals in earnest, and not just buildings named so in the time after the Collapse.

The stone walls of these buildings endured centuries but most no longer had roofs, and the windows were long since lost.

The broken cathedrals of the Street of Gods made me sad. They were a reminder of how much had been lost after the Collapse. Someday, if we could put the wars behind us, perhaps we could reclaim the glory of the golden age before everything fell apart.

The Street of Gods slowly became a landscape not unlike Downtown as we travelled north. When we reached the north-east corner of Downtown we turned east and pressed on into the great district of Three Branches.

There were two deep valleys that intersected the city of Trana. For the most part the city rose along a gentle slope from the lake inland, the only exception were the points where the valleys cut across the landscape. Three Branches was a series of hill-tops created by the spread of one of these river valleys along three separate paths.

The primary valley ran from the lake north-by-north-west and then east before forking to the north, the east and the southeast. In order to reach the Scar a rider either had to travel through the low-lands of Blasted Port, through the moderately flat country of north 'Tobico and the northern districts, or across the river.

"The northern path will be carefully watched," Mr. Chamblais said. And I could see why. After what we'd done to the garrison, which lay directly along the northern path to Confederation camp, there would be many eyes on that road. "The southern road passes through Blasted Port and Queeneast. The first is home to bandits and the second is densely populated. It is the most direct route but not the safest. We could probably handle the bandits, but it is certain that there'd be spies along the route. Queeneast has never been friendly with the Black Trillium even at the best of times."

And so we'd taken the compromise route, risking the crossing at the viaduct in order to pass through the more sparsely populated district of Three Branches.

I didn't come out to the viaduct much. It wasn't a safe place. The ancient bridge, spanning the parent valley of Three Branches, was at least five hundred years old, all blackened steel and crumbling concrete.

That it had survived the Great Collapse was nothing short of miraculous. The fact that it had not been stripped down by scavengers since was a matter of local superstition.

In the days following the Collapse, a team of ten men had tried to harvest the steel from the viaduct. All ten were caught by a gust of wind and fell to their deaths. People said a fierce god lived in the viaduct.

With fear of vengeful spirits, crumbling concrete and rusting girders, few people crossed the viaduct unless their need was great.

I could almost sense my horse trembling beneath me as we crossed it. Whether the steed was reacting to the presence of an angry spirit or whether it was my own trembling I felt I did not know. Savannah seemed perfectly at ease. In fact, when we reached the center of the ancient bridge she looked up into the sky, stretched her arms out wide and breathed a deep breath, as if she couldn't have been happier.

I was happy to see the other side of the hulking bridge.

Three Branches was a large and well-ordered district. The ruling council was not an ally of the Black Trillium but they were not our enemies either. The district was home to a full tenth of the population of Trana, five thousand souls, but it was so spacious that it still never seemed crowded. Tobico and the Scar, the border districts, were larger, but it was, by far, the largest single interior district of the city.

Once, the district had housed large clusters of low, wide towers, each a home to a thousand souls but these had all been pulled down long ago. Now the district was clusters of wood and brick homes with neatly papered windows and large yards holding crops of beans, squash and corn.

The district was peaceful and the people kept to themselves. They paid us no heed and we passed quickly through and into the wide corn fields of the Scar.

We entered the boundless rows of corn and crossed the fields to a long, narrow strip of trees running near the camp. At least they should have been boundless rows of corn. The fields lay fallow. The harvest had been taken in too early.

"What's this?"

"You didn't notice the refugees while you searched for Old Saul," Mr. Chamblais said. "The Confederation stripped the Scar of its crops to feed their army."

"Why would they do that?" It boggled the mind. I hardly considered myself a military thinker, but surely the leaders of this army didn't want to needlessly make enemies of the locals. It'd only make our side stronger.

"Somebody burned their granary. They, of course, blamed us. But it wasn't. A third party was acting against them, and doing so more effectively than we have managed. We never were able to find out who."

"It wasn't Boyd, or any of his people," Savannah said.

"What about the man in the demon mask?" I asked.

"There was no talk of Broken in the attack on the camp." Mr. Chamblais said. "So I do not know if he fits the act. But one thing is sure, Trana has become a pit of conspiracy and intrigue."

"Which you've contributed to," Savannah said.

Mr. Chamblais nodded sadly and did not try to argue with her. A few kilometers south of the enemy we left our horses in a glade and crept on foot to the camp.

There was a little ravine with a little stream running through it that led up to the camp. The water was fouled with the filth of the soldiers. I sighed heavily in disgust. Savannah and Mr. Chamblais shared an enigmatic glance but said nothing. None of us felt like talking, not this close to the camp of our enemies.

The sun was low, painting the world in orange and gold, when we arrived at the edge of the camp.

Our reports had said that there were one thousand men and horses in the camp. As we rounded the last bend and hid ourselves in the sunset-coloured woods we discovered how wrong our reports had been.

There were no less than two thousand men and fifteen hundred horses. The camp was bursting at the seams. Confederation had sent for reinforcements. This was going to be difficult.

CHAPTER 38

Savannah

MR. CHAMBLAIS HAD TOLD us that there were a thousand men in the Confederation camp. The truth was that there was twice that number, and they were crowded in. It struck me that the site for the camp had been chosen to fit a thousand men. More had piled in later.

"Shit," Kieran whispered under his breath.

"If you want to turn back," I said in an equally hushed tone, it wasn't likely that the soldiers would hear us over the din they were making but caution made me quiet, "I would understand, this isn't what you signed up for." The truth is that I was seriously considering turning back and all. Two thousand pale Confederation infantrymen in steel armour, how would I ever manage to blend in enough to find Dave Boyd?

"No," said Mr. Chamblais. "This changes nothing. If anything it will help us—as that has the look of a camp in chaos." He seemed almost offended that I'd suggest such a thing. My opinion of the gruff old rebel rose sharply in that moment and I felt a pang of shame that I had been so close to throwing in the towel.

"So what's the plan?" I asked.

"We wait until the guard changes about an hour after dark, then we will enter the camp. My friends told me the general position of the hospital tent. We will look for Boyd there and then, if he isn't there, we'll try the gaol." Great, we were going to break into the cells. No way that could backfire.

"OK."

"Kieran tells me you have an expert grasp of Kite-Stepping. While we make our way through the camp we will neutralize the guards. You can use your Kite-Stepping skill to move silently along the tops of the tents and keep us alerted to any guards in our path that we can't see."

I looked quizzically at Mr. Chamblais, surprised he'd even heard of Kite-Stepping, let alone understood what it could do.

"I've travelled this world a long time, girl. There are many strange talents out there."

"I'm not sure my Kite-Stepping is quite that good just yet."

"Then we should go back and retrieve Monsieur Shatterfield," Mr. Chamblais said flatly.

I thought of Old Saul trying to scout out a safe path through a camp of two thousand crowded souls and my mind rebelled. "No, I'll try my best." I bit my lip absent-mindedly.

Kieran didn't look thrilled at all with this turn of events. I wasn't either but I was damned if I was going to let him play up like I was some sort of helpless damsel. I stared him down and he looked away.

We waited.

The sun set.

We moved.

I slipped across the tops of the tents, as quiet as a rustling in the breeze, as light as a feather. It was actually easier than I'd expected. I just had to make sure I landed on a support pole and not on loose fabric.

Below, Kieran and Mr. Chambais moved along the aisles between the tents like two shadows in the night. Using their paralyzing finger strikes and daggers with charcoal-blackened blades against any sentries who stood in their path, they cut a silent path of destruction through the camp.

I worried about what would happen when somebody discovered one of the guards missing, or when one was found stuffed in a shaded gap between two tents with his throat cleanly cut, dead eyes staring in the terror of knowing that he would die unable to move, but I tried to set aside these thoughts.

I felt pity for the soldiers. Most of them only signed up to be pointed in a direction by somebody strong. Still, they were an invading army.

In short time we made it to the hospital tent. It was a long canvas affair with a green roof. It was held up by four central support poles and had two entrances, one at the north and the other at the south.

The guards around the tent were unusually thick, there had to be a dozen clustered mostly around the two doors. We came from the south and so we concentrated on eliminating the guards from the southern end of the tent first. We needed to silence all six before they could shout out. This was the hardest part of our mission. We'd regrouped briefly before moving to the hospital tent and agreed to strike simultaneously, each taking two of the guards. To facilitate the task Mr. Chamblais slipped me two knives weighted for throwing.

"Do you know how to use these?" he asked in a hushed voice.

"Actually, no."

"Make sure the sharp part goes into the enemy. It's easy, no?" He sounded almost like he was joking. I didn't laugh. I gave him back the knives.

"I don't need these," I said as I summoned up every bit of my skill at Kite-Stepping and drifted high into the air. I dropped silently behind them and struck each across the back of the neck with an open hand. Snapping bone was easy beside pulling rebar from a wall with bare hands. The two men fell silently. I felt a quiver of disgust with myself but it had to be done. We were committed now, and they'd do worse to us if we were caught.

Kieran and Mr. Chamblais were equally effective. Nerve-Shocking Fingers was a powerful tool for assassination, muting the guards before they had a chance to cry out. They fell easily.

And then we stepped inside.

There were only two people in the tent. One was the old doctor. The other was Sophie, looking pale and sickly.

When the three of us slipped into the tent like spectres of death her eyes widened and she screamed. Damn.

Things started happening quickly then.

Kieran and Mr. Chamblais rushed forward just as the six other guards came into the tent shouting. The old doctor gave a surprised little yell and bolted from the tent, cutting his way through the side of the tent with a doctor's knife, again showing greater speed and agility than most old men. In fact, when I thought of it, his reaction reminded me almost of how I'd expect Old Saul to act.

We'd had a contingency set up for if something like this happened. We were all to get out as fast as possible and we'd meet up at the glade where our horses were by dawn.

"I'll get the doctor, you get Boyd!" Kieran shouted at me as he took off through the slit in the side of the tent.

Meanwhile Mr. Chamblais took on the six guards from the north end of the tent. I ran to help him but he shouted, "Go!"

"But what if one of you gets captured?" I asked.

Mr. Chamblais had a pained look on his face. He cut down a guard and said, "We'll worry about getting ourselves out, you find Boyd."

I paused, sword in hand, unsure what to do.

"Go!" Mr. Chamblais roared.

I turned and ran.

As soon as I left the tent I leaped up, Kite-Stepping into the air and carrying myself over the heads of guards who were rushing up to see the source of the commotion from the tent. I had to find Kieran. I didn't care about Boyd anymore. What worried me was all the trouble Kieran would get into on his own.

I took off over the roofs, looking for him.

I found him quickly. He was where the fighting was thickest. There were ten men on the ground around him, but he was on his knees, at sword point. There were fifty men in a circle around him. He was fucked and there wasn't a thing I could do about it.

Damn.

There were too many people running around, and I was nearly exhausted. I needed to catch my breath, hide for a second. I chose a darkened tent and cut a slit in the roof, dropping into it.

I landed on something soft and warm. The something went, "oof."

I scrambled off and pointed my sword at whoever I was with. There was a brief flare as a flint and steel set was sparked, a lamp lit. It was Dave Boyd. He was grinning faintly though he mostly looked sick from his wounds.

"Savannah, Savannah, Savannah. If you've come to rescue me you've done a damn poor job of it."

Screw it, Boyd had landed in my lap (or more to the point I'd landed in his). In for a penny, in for a pound. Boyd was clearly still injured. I'd get him out first and then go back for Kieran. He'd just have to hold on until then. "A friend of mine was taken trying to rescue you. Don't make it in vain," I snarled.

"I suppose we're just going to fly out."

"That was kind of the idea," I joked.

"Savannah, I saw you move when you found me in the tunnels and I suspect I know something of your skills. When I was younger I even learned a small measure of the Kite-Stepping talent from the first master of it. But I'm far too injured to make use of those skills. I can barely walk."

Boyd's admission shocked me. I'd assumed Saul to be the first master of Kite-Stepping, but he'd not taught Boyd anything, nor was it mentioned in his books. But that would have to be a matter to deal with some other time.

"I'll help." I felt almost sick thinking of leaving Kieran behind. But I was coming back, and he'd known the risks. I needed Mr. Chamblais if I wanted to get him back. I needed a plan. I needed not to be hindered by an injured former prisoner.

There was no other way around it. I needed to think of the mission first. Somehow I knew it was what Mr. Chamblais would have done too.

"Hurry up," I said to Boyd, who was slowly getting out of bed.

"Alright," he said, looking pained to be standing. "Let's go."

By sunrise Mr. Chamblais should be back at the glade. Together we could get Kieran back, but first I had to get Boyd out.

Even with him trying to help as much as he could, carrying him was very taxing. Kieran would just have to hold on.

CHAPTER 39

Kyle

I WAS BEING RUDELY escorted by one of my father's guards into his august presence when I heard the commotion coming from the hospital tent. I felt like my gut was full of burning ice. Assassins had come for Sophie again, or her father. Considering Boyd's warnings I wasn't sure which was worse. I turned toward the fray, and the soldier tried to stop me.

"I can't allow you to go running off before you've seen your father, Prince Kyle."

I pointed in the direction of the tent. "My betrothed is in there. There has been one attempt on her life this week. I must see to her protection."

"I have orders to restrain you if necessary."

"I don't have time for this," I muttered. I drew and cut down my father's bodyguard before he even realized I'd turned against him. I looked around, and saw a few of my own soldiers nearby, none of the new troops. "It was the rebels who killed him," I hissed.

One of the soldiers saluted. I didn't know if I could trust them, but I'd have to cross that bridge when I came to it. I had other matters to address.

Halfway to the tent I came upon that would-be assassin, Kieran if I recalled correctly.

So he'd had finally come to face me. He'd come to die.

I roared and attacked him.

He looked almost surprised when I jumped out at him, as if he hadn't been expecting to see me. He probably expected to take us sleeping in our beds, the scoundrel. He parried my sword, his movements almost mirroring mine. He'd improved even in the last few days. I cut left, he parried left, I thrust down and right, he dodged aside. He had improved.

But he hadn't improved enough, I was going to win.

Almost too late I remembered his finger-strike skills, the ones that paralyzed. I barely avoided getting struck by his outstretched hand.

Still, it was all over. The sounds of fighting had drawn men to me. My men, loyal men who'd been with me from the beginning: they crowded in, blocking his escape, cutting away his room to maneuver. "Take him alive. I can't question a corpse," I said.

"Fight me, coward!" Kieran shouted but I didn't care. He was the idiot who waded into my camp alone. I didn't feel a pressing need to prove myself to him in single combat. Let him scream insults. They didn't matter. I'd won.

He cut down ten of my men with lightning speed. I was impressed with the boy's skill, he'd had a talented teacher. I couldn't wait to track the man down and gut him, whoever he was, for the crime of training rebels with such skills.

The more he fought, the more tired he became, the more obvious it became that he'd lost. In time his sword dropped from his numb fingers and my men pushed him to his knees and set about binding him.

"Take him to the gaol. I'll be along to question him shortly."

"Yes, sir," one of the soldiers said and led Kieran away. Kieran struggled as he was dragged away, shouting insults and threats, but he'd lost. There was no escape for him.

I went to the hospital tent, the source of all the commotion, and the triumph I'd felt melted away. There was a huge gash in the side wall of the tent. Doctor Fletter-Daish was gone. Sophie was gone.

Sophie was gone.

They'd taken her.

And my father was standing in the tent, looking disappointed. I guess my father and I look the same. He was bigger than me, a bear of a man, standing a head taller than most. Even Brutus didn't seem so massive beside him. He had long, black hair streaked with grey. It was naturally curly so my father held it back from his face with a leather thong terminating in sapphires and he wore a small gold and steel circlet also bejewelled with sapphire.

The blue crown of Confederation. One day it would be mine. He had many expensive rings on his fingers and his clothes were rich and clean even here.

He was frowning when he saw me.

He started softly enough. "You have a lot to answer for, son. No messages have reached me since you departed. My own messenger disappeared without a word. I arrive and I hear how you allowed enemies to raid the camp not just tonight but once before. I hear that your second in command sits in prison charged with treason. Your third in command is dead. His replacement is dead.

Your own betrothed nearly dead, your command structure in disarray. And there are enemies raiding your camp again!" By the time he finished he was roaring.

"I caught the intruder."

"You caught *an* intruder," he said, bitter emphasis on the fact that the intruder was probably only one of many. "For once."

"The first incident was almost surely the work of Marc Antonelli."

"Yes, I heard about that. And I had to say that, while I had a low opinion of you before you went off on this fool's errand I never once expected you'd be this much of a fool. Do you expect me to believe that Marc Antonelli is a traitor? His father was a good friend of mine. His son has been your closest companion your whole miserable life."

"Do you think I came to this conclusion with ease or comfort, father? Yes, my best friend betrayed me! Everybody has betrayed me, or been taken from me!" I looked at the ground and darkness piled up behind my eyes. "They took Sophie."

He looked away from me, his back rigid. His face in profile was as hard as a granite bust, and as unforgiving. "Perhaps that is for the best."

"She would have been my wife!"

"You presume too much. You assume I'd have ever let you keep her."

I stared at him, dumbfounded and searching for words to throw at my father, to show him that I would not be cowed by him, when a soldier arrived. He was one of the new soldiers: one of my father's. "Majesty, we've found approximately twenty dead guards secreted throughout the camp. There are no signs of any additional intruders. But, Dave Boyd is missing."

When my father struck me across the jaw with an angry backhand I at least had the strength to stay standing. A trickle of blood ran down from beside my eye where one of his heavy rings had cut me. I put a hand to my head and felt the sticky blood. I stared at him silently cursing him, the way he treated me, like I was still a child.

"What was Boyd doing alive if he was in your custody?" he asked, his voice quiet and dangerous. "Revenge on him was the entirety of your mission."

"He had information we needed."

"Your orders were to send me his head in a box." My father loomed over me, hands bunching, veins in his head sticking out. How could a man so angry remain so quiet?

"He was connected to the Black Trillium," I blurted. I hadn't wanted to tell my father, not without proof at least, but he had to know.

He turned away from me. "They're dead, you fool."

"Father—"

"Get out of my sight before I have you removed," he cut me off, turning his back on me. I left in wordless wrath.

I set out for the gaol with my thoughts a maelstrom of wrath. My mind flitted from topic to topic, fury and insult piling up into huge storm heads. I wanted to unleash the thunder of my wrath but I couldn't afford that luxury. I needed to be cold, pragmatic.

Boyd was gone, Sophie gone. I had Kieran. I was going to inflict tortures upon him that would go down in the annals of history until he gave me both back. And then, when Sophie was safe once more, I'd give him an inglorious death, put him down like a dog.

I thought about the things I would do to him, cut away his fingers, a joint at a time, peel his skin from his bones in narrow strips, put out his eyes, cut off his nose. But I'd leave him his ears and his tongue. He'd sing for me by the time I finished with him and his screams would be sweet.

Some blood dripped into my eye and stung. How dare my father strike me? I was the heir apparent to his kingdom! When I had the Black Trillium in my hands, when Sophie and Boyd were both back safely in camp, I'd show him. He was an unnatural father.

I was so wrapped in my anger that I almost walked into the assassin they'd left behind.

The man was masked, he had an axe, and he was another big man. He could have been the brother of the assassin who wounded Sophie.

The axes were the same, identical.

I stumbled away from the blow and drew my sword.

"Not tonight," I snarled.

I drew out of 'Sheathing the Drawn Blade in Flesh' and the assassin's axe flew into the night air, spouting a little gout of blood from the wrist of the hand that went with it. The assassin had fallen back a step and was gripping the stump of his bloody hand.

I stepped toward him and he backed up as fast as he could, shock playing across the tiny slit of his face I could see above the edge of the mask on his face.

What a coward, hiding behind a mask. I cut it from his face and it was a face I knew.

I didn't know him well. He was a soldier, cavalry, often served as a guard around the camp. His family wasn't important enough for me to know him well but he was a respected soldier, a respected warrior.

He was one of my men. Why would one of my men try to kill me?

"Not tonight, traitor. I won't die tonight." I forced him back, the tip of my sword drawing a little bead of blood on his throat.

"I wouldn't ever kill you, sir," the assassin gasped, cupping the ruin of his wrist. Right, that was about as believable as a whore lying to her man about how she was faithful while her poxy client lay spent next to her in bed.

I said so.

"I was just sent to scare you, sir, hurt you enough that you'd go home. Please, I have a family." Wrong thing to say.

I drove my sword through his throat. He didn't scream as he died but it wasn't for lack of trying.

Somehow, even from within the gaol, Marc was directing my own men against me. The camp wouldn't be safe until I cut out this infection. Sophie was gone and that bastard assassin Kieran was my only lead.

I set off for the gaol, sword at my side. When I got there, there would be ample chances for me to vent my spleen.

CHAPTER 40

Kieran

THEY DRAGGED ME AWAY. I shouted out, called MacMillan a bastard, a coward, said he wasn't a true man. He ignored me. I struggled against my guards, but they'd taken my sword, bound my hands. I was helpless.

The gaol was unimpressive. Before the Confederation set up their filthy little camp it had been a stable. They dragged the horses out and put bars on the windows. Other than that it was the same fetid place it had been before. I wouldn't even keep a horse in here.

The walls were crumbling lath and plaster. The roof was mouldy thatch. The door was strong, reinforced with steel bands and bars. Probably the wall would crumble before the door would give way. The floor was dirt and was strewn with mouldy straw and horse shit. Cockroaches and other filthy bugs skittered along the floor and scaled the walls.

When I was thrown into the gaol I landed square on a fetid pile of shit-smeared straw. On the other end of the room was another man. He was gaunt, though he may have once been stout, his eyes and hair were dark and his hair and beard were unkempt. The bags under his eyes suggested he hadn't slept in a long time.

"Hey there," I said to him after the door slammed shut. "Do you want to give me a hand?"

He just stared at me, a disgusted look on his face.

"What are you in for?"

"I want nothing to do with you," he said and looked away.

"Fine, whatever," I said. "Could you at least help me with my hands?"

He didn't answer.

I said nothing more and began working on the rope they'd bound my hands with. It didn't take long to find a loose nail in the wall. After a bit of work I managed to get my hands free.

My cell-mate just looked at me like I was one of the cockroaches on the floor.

"We might be rooming together for some time. Could you at least tell me what your name is, why you're in here with me?

"Marc," he sighed. "And I can hear what goes on in camp through the walls. I heard them bringing you in. I want no part of your business."

"I was thrown in here for trying to rescue a friend."

"You're an assassin and a spy—and you may be the one truly to blame for my situation. Be content that all I wish of you is silence, and give me that."

I made no further attempts at conversation and started looking for a way out. The door was solidly locked. Savannah could have gone out through the roof but it was twenty feet up and I couldn't jump that high.

I saw plenty of spots in the wall that I could possibly climb up but the walls were in such awful condition I doubted that would work.

The ground was hard-packed earth, I might be able to dig my way out but it would take some time.

All in all the weakest part of the gaol seemed to me to be the walls.

I could probably put a fist through them, though I suspected punching a hole in the wall would be more likely to attract attention than trying to sneak out.

I picked a spot on the back wall, far as possible from any windows, far as possible from any doors and began peeling strips of lath out of the walls, one chunk at a time.

After five minutes I'd managed sore fingers and to remove the main source of support from six inches of wall. I tested the plaster underneath the lath, and sure enough, it was very crumbly. The outer wall of the stable had been plaster too, if I could strip away enough of the wall from the inside I might be able to burst through and run off before anybody noticed I was missing.

"What are you doing?" Marc asked angrily.

"Trying to escape." I concentrated on the wall, not looking at Marc. "Want to help?" And I pulled another strip of lath out of the wall.

"I can't let you do that."

"What? Are you a rat or something?"

"No, just a loyal man," Marc said, and I could almost feel his breath on my ear. I didn't really care who he was loyal to, it clearly wasn't me.

I felt, rather than saw, the blow he aimed at my spine and twisted out of the way. His hand thumped into the wall and knocked out a chunk of plaster from where he struck it. He swore, loudly.

"What's going on in there?" a guard called from outside.

Marc looked like he was going to shout so I hit him with the 'Silent Needle,' one of the most advanced nerve-shocking techniques I knew. He tried to speak, but no sound came out.

His ruddy face flushed with rage and his dark eyes flashed. He lashed out at me with a powerful kick. This man was not a beginner in combat. His wrestling and kickboxing were, if anything, better than mine.

Still, he didn't know the Nerve-Shocking Fingers, and that gave me an edge. Every time he got the best of me I would hit a new vital point. Every time I could see parts of his body falling numb, I could see the pain of the blows on his face. He landed a few strong blows on me but I'd taken worse, and I won the fight.

Then I screwed up, and, while trying to apply the 'Leg-Deadening Palm,' I freed his voice. Immediately, he shouted, "Help! This man is trying to escape!"

Even with his voice freed, the treacherous Marc was wounded from my repeated use of my esoteric skill. A less talented fighter probably wouldn't have survived the blows I'd delivered to him, but Marc was apparently made of sterner stuff than most. I tried the final strike, 'The Sword of the Broken Heart.'

I'd seen Mr. Chamblais use it earlier that night, with this powerful technique you could kill with a single touch, stopping the heart of your foe. I'd never been able to apply it.

I got it almost right. The blow threw Marc from his feet. He roared and writhed in pain, clutched at his chest, but he didn't die.

And as he bellowed and cursed the guards burst in.

There were a dozen of them and they were armed with clubs. They pummeled me with their clubs. I curled into a ball and tried to protect my head and my vital organs from the hammer blows that came crashing down on me. The guards kept beating me, cursing me the whole time for fighting, for trying to escape, for disrupting their evening. It didn't matter. Eventually the curses blurred together into a litany of abuse and pain. Blackness swallowed my senses.

When I came to I was on the floor of the gaol. I was tied, like a pig, hand to foot, with a tight leather thong, and I was alone.

CHAPTER 41

Savannah

WHEN WE ARRIVED AT the glade there was no sign of Mr. Chamblais and all of the horses were still there. I dropped Boyd on the ground, as gently as possible, and leaned against a tree, exhausted.

"Thank you for rescuing me. And for keeping the manual from them."

"I don't give a shit about the manual," I said sharply. "I came back for you."

"Of course, I appreciate that. But I'd told you, protecting the manual was the important thing. I already nearly gave my life for that once." We were silent for a few tense minutes after that, the quiet broken only by the wind through the trees, the gurgle of the water, and the gentle snoring of sleeping horses. "You didn't have to come back for me."

"What sort of person would I be if I hadn't?"

"I haven't seen many people like that in a very long time."

I crouched and looked at him, the hard contours of his face seemed to have softened a bit, whether from fatigue, the alcohol on his breath or simply the ordeal he'd been through. I nearly felt sorry for him. But then I remembered how many secrets he'd kept from me.

"Maybe you should be more trusting."

He scoffed. "I know I have kept things from you."

"You think? Like how you learned how to Kite-Step? Or why you were keeping the manual in the first place? How you know MacMillan's woman? Who her father is? Don't you think that some of this might be information I should know?"

"You're right. I owe you that much."

"Yeah, you do. But for now it'll have to wait. You should be safe here. I have to go back in."

"What? What the hell are you thinking? You'd risk giving them the manual again?" His voice sounded harsh, coarse. I noticed a rope burn around his throat, another injury he'd taken since we'd last met.

"I have to rescue my friends." At least I could say that honestly about Kieran. I wasn't sure about Mr. Chamblais. But he was Kieran's friend and he should have been back by now. I was faster than him, even with Boyd, but it was getting late. If he wasn't here it suggested something had happened to him, he was in some sort of trouble.

"Then give me back the manual."

I reached into my pocket. "Here." I threw it to him. "Sorry about the stains."

He thumbed through it, came across my notations from Saul's wall. "What's this?"

"Medicine, from Old Saul. I didn't write over any of the diagrams. It's all fine."

He grunted. "You still shouldn't go. Sophie was willing to torture me. When I talked her out of that she wanted to kill me and find you—to torture the secrets you learned from that manual from you. It's crucial that your skills don't fall into her hands, or MacMillan's."

"I don't care. I'm going back for Kieran."

"Don't be a fool," he snapped and tried to stand. His wounds pained him and he winced, slumping back against the tree.

"How do you intend to stop me?" I asked, feeling an edge of anger that, after all this, he would still try to command me.

"I can't."

"But I might if I deem it appropriate," said another voice, sharp and imperious, coming from the woods away from the direction of the camp.

I put my hand on the hilt of my—Dave's—sword. "Show yourself."

He laughed and stepped out of the shadows.

Have you ever had a nightmare so real that you wondered if you were awake? That's the experience I felt when I looked at the face of the man who appeared from the woods. He had dark hair, straight and neat. His beard was neatly trimmed and framed a strong cupid's-bow mouth. He had a youthful look about him, until you looked at his eyes: the green of heavy moss and as ancient as the ruined towers from before the Collapse.

He carried a sword with a basket hilt, crusted with emeralds. That sword was probably, alone, worth all the steel in Boyd's vaults twice over, and he was wearing green robes. All westerners knew about the Wizard in Green, the Duke of Seattle.

And every westerner feared him.

Boyd tried to rise and stumbled to take a knee, head bowed, with the manner of a retainer hailing his lord. Boyd knew the Duke of Seattle.

My jaw hung slack at the sight of him. The terrifying conqueror of California, the master of the ancient machines was here in Trana. Why was he here?

"Where do you think you are going, young lady?"

Legend said that the Duke of Seattle could see through any lie, and that he was a capricious beast who would kill anybody with the gall to attempt to mislead him. I decided to go with the truth. "To rescue my friend."

"And Boyd would not go on your behalf?" He seemed arch. Boyd looked terrified. I'd seen Boyd desperate. I'd seen him angry. I'd never seen him terrified before, even when he was preparing to sacrifice his life.

I repressed a shudder and said, "He's injured, he needs to rest. And besides, I don't need him to fight my battles for me."

"Is that how you came to be carrying his sword?"

"I'm carrying his sword because he gave it to me. Begging your pardon, but why is it any business of yours?"

Before the Wizard in Green could answer, Boyd interjected, "This lady has saved my worthless life three times, Lord. I owed her a debt."

It was bizarre seeing Boyd being so submissive. This was the man who spit in the eye of kings and rebels. And he was all but grovelling to this man. Then again, the man he was grovelling to was the single most frightening person in the west.

"Does she understand what you have given her?"

"Hey, I am standing right here," I snapped at him.

"I am aware of that." He was trying to get under my skin, I knew it. Trouble was, it was working.

"So what's the big deal if Dave gave me his sword? If he wants it back he just has to ask."

"You know who I am, yes?"

"I can guess. But anybody could put on a set of green robes."

The Duke of Seattle threw his head back and laughed. "I can see why you like this one, Boyd." He turned his attention to me. "I can assure you that I am precisely who you suspect me to be. Which means you probably know how much I like a good wager." Folk stories from my childhood of the Wizard in Green flickered through my mind. Yes, he did like a bet. It was about the only way of safely dealing with him.

"What's the wager?" I asked.

"Like you I have come to recover somebody from the Confederation camp. I propose we make a race of it. Whoever makes it here with the person we set out to rescue first wins. If you win I'll teach you what is so special about Boyd's sword."

"What if I lose?"

His grin turned nasty. "The sword you took was not Boyd's to give nor yours to accept. In my country you have committed a grave crime by holding it. If you lose, or if you refuse this bet, I'll take you back to Seattle as my slave."

I laughed in his face. "Do you seriously think I'd just trade myself into bondage?" I said and looked around myself for any weapon I could use, any avenue of escape; but this was the Wizard in Green. There was no escaping him. My only real hope was to play his game, and win. Of course part of that was setting proper terms.

"For taking that sword, you have forfeited your freedom." His green eyes looked flat and lizard-like.

"This is my fault, Lord. I gave her the sword in a moment of weakness, when I thought I would die. I felt it was better than letting it fall into the hands of who-knows-who. Your daughter..."

I didn't see the blow that knocked Boyd from his knees, sprawling across the ground on the other end of the clearing, but I heard it, nearly felt it in my bones. I closed my eyes and suppressed another shudder. I was playing a dangerous game with a reckless opponent.

"Don't mention my daughter to me."

Boyd moaned a little, felt his jaw, but didn't try to get up.

The Wizard in Green returned his attention to me. "I believe we were discussing our wager."

I could try to escape. I knew how to Kite-Step and that was a powerful skill for avoiding a fight, but I didn't want to run. I'd sworn never to run, sworn to myself an oath as strong as any you can make to yourself. I would not run. "This wager isn't fair. Whatever secrets the sword holds, I can find on my own. I am risking my freedom here. When I win, I want a greater prize."

The Wizard in Green threw back his head and roared in laughter. "Well spoken, young lady. Name your prize. But beware asking for too much of me. I am quick to anger and have less than subtle ways of venting my wrath when it is stirred up."

I bit back my fear. "When I win, you will tell me the secret of the sword. But I have two further requests, minor matters that should not be beyond your talent."

"Go on." His fingers drummed on the pommel of the bejewelled sword.

"I want a promise from you to do one task for me, of my choosing, and at the time I ask for it. And I want you to swear to be my friend for as long as I wish you to be. You will not be bound to serve me in any way nor to stay at my side. Only to be kind to me when we are together, and polite." Was it cheeky? Damn straight it was, but I didn't care.

The Wizard in Green stroked his beard in thought for a while before answering, "This is a fair bargain, but I'm setting one limit on it. You may not ever compel me to act against my family or my students. Furthermore, should you ask me to do so, our friendship will be over."

"Agreed," I said, but I couldn't help but wonder what I'd gotten myself into.

"When we have rescued our charges, or failed in our tasks, we will return here, and this failure of a man will adjudicate the winner. He may have squandered the gifts I gave him but at least he can do that."

"Fine." As I spoke, the Wizard in Green vanished into the forest with blinding speed. I put my hands on my hips and glared down at Dave Boyd. "When I get back we are going to have bitter words about the shit you've gotten me into, Dave."

"I already promised you answers."

I didn't waste any further time on him, Kite-Stepping into the tree-tops and into the night. Once more into the breach.

CHAPTER 42

Kyle

WHEN I ARRIVED AT the gaol it was in chaos. My guards all crowded around Marc, who was lying in the earth, writhing and clutching his chest.

As soon as he saw me he reached out his hand and said, "Kyle, I think I'm dying." When I looked into his eyes I believed him.

"Take him to the hospital tent," I said.

"Are you alright, Lord MacMillan?" one of them asked me. I realized my hands and my face were spattered with the blood of the assassin, and the gash in my face where my father had struck me was untreated. I must have looked frightful. But I had no time to reassure my men that I wasn't the one in need of care.

"Hurry!"

They carried Marc to the hospital tent but it wasn't easy going. He thrashed and writhed in pain the whole time, as if he were being stabbed with invisible knives. Whatever had happened to Marc, it was terrible. For the moment, all thought of Sophie, of my father, of the bastard in my cells faded. There was only the man who had been my friend for a long time, the man who may have been my betrayer, but it didn't matter. He was my friend, regardless of what else he may have done. If he really was dying, perhaps we could make our peace.

When we arrived at the tent there was nobody there. My father was gone. The gash in the side of the tent, where the assassins had entered, was like a ragged wound.

My men set Marc down on a cot and he nearly thrashed off of it in seconds. I pressed down on his shoulders. "Be calm."

He nodded and grit his teeth but the phantom pains that wracked him didn't cease and, although I could tell he was trying to be still, he still twitched and writhed.

"Get a medic," I said to one of the guards. "And once the medic is coming find that damn doctor if you have to turn Trana upside-down."

The guard saluted and, wordlessly, half of the guards filed out, to find medics or to return to the gaol, I didn't know which.

"Marc, what happened to you?"

"You locked me in a cell with a maniac." His tone was accusing. "Listen, I don't think I have much longer and there are things you have to hear."

"Don't be silly," I said. "You aren't dead yet. We'll get you a doctor. We can sort this all out."

"My heart, it's wounded. I know I won't survive the night."

I should have remembered that this Kieran was an assassin. No doubt he used those bizarre empty-hand skills he possessed to hurt Marc.

The medic rushed in, my father's personal one. He was a gruff man with a grizzled grey beard and salt-and-pepper hair.

"I was told Colonel Antonelli was injured," he said. "Out of the way, please."

I stepped aside and let the doctor past. He checked Marc's eyes, took his pulse. "Sweet merciful gods."

I tried to back away but Marc grabbed my wrist and said, "No, please, stay."

He said it so weakly, so pathetically, it nearly broke my heart. What had that assassin done to Marc? I gave his hand a squeeze. "I'll stay."

"Have you been given poison?" the medic asked.

"No, he struck me."

"Where?" the medic asked. Marc, with a shaking hand, touched a point just above his heart. The medic grunted and cut away his shirt. There was a small bruise there, the shape of three finger tips.

"It is what I feared," the medic said.

"What?" I asked.

The medic grimaced and sighed, his expression was pained but his tone became one of recollection of the ancient past as he answered. "When I was a young man, I served as an apprentice to your grandfather's personal medic. On the night we took Quebec City, five men were brought to the tent with a three-finger bruise just above their hearts. We called it the 'Black Flower of Death' for lack of a better name."

"So it's Black Trillium witchcraft."

"Undoubtedly."

It took conscious control not to crush Marc's hand because my muscles wanted to clench, I wanted to smash something. And I realized I'd been a fool.

Marc was no traitor. The assassin, Kieran, was Black Trillium and he'd struck a lethal blow on Marc for trying to stop him from escaping.

"So, you've seen it before." My voice sounded more threatening than I had intended it to be. "Fix it. Make him better."

"I'm sorry, My Lord," the medic said. "I can ease his pain, but I've never seen a man survive the 'Black Flower of Death.'"

"It's alright," Marc said. "The pain isn't so bad now."

"Nonsense," the medic scolded kindly. "I've seen how this goes. If there were a way to save you, sir..." He glanced up at me furtively, afraid to meet my gaze, afraid to say what was on his mind. "You do know what this means, My Lord."

"Kyle," Marc said with a pained expression. "I don't have much more time. There's something I have to tell you, before the end."

"You are sure you can't cure him?" I asked the medic.

"If there were even the faintest hope, My Lord..." The medic ducked his head. His face was a picture of helpless disappointment.

"Leave us, then. Everybody, get out."

The medic bowed and backed out the door, followed by the guards. Even with my father in the camp, these men were mine and followed my commands.

Marc squeezed my hand. "Before I die, there is something I have to tell you."

"It's fine," I said. "No matter what you say, I will not dishonour you in death. Whatever you have done I'm sure you thought you had a good reason."

"No, you don't understand." Misery and pain radiated from his body in waves of heat.

"Help me understand."

"I'm not the the traitor. I never was," Marc hissed.

"I know."

"Good. It will make what I ask of you easier if you know I was never disloyal."

"Marc, can you forgive me? Please, I didn't know."

"Here, at the end, it doesn't matter. I forgive you. But please, be quiet, hear my last request."

"I can deny you nothing." Marc, my oldest friend, childhood playmate and stalwart companion, hero of the Confederation a dozen times over, I had wronged him more thoroughly than any other person. If he asked me to join him in death, in that moment I would have done so.

"Your father, he lacks vision. He gathers his men about him in Fredericton and, year after year, they rust. Promise me you will bring the Confederation to glory." These words, had anybody else been here to hear them, would have been treason.

"I promise," I said.

Marc thrashed on his bed and his eyes squeezed shut. His face was almost purple and a trickle of blood dribbled from his nose. His breathing was fast and ragged and shallow. He opened his eyes a slit and they weren't bloodshot—but red, as if every capillary in his eyes had burst at once. "The end comes quickly now. I can't see you any more. Kyle, promise me, please, there is another thing."

"Yes, anything, just tell me!" I said, my voice filled with panic.

"Avenge me." Then, as if his spirit escaped his body with the words, he spasmed once more and his heart stopped and he lay still, face made ugly in death with the grimace of pain laid upon it.

"I promise." I stood to leave the tent.

As I stepped outside I found Brutus, stolidly waiting at the flap of the tent, silent as always. Just as well that my bodyguard was a mute, no tongue to wag over what Marc asked me on his deathbed.

"Go round up an executioner," I said. "At sunrise we execute a rebel."

CHAPTER 43

Kieran

I COULDN'T MOVE. BOUND hand to foot, I struggled just to shift myself to see the doorway, to be able to see trouble coming at the very least. I wondered if Mr. Chamblais had escaped, if Savannah escaped.

Gods, let Savannah be alright.

I took stock of my situation. Unarmed, in an enemy camp, no friends, no tools, bound so tightly that I couldn't move. Right, situation stock taken. It added up to a whole lot of Kieran-in-trouble. At least I couldn't see the almost-hole in the wall where I'd nearly escaped until that bastard Marc stopped me.

I wondered if he was still alive. Had I done for him the same way he'd done for me? Slowly and painfully? The door opened and the biggest man I'd ever seen walked in. He was stark, skeleton white. Even his eyebrows were so pale they were barely visible. His pink eyes stared out from the stark white face with a dangerous intensity. I couldn't help but notice two axes strapped to his back. Was this my executioner?

He closed the door gently and crouched down to my level. "Some people see big and think stupid. I would prefer you didn't make that mistake. So I've taken the liberty of arranging for us to be alone. So that you understand the situation clearly, my men believe I am going to put the boot in a bit before you are killed to get some revenge for you framing and subsequently murdering Marc Antonelli. You would be well advised, when you next leave, to act as if you were freshly beaten. Do you understand?"

"What do you want with me?" I couldn't think of anything better to say.

"I haven't decided yet. Perhaps to give you a chance. I am not Black Trillium, but I am somewhat sympathetic to your cause." His voice had rough edges, like he hadn't exercised it much lately, but he was clearly an erudite man, however grotesque his appearance.

He took me by surprise. I'd never revealed myself as being a member of the Black Trillium to MacMillan or any of his servants. Only Savannah and members of the order knew. "How did you... I'm not Black Trillium, don't be absurd." I hoped he wouldn't notice my little slip.

"Giving you a chance could be as simple as making sure the axe is sharp when they cut your head off, Trillium man," he said as if I'd said nothing at all.

"I'd rather they didn't chop my head off. OK, yes, I'm a member of the Black Trillium. I guess it won't harm me much to admit it now. I'm a dead man anyway, aren't I?"

He just smiled. "I told you, some people mistake big for stupid. A hint, when you are trying not to reveal yourself, don't kill somebody with a technique named after your sect."

"The Sword of the Broken Heart?" That wasn't named after the Black Trillium. I was missing at least one key fact here.

"You honestly don't know what they call that technique you used in Fredericton?" The big man seemed genuinely surprised at my ignorance.

"I've never left Trana, I was born here."

"You're going to die here. Convenient, that. Nobody will have to travel far for the funeral."

Ha ha. Oh how I'd have laughed, at least if I hadn't been tied hand and foot on my side on the shit-smeared floor of a cell in the camp of my sworn enemies.

"They call it the Black Flower of Death."

Damn.

"Why do they call it that?" I asked, dreading the answer.

"They call it that because, if executed inexpertly, for instance by a man who hasn't had to use it in combat before, it leaves a bruise where it hits that looks almost exactly like the tattoo that I'm certain I'd find over your heart." Who was this man?

"How do you know all this?"

"How long has Jean Chamblais been in Trana?"

"Longer than MacMillan," I said, nice and vague.

"Let me tell you a story."

"I can't exactly walk off on you." That elicited a chuckle.

"Forty years ago I was one of three young men, barely more than boys really, who had been selected to study soldierly arts under the great warrior Miguel Jesus Arroyo y Lopez. The ancient man had wandered for forty years, travelling from the Yucatan Republic, through the dangerous lands of the Southlanders before coming to the lands that would eventually be

Confederation.

"By the time he arrived in Quebec City he was old and he wanted to pass on his skills, but he was afraid that he could not teach one man to master all the powerful skills he'd learned.

"Instead he taught each of us one third of his skills.

"I was the youngest of his students. He taught me the Stone Axe skill. I mastered it willingly. I've always been strong.

"The middle student was Paul Magritte. He became cruel, using what my master taught him to terrify and dominate. My master drove him out of Quebec City and I know not what happened to him.

"The eldest was Jean Chamblais. He learned the pillar of our master's skill, the Nerve-Shocking Skill. He wished to follow in our masters' footsteps and become a roaming hero.

"When the MacMillan founder began his campaign of conquest, Jean was one of the men who founded *La Fleur Noir*, a secret society dedicated to the defence of Quebec City. He asked me to join him but I refused."

I was dumbfounded. In a short time I'd met not one but three legends—the Wizard in Green, and now, one of the Three Brothers. What's more, he'd implied that my own mentor was also one of those legends. Why had Mr. Chamblais hidden it if he was the eldest brother? And why had this giant refused to fight for his home, why had he ended up in the Confederation camp armed and free?

I struggled to find something to say to him. "Why didn't you fight? Surely you weren't afraid. You were a legend, a hero!"

He smiled gently and said, "No, I wasn't afraid. I've always been a large man, freakishly so. I've always had to be careful, to avoid hurting somebody by accident. I don't like hurting people. Even now, after everything I've had to do," he sighed heavily, "I'd still rather have a peaceful life.

"I tried to convince Jean that we should just go with our master out of Quebec City, find a peaceful life in 'Toba. But he refused. He said it was his duty to protect his home from tyranny.

"The city fell, and our master, an ancient by then, died at the hands of soldiers for carrying a sword that he never even drew. Jean disappeared as thoroughly as Paul before him and I was taken for a slave."

"You should have avenged your master."

"It's easy to say that," the big man said, "but when does the cycle of revenge end? No, I was taken a slave, and because of my strength they made me into a soldier. I tried faking being mute, being an idiot, but it didn't matter. They would just whip me to fight. I was never comfortable killing but my masters noticed I excelled at protecting. I was given guard duties and performed them admirably. I protected generals. I watched. Eventually I became accustomed to protecting these petty warlords while they looked down on me.

"Eventually I was promoted to guarding the crown prince himself and he was no different. He thought me an idiot."

"And you ended up here," I said, believing the story over.

"You are getting ahead of yourself. First, I discovered that *La Fleur Noir* had arisen again in Trana, when the prince announced on the road that this was so. I knew Jean would be here. I couldn't allow the man who was a brother to me to be killed by the man I'd sworn to protect.

"I tried to force the prince to return home. I failed.

"I had students among the guards, other men with consciences, men who I trusted with my master's teachings. I sent them to frighten the prince into turning around, to hurt him without endangering him. They failed too."

"Marc said there were assassins loose in the camp."

"Probably he was referring to you, and your friends. But, yes, my men were about tonight. We'd tried several times to send the prince home. Each attempt was more desperate. My best student died at the hands of the prince tonight. And I stomached it. And I came here to you, and told you this story, instead of getting revenge."

"So you don't want revenge. It doesn't matter. You're still his servant. I'm still his prisoner. He'll still kill us both if he knows."

"It matters because I have the chance to save Jean's student. But if I save you, you must promise me that you will not continue the cycle of vengeance. Do not pursue the prince for the things he has done."

"You ask a lot of me. You didn't see the torture chamber at the Confederation garrison."

"I saw what you left behind."

I hadn't been subtle there, true. "OK, you have my word. I won't perpetuate a cycle of revenge, but I will still protect the people who I care for."

"As will I. And do tell Jean that Brutus lives still, and hopes his brother lives long enough to see some peaceful days." He cut the straps that held me in place.

And then MacMillan walked into the shed.

"Brutus. Is the executioner ready?"

Brutus grunted and nodded his head.

"Excellent. Take the prisoner. The sooner he dies the happier I'll be."

Brutus grunted and lifted me over his shoulder. As he did, he reached to my feet and I felt another bond snap. My hands were free, and my legs. I had a chance, if only I knew how to use it.

CHAPTER 44

Savannah

I DIDN'T WANT TO return to the crowded city of canvas tents, stinking of horses and unwashed men, again, but my desire to rescue Kieran and to avoid a life of slavery to the capricious Wizard in Green was far greater than the revulsion I felt to be returning to the Confederation camp.

The sun had not broken the horizon when I came into the camp but the sky had already begun to brighten; it was more bruise purple than midnight black. The stars were fading and the moon looked pale and sick, not the silver globe that shone above Kieran and I just a little more than a night before.

This meant greater danger for me. I no longer faded into the darkness of a night sky. I would have to be careful.

Skipping with feather steps from tent-top to tent-top I kept an eye to the ground, watching for guards, for soldiers stirred up by the confusion of the night. My only chance lay in being a ghost, a rumour, invisible.

I needed to find the gaol, but I realized I wouldn't know it to see it. Mr. Chamblais seemed to have an idea of where it would be, but he was missing.

I couldn't just ask directions. I was at a loss. If I didn't act soon that horrible old Wizard in Green would rescue whoever he was after and I would be thoroughly screwed.

I was not going to be anybody's slave, I'd die first. If it looked like I might lose I was tempted to forget subtlety, attack and get myself killed in the attempted rescue rather than face death by degrees as a servant to the Wizard in Green.

I had to rescue Kieran, I just had to.

I had stopped, trying to figure out my next step, when the noise started. It was coming from the hospital tent. I knew how to get there surely enough. I figured, what the hell, it wasn't like I had any better idea for where to go next. I slipped across the tent-tops toward the sounds of commotion.

When I got near I saw Kyle MacMillan leading a dozen soldiers and carrying one of his men, the handsome one who'd been at his side when he first arrived, into the tent. He didn't look handsome anymore. His face was flushed and locked in a rictus of agony. His back arched, his body twitched, his teeth gritted. His beet-red face was a network of newly scabbed-over cuts and bruises. There were huge shadows under his eyes from lack of sleep.

He looked like a man about to die.

MacMillan was paying attention only to the dying man but, with so many guards nearby, I was afraid of being spotted.

Dropping to the ground, I slunk into a shadow between two tents and hid, waiting for a chance to move closer. After a while half the guards left in a hurry. I waited a little longer and the other half of the guards left.

I crept out of the shadow between the tents, but, as I moved, a giant hand clamped onto my shoulder. I was caught, found out, I was dead. I bit my lip to stop myself from screaming and turned to look into the face of my captor.

I had to look up (way up) to meet the pale pink-eyed stare of another of MacMillan's men, the giant. He must have thought I was about to scream, because he put a finger to his lips and took his hand away, silently beckoning me to follow him the opposite direction, the long way around the tent.

Past the guards I would have run into had I gone the direction I'd originally intended.

Why was he helping me? Who was this man? I didn't have time to think about this much. Soon after we passed the guards we were crouching behind some sacks of grain near the entrance to the hospital tent.

I thought of the image of a petite, dark western girl and this hulking, pale giant hiding behind a stack of corn and had to stifle a laugh. From inside we heard a voice say, "Avenge me." The words were pained. I didn't recognize the voice. Even if I knew the speaker I doubted I would have recognized his voice, it was distorted with pain.

There was a dead sucking silence for five unbearable heartbeats and then MacMillan, voice quiet and full of loss, said, "I promise."

The giant put his hand on my shoulder again and gestured for me to be still. He stood, went to the entrance to the tent.

"Go round up an executioner," I heard MacMillan say, his voice full of fatigue. "At sunrise we execute a rebel."

Sunrise. Shit, I didn't have long.

MacMillan returned to the tent and the giant glanced at me, beckoned for me to follow, to take to the rooftops again. I didn't need to be asked twice. I didn't want to be on the ground in this camp, trying to out-run Kyle MacMillan.

As I followed the giant I thought about how clever he was. He must have seen me as I snuck into camp. He wanted to use me for something, but he didn't want to turn me over to MacMillan. I was afraid but also intrigued.

I followed him to a dingy stable, hastily converted to a cell. He went inside as I settled on the lip of the mouldy thatch roof, careful not to fall through.

I heard a hushed conversation inside but couldn't make out the words. They talked for quite some time though. I was starting to get bored. I wanted to get Kieran and go. I was seriously worried about losing the wager. But Kieran couldn't Kite-Step. Even assuming he was in the gaol, I wouldn't be able to get him out on my own.

The giant had plenty of chances to betray me. He hadn't done so yet. I'd have to take it on faith that he meant me no ill, had to hope that he was helping.

And then MacMillan arrived and, after more muted conversation that I still couldn't follow, emerged from the gaol, leading the giant and a dozen guards.

Kieran was slung over the shoulder of the giant, bound hand and foot with thin, cruel, leather thongs. His face was bruised, swollen and cut. He looked beaten. He didn't look up. He couldn't see me.

But the giant did. He met my gaze and then he snapped the leather thong binding Kieran's feet.

CHAPTER 45

Kyle

I WAS BUZZING WITH anticipation, drunk on the heady feeling of righteous revenge. This man, this member of the Black Trillium, had killed Marc, my friend. I longed to swing the axe myself, damn how unsightly it might look in front of my father.

Even my father would respect the fact that I had earned this death. He was my prisoner. And no matter how angry he was with me, my father would not deny me the right to dispose of my prisoner.

We marched to the assembly grounds in the middle of the camp. Even this space was crowded, filled in by my father's command tents, dwarfing my own. He had to have a larger one. We mounted the platform as the first rays of sun broke the horizon.

Tinted in purple and grey I strode to the front of the podium and addressed the assembled men. "Today, we execute a rebel."

The sound of my men banging shields was deafening. They all knew about the disturbances over the night. And now the perpetrator, the one who helped to murder more than twenty good men, would die while they cheered.

I spread my arms wide. "Kieran, who is of no house of note, murdered twenty good soldiers to fulfill the forbidden rites of the Black Trillium!" As the hubbub of my pronouncement spread in rings throughout the crowd I saw my father emerging bleary-eyed from his tent. I guess he went back to sleep while assassins tried to cut me down. I felt a hot twinge of rage and looked directly at him. "Do not believe the men who would tell you the Black Trillium is dead. They are mistaken."

I could see the flash of wrath in my father's eyes. By the gods, did I love having the chance to publicly rub his nose in it.

"I will personally bring this murderer to justice." I reached for the headsman's axe. As I took the weapon from the headsman, I saw that the design of the axe was precisely like that used by the assassins who had plagued the camp.

I stared at the axe in disbelief. I heard shouting from the edge of camp but, entranced by the headsman's axe I paid it no mind for a moment. The shouting grew louder and I looked up from the all-too-familiar weapon, and saw the disarray of the camp. A sergeant was pushing through the crowd, white with fear and spattered with blood. He was calling for me by name.

Unthinkingly I jumped down from the platform and met the messenger who collapsed to his knees, gasping. "Lord, there is a demon in the hospital tent."

"What did you see?" I rather doubted it was a demon considering all the much more real threats about in the camp today.

"A creature that looked like a man. He had green robes, a sword covered in green gemstones, and he was killing everybody." Green robes and a sword covered in emeralds. It sounded like the Wizard in Green who so resembled my Sophie. And they were not demons. They were just foreigners with access to ancient remnants of a forgotten world. "Come with me," I said.

The sergeant saluted weakly. "Yes, Lord." He struggled to his feet, leading me off as fast as he could.

Behind me the assembly fell into disarray but I didn't look back. This man, this Wizard in Green, was connected to Sophie. Getting her back mattered more than anything else, more than my army, more than the Black Trillium, more than getting one up on my father. Marc would have his vengeance, but first I would address the living. There was no greater priority, and the Wizard in Green would be a powerful ally.

When we arrived where the hospital tent should have been, there was nothing but ashes. The flames had been hot enough to scorch the walls of other nearby tents even damp with morning dew.

Burnt and twisted bodies lay thick around, some missing limbs. When I saw them I was transported back to the garrison, to the destruction I'd witnessed there. I would get my revenge on the Black Trillium for that, I swore I would. But only after I spoke with the Wizard in Green and calmed this situation.

The Wizard in Green stood in the center of the field of ash. His robes were untouched by the flames but there was fire in his green eyes, a look of unconfined fury in his face.

"You," he snarled and leaped toward me, sword outstretched, expertly executing as his opening move the same technique that Dave Boyd had used for his opening gambit months ago when we'd last fought.

The Wizard in Green knew the Triumvirate sword art! And now everything made sense. Boyd's threats of Sophie's father's wrath, her noble bearing, her disdain for the primitiveness of our court, the frenzied quest for the sword art: there was one answer to all of it. Sophie's father was the Wizard in Green.

I drew my sword and parried with 'The Soldier's Salute,' a sticking technique that was designed to redirect an aggressive thrust.

The Wizard in Green responded with 'Cracking the Snake's Tail,' a technique from the Form of Limitless Cunning, and precisely the counter I would have used to 'The Soldier's Salute.'

Over the course of five more passes my nemesis continued blending techniques from the Form of Limitless Cunning and the Form of Limitless Aggression with perfect precision and grace. I was losing. Had I been twice the swordsman I was I still wouldn't have had a chance.

"Please," I said. "Can we talk this through?"

"What have you done with her?" He didn't seem to be paying any heed to my words.

I parried again, barely deflecting the blow in time. I felt a burning on my ear, felt a sticky trickle of blood from the notch left behind by the Wizard in Green's sword. "I don't know where she is, she was taken from me by the Black Trillium."

"Lies," he said, another attack, another scratch, across my cheek this time.

Desperately parrying, I struggled to speak and maintain my rhythm; even the slightest mistake would mean my death. "I want her back as badly as you."

"Lies!" The tip of his sword scored a long hot line across my left thigh, cutting into muscle, a line of fire stretching out of the leg and through my body, washing out my other senses.

I wobbled and nearly fell. "I love her," I said, thinking them to be my last words. And the sword stopped.

"I believe, at least as far as you know, you are telling me the truth about that at least."

"I'm telling you the whole truth."

I chanced a look over my shoulder. Soldiers had ringed around us, locked shield to shield. Of my father there was no sign.

"The Black Trillium is known to me. They kill but they rarely kidnap."

"I caught one of their number here tonight. The same night she was taken from me." Some fire returned to my voice. My throat was bone dry, fear and pain stealing my breath. I must have sounded baleful.

"I suspect you are being deceived, but I will afford you this courtesy: I will give you one day to find out where she is. If you haven't found word of her by then..."

He swung his sword again, and instinctively I parried. My sword shattered. I was peppered by flecks of shattered steel and thrown backward with the force of the blow.

"Do you understand?" he asked.

"Perfectly."

Then he disappeared, knocking my guarding soldiers aside as if they were stalks of wheat and blurring away faster than any ordinary man should while seeming to fade into the background.

One day to find Sophie before that mad Wizard in Green came back to kill me. I'd have to spare the Black Trillium for the moment, at least until he divulged the location of my love.

I staggered back to the rallying grounds and found them in total disarray. Soldiers ran to and fro, messengers passed messages from my father's command tent to all corners of the camp. There was nobody on the execution platform. The headsman's axe remained where I'd dropped it.

I ducked into my father's tent and found him poring over maps, giving orders, being a true commander of men.

He glanced up at me and looked away in disgust.

"Where is my prisoner?" I asked. Nobody spoke. "I am in command of this camp," I said to the world at large, irritation radiating through my voice.

My father looked at me disgustedly. "No, you aren't."

"I had to go and defuse that situation at the hospital tent. Nobody else would have been able to stop the killing."

"I'm sure that nobody else was up to the task. After all, you've succeeded so wonderfully at every other task you've been set. You, son, are the true paragon of competence." My father turned his back on me. I felt a wave of wrath burn through me. Even with the gash in my thigh I strode across the tent and grabbed my father on the shoulder, to force him to confront me.

He punched me hard in the gut. I wheezed and almost doubled over. "You damn fool." His voice was hard and cold and low. "You let the rebel escape." I wheezed and tried to express my disbelief but I couldn't gather the breath. How could he have escaped? He was alone and bound.

My father grabbed me by the hair and forced me to look him in the eye. "Your camp has suffered constant lapses of security under your command. You aren't worthy to keep it."

"I'm your son," I said weakly.

"Right now you don't even have enough honour to call yourself my dog." And he meant it. I could see the bitterness, the hate in his eyes, could hear it in his voice. "You are relieved of command."

I'd lost my friends, my love, my command, even my father's respect, for what little that was worth. I was desolated. And in the wasteland of my heart was only one word: death.

CHAPTER 46

Kieran

THE FEEL OF THE headsman's block under my chin was coarse and hard. It stank of mould and copper, it smelled faintly of death. There was a man with his hands on my back, pressing me down. He hadn't noticed that my hands were no longer bound.

I ached from the discomfort of having lain in the restraints, with the pain of the beatings I'd suffered in the night. I just wanted to lie down and sleep for a week. It looked like I'd be sleeping longer than a week though. The eternal rest didn't seem very restful from this vantage point.

My world was reduced to the floor of the stage, the wall of shields, spears, and swords of the soldiers in the square, and the legs of MacMillan as he revelled in his chance to kill me. "Today, we execute a rebel."

The Confederation bastards banged their swords. Big men, an army to kill one rebel.

MacMillan continued to expound on the glory he'd get from murdering me. I hated him. And it wasn't a selfless hate. Certainly, I hated him for the cruel things he'd done, for the occupation of my city, for the cruelty in the garrison, for the sins of his family that he'd perpetuated. But this was merely an echo; a candle flame beside the bonfire of hatred I felt because he wanted to kill me helpless and bound. In the end it didn't matter to me that he believed me trussed up like a feast day hog. I only cared that this man wanted to end my life, and, oh, did I want to end his.

"I will personally bring this murderer to justice." He might succeed. He might kill me, even with my hands free. I tried to relax, to control my breathing. I saw him take the axe, waiting for the one little moment where I could strike, could try to escape.

The moment stretched out. I watched desperately for any sign of movement but all I could see was him, standing still, lost in thought, and holding the axe, not at the ready. I struggled to turn my head. The man pressing on my back pushed back but he was weaker than me and I was able to shift enough to see MacMillan.

"Settle down, it'll hurt less that way," the soldier holding my neck said.

The axe was disturbing MacMillan for some reason. I wasn't certain why it was that he chose this moment to lose his nerve but I almost wished he'd snap out of it, strike at me. I was anxious to lash out at him, to take him down in his moment of triumph.

The moment crystallized around MacMillan, axe in hand, staring dumbly at the blade. It shattered in the sounds of death from far away.

The screams of battle seemed to resonate up through the wood of the chopping block. I could have sworn I heard the shouts and the clashes of metal on metal a second before anybody else. But they broke MacMillan out of his reverie.

He crossed the rallying ground and started talking to a soldier from his army. From my position I could see the soldier but just barely, indistinctly in the corner of my eye. I could tell that the soldier was injured, fatigued from battle. He couldn't even stand, falling to his knees before MacMillan. I couldn't hear what they were saying but as the soldier spoke, MacMillan's face broke into panic and despair. He commanded the soldier to his feet and left as quickly as he could. I wouldn't have a better chance.

With a shout of defiance I lashed out, striking the man who was holding me down with a perfect paralyzing blow. He fell away from me and I rolled to my feet.

The man who I'd struck was a big man, one of the dozen who'd beaten me in my cell. I remembered he'd been the one who'd beat me longest. I stomped on his throat and he made little gagging noises. I was free, but unarmed, and facing a whole army.

The men guarding the podium were the same twelve who had beat me in the cell. One had fallen. The rest were on the podium, already advancing on me with their clubs raised. I attacked the first ferociously, using the boxing and wrestling techniques taught to me by my uncle. These weren't as deadly or refined as the Nerve-Shocking Hands but they were perfect for dealing with thugs armed with clubs.

When the guard attacked, swinging his club in a big, clumsy side-swipe, I slipped around his arm, taking his back. I spun into a throw and, with the dazed guard on the ground before me I took his club from his unresisting fingers and went to work on the other ten.

They fought fiercely, but I wasn't trapped in a cell any more, and I was armed, and my life hung in the balance. I forgot pain, forgot fear. I was beyond fear of death. I expected to die in this field. I only hoped to take as many Confederation soldiers with me as possible. I threw down the podium guards, breaking arms, knees, wrists, skulls.

Only seconds had passed since I'd begun to fight back. The podium was empty but for the groaning, fallen, wounded but that wouldn't last. Already men were climbing onto the stage, readying weapons to bring me down.

I brandished the club and beckoned on the mob. "Come on, what are you waiting for?"

"I'm waiting for a pause in the fighting." I turned to look, prepared to face whoever was behind me. I saw her, standing on the roof of a tent, light as a feather, despite the huge sword in her hand. She had a strange little grin on her face and looked ready for battle.

"Savannah!"

She gave a little bow and leaped down from the tent, drifting to the stage like a feather. I had to learn how she did that trick sometime. She landed next to me and her black eyes flashed. She held her hands on her hips. The fact that she was holding Dave Boyd's greatsword in one of those hands made her even more impressive, and more disturbing than she would have been otherwise. "You didn't think I'd leave you behind, did you?"

The forces of the army recovered from the surprise of Savannah's arrival and began to close on us again. "Let's discuss it after we escape, eh?"

Savannah nodded curtly. She jumped toward the soldiers now on the podium, cutting down three with that huge sword before they even realized they were fighting.

I joined her, clubbing aside two soldiers who attempted to round behind her. From one I took a sword. It felt good to have a blade in my hand again. The swords of the Confederation weren't all that different from the swords I'd practised with.

"You take the thousand on the left." The flush of battle made me almost drunk on braggadocio and fear in equal measures.

"I'd rather just haul your ass out of here," Savannah said, but I could almost feel her nerves quivering with anticipation of the battle. When the soldiers closed with us again she gave a wild, feral scream and lashed out with unrestrained savagery against the soldiers.

Fighting side by side we were a terrible sight to behold. Our two styles, the two halves of a much greater whole, complemented each other, making the whole greater than the sum of its parts. We cut and stabbed and parried and dodged, back to back, and waited for our opening.

We fought and soldiers fell but there was an endless supply. As things were going we might fight, and die, standing on a hill of the dead, but die we would.

And then the soldiers fell back by inches, gave us the tiniest room to breathe. "Get ready," Savannah said. "On my mark take my hand, we're leaving." We were going to win through.

I failed to see that the soldiers had been slowly working Savannah and I around, maneuvering us into a position where we unknowingly had a tiny blind spot.

I turned to grab her wrist, and in that moment, I saw three soldiers, spears at the ready, approaching me from behind. The tips of their spears glittered in the early morning sunrise glow. I was struck by the bizarre notion that the tips of spears sparkling in the sunlight would probably be the last beautiful things I ever saw. My life would end soon, and it would end bloody. The men lunged forward, and I knew I could not evade them, could not bring my sword to bear.

CHAPTER 47

Savannah

WHEN I WOKE UP yesterday, I'd say that the number one item on my list of things to not do was to enter into an apocalyptic battle with the entire Confederation army. And yet, here I was, fighting the whole damn Confederation army. We'd killed a few dozen. I knew their faces in dying would come back to haunt me but I wasn't worrying about it in that moment. If we lived long enough for me to feel remorse then I'd have come out ahead.

Three spearmen had got past Kieran and were positioned to cut him down. They lunged at him and I threw myself on him at the last moment, knocking him to the ground as the spears stabbed over us. I used my momentum to roll back to my feet and chopped at the spears. My sword sheared through the shafts of all three spears like a knife through soft butter.

Nobody was more surprised than I was. I'd never seen such a thing. I guess Kieran might have been more surprised, he'd clearly thought he was about to die when he'd caught sight of the spears. He staggered to his feet and I grabbed hold of him, drawing my arm under his, carrying his weight, in part, on my shoulder.

Kite-Stepping carrying Kieran's weight was precisely as hard as I thought it would be. He tried to help but he'd had absolutely no training and, half the time, his ham-fisted attempts to lighten my load just made things harder.

I couldn't clear the soldiers. Instead I had to go over the tents north of the podium and circle left across the tent-tops. Arrows fell around us like deadly black raindrops.

Swords flailing to parry, we landed roughly on the ground halfway to the edge of the camp. The Wizard in Green was stirring up a hell of a commotion, and I thanked him much for that. The camp was all but empty. We stumbled, half dead and exhausted, back to the clearing.

Nobody followed us, but Dave Boyd was still there, sat under a tree. He looked up at us and stood, crossing the clearing with a limping gait that suggested that, for all of Kieran's abuse at the hands of Confederation, Boyd was still worse.

Kieran, for his part, collapsed to the ground, propping himself with the palms of his hands as he dry-heaved. "I miss the adrenaline already."

"You look like five miles of bad road. What happened to you?"

"The amenities at the Confederation camp left something to be desired." He always had to make some sort of a smart answer.

"You got beat bad, eh?"

"Just a little." He smiled weakly but made no move to stand.

"Well I'll be damned," Boyd said. "You actually did it. You beat the Wizard in Green."

"Wizard in Green? Did you meet the old man with the green robes?" Kieran asked. He was exhausted, beaten half to death and confused. I felt a searing feeling of pity and of tenderness. The tenderness was strange. So we'd been close, so we were friends, it was no reason for me to feel all mushy.

"You know him?"

"Yeah, I think so. He helped me find Old Saul, and assisted me in improving my understanding of the Triumvirate sword art."

Hah, now there was a thing. The Wizard in Green meets Kieran and he gives him a hand, helps him on his way, teaches him how to fight. He meets me and it's all, 'I'm going to take you for my slave.' There ain't no justice. "I'm glad you got on so well with him. Considering who he was, you're lucky he didn't cut your eyes out for looking at him funny."

"I wouldn't cut the eyes out of one of my legitimate martial descendants," said a clear voice from behind me. It was the Wizard in Green. He would show up just as I was talking about him. "It appears you have won our wager, miss."

"Savannah."

"Savannah, yes." He smiled warmly. That was almost as frightening as seeing him all intense. "I need not ask Boyd to rule. I concede defeat. The one who I went to rescue was not in the camp any longer. The Black Trillium has her. Or at least that fool Kyle MacMillan believes as much."

I was about to say something maybe just a little bit boastful when Kieran piped up. "You came for your daughter."

"Yes, I came for my daughter," he supplied. Kieran was absently nodding his head.

"The Black Trillium doesn't have her," Kieran said firmly. I wondered at his decisiveness on this topic.

Clearly the Wizard in Green did too. "Oh?"

"If any member of the Black Trillium got their hands on your daughter, no offense intended, but they'd kill her on the spot."

I was shocked that Kieran dared speak to the Wizard in Green this way. The ancient trickster would kill on a whim, if the stories were true. The terrifying man who was now my 'friend' just frowned sadly. "All the more reason I get her home, where she belongs." We all fell silent.

Eventually the Wizard spoke again. "I am always good to my word, where a wager is involved. Savannah, you may call me your friend. I owe you one favour, and one only. Remember, do not ask me to act against any of my students or family. This protection extends to Kieran here, my daughter, and, as much as it pains me to say it, Kyle MacMillan."

I opened my mouth to protest, but the Wizard cut me off with a gesture. "I understand that there is deep enmity between you two, MacMillan and my daughter. I will act to preserve her life, but I am oath-bound never to lift my hand knowingly against any student of my lineage. I must, in this conflict, stand aside.

"One thing is clear, though. Dave Boyd has not been a satisfactory guardian of the manual or my sword. I entrust these duties to you."

Boyd tossed me back the battered book.

I wasn't sure how far I'd trust the strange old man. I didn't suppose I had much choice.

"Where is Mr. Chamblais?" Kieran asked. "He should have been back by now. He wasn't captured..." Kieran trailed off, unwilling to complete the thought.

"We haven't any reason to think he came to harm," I said. "Maybe he was just delayed, diverted."

"I..." Kieran was clearly divided. "Want to get back home. I'm worried about uncle Stephen." And that was the other elephant in the room right there.

"I think this is where we must part," the Wizard said, "for the time being. Before I go though, three things." He rummaged around in his robes and produced two small disks of flexible plastic. "Each of you put one of these on your skin near a major vein. They will help mitigate the effects of fatigue and minor injuries."

"Wizardry?" I asked.

"Inasmuch as wizardry consists of knowing just a little bit more than everybody else, yes. This is medicine from before the Great Collapse. It was, at the time, a trifling little thing, but in this crude age it would seem nearly miraculous."

I took the disc from him. It was slick and yet sticky at the same time, clinging to my skin as if by static electricity. I slipped it on my neck and almost immediately the fatigue of the night began to fade. It really did seem miraculous.

"Second," the Wizard said, "I must remain behind, close at hand to the Confederation camp for the next day. I have business to conclude with Mr. MacMillan. However, should I see your Mr. Chamblais, I will let him know that you have returned home."

Kieran nodded. He looked more alert too, and while his bruises were still terrible, he seemed more mobile. He stood without pain.

"Third," the Wizard said, "the secret of your sword. Come close, Savannah." I walked over to him and leaned close. He whispered in my ear. "It is one of two swords I crafted myself. The other I carry. You may carry it, for now. By besting me you earned that right, but it is mine and when you no longer have need of a sword, I will take it back from you." The Wizard's own sword, forged in the first days of the Great Collapse. Well that was something, and no mistake. "Goodbye." He flourished his sword, bowed dramatically and faded into the woods like a ghost.

"Dave, are you coming with us?" I asked.

"Yeah, I'm coming. I'm surely not going to walk back to Broken Tower from the Scar in this state." He chuckled.

We mounted our horses and rode back to Kensington.

I almost wish we hadn't. When we arrived a pall of smoke hung over the district. The colourful paint on some of the brick houses was charred, a few buildings gutted, others torn down. People huddled in doorways, crying, holding loved ones with bloody wounds.

While we were away, Kensington had experienced a battle.

Kieran, wild eyed, kicked his horse into a frenzy. He rode to the front door of his home and charged inside, looking furiously about himself. There were no enemies in sight. He charged up to the stairs, Boyd and I close on his heels. We found nobody there.

"Uncle!" Kieran shouted, while Boyd and I called for Saul.

We began searching the house. We found Old Saul cowering in the basement. "Saul," Kieran said. "What happened?"

Saul rocked back and forth, banging his head lightly against a wall. He was muttering a single word under his breath, over and over again. I leaned in close to listen, putting my hand on his shoulder to calm him. I strained my hearing. The word Saul said, over and over as he cowered in the cellar: "Defiled."

CHAPTER 48

Kyle

WHEN FRIENDS FALL AWAY, when family fails you, when you reach that awful point that you realize you are alone, there is no help, no companionship, nobody you can rely on, all that remains is to decide your own fate. As I walked out of my father's tent, all but disinherited, I was lost in thought about how to do just that. I decided that, in the short term, the best thing to do would be to have a very strong drink.

I went looking for Brutus, he might be a mute and an idiot but at least he would be company. But even my stalwart bodyguard had abandoned me. I was entirely alone. I thought about the axe. Was he the traitor all along?

I returned to my own tent and drank myself into a sleepless abyss, feeling no comfort, feeling no peace, just the blackness of despair followed by the oblivion of unconsciousness. I awoke clear-headed and free of a hangover. There was a tingling sensation on my neck and when I slapped my hand there, it came away with a small plastic disc. The Wizard in Green was standing in my tent.

"Your day is drawing to a close." He was calm and collected, not the raging demon I'd confronted this morning. "I'd think you had better ways to spend it than drinking."

"What can I do? I've lost everything to the Black Trillium. They've defeated me." I sounded pathetic. If I'd been drunk I might not have cared that I sounded pathetic, but thanks to the Wizard in Green's pre-Collapse devilry I didn't even have that to fall back on.

"The Black Trillium doesn't have her, you idiot." The last words hurt. I'd been an idiot, I knew that, but I didn't enjoy being reminded. And I didn't like the insinuation that the Black Trillium wasn't to blame.

"Who else would have done that?"

"The Black Trillium would have killed her in her bed if they'd had the chance." His eyes flashed angrily as he said that. I didn't understand why it seemed like he was angry at me for that.

"If I could get her back..."

"So go do it. This self-pity is pathetic." His voice was loaded with scorn. He really did see me as pathetic. And I was pathetic. I was broken.

But I didn't have to spend my days moping uselessly around the camp. I was stripped of command. I could go where I would. But I'd have to speak to my father. If I left without even telling him I was certain I wouldn't like the consequences. I knew that much at least. "I will inform my father that I am leaving. I'll find her."

"Then I may spare your life." The way he said 'may' didn't fill me with much confidence.

I left my tent and crossed the short space to my father's command tent. It was buzzing with activity. As I walked in, he glanced at me and grunted, "Stopped wallowing in your tent like a child, eh? I won't have you underfoot here. You've proven yourself incapable of command."

I bit back my hatred and wrath. "I'm leaving the camp."

"Fine." His voice was flat, bored, as if what I did really didn't matter.

"I don't know how long I'll be away."

"Good."

I turned to leave and almost ran into a sergeant carrying a message. He looked panicked, and, with jittering nerves, he dropped the letter.

I picked it up, read it over out of habit.

To Kyle MacMillan,

I have Sophie of Seattle, your companion, in my power. Her life lies entirely at my discretion.

Bring your army to the University of Toronto and surrender it to me by the end of the week and she will be returned unharmed.

There was no signature but there was a single, three-petaled flower sketched in below the text, the mark of the Black Trillium. I felt my wrath boiling over but fought to tamp it down. I had a lead. I had a chance to rescue her.

My father snatched the letter from me. Everybody in the tent stopped to watch—they probably wanted to be able to tell their friends what indignity would be heaped on me next.

He read it over tersely and snorted out a laugh, an ugly chortling sort of sound. "What sort of a fool would make such a preposterous demand?"

"It's the Black Trillium." The Wizard in Green had been wrong.

"That hardly matters, the only objective we have here is to recover and execute Dave Boyd. Your... dalliances... with the remnants of those pathetic rebels have caused nothing but grief for this army." My father turned his back on me.

"We can capture them in their base and rescue Sophie."

"No."

"I'll go alone."

"Go ahead."

"Without the army to protect me they may very well capture me, kill me," I said, trying to call his bluff.

"I have other sons." He said it so matter-of-factly, tone flat, uncaring. He crumpled the ransom letter up and stuffed it into my jerkin pocket. And then he turned away from me, gathered his men around him. I was dismissed. I felt my fists clenching in rage, and stormed out of the tent, returning to my own.

The Wizard in Green was still waiting for me. "Well?"

"You were wrong. The Black Trillium has her. They are holding her ransom." I took the letter from my pocket, smoothed it as best I could, and handed it to the Wizard. He read it.

"And you will pay," he said when he finished.

I began putting on my armour. "They want my army. My father has taken it from me. I'll have to rescue her alone."

"Unacceptable."

"Then kill me now and never know where she is. This is all I have." I wasn't playing around with this guy anymore.

"If you go alone there is a good chance she will be killed."

I agreed with him, refusing the demands would be a very good way to get her killed. Of course I wouldn't actually surrender my army to the Black Trillium, they knew that too. They just expected that using Sophie as the bait in their trap would be irresistible. They were right.

"Take it up with my father."

"This is your responsibility. You took her for your own, you involved her in your ghastly political schemes. You brought her to Toronto. I will not take this up with your father." The more he spoke, the louder he shouted. I was sure he would kill me.

"I'll figure out something."

"You will pay the ransom for my daughter or I will end you, and your entire miserable family," the Wizard in Green said. And I believed him. I didn't really care about his threats to my family. I didn't have any great love for my brothers, they were the competition. As for my father...

I needed an army. He'd taken mine.

"I don't want to die," I said. "I'll find a way."

"I will be waiting at this university. I expect to see your army there within two days or I will return for you. And next time, we won't speak." He turned to leave, then stopped again. "And keep this in mind. Anybody can draw a black flower on a piece of paper. Your hatred for the Black Trillium is obvious. A cunning enemy might use that against you. Be wary—this may not be what it seems."

I poured myself a drink, but just one. I needed steady nerves for what I planned.

Night fell quickly. The pace of the camp slowed. I was ignored by all, forgotten by all. I dressed, not in armour, but in dark clothes, and secreted several knives, and a wire attached to two wood handles on my person.

I'd taken the tool from a potter years ago. I'd learned that it was as good for quiet killing as it was for cutting clay.

I snuck up to my father's tent. Brutus was still absent and my personal guard was all but wiped out thanks to the Black Trillium. My father's personal guard were spread out around the tent. They didn't pose a serious impediment, not after what I'd learned from Sophie.

Two were standing guard in front of the tent. Two more were patrolling the perimeter. I waited until they couldn't see each other and struck. The first fell easily. I was nearly spotted by the second as I struggled to drag the body into a shadowed nook but he glanced the wrong direction at the right moment and I escaped from sight long enough to silently dispatch of him too.

I decided not to chance the two men in front of my father's tent. Instead I took a page from the book of the assassins who'd kidnapped Sophie. I carefully and quietly cut a gap in the fabric of the tent. I knew my father well enough to know that he'd have no guards inside, not while he slept. He didn't like being 'watched over like a baby.'

My father was in bed, snoring contentedly. He didn't stir as I crossed the tent to where he lay. I pulled the garrote out of my pocket and positioned myself to strike. I looked down at the great Bart MacMillan as he slept, untroubled over having shamed me, beaten me, declared his army more valuable to him than his son's own life. My stomach hadn't been so full of butterflies since the moment of my first killing, when things in the world had still felt right.

I took the garrote in both hands, clenching, white-kuckled, the wooden handles in my fists, and I slipped it under his granite jaw. I tugged fast and hard, pulling the wire tight, cutting off his air. He awoke, tried to scream, but he had no breath.

"This was how you took the kingdom from Grandfather. Wasn't it?"

He couldn't answer. The wire was too tight. Making horrible croaking, choking noises my father thrashed around, desperately trying to escape the sting of the wire.

I let all my anger, all my pain, flow into my arms. I pulled the wire tighter, and it began to bite into his neck, digging so deep that it drew blood.

My father thrashed around the tent, trying to make a racket, trying to shake me off, but no matter how hard he struggled I found the strength to hold on, to choke the air from him.

His ears turned red, then purple, and then he went slack, sinking to the ground. I pulled the cord tighter. After five minutes that seemed like a decade I let the cord drop. I took my father's pulse, there was nothing. A collar of blood ringed his mangled neck. His face was bruised, almost black. His eyes had rolled up in his head, he was dead as a stone.

I spat on his corpse and dragged it back into bed, making sure to pull the covers high, over his wounded throat. I went out the front of the tent and buried a knife in the eye of each of the guards standing there before they could call out. It was a matter of a little work to hide the four bodies so that they wouldn't be found before daybreak but somehow I managed.

Then I went looking for the medic.

I found him in the make-shift hospital tent that had been erected to replace the one the Wizard in Green had burnt. I dragged him out of bed. "Come quick, I think my father is having a heart attack."

Now came the hard part.

I led the medic back to the tent and he asked where the guards were.

"Off looking for help, I daresay," I said. I saw him glance at a spatter of blood on the canvas of the tent. I smiled widely at him. He smiled back, nervously, and said nothing.

I led him to the bed, where my father lay. He drew back the covers. "I know what you want from me," he said.

I took one of my trusty knives out and said, "You're a smart man. And I'm sure you're very sad since it's clear that I dragged you out of bed for no reason. The heart attack must have claimed his life before you had the chance to save him."

"Yes," the doctor agreed. I saw a bead of sweat forming on his brow and he swallowed uncomfortably, painfully aware of how close to death he was. "He was dead when I arrived."

"From a heart attack, yes? Because that's such a cleaner option than saying that the Black Trillium invaded the camp again: killed my father, his guards and his chief medic before disappearing. I'm sure you would agree." I twisted the little knife a quarter turn without adding any pressure... yet.

"Clearly a heart attack."

I withdrew the knife, put it back in my boot. "As Kyle the First, third monarch of the Confederation, I will see you well rewarded for your efforts on behalf of my family."

"Thank you, Majesty."

"You may go."

He fled the tent at just a little faster than decorum would dictate when leaving the presence of a king.

I would have to see to the bodies before the night was out. There would be questions about four men abandoning their post, but I was sure I could explain that away as loyal retainers leaving to grieve the death of their king in private. The bodies were hidden well enough for now but once the camp got busy there were bound to be uncomfortable questions.

I tried to think of who was left in the camp that I could trust. Perhaps some of Messier's old men. I stripped the corpses of their uniforms and dressed them in some of my coarsest, most worn, riding clothes. The fits weren't perfect but they'd do. I hid the uniforms in my tent and then awoke the troops I'd chosen.

"There's been another attempt to raid the camp," I said to them. "I managed to deal with the attackers, but I am in enough trouble with my father without worrying him about that. I need some men who can handle a shovel and keep their mouths shut afterward. A big payday and a promotion for each of you if you do."

The soldiers agreed and helped me bury the bodies in a clearing in the woods near the camp. They held their tongues.

There was just one more thing to do before daybreak. I searched around the tent until I found it in a gilt box of dark stained rosewood under the bed. I drew back the lid and it lay there, blue and grey, gold and sparkling. The crown of Confederation. With trembling hands I lifted it from the box and seated it on my head.

It was cool and light on my brow.

CHAPTER 49

Kieran

"DEFILED," WAS ALL WE could get out of Old Saul for a long time. Savannah explained it was what he called the Broken. She didn't know why.

With a great deal of effort and a whole lot of time Savannah managed to calm Saul and we led him out of the basement. We sat him down in the garden and poured him a cup of peppermint tea. But for the stench of smoke hanging over everything like a pall we could have been enjoying a relaxing summer day.

"The Broken again?" Boyd asked. "Where are they all coming from? There isn't any way that they could be coming in from Cleveland. Somebody would have noticed."

"These ones are acting wrong," Savanah said. "They're organized. Hell, they are using fire."

"Don't the Broken do that?" I asked. I had heard stories about the Broken, of course, I'd even fought them once, but I didn't really know much about them beyond the stories.

"No," Savannah said. "They don't."

"The Duke had a problem with the Broken shortly after he came to Seattle," Boyd said. "He used fire to purge their hives."

"You mean the Wizard in Green, right?" Savannah asked.

"Yes."

"How did you know him?"

"I was a powerful lord in the south. I came from an impeccable family, heroes of the Collapse. He believed I could unify the counties of the Southlands and brought me to his court. He gave me gifts, the manual, a sword, gold."

"Did you fail?"

"Not entirely. I managed to unite a great deal of the Southlands. It's what bought MacMillan his peace since his failed invasion. But I was betrayed. Not everybody was as happy with a unified leadership as they'd led on when they thought it might be them at the top of the heap. There was a coup. Some of my most trusted men. I fled back to Seattle but Sophie had already left, looking for me. The Duke, the man you call the Wizard in Green, blamed me for her disappearance. As penance, the Duke told me to bring the manual to Old Saul. They had been friends long ago. He was the one who taught Saul Kite-Stepping. Saul had shared a few of his secrets of pre-Collapse medicine with him. He said I was an unworthy guardian, his old friend would be more fit. Then I saw Saul's condition..."

Old Saul didn't pay any mind. He sipped at his peppermint tea, huddled in on himself, shaking and twitching pitifully.

"He doesn't like the Broken," Savannah said. "He always hid from them when we were in the Cathedral of Broken Glass."

"That strikes me as strange," Boyd said.

"Why? I don't much like them either," I said. I was feeling a little bit left out of their conversation. I figured that the Triumvirate sword master was this wizard or duke or whatever he liked to be called, but I didn't know much about the west. I knew there was a place called the Duchy of Seattle and I knew the ruler was strange. Beyond that...

"Saul isn't a traveller," Boyd said. "The reason the Duke sent me to him was partly because he could depend on Saul being at the university."

At the mention of the university, Saul began trembling much more visibly. "No, nononononono, Shatterfield is dead. Died in a fire, no more Shatterfield, just Old Saul. I won't go back there. No, not even if the Defiled take me."

"There was a fire at the university. The herbalist who sold me the herbs mentioned it. He said he thought Saul had died there. Saul, what do the Broken have to do with the university?" I asked.

He hid his head behind his arms and averted his eyes. "No, can't go there. It's dark, empty."

"The university?"

Saul just hunched in on himself, shaking like a leaf and muttering indistinctly.

"Lay off him, Kieran," Savannah said.

"I'm not trying to push him," I said, feeling a bit defensive. "But if he knows where my uncle is..."

"Gone, gone, the Broken took him into dark places where Old Saul can't go, he was there once, but Shatterfield is gone, dead, just Old Saul left." Saul spoke almost fiercely, he was shaking even worse, looked like he was on the edge of a seizure.

I wanted to say 'I didn't do it,' but that would have sounded childish. Shatterfield was melting down over uncle Stephen. What had happened? "It's going to be OK," I tried but it had no effect. I guess I didn't sound that convincing. Savannah pulled Saul into a gentle hug and tried to calm his shaking. She gave me a look, equal parts understanding, frustration and sadness.

"Back off of Saul. He's fragile." Boyd sounded very hostile. Savannah rolled her eyes at him but she didn't gainsay him.

"If you have a better way of figuring out what went on," I said.

"Have you tried talking to anybody on the street?"

I felt really stupid. As the peacekeeper it's what I should have been doing anyway. As a member of the Black Trillium too. Instead I'd holed up in here and... and... how dare he be right! It made my blood boil. "You're probably right," I admitted.

"Both of you go," Savannah said, heaping irritation into her tone. "I'll look after Old Saul."

"I'm not sure I'll have the stamina to wander the streets that long," Boyd said. "But if this kid can't be trusted I suppose I'll have to go."

I didn't relish spending time walking around Kensington in ashes with this asshole but there was nothing to be gained by taking his bait. "Fine. Coming?"

We hit the streets.

"What's your problem with me?" I asked Boyd as we left.

"You're Trillium, right?"

"Yeah."

"So if your order would have just allied with me to begin with, none of this would have ever happened."

"That's not my fault."

"Perhaps not. But perhaps you should think about that anyway."

The house next to mine had fire damage, the house beside it was gutted by the fire. We looked through the house but there were no survivors. The owner of the burnt-out house had been an old woman with three grandchildren. We found their charred remains huddled together near the rear door.

I scowled down at the blackened things and my heart filled with rage.

"You should have been there for these people. Instead you were playing at rebellion."

I wheeled on him, decked the older man in the face. "I risked my life rescuing you," I said, hands up, ready for a return blow that never came. "I almost died! You were almost dead too, and who knows what would have happened if we hadn't come for you."

"You had a responsibility to these people. Whatever romantic notions you had of heroism, you should have been here instead."

"Yeah, whatever." I walked out of the ash-filled ruin, but his words stung; perhaps because I was telling myself the same thing.

The next house actually still had people inside. They were cowering in the basement and were almost in as much of a state as Shatterfield had been. None of them were injured, but every single member of the family, father, mother, and flock of small children alike, had the same terrified expression in their eyes, a psychic wound rather than a physical one.

"It's OK," I said. "The Broken are gone." By degrees I coaxed them out of their basement and got them to open up to me.

The Broken had come from within Kensington, or from somewhere west of the district, somewhere in Queenwest they speculated.

They hadn't seen where the Broken had carried uncle Stephen. They hid as soon as the trouble began.

"It's alright. You did the right thing." I was thinking, 'cowards,' but I'd never say it. Boyd kept his mouth shut. I'd given him a fat lip and he looked surly.

Bit by bit we traced the path the Broken took back to the source. Eventually we came across a boy, huddled under some crates in an alley. He said he'd seen the Broken come out of a house within the district, not from west of it.

"Can you show us where?" I asked.

"Yeah, I can show you. But my leg ain't working too good on account of how I twisted my ankle running from the monsters." Monsters, as good a word as any for the Broken, I supposed.

Boyd grunted. "They're only people." Which was an odd thing to say; the Broken hardly seemed like people. They didn't act like people either.

"They didn't seem like people," the boy said, echoing my own thoughts.

"They've had everything taken away from themselves, even their sense of who they are."

I almost liked him in that moment.

Holding the boy between us, we carried him out of the alley. "Turn left."

We turned left, south of Augusta, back into the heart of Kensington. "Are you sure it's this way?" I asked.

"If you think you know better you can find them Broken on your own."

"It's fine. We believe you."

"Alright, now head on that way for a ways." We were walking right toward home. I doubted the kid, I really did. But he said he'd seen where the Broken came from. We had to at least check it out.

"OK, now stop. It's one of these places around here." He wrinkled his brow up in concentration. I recognized the houses. I'd been here, recently. When he pointed to the house, with the door hanging open like a gaping, cavernous maw, I wasn't surprised.

"It's that one."

The house was an ordinary one. It didn't appear to have been seriously damaged in the fighting. There was a foreboding sort of emptiness to it, but it wasn't strange the house was empty. I knew precisely why there wasn't anybody at home here.

Beside the door, a discreet wooden plaque bore the legend: "Fletter-Daish, Doctor," adorned by a scarlet red staff entwined with venomous snakes.

CHAPTER 50

Savannah

DAVE AND KIERAN WERE gone a long time before I began to get nervous. "Where are they?" I asked Saul.

"Gone, gone, dead and dust." His answer didn't ease my mind at all.

"Do you know anything about the Broken, Saul?" I hated to do it. He was worse than ever since the attack, but if he knew something, if Kieran and Dave were in danger... I didn't think I could stand it. I had just about taken as much as I could from Trana. Perhaps it was time to move on. No. If I left now it would be running. No running, absolutely no more. I'd just have to stick it out until we'd dealt with the situation here, if we ever did. An army of Confederation troops, the Broken coming into the city. I had a sinking suspicion that we were all going to die in this city, and not in the ninety years old, surrounded by grandchildren sort of way.

"Know where they came from." He was better, calmer when it was just me around. He trusted 'Little Leiurus' in a way that he didn't trust even Dave.

"Saul, I know it's frightening but I need to know where they came from."

"Fire and ash and things man was never meant to know."

Who could make heads or tails out of that?

"I don't understand, Saul." The fear I felt if Kieran never came back, if Dave vanished, blended with the apprehension of what would happen if they came back and found nothing.

"Old Saul can't say the name of the place. It was Shatterfield's place."

I remembered Dave talking about how the Wizard in Green expected Old Saul to be at the university. And Kieran said that Saul had been at the university during a fire. I needed to find Kieran and Dave. "Saul," I said, trying not to sound too nervous, trying not to panic him. "I need to go out for a few minutes. Will you be OK if I leave you alone?"

Saul nodded weakly.

"Thank you." I walked to the front door, careful not to start sprinting there. I was reaching for the doorknob when I heard a click and the door swung open.

Startled, I stepped back from the door and drew the Wizard's sword. I still hadn't fully grasped what that really meant, but I expected, at the very least, I hadn't seen the last of the Wizard in Green.

Framed in the open door was Mr. Chamblais. He had dozens of little cuts and scratches and he did not look happy. "*Merd.*" I might not know how to speak the damn language but I could tell a good curse when I heard it.

"And it's nice to see you too, Mr. Chamblais," I said, loading irony onto my words.

"I'm sorry. I just didn't expect to be put at sword point in this house. I've had a long night."

"You and me both." I sheathed the sword again. "Come in."

"Did you and Kieran get out alright?"

"Eventually. But only just."

"Oh?" He was trying to hold things together, keep his tone conversational. I was trying to do the same. I wondered which one of us would crack first.

"Kieran almost got his head chopped off. But we managed to escape in time to get back here and find his uncle missing, the neighbourhood put to the torch." I sounded pissed off with him. I know I did. I just was overwhelmed. I needed to take it out on somebody. "And where were you?"

"After that awful woman started screaming I managed to escape by fighting my way to the northern edge of the camp and disappearing into the corn fields. It took me the entire night to shake off my pursuers. By the time I returned to the clearing, you were gone, with my horse I might add."

Oh yeah, hadn't really thought that through too well. "We needed something for Dave to ride and we weren't even sure if you made it out alive."

"It is nothing. What is the situation here?"

I led him back to the courtyard, talking as I went. "The Broken attacked Kensington. They took Kieran's uncle, burnt a bunch of houses, scared a lot of people. Kieran and Dave are out investigating now."

"I need to speak to Kieran and Boyd both immediately."

I heard the sound of the door opening, reached for my sword again, stopped myself until I saw who was coming through. "Looks like you're in luck, here they are now."

"Mr. Chambais," Kieran said, surprised. "I'm so glad you are alright."

"I hear you had a misadventure or two of your own," Mr. Chamblais said.

"I think we need to talk, about the Three Brothers."

"I saw Brutus in the Confederation camp. But now isn't the time." He looked to Dave Boyd. "You have been playing both sides against each other for a long time Mr. Boyd, but you once asked for an alliance with the Black Trillium. Were you sincere?"

"The last time I made that offer it didn't go so well for me," Boyd said. "I take it that means you're also Black Trillium."

"Well?"

"I just want to protect Broken Tower," Dave said. "It's my home."

"Would you step down from your throne, let the people you wish to protect forge their own destiny?" Mr. Chamblais asked.

I could tell a lot hinged on what Dave said next. You could have cut the tension with a knife. "Yes, I seem to have a habit of being kicked off of thrones. Might as well at least leave things for the better for once." He sighed. He looked so tired. The poor man had been kicked around the entire continent, always thinking he could make something better, never quite managing it. And everywhere he went all he collected for his effort was scars. His time in Broken Tower had nearly killed him. I felt a surge of sympathy for him.

"Confederation soldiers are marching into Trana. All two thousand of them. We need every person with cause to fight the Confederation out in the streets and armed."

I glanced at Kieran.

His face was pale but he didn't look surprised. "Looks like we stirred up the hornets' nest."

"What precisely did you do?" Mr. Chamblais asked.

"Escaped from an execution platform in the centre of the camp, killed a few dozen soldiers on our way out," I said. "But it wasn't any running through a corn field."

Mr. Chamblais laughed harshly. "No, running through a corn field doesn't generally stir up an army for immediate assault. Oh well. It would have happened eventually. It's just unfortunate it happened now."

"How much time do I have to muster soldiers?" Boyd asked.

"Not long. The chances are good that they've reached the viaduct by now." That put them only a couple hours away.

"I'll open the armouries at the dome now."

"So," I said to Kieran. "Black Trillium, eh?"

"I couldn't tell you," he said, "not without..."

"I kind of figured it out anyway. Besides, we're all rebels now."

"Can we discuss this later?" Mr. Chamblais asked. "We have to prepare the defences."

"We've got more pressing problems than the Confederation army," Kieran said. "You should come with us: see what we found."

"If it's all the same to you," Dave said, "I'll leave the show and tell to you and head back to Broken Tower. I won't be much good in a fight, but at least I can get the soldiers organized if I leave now." He shot Kieran a dirty look. I noticed he had a fat lip. I'd have to have words with Kieran about hitting my friends at some point.

"My people will be along shortly," Mr. Chamblais said. "They will ask about planting flowers in steel."

"Code words, wonderful," Dave said sarcastically as he hustled out.

"What did you find, Kieran?" Mr. Chamblais asked.

"Something terrible. Follow me."

We went back into the street and hurried past the burnt-out ruin of nearby houses. Kieran averted his eyes and I guessed he knew what lay in some of those houses. We rounded the corner and ended up in front of Dr. Fletter-Daish's house.

"Is it in there? What did you find?" I really wanted to know.

"The way the Broken got into Kensington," Kieran said.

This I had to see.

We went into the house and Kieran led the way to the basement. Mr. Chamblais and I both drew our swords. I was a bit surprised that Kieran did not.

The stone walls of the basement were damp with slime, mold, condensation and misuse. I was a bit shocked that Dr. Fletter-Daish would have kept his home in such awful condition. It was dark down there, so Kieran lit a candle. In the gleam of the weak light I almost wished he hadn't.

There was a gaping hole in the wall, burrowing like the tunnel of a monstrous worm through the core of the city.

"They came in through this hole?" Mr. Chamblais asked. "You are sure?"

"And they came for uncle Stephen," Kieran said.

"But that means..."

Oh, come on, did I have to say it? I knew what they were thinking.

"Dr. Fletter-Daish has something to do with the Broken attacks," Kieran said.

"Where does the tunnel lead?" Mr. Chamblais asked.

"Sewers, old tunnels, some of the blackest parts of the Long Dark."

"So they could have come from anywhere." Mr. Chamblais seemed really upset by this. Time for me to be helpful.

"They came from the university," I said as nonchalantly as I could standing before this mouth to the underworld.

"What?" Kieran and Mr. Chamblais asked in unison.

"I managed to work it out from what Old Saul told me."

"But if the doctor is working with the Confederation, they will have a second army close at hand when they attack," Mr. Chamblais said.

Kieran was furious. The scowl on his face was frightening. "If the doctor was behind the Broken then he set up the whole thing. But if he was the one poisoning uncle Stephen why did he send me for Old Saul to cure him?"

"He wants Shatterfield back," said a weak voice from behind us. I wheeled around. Old Saul was standing in the stairway, trembling and twitching and looking absolutely miserable.

"What do you mean, Saul?" I asked.

"He always wants Shatterfield back, but it's his fault Shatterfield died. He can't get him back. Not ever."

"Saul," I said. "He has Kieran's uncle."

Saul slumped against the wall, whatever willpower had kept him upright so close to the cause of his terror exhausted. "Can't go there. Just can't. Not ever."

"We have to get my uncle back," Kieran said.

"What about the Confederation?" Mr. Chamblais asked.

"Somehow the doctor is controlling the Broken," I said. "If the Confederation has an army of berserkers at their beck and call your fight is going to be an awfully short one."

"I am just one man," Kieran said. "I can't do much against an army, but alone I can get into the university, try to rescue uncle Stephen, try to figure out what the doctor is up to."

"No," I said.

"Savannah. I need to do this."

"I know, but you aren't going alone."

CHAPTER 51

Kyle

I HAD TO MOVE quickly to consolidate my army after the deed was done. My father had an elite unit of one hundred men—warriors who would have died a thousand deaths for him, some of the greatest swords in the Confederation. I'd been lucky that he'd thought himself secure in the center of camp and only posted a few of them as guards. He'd been over-confident. It had been his downfall. Still, as much as it might bother me, those hundred men had to go.

My first act as monarch of the Confederation was to have all one hundred of them killed in their sleep, throats slit, bodies tossed into the stripped corn fields, food for the crows.

After that I called together the officers I believed I could trust. With Marc and Oswald dead, Brutus missing, Sophie taken and my father's best generals in command of the army at Fredericton I had slim pickings to choose from, but I was able to assemble a war council by the time day broke.

"The Black Trillium holds Trana," I told them. "Forget what you think you know about the situation here, they are our true enemy."

There was a lot of grumbling around the table at that declaration but the officers knew well enough which way the wind was blowing. The presence of my own most loyal knights (the same men from Messier's units, now promoted and provided horses and armour as per my promise for their silence) around the tent sent a clear message to any halfway intelligent officer who survived the night of knives. Kyle MacMillan ruled here.

"They have taken my fiancee hostage," I said. "And they have demanded we surrender to them at a district called the 'University of Toronto.'"

"University of Toronto?" asked Colonel MacPherson. The Colonel was of middling skill as a commander but his family was related by blood to my own. He was sweating right now. He had been close to my father and, if not for his rank, he probably wouldn't have survived the night. He was aware that if he wanted to stay alive he'd have to prove both loyal and useful.

"Some archaic spelling of Trana," I said dismissively.

"Surely, Your Majesty," MacPherson said. I liked being called 'Your Majesty,' it had a nice ring. "We aren't going to do it."

"To the contrary, we are going to march straight into this trap." I said. More grumbling. "But not without an ace up our sleeves."

I had a small dish of black powder on the table in front of me. I took a long candle and dipped the flame into the volatile powder. The resulting conflagration was sufficient to shock several of the more nervous officers out of their seats.

"We have fifty pounds of this black powder. Sophie instructed me in its production before she was taken and I have been having it made ever since. We will be putting the powder on wagons and placing them at strategic positions on the battlefield. When the time comes, we will use it to throw our enemy into confusion."

"We are walking into a trap," MacPherson said.

"Yes, but we are doing so with our eyes open. I have faith in my army to take the day."

We broke soon after and set about marching on Trana.

We met no resistance for a long time. Word had gone ahead of our coming and the civilians had made themselves scarce. Three Forks was all but empty and we crossed the viaduct unhindered. I knew that the university district was immediately east of downtown. The northern boundary of both districts was a wide street called 'Blur Street.' Blur had tall towers in very poor repair to the north, but the southern side of the street changed, a hodge-podge of times and places, sometimes even represented in a single building, added to and expanded over time into a chimerical and monstrous combination of limestone, steel, plastic and other, stranger materials.

My hand came to rest on the pommel of my new sword. It had been my father's, but he didn't need it anymore. I had a pressing need for a good blade.

We'd just passed the chimera building when the ambush was sprung.

I'd half been expecting it for some time. If we expected violence at the university it made sense for the Black Trillium to spring it on us sooner.

They surged out of a narrow valley between two large buildings to the south of us. Archers rained down arrows on our heads.

At the lead of the infantry were Dave Boyd and a man with wild eyes and matted hair. He matched the description of one of the warriors who raided the camp the night Sophie went missing. Boyd looked haggard and misused, but he had fresh bandages around his wound and a sword in his hand. Even injured to the brink of death he was a more lethal killer than a dozen soldiers.

My men were ready for the ambush. The carts, loaded with black powder, were sent rolling into the valley. Sophie had taught me how to make fuses, twisting together black powder and cloth, and these long fuses were uncoiled as the wagons rolled.

My cavalry was next to useless in the city-canyon of towers and monoliths between downtown and uptown and so they'd dismounted and were using their large jousting shields to shelter themselves and my infantry from arrows.

The initial rush of the Black Trillium had been damaging. My left flank hadn't responded well, lacking strong commanding officers was a problem.

I saw MacPherson fall under the sword of the wild-man, and realized he was using the Triumvirate sword art. "Is there anyone who hasn't learned that damn sword style?" I muttered and gave the signal for the fuses to be lit, the black powder being detonated.

Nothing happened.

I gave the signal a second time.

Still nothing.

I rode toward the wagons and discovered why my explosives hadn't detonated. "Brutus," I shouted. "What are you doing? This is treason!"

His bloody axes had shattered all of the barrels and taken the heads off of five of my guards.

"You should have gone home," Brutus said. He could talk? My mind reeled with the extent of his deception. "I didn't want to do this."

He charged at me, axes raised. I ducked below his axe swing and executed 'Sheathing the Drawn Blade in Flesh,' the same technique that had taken the hand of the last axe-wielding assassin to try for my life.

So it had been Brutus all along. I should have known. All those times I called him an idiot to his face. He must have been laughing at me.

He was much more skillful than the last assassin. I didn't take his hand. Instead the butt of his axe crashed down on my hand. I felt one of my fingers break under the force of the blow but I held onto my sword.

The wild-man arrived, cutting a swath through my men like a salmon swimming against the tide. "Brutus, I thought you'd gone over to the Confederation. Whose side are you on?"

"I think I'm on the side of peace," Brutus said. "But for the moment that side appears to be yours."

"Is this the day we avenge Master Arroyo?"

I tried to use the distraction to stab Brutus, but he seemed perfectly capable of fighting and talking at the same time. He slapped my sword aside with contemptuous ease and elbowed me in the jaw. I reeled, saw stars, fell backward into the shattered ruins of the gunpowder barrels. The black powder had an acrid scent.

"Young Master MacMillan has already done the deed for us. Bart MacMillan died last night. You know it was him, not his father, who did the deed."

"Then all that remains now is to free the Confederation from tyranny," the wild man said.

"That struggle is yours. All I ever wanted was peace. When this battle ends, I intend to disappear."

"I'm sorry to hear that, my brother."

My head was clearing enough to try standing. The black powder clung to me like explosive sand. I shook my head, fumbled in my pockets.

I had flint and steel. I could destroy the traitor and his 'brother' in one blow. The fact that the blow would kill me too was a problem, surely, but they had me under their power. I was sure I was a dead man anyway.

They were busy fighting my guards, killing them, sadly. But, for the moment, they had taken their eyes off me.

I touched the flint to the steel, prepared to make the last, fatal spark.

And then from the east came the scream from a hundred mouths.

"The Broken!"

I dropped the flint and steel, picked up my sword again, and, just like Brutus and his 'brother,' turned to look to the east.

A frothing horde of the twisted sub-humans was charging from behind our army, out of the entrances to the Long Dark that riddled the buildings of Blur Street like the chambers of a hornets' nest.

Unarmed, without armour, without tactics, but entirely fearless, the Broken attacked indiscriminately.

Everybody was stunned by the brutality of the attack. They'd taken both armies' flank and the battle had become a free-for all. The Broken outnumbered us, there seemed to be Broken without end, hundreds upon hundreds of fearless killers.

Brutus had his back to me, preparing for the onslaught. I had a chance to do one important thing before I was trampled under an endless wave of nightmares.

My sword slid between his ribs with sickening ease. "No!" shouted the stranger, but he was far too late to stop me.

The sword burst out of Brutus's chest. He grabbed at the blade and roared in pain. He twisted, jerking the sword from my hands and spun away from me.

Disarmed, I was sure he'd make me join him in death. But he didn't. He just staggered away a few paces, still standing despite the mortal wound. Then the Broken swarmed our position, knocking Brutus down and crushing him under their feet. I saw the life fade from his eyes and I knew I'd ended the traitor.

The wild-man reached for me, cutting through a dozen Broken in his frenzy to face me, but he fell too, buried under countless clutching hands. I could hear him roaring in defiance, but I couldn't see him in the middle of the nihilistic frenzy.

A naked, filthy man, with rotting teeth and open sores on his face reached for me with dirt-caked hands that looked like talons. His eyes glowed sickly green. I tried to fend him off but I didn't have my sword and my boxing skills were no match for the numbers of Broken who crowded around me, pulling me to the ground. I felt a bare foot stepping on my head, felt the crushing hardness of the street against my cheek, and everything went black.

CHAPTER 52

Kieran

I FELT A PANG of shame as Mr. Chamblais set out to do battle with Confederation. They outnumbered us, and open battle had never been a good idea. That was why we had limited ourselves to little raids and surgical strikes before.

We needed every member of the Black Trillium and every ally we could muster too, otherwise we'd never have let Boyd in on the secret of our affiliation. And yet, I needed to rescue uncle Stephen, I needed to unravel what game Dr. Fletter-Daish was playing, how he was controlling the Broken. If I did not, it might not matter how many warriors were holding the line.

"You ready to do this?" Savannah asked, seeing the frown on my face, guessing at my reservations.

"Yeah," I said. "Just worried about Mr. Chamblais."

"Worry about us a little too." Savannah punched me lightly on the shoulder. "From the way you tell it, people don't come out of the university."

"We aren't just anybody. We'll be fine." But I wished I felt as confident as I'd tried to sound.

"Yeah. We got out of the Confederation camp, didn't we? It's not like the university can be much worse. After all, what is it? Just a big old ruined school right?"

"Right." I thought back to an old school book with a formula in it for a powder that could destroy buildings, and I felt uneasy. That was a parlour trick in the time before the Collapse. I was terrified about what horrible secrets a university might hold.

We set out, subdued and worried, through a Kensington transformed by fear into a very different place. Black soot marks marred the colourful murals and brownish stains of drying blood adorned the concrete walkways. The sickening scents of ash and death still lingered in the air.

I'd always loved my home, but just that once, I was happy to be leaving, even if I was going somewhere far worse.

We walked north up the middle of the divided street, feet finding the cracks where the metal rails had been once, and spoke little as we walked north to the university, possibly to our deaths. There was nobody in the street south of the roundabout, but there was a single man sitting on the step of the hulking building that sat in the overhang, an ancient limestone affair, missing the roof and overgrown with ivy so heavily that the shape of the building beneath was occluded.

We almost missed him, his robes were very nearly the same green as the ivy. "Look," Savannah said. "It's the Wizard in Green."

I guess calling him a wizard was close enough to the truth at that. He seemed to be everywhere and, from what Savannah told me, to be capable of just about anything.

"You said he's your friend now, right?" I asked in hushed tones.

"What are you worried about? You're part of his lineage, he's sworn oaths not to hurt you." I guess she felt bitter that the Wizard saw me as a member of his lineage, but had only agreed not to enslave her because she'd beaten him in a bet.

"I'm not worried."

Savannah didn't look like she was buying into my bullshit.

"Are you two going to come over and greet me or do I have to wait here until I'm as covered in ivy as the building behind me?" the Wizard asked, his voice terribly loud and clear in the silence of the day.

"We're coming over," Savannah said. "But, as happy as we are to see a friendly face," I hoped the Wizard didn't pick up on the sarcasm she heaped all over that statement, "we couldn't help but wonder what brought you here."

"I came to recover my daughter. I don't trust MacMillan to do the job without mucking it up." I wouldn't have trusted MacMillan to clean the shit off my boots so I could see his point. I found myself resisting the urge to nod my head.

"Is she in there?" Savannah asked with her face contorted into a look of absolute concentration.

"No. I saw the two of you coming up the road here, and decided to wait on you. I am guessing you need to get into the university too."

"How did you know that?"

"Because I know for a fact that the Black Trillium didn't take my daughter, whatever that fool of a king might think." He was looking right at me as he said that.

So Kyle MacMillan was king now. An interesting turn of events, surely, but hardly important just now.

"How did that lead you to the conclusion we needed to get into the university?" I asked, trying hard to sound polite.

"Whoever it is who took my daughter took pains to implicate the Black Trillium, to bring MacMillan and his army here. I'd expect that if they were trying to manoeuvre one army here, in a town with two armies that might oppose him..." The Wizard was certainly no slouch.

"He's controlling the Broken."

"Is he now? I've long wished that particular horror of the old world could be ended once and for all. Alas, that may prove difficult. But it is getting hot, let's walk as we talk."

The three of us set out together to the north, heading for the Harbord gate to the university, the only known entryway in the warren of boarded-up buildings and walled-in roads.

"How much do you know about the Great Collapse?" he asked.

"Wars, famines, plagues, and the cities falling." It was from the Under-God's prayer and I didn't say it lightly.

"A fair enough assessment, if a bit simple." I knew he was powerful. I tried very hard not to act offended at being called 'simple.' Don't poke sleeping bears and all. Savannah, for her part, tried very hard not to laugh at the stupid expression on my face. I think I was slightly more successful than she was.

"A few scholars survived the Great Collapse. Their families passed down the knowledge of the ancient world. They formed enclaves where the old ways were remembered—Seattle, Toronto, Cleveland."

"Where the Broken came from," Savannah said.

"In a way. The Broken were created in Toronto during the Collapse. The technology was unleashed on Cleveland. The enclave there fell eventually to them."

The thought that the Broken came from Trana originally sickened me. You think of atrocities as things that happen in far off places—to somebody else, somewhere else. Then I remembered the garrison and the terrors I saw there. And I couldn't help but think what some people, people from here, people who might be my neighbours, might do with a weapon like the Broken. "And now they're being used here," I said, repressing the urge to be sick.

"You do realize that the Broken are just sick people."

I thought back to all the Broken I killed and felt like my stomach had filled with molten lead. I might have been acting in self-defence, they might have been people perverted to such a degree that any humanity left in them was smothered under the weight of the horrors they'd perpetrated, but had I ever stopped to think of that before I killed one?

I glanced at Savannah and she didn't look much happier.

"Perhaps you didn't realize that." The Wizard looked a bit taken aback but forged on ahead. "Illness may be too weak a word. They're warped, given thicker skin, claws, the ability to see in darkness. They're made aggressive beyond reason. But, like any weapon, they can be controlled, if you know the trick. In my youth somebody attempted to destroy Seattle with the Broken. It was clear the secret of their creation and control lived on and I looked to Trana."

"Looks like you slipped up."

"I had an ally here, a scientist who was looking for a way to cure the Broken."

I could take a wild guess what name was going to pop up. "Saul Shatterfield."

"Yes," the Wizard said, smiling. "But the last message I ever got from him was warning that he feared that others at the university were researching the Broken, changing them. He seemed quite worried. When Boyd was deposed after his attempt to unify the Southlands, I sent him here with the sword and the manual to protect him."

"Why send only half the manual?" Savannah asked.

"Because the entirety of the Triumvirate sword art was not meant for anybody but me."

"That's why you held back the third part from everybody," she said.

"I didn't precisely. Though it surprises me you even ascertained there was a third part. Ah, but each of you learned different halves of the art. You must have noticed the little something missing. Yes, there was a third part to the Triumvirate sword art, as one could guess from the name. I sent it to Saul too, in a sealed envelope. I never told Boyd what was in it."

"Why did it take you so long to follow up on this?" I was furious with him. He'd known that we were sitting on top of an ancient weapon from the time when the whole world burnt and he'd done nothing.

"I was looking for my daughter. I forbade her from studying the Triumvirate sword art. It was her mother's dying wish that she be raised to be a lady, not an adventurer, and I intended to honour it. But she went behind my back and stole the half of the manual I'd kept from my library."

"When she mastered the first half she came out here looking for the rest," Savannah said.

"Yes." The Wizard's eyes flashed with anger. "She was following Boyd. She knew he'd brought the manual with him."

"You came all the way here for her?" I asked.

"She is my only reminder of her dead mother. Her place is at my side." There was a finality to the Wizard's words. I felt it would be awkward to bring up the way she'd been involved in trying to get Savannah and I captured, tortured and killed.

We had come to the Harbord gate.

Standing between the facade of the Glass Palace to the north and the squat concrete building to the south was a group of twenty people. Their faces were dirty. They had sores and a certain vacant expression in their eyes which glowed with green hate.

When they saw us, they came to us, slowly, patiently.

Savannah reached for her sword, but the Wizard stayed her hand. "Not yet, I think."

The gang of Broken crowded in around us and groping hands reached for arms, shoulders. They gripped hard, but not cruelly so. I felt a little shove on my back. They were leading us into the university.

"I don't like this," Savannah said angrily.

"Think of them as the welcoming committee," the Wizard said.

"Some welcome," I said with minimal snark and, with those words, we entered the university that no living soul ever left.

CHAPTER 53

Savannah

I COULD SMELL THE stench of the Broken's breath on the air. I wanted to retch, but I didn't want to be the one that freaked out first. I swallowed back the bile I felt rising in my throat and walked along with the Broken into the university.

I'd expected hell on earth. I had expected pits full of corpses, mountains of skulls, ash-black buildings. Instead it was all green lawns and well-kept buildings. There was a lot of ivy crawling over all the buildings, like whole buildings covered in the stuff everywhere I looked. Aside from the mob of Broken it was almost pretty, tranquil.

That combination of sweet and sour smells, flowers and the stink of sick people, was nearly enough to make me toss my cookies and, for a second time in as many minutes, I had to bite back the urge to vomit.

I bit my lip and kept my mouth shut, tried to breathe shallowly, to avoid taking in too much of the stink all at once. Kieran and the Wizard were making similar faces, although, unsurprisingly, the Wizard in Green was handling himself better than either Kieran or I; the show-off.

The Broken led us past gardens and crumbling houses until we came across a veritable mountain of green. It loomed up into the sky, far taller than any building nearby. Under the dense canopy of green, I could barely make out grey concrete walls. The building loomed, bulky and brutal, made of strange angles. Whoever designed it had ventured to create a mountain for a building, and they had been successful. What few windows the building had were high and narrow, black slits peeking out from behind the dense growths of ivy that clung to every surface.

"What is that place?" I asked, trying hard to keep the wonder out of my voice. I'd seen many towers in Trana and yet this building, though not as tall as the towers to the south, was far more terrible.

"A library, if I'm not off my guess," the Wizard in Green said.

"Looks like a fortress to me," Kieran said gruffly.

"Libraries often did." The Wizard offered no sort of explanation for what that might mean.

The Broken began shoving us gently but insistently up the steps towards a single door clear of the masses of ivy. This door, a heavy wood one, bound with bands of blackened steel or iron, seemed out of place on the building. Certainly the door had the same sort of brutal grandiosity to it that the building, library, whatever it was, did, but it seemed much more modern—not a product of a forgotten age.

"Do we have to go in there?" I asked, feeling out of ease in the shadow of the ancient building.

"No, we can just fight our way through the gang of Broken and escape back to Kensington again," Kieran said sharply.

I thought about sniping back at him to repay his sarcasm, but really, it wouldn't help. I knew that, so I kept my snark to myself and walked into the building.

The mountain was hollow. A whole tower, a single cylinder of concrete rising into the sky. Rings of balconies rose up around the central atrium. I looked up and the ceiling was nearly lost in the gloom. I'd never seen such a massive single room.

I was awe-struck. If not for the Broken prodding me on, I'd have probably stood in the doorway all day, just taking in the sights.

I think the most awesome sight, though, were all the books. Each balcony was stacked high with them, shelves and shelves of books, old and crumbling.

I'd seen books. My family had owned an ancient, out of date almanac. It's what I'd learned my letters on.

"So many books!" Kieran said. I guess he felt the same as I did.

"Almost as great as my own collection," the Wizard in Green bragged, but I didn't really believe him. The idea that there were enough books in the world for two such collections defied belief.

The Broken led us through a set of doors, away from the mesmerizing sight of all the books, and into a narrow concrete shaft with a long flight of stairs. Without windows I didn't want to hazard a guess how high up we were. I felt disoriented, like I was in a cave somewhere far from the sun. They led us out into a covered walkway. There were windows here, plastic ones that had survived the ages, but they were so covered with ivy that there was only the barest hint of sunlight filtering through in yellowish green.

We crossed into another mountainous building, this one lighter, though the spaces were closer, the space divided into strangely triangular configurations.

We were led into another cavernous room. I was starting to feel numb from awe. I'd seen so many wonders in this building that I was becoming immune to the awesomeness of it all. There was a dais at the far end of this room, black stained wood, heavy and permanent looking. At the top of the dais was a big, fancy, wooden chair. A lot of work went into carving that bastard. Sitting on the chair was the old doctor, Fletter-Daish. There were two other chairs in the room. In one of them sat Kieran's uncle. He looked unwell, but awake, not in danger of sudden death. I guess the time under Old Saul's care paid off.

The other person seated in the room was Sophie, daughter of the Wizard in Green. She looked whole, but tired. The wildness in her eyes was faded.

"Welcome, at last, to my true home," the doctor said.

The Wizard in Green ignored him and spoke to Sophie. "Are you well, my daughter?"

"I won't go back with you," she replied. I guess there was no love lost between the two from the way she said it. I'd never heard somebody speak to a parent with so much hatred before.

Meanwhile Kieran said, "Uncle Stephen!"

"Hello Kieran. I'm sorry you've fallen into this trap too, but I'm glad to see you alive and well."

"There will be time to greet each other later," the doctor said. "First there is the matter of my brother."

And a few things became clear to me. I'd always felt like the old doctor seemed familiar. If you added a dozen years, took off twenty pounds, and covered him with dirt, he'd have been a dead ringer for Old Saul.

And he'd been trying to get us to bring Old Saul to him since I'd first met Kieran.

I remembered Old Saul insisting that he would not be returned to a man who he would not name, somebody related to his past, to the university.

This man was Old Saul's brother.

This man wasn't a Fletter-Daish, he was a Shatterfield.

"An anagram alias, Mr. Shatterfield?" said the Wizard in Green. I saw Kieran silently coming to the realization of how he'd been manipulated. His face hardened with anger and resolve.

I wasn't entirely clear what an anagram was, but I was happy enough to have figured out before Kieran how the two doctors were related.

"I do so love to have intellectual company," said Saul's brother. "You would be the inestimable Duke of Seattle."

The Wizard in Green bowed graciously. "I am only here for my daughter. I will take her and I will go."

"As soon as I get word that Kyle MacMillan has surrendered to my forces I will release her into your care."

"Release my uncle too," Kieran demanded.

"I will, when you bring my brother to me."

That was strange. The Broken had raided the house when Kieran's uncle was taken. Old Saul must have outfoxed the Broken, avoided detection altogether. Good for Saul.

"Saul doesn't want to see you," I said, mustering my courage.

"Poor Saul isn't in his right mind. As I'm sure you are well aware," said Saul's Brother in a mawkishly sad tone, dripping in sarcasm.

"Don't worry about me, Kieran," said Kieran's uncle. "Whatever he's up to can't be any good."

"What I am up to is not your concern," said Saul's brother. "Bring my brother to me and I will release your uncle as good as new."

Kieran opened his mouth to speak but a trumpet sounded loud and clear at that moment. "What was that?"

"That was the sound of my victory," said the doctor. "The Black Trillium and the Confederation have fallen to my army. Trana is mine, and soon the entire Confederation will follow."

CHAPTER 54

Kyle

I REMEMBER THE CHOKING, musty smell of the burlap sack over my head. I suppose I should have been happy to be alive. By all accounts these creatures should have been eating me alive by then. Instead I was a prisoner.

Considering that I'd started the day as the monarch of the entire Confederation, I wasn't sure being a living prisoner was much better than being dinner. At least, I supposed, I'd have a chance to get revenge.

I felt every crack in the pavement, every bit of rubble so frighteningly clearly. Not being able to see was part of that I guess. The Broken weren't gentle as they drove us somewhere.

I could guess where.

Not long after the Broken piled on top of me and everything went dark I'd been stood up by rough, clumsy hands. I heard Brutus's friend swearing in French.

So he was a prisoner too.

I remembered the warning of the Wizard in Green—that it might be somebody other than the Black Trillium behind Sophie's abduction. They'd come but there was no sign of her. I wondered if I might have been wrong.

He continued his endless tirade of profanity for a few minutes as we trudged blindly through the city before my resolve wavered and I spoke to him. "Do you have to make such a damn racket?"

"MacMillan," he spat. "They took you alive too. That's too bad." I guess there was no love lost with this man.

"You have me at a disadvantage." My throat felt raw and vicious.

"Jean Chamblais."

"You're Black Trillium, aren't you, Jean?"

"You were looking for us, I understand."

"The Black Trillium sent me the letter demanding I bring my army into Trana, surrender it in exchange for my betrothed, the woman you kidnapped." I didn't expect him to respond, but I couldn't take the sound of the silent army, the scraping of feet and the sounds of ragged breath, unbroken by any speech. Accusing him gave me something to fill the silence with.

"You are mistaken. I have kidnapped nobody, and I certainly have never written you a letter."

"You didn't want to ransom my fiancée for my army?"

"Ask your father whether the Black Trillium is interested in ransoming aristocrats."

"My father is ash in the wind." I shouldn't have said it. I was giving ammunition to my enemies, but I had won the crown, damn it.

"Congratulations on the start of your reign." Jean chuckled. It wasn't a friendly sound or a happy one either. "You're off to a wonderful start."

"I'm no worse off than you are," I shot back.

"I am nobody, just an old sword-hand. You are the self-styled king of the entire Confederation. If we are standing in the same field you have fallen much farther than I."

I knew he was right. And I hated him for it.

"So, if we aren't prisoners of the Black Trillium, who are we prisoners of?" It had to be somebody local. I figured if Jean wasn't behind the Broken he might at least know who was.

"I don't know. I've never heard of somebody being able to control the Broken before."

"They're taking us to the university. I'm sure of it."

Jean said nothing.

We walked in silence for a while, the heat of the breath of my captors burning my neck, the air muggy, humid, pungent. "Why so quiet?" I asked.

"You hear stories. About the university." We were turning. Still walking on a road, I could feel it through my shoes, but at least we were going somewhere. I momentarily entertained the idea of being marched to the west until I collapsed of exhaustion, or walked into Lake Huron.

It wasn't a pleasant thought to entertain.

"Yeah? What sort of stories?"

"That nobody ever leaves," Jean said darkly. Just great. I was being marched by an army of the damned into some abandoned school that nobody ever left. I was pretty sure if you looked up this situation in one of my father's books on strategy (my books if I could ever get away) it'd just say, 'don't let this happen.'

"Got any plans to escape?" I asked.

"None I feel like sharing with you. Or did you forget that I still want to kill you?"

"We're in the same boat." I tried for reasonable. I mean, yeah, first chance I got I'd put a knife in his back, but that didn't mean we couldn't work together to get to the point of being free to try to kill each other.

"You killed my brother." Even through my burlap hood and his, I could easily hear the hatred and venom in his voice.

"He betrayed me so many times first. He earned his death."

"And you haven't?" I could hear the wrath in his voice. This man truly wanted me dead. And he'd do it. Even now, he'd kill me, if he got the chance.

I thought about trying to provoke him just so that I could forget the terror of my own position, even for a moment. It wasn't wise. He already wanted to kill me, and from what I saw of him on the battlefield he probably could if he got an opening. But I needed to talk to somebody, to forget for a moment the terror of my situation.

"He didn't leave me any choice. He'd tried to have me killed twice, tried to have Sophie killed too. His actions led to my best friend's death." I decided to gloss over the fact that it was my blaming Marc for his actions that led to Marc being in the cell with Kieran, that led to Kieran killing Marc before escaping with his little girlfriend.

I fell silent, imagining all the terrible things I'd do to Kieran the next time I saw him. The little bastard had taken my best friend from me. He'd humiliated me in front of my father. I'd never done anything to him to deserve such treatment; I was the wronged party here.

"So you lost people too. It doesn't justify your tyranny."

"Somebody has to rule."

"Has it ever occurred to you that the people might want to rule themselves?" His voice sounded nasty, accusatory. I would have punched him if I were free.

As it was though, all I could do was talk back. "I suppose that the Black Trillium doesn't have any intention of ruling the Confederation."

"The Black Trillium serves the will of the people, we do not rule."

I had nothing to say to that.

We walked in uncomfortable silence for a ways longer and turned again. The day was silent, and I could smell very little behind the must of the sack and the sour stink of unwashed bodies, but I thought that I could smell, maybe just a hint, the scent of summer flowers.

"Do you smell that?" I said to Jean.

"I think we've arrived inside the university. There were supposed to be beautiful gardens there once."

"So whatever happens to us, it'll probably at least happen soon."

"I don't know. Your people have ways of drawing out how long it takes for..." he paused for dramatic effect, "something to happen to somebody. I'm sure whoever commands this army is likewise equipped."

In other words, expect to be tortured before being granted the mercy of death.

"You are such a cheerful man."

"What can I say? Adversity brings out the best in me."

We were stopped.

"We seem to have arrived somewhere," I said.

"Really?"

We started walking again. We climbed a flight of stairs, I tripped and stumbled a dozen times, but rough hands caught me and pushed me up the steps. We entered a building. I could tell even through the sack because the quality of the light changed. It was darker in here than out in the street. A building without many windows maybe.

We crossed a smooth floor, heels ringing on the tiles beneath our feet, and then ascended a second staircase.

The Broken prodded us forward at the top of the staircase. "Any idea where they are taking us?" I asked Jean.

"Maybe they want to push us off the top of the building." I could hear him grinning. I hated the bastard more with every word he said, but he'd become the circumference of my world, him and the coarse hands of the slave army.

I didn't rise to his bait. We crossed another floor, it felt like concrete, and then went down a flight of stairs and across a hall. I heard other voices in the distance, indistinct.

We stopped. The bag was pulled from my head. I blinked in the sudden light, although it was dim in the room.

Dr. Fletter-Daish sat on a throne. He was staring down at me.

The Broken ringed the room, guarding every exit. Besides the doctor, Jean, the Broken and I, the room included Sophie, Kieran, Savannah and the Wizard in Green along with a man I didn't recognize. Everybody was looking at Jean and I.

"Ah good," the Doctor said. "At last, everybody is here."

CHAPTER 55

Kieran

As THE BROKEN MUTELY lifted the hood from off of MacMillan's blond head, it seemed like I should have felt some sort of vindication. MacMillan was beaten, his army cast down. Alright, it was because of Saul Shatterfield's mad brother and his army of monsters, but still.

I probably would have felt vindication anyway, but Mr. Chamblais was there too, hands bound in front of him, looking just as thoroughly beaten as MacMillan. The bad guys may have lost, but so had the good guys. Our victory was no cause for celebration.

"I won't surrender to you," MacMillan said. "You might as well kill me."

"In due time I might, but for now you are more valuable alive."

That wasn't very heartening either. After all, we were only 'more valuable' alive right up until we delivered the madman's brother to him. He'd tried trickery, toyed with the life of uncle Stephen, but that hadn't worked. Still, something didn't make sense. Why had he gone to the Confederation camp? Just to capture Sophie? He could have done that without abandoning his ploy to recover Saul. What were his priorities? How badly did he need Saul to enact his plot? He seemed to have won handily without Saul.

I made a note to discuss it with Mr. Chamblais, uncle Stephen and Savannah if we ever got the chance. Not that I was too confident in that.

"You don't need the surrender of the Black Trillium to rule," Mr. Chamblais said. "Why are you holding us?"

"Initially, using the Black Trillium to get access to my brother was a matter of convenience only," said the doctor. "I could monitor your actions, distract you from your own plans, and use you to accomplish my own goals.

"Now that I've neutralized your pathetic little army, it's simply a matter of you being the best lead I have to find my brother, and I do want to see my brother very much."

"Why do you want your brother so badly?" I blurted out. "You won!"

"Would you accept that I love my brother and that I want to care for him?"

"No," Savannah said. "Saul hates you. Fear of you ruined him."

"Then accept that he is crucial to my long-term ambitions. The reason why is something beyond your limited ability to comprehend." He glared at Savannah like she was some particularly unsightly insect.

The Wizard in Green scoffed. He couldn't hide his disdain. "You're afraid your brother managed to develop a cure."

"You are far from home, Wizard in Green."

"No thanks to you. It was you who sent the Broken into Seattle, wasn't it? I destroyed them all."

"A failed experiment. But that is irrelevant. No matter how powerful you are you won't escape."

"I don't intend to escape. You will give me my daughter, two fresh horses, and parting gifts by way of apology for the inconvenience you've caused me."

"I won't be doing that."

"Then I'll leave over your corpse," the Wizard said dryly. Had to give him credit, he was cool under pressure.

"You may be powerful enough to kill me," the doctor said. "But your daughter is not. She already tried to escape from me, and failed. I promise you, if you try and cut me down now I will gut her first."

"Do it," Sophie said. "I'd rather die than go with him."

"Such a happy family," the doctor said.

The Wizard in Green took a step toward the doctor's throne. All the Broken in the room crept closer at the same time, closing around us, making themselves more visible. There must have been hundreds.

"I have some cells in the basement," the doctor said. "You can rest there, together, while I decide what to do with the lot of you. The Duke of Seattle will go first. Once he's safely in a cell I'll send down his daughter. Don't try to escape. Even you, with all your craft, couldn't make it to the edge of my domain, Wizard in Green."

With a gesture, he summoned silent guards who proceeded to manhandle us all out of the throne room.

"This isn't over between the two of us," the Wizard in Green said. "There will be a dreadful reckoning."

Broken guards escorted us one-at-a-time to a holding cell in the basement. It was a single windowless room with one heavily reinforced door. When the door swung open one last time, Sophie stumbled in. The Wizard in Green made his move but as he rushed toward the door, the voice of Doctor Shatterfield shouted back, "I have a crossbow trained on her neck. I suggest you keep back."

Glowering fiercely, the Wizard complied.

So there we were: Kyle and Sophie, my uncle and I, Savannah, and Mr. Chamblais and the Wizard in Green, all standing together, trapped in a cell in the bowels of the university. And they'd left us our weapons. I felt like maybe we were being toyed with again.

Kyle approached Sophie first. "I was so worried about you," he said.

"Get away from me," she snarled and turned her back on him. "After all that we've been through, I saw him in our tent that morning." She pointed at her father, thrusting her finger like a spear at him. "You're going to return me to him, aren't you?"

"I only wanted to save you."

"Then save me from living death, stifled by his walls and rules. Kill my father!"

The Wizard in Green looked sadly at his daughter. "I only ever wanted the best for you. Your mother..."

"Don't you speak to me about her, I hardly knew her and yet she dominates my life. All because you refuse to bend enough to break a promise!" She lashed out at her father, trying to take his throat but he drifted aside from the blow, never in the slightest danger.

"The boy couldn't kill me anyway. I would prove a more challenging target than his own father."

"What do you mean?" Sophie asked.

"Kyle MacMillan rules the Confederation now, in name at least," Mr. Chamblais said. "Patricide is the usual method for you to pass the crown, is it not?"

"I did it for you, Sophie: to take control of his army to rescue you."

"And like usual, you screwed it up."

Uncle Stephen let out a loud, deep laugh. "This is the terrible Confederation that had us all shaking in our boots?"

I went to my uncle. "It's good to see you getting better. I've struggled so long to try and find a cure for you."

"So I've heard." Uncle Stephen smiled at me. "Your parents would be proud of you, Kieran."

"As if anybody cares," Kyle snapped.

"Oh, for once Kyle, shut up," Savannah said.

"For once, I agree with her," Sophie said. "I've heard enough of your voice to last me a lifetime."

"After everything I've done for you. I moved heaven and earth for you."

"You moved heaven and earth to land me trapped in a cell with my father—the one person I least wanted to see."

"When I take my throne..."

"Kieran," Mr. Chamblais said, "I don't know how you three managed to keep your swords, but do me a favour, cut down this scumbag."

"Gladly," I said, drawing my sword. I saw the fear in Kyle's eyes. He was unarmed, outnumbered by his enemies, stripped of his army.

My sword was halfway out of its sheath when he blurted, "I'll give you Trana!"

"What was that?" Mr. Chamblais said threateningly.

"If you spare me for now, I swear, as soon as we escape from this place, I'll leave Trana and I'll take my army with me."

"And you expect me to believe you?" I continued, drawing my sword.

"I promise, on my life!"

"I will adjudicate that," the Wizard in Green said.

"Begging your pardon," Mr. Chamblais said. "But why?"

"This is a dispute within my lineage. You are a student of one of my students. Kyle learned through Sophie. And while she stole the sword art from me she is my daughter and I am prepared to forgive her for that."

"As if I want your forgiveness," Sophie said.

The Wizard in Green ignored her. "Ultimately every person in this room learned their talents through me. You are my lineage, here in this room. This makes it my concern, and disputes within my faction must be adjudicated by the faction master. Me."

"Those rules don't hold so much in the Confederation," Mr. Chamblais said. "That may be how they do things in the Southern Counties but—"

"Do you think I care how they do things in the Confederation?" the Wizard in Green cut Mr. Chamblais off. "My grand-student has a dispute with my great-grand-student, his junior but from a different branch of my lineage. In a matter like this, only I can adjudicate. Only I am master to both.

"Kieran, put up your sword. Kyle will leave Trana after we escape, and he will take his army with him. If he does not, I will collect his life."

"That raises the matter of how we are going to escape," Savannah said.

"Aren't you going to argue with him about this?" Kieran asked.

"Not likely. He's got a thing about people in his lineage. He's already made me promise not to ask him to lift a finger against anybody who could claim to be a student of his. If he's deciding to act as judge in this matter, hell, I'll sit back and figure you guys just won Trana. You know, if we can escape."

"It's clear we'll have to kill Doctor Shatterfield," Mr. Chamblais said.

"Yes. But it's not the first thing we must do," said the Wizard in Green. "He needs his brother for a reason. Before we deal with him we must know what that reason is."

Sophie sighed in frustration. "Honestly father, can't you ever visit a library without stopping to pilfer books?"

"Never," the Wizard said, and he almost smiled. "Do you think I couldn't just take you from here and escape now, Sophie? There's something more important here. I'm sure of it: possibly a cure for the Broken. And I'm sure Saul Shatterfield is at the heart of it all. I'm not leaving without it.

"So, I'm going to go read some books. I suggest you all do the same. Unless, that is, you fancy your chances escaping without my help." He walked up to the door and put his palm over the lock plate. He stood there, concentrating for a moment and then shifted his feet and shoulders slightly. The lock split like the sound of a bell.

"Meet back here in no more than three hours," the Wizard said. "I will make sure no Broken block our path to the stacks."

He walked out the door. Faint sounds of fighting emanated from the hallway. They didn't last long.

"Well, I guess it's not the worst idea ever," Savannah said. "If Doctor Shatterfield needs Old Saul for something it can't be good. Maybe it'd be a good idea for us to find out why. Kieran, you coming?"

"Yeah," I said. "Uncle Stephen, are you going to be alright?"

"I should be just fine, I'm just tired. Jean can you stay here? I would like to catch up with you."

Sophie rolled her eyes. "Come on Kyle," she said. "If you want a chance to win back my good graces at all you'll help me look for a way out of this hellhole. Perhaps we can get away from my father while he's distracted rummaging through somebody else's library."

"Are you sure that's the best idea? I mean, Kieran and Savannah are right here."

"And I'd rather not fight them unarmed," Sophie said. "You two are planning on playing by my father's stupid rules, aren't you?"

"I'd rather not get on his bad side," Savannah said.

"You're a fool to deal with him at all. If you had any sense you'd try to run too. But that's neither here nor there. I propose a truce. Two hours. We won't accost your little book hunt. You keep out of our way."

"Whatever," Savannah said. We left the cells together, but very pointedly two groups apart. There were Broken scattered throughout the hallway. They were all very dead. But clearly the Wizard in Green hadn't seen fit to draw his sword.

Taking Savannah's hand in my own, we walked away from Kyle and Sophie, up the stairs, into the stacks.

"Do you know much about libraries?" Savannah asked.

"Uncle Stephen has ten books," I said. "I thought that was a large library."

"Yeah, um, looks like it wasn't," Savannah said with a weak chuckle.

"Do you think we're really going to find something here to help us escape?" I asked.

"Can't hurt, right?" Savannah replied.

"I suppose it can't get much worse," I agreed.

"Come on," Savannah said, "let's pick that shelf." She rounded a corner. We were far away from the others now, surrounded by books. The smell of them, old and musty, and dry, almost made me want to sneeze.

We started rummaging through the shelves. The books were on some sort of scientific topic, and the mathematics was beyond my level of capability. "Can you make heads or tails of this gobbledygook?" I asked Savannah.

"No," she said.

I heard a faint sound, clicking.

I slowly closed my eyes, breathed in slowly, quietly.

"What's wrong?" Savannah asked.

"I'm listening."

She fell silent. Again I heard a clicking sound, almost like a laugh, if insects could laugh. "I think we're not alone in here."

"The Broken," Savannah said. "I heard them."

I opened my eyes. "Get ready." But Savannah had already drawn her sword. They must have found us before we found them. The creatures took up positions, blocking off our exits, and when they attacked us it was in a wave. There were dozens of the creatures: not the shambling animal types but the other, stronger, more controlled ones that Doctor Shatterfield kept around him.

Savannah pressed into the horde with cuts left and right. Occasionally one of the Broken would slip too close for her sword to handle, just by the press of numbers and she would seize it, rip flesh off in gobs or shatter bones with a snap of a single hand.

I'd never seen such a brutal bare-hands style before, but now was not the time to marvel at the secrets she hid. After all, I had a few tricks up my sleeve too.

Sword in hand I came to Savannah's aid. Our complementary styles served us well and we seemed to be winning for a time. But the Broken just kept coming and they seemed to have no sense of self-preservation.

I sliced limbs from some, cut throats and pierced hearts. If more than two came at us at once, I'd paralyze one with Nerve-Shocking Fingers and let its falling body obstruct the creatures behind it.

But it was no good. There was always another Broken to replace it.

"Grab on," Savannah said, and I took hold of her as she Kite-Stepped above the heads of the mob, bounding over several stacks deeper into the library. The Broken surged up the book shelves, but the spaces above the stacks were high and dark.

With high leaps and silent feet, Savannah slowly shook the horde off. When we thought we were safe, we went to the ground.

"We need to find somewhere to hide," I said.

"You think?" Savannah snapped quietly. She frowned and leaned against one of the book shelves. "Sorry," she said.

"It's fine." I looked down the aisle between the shelves but I saw nothing but the faint outline of shelves in the shadows. "Look, between us and the Wizard in Green stalking the aisles and those two Confederation psycopaths trying to make their escape, this place is pretty much a kicked wasp's nest. But I bet they'll be expecting us to try to escape. If we move further into the stacks, away from the exits, maybe we can find a spot to barricade ourselves in, somewhere defensible."

"And starve to death? We can't eat books."

"I know, but it'll give us some time to come up with a plan."

"I don't like it," Savannah said, crossing her arms. "But it's better than doing nothing, or letting those Broken grab us and throw us back in that cell. Alright, let's go."

Without further discussion we proceeded deeper into the library: away from light, away from noise, into the dark and the smell of books.

Eventually we found ourselves in a small room with no lamps. The door in was dusty and cob-webbed. We slipped inside, carrying one of the little lights from outside with us, and found the room full of hand-bound books. They looked more modern, not relics of the time before the Great Collapse, but things people made since. They were all dusty. Nobody had been here in a very long time.

I opened one. It was the diary of Stephen Shatterfield, a scholar. "Take a look at this."

"Yeah," Savannah said. "And this one too."

We went from book to book and every book in the little room was a diary of a member of the Shatterfield family. They'd lived here, in the library of the university, since the Great Collapse, and they had all kept their records here.

The last one we found, the diary of Moira Shatterfield, related the birth of twins, Saul and Paul. I guessed that the doctor was Paul. We could not find a diary for Saul or his brother, but I did find an empty place, at the end of a shelf, where a book should have been.

"It's too bad that Old Saul's diary isn't there."

Savannah frowned at the open space in the shelf. I could see something dawning on her. "It's hidden," she said. "In the walls."

"What? How do you know?"

"He kept bits of his diary written on the walls of his home in the Cathedral of Broken Glass. He used to talk about the diary in the walls. I just thought it was more of his..." She paused. "Well..."

I understood. She didn't want to be uncharitable to the old man. He was mad, but he was her friend.

"You think that maybe he was telling you where he hid his old diary?"

"Couldn't hurt to check."

And that was how we ended up banging on the walls of a dusty old room in the back of an abandoned section of a library in the forbidden university. I was shocked when I heard Savannah crow, "Found it!"

"Really?"

She dug her fingers into the old plaster like it was soft dough and tore away a large chunk of the wall.

"Where'd you learn how to do that?"

"Saul taught me. Only, when he does it, he uses rebar in concrete."

"Remind me to be nice to Saul." I grinned wanly, I'd not ever thought the old madman would have skills beyond his Kite-Stepping and some swordplay.

"You should be anyway," Savannah said. She cleared away some plaster dust and raised her little lamp to the hole in the wall.

A single diary sat in the gap.

With trembling fingers, Savannah reached for the book. She drew it out of its hiding-hole and slowly opened the cover.

A single page of yellowing paper drifted to the ground.

I picked it up.

It was covered in images of men standing in sword poses, filled with instructions on balance, posture, timing.

Savannah pulled her stained and battered manual from out of the recesses of her clothes.

It was a perfect fit.

CHAPTER 56

Savannah

I COULDN'T STOP MY hands from trembling as I picked up the dusty old book. I cared deeply for Old Saul. That hadn't ever stopped me from wondering how he'd come to be as he was. I accepted him, damage and all, but that was different than understanding.

It almost felt like a violation to open the book, to look inside the covers of Saul's life, before he was broken, before Shatterfield died, before he became Old Saul, hiding in the crumbling ruins of the Cathedral of Broken Glass.

Had our situation been different I might not have opened the book. But our situation wasn't different. It was grave. We needed to know what answers might lie in the book.

I opened the cover, and a page fell out. It was a smaller page, from a different book. It appeared to have been jammed in between the pages of the diary as a book mark. Kieran stooped, picked it up, and then his hands started trembling too. Mutely, he held out the page. It was all too familiar.

Through everything we'd been through I'd kept the manual entrusted to me by Boyd close to my heart. I took it out. It had to be. It was the missing page.

"Do you realize what we've found here?" Kieran asked.

"Something that could get us killed," I said. "Especially if Kyle and Sophie realize we have it."

"We should commit it to memory, hide it again."

I nodded. His reasoning was sound. With the information on this page we would be able to master the two parts of the Triumvirate sword art that the Wizard in Green had written down. I liked that idea.

"Alright, but as soon as we have, we have to read the diary. The sword art won't do us much good against an army of the Broken."

Kieran nodded in agreement. And then we went to practicing.

It was so simple! The missing piece was a series of postures designed to quickly redistribute balance from the aggressive forward postures of the Form of Limitless Aggression to the cautious, careful positions of the Form of Limitless Cunning and back again.

Once you saw it you couldn't help but be struck by how obvious it should have been. I felt like slapping myself on the forehead and shouting 'of course!'

We committed the page to memory in half an hour. "Alright," I said. "The diary."

Again I opened the book to the page that had been marked with the sword art page. This time, nothing fell out.

The pages were brittle and yellowing. I had to squint in the dim light of the single lamp to make them out. I read aloud, hands trembling, stumbling over the pain in the pages. Here was Old Saul's heart laid bare. It was all I could do to read it. Having Kieran there helped, but only barely enough to let me make it through one desperate page after the next.

"December Fifteenth,

"The Five Venoms toxin worked! Within fifteen minutes of administering the dose the subject had begun to return to lucidity. It pains me to think how little he had to return to. These Broken, many of them are from families of the original victims. They've never known another life beside the one they were born to. And though the cure restores their minds it does nothing for the crippling deformities thrust upon their bodies.

"It also pains me that the Five Venoms toxin proved entirely lethal at the doses necessary to treat the Broken condition. The subject passed within 24 hours of treatment.

"I am increasingly concerned about Paul. He remains committed to the cause, at least he says he wants to find a cure, but he shuts himself in his lab, I hear screams from in there sometimes...

"Yesterday he complained about running low on test subjects. I don't like buying the Broken from slavers. People shouldn't be bought even if they have lost their faculties."

"Five Venoms toxin," Kieran said with a sense of wonder, "cures the Broken?"

"For what good it did them," I said. "It killed them too." I could understand a little better the pain that Saul felt, the fear of the Broken. He felt guilty. He'd wanted to help them, who knows how many he'd killed trying to cure them. I turned the page.

"December Twenty-First,

"Paul said he had something important to show me yesterday, a breakthrough. I went to him, thought he'd found a cure. I was wrong.

"He's been studying how to control them. He told me that there was no hope of a cure, but that they could still be made useful, that we could use them to create a new order.

"He sent them to Seattle to test. He said that they'd disappeared after they arrived but that they had got there as directed. He said his principles were sound, in theory.

"I don't want to be a ruler. I rebuffed him. What he's doing, he's creating slaves who don't have the ability to resist slavery. It's wrong, disgusting. I hate my brother today." I looked up from the page. "He has had the ability to control them for so long."

"And yet he's waited," Kieran said. "I wonder why."

I turned the page. It was getting even harder to go on. Reading about Paul Shatterfield's descent, Saul's growing sense of his own brother's monstrousness. It was almost too much. I bit my lip and brushed away a tear, and then began again, slowly. "December Thirty-First,

"I should have known. I should have known. Already I can feel it working within me, trying to strip me of my faculties, of my will, my reason. He is mad, totally mad. He wants to create a world of slaves, obedient to his will and nothing else.

"I have no choice. I will have to take the Five Venoms toxin. The bio-weapon takes time to be effective. If I can get the dose just right, perhaps I can stave off the effect without killing myself.

"When did he start? When did he begin making new Broken? Why did he revive this terrible science? It should have died out, it should have been allowed to be forgotten.

"I have a friend in Seattle. I've written to him to send for help. He did away with Paul's army.

"If I hadn't looked for a cure, if our parents hadn't given us this fool's quest, things could have been so different. Paul wasn't bad to begin with. He was a kind man once, a compassionate man. When did he change?

"We shouldn't have looked for a cure. We should have just let the Southlanders, the Confederation kill them all off, put them out of their misery.

"But that isn't right, a cure is needed. The Broken didn't ask to be what they have become.

"If I can't find a cure I'll be cursed to either die by degrees physically from the poison or mentally until I become just another unthinking brute."

The book fell from my numb fingers.

"He didn't end up that way," Kieran said.

"No. He just ended up driven mad from pain and grief."

"Maybe we can help him..."

"Help him? How can we help him?" I was shouting, I was furious, I shouldn't have been taking it out on Kieran, but nobody else was close at hand.

"If he found a cure, if he was able to save himself... Maybe there's another page." Kieran said placatingly. "Maybe he left some other clue."

I nodded, swallowed my fear, and stooped, picking up the book. I turned to the next page.

"The Last Day,

"Fire, fire is the only cure. I can't allow this to continue. I can't allow the Shatterfield name to go on. We are cursed, cursed. No. Only fire can save us. Only fire can stop what he's done here, what he will do...

"The lamps. The lamps. It is a dry night tonight. I just have to hold together for one more night.

"The poison burns, I took so little, but it gives me clarity. It holds back the curtain of death. These people, not just Broken but Defiled. I will hide the book. He must not know. Can't know what the cure is. The terrible cost of it. I will make a hole and bury Saul Shatterfield in it until he is gone, all gone. I've burned his diary. It will set him back.

"All that will remain is ash."

"Old Saul lit the fires that burned the university," Kieran said.

"But he didn't stop Paul," I said. "He just slowed him down."

"All the people who disappeared. He must have made them into the Broken."

"I know," said a voice from behind us, the voice of Paul Shatterfield, "it's a blunt instrument but it is the best one I have. I needed subjects. However did you find my brother's diary?"

"You!" Kieran shouted.

"I have been watching you ever since you came across my servants in the stacks. Did you really think I'd simply let you run loose in my library? It's bad enough knowing the blasted Duke of Seattle is rummaging around here. But he'll come to heel too. I caught his daughter and her friend trying to escape."

Kieran lashed out, drawing his sword and cutting at Paul Shatterfield. A dozen Broken threw themselves on him. One jumped directly onto Kieran's sword, taking his own life to bind Kieran's weapon.

I wanted to be sick.

Paul Shatterfield walked casually over to me, snickering at the sight of Kieran struggling wrathfully on the floor against the mass of poisoned souls who held him there.

He plucked Saul's diary from my unresisting fingers.

"I've decided how to best make use of all of you. My servants will escort you to the throne room."

He took my sword, passed it to one of the Broken and then he left again, whistling a jaunty little tune, and more Defiled came in, my hands bound behind my back. Kieran, still struggling fiercely, was bound hand and foot and carried out ahead of me.

CHAPTER 57

Kyle

SOPHIE AND I NEVER got far. The Broken were on us less than a minute after we left the cell. Unarmed, we surrendered and returned to our cell. Kieran's uncle and the wild man were still there. Kieran, Savannah and the Wizard in Green never reappeared. Instead, Broken guards ushered us back to the throne room. As we arrived, Kieran and Savannah also returned. They'd been disarmed, and a Broken carried their swords.

Savannah walked, though under heavy guard. Kieran was carried in, bound again, shouting and fighting the whole time.

The man was fierce. As much as I hated him, I had to respect his fighting spirit.

We were assembled at the foot of the doctor's throne, Kieran dropped like a sack of potatoes to the floor, his ankles bound as well as his wrists. I noticed one of the Broken was carrying his sword, stained with blood.

The Doctor spoke loudly into a metal box and his voice boomed through the building as if it came from everywhere at once. "The Wizard in Green will attend the throne room or I will kill his daughter within five minutes."

He arrived in three, sword in hand. He was spattered in gore but unharmed, and I knew that somebody wouldn't be leaving this room alive.

"Now that you're all here I have an announcement." Doctor Shatterfield said. "I've decided to show mercy and let you go. I only ask that you sit down for a meal with me first so that we might bury the hatchet between us." Something in his tone of voice told me this wasn't as nice an option as it might have sounded on the surface. Certainly Savannah and Kieran didn't think it was.

"You won't make me into one of your slaves," Kieran shouted. "I'll die first!"

"You wrong me," the doctor said. "I said I'd let you go."

"We don't believe you," Savannah said. "Wizard, he's found a way to make new Broken."

That electrified the Wizard in Green. "You have proof?"

"Saul's diary. He took it."

All eyes fixed on the doctor. There was a black book in his hands. I'd hardly noticed it. But he didn't look pleased that Savannah had pointed it out.

"I don't need to put the Broken drug in your food. I could gas you with it. I was going to make your passing easier."

"Like you made my passing?" said a weak voice from behind us.

I turned to look. There were two men standing in the doorway, one I recognized, Dave Boyd somehow escaped from the battle. The other I did not know, though he was the spitting image of the doctor.

In fact, if he were twenty pounds heavier, if he didn't have that half-crazed look of fear around his eyes he might look exactly the same.

Savannah looked shocked. "Saul, what are you doing here?"

He smiled weakly at Savannah. "Trying to face my past while I still have the strength to."

"If I knew you would come home on your own I wouldn't have exhausted so much effort looking for you, Saul," the doctor said.

"Let my friends go, Paul." Saul and Paul, eh? I bet they adored their parents.

"I can't do that. But I am still glad to see you home, and looking so well. I'd heard reports you lost your mind." Saul didn't look exactly sane to me. He kept twitching. In fact, I think he'd probably have fallen over if it weren't for the support Boyd was providing, propping him up.

"Saul still hasn't recovered from what you did to him," Boyd said. "If not for the love he feels for Savannah and her friends I couldn't have got through to him even this much."

"I will have it out with you," Saul said. "If I must."

"So be it," Paul said. He gestured and the Broken attacked en masse.

Saul jumped high, higher than I've ever seen a person jump, higher than I thought it was possible to jump. I'd seen Savannah and Sophie use similar talents. But theirs paled compared with what he could do.

He cleared the mass of the Broken, kicked off a wall, jumped higher off the kick and then plummeted like a stone toward Paul, who leaped straight out of his throne, with meteoric power. The sound of their collision in the air was more like two boulders slamming together than two men.

They both fell to the ground and a huge plume of dust billowed into the air, obscuring both from view.

The others wasted little time. Savannah struck at her captors, striking one so hard that it crashed into a second, throwing both in a twitching heap on the ground. She leapt to the Broken carrying her sword and struck it on the side of the neck in mid-air. It gurgled and dropped to the ground motionless. Sword in hand, she cut Kieran free of the ropes binding him and he jumped to his feet. Sophie's father drew his emerald sword and stepped in front of her. Barely five seconds had passed.

The dust settled.

Saul and Paul were trading blows still. Each shot fell like a hammer in a forge. Each blow that landed resounded.

Saul was losing the fight.

"We have to help him," Savannah said to Kieran.

"Yeah," Kieran said. The Broken who had attacked Saul before his leap were milling uncertainly. Whatever power kept them chained to Doctor Shatterfield's will held them enough to prevent them from going berserk, but they seemed confused, uncertain what was required of them.

A few of them were carrying weapons, the ones stripped from me, from Chamblais and from Kieran.

Kieran made a bee-line for the Broken carrying his sword and poked it in the chest with three fingers. It fell to the ground, twitching and screaming, much as Marc had. He picked up his sword and joined the fray.

Savannah hadn't waited for Kieran to go to Saul's side. She brandished her big sword and charged in with the power of the Triumvirate sword art behind her.

Paul delivered a hard blow to his brother's jaw, throwing him to the ground. He lay there and was still.

"No!" Savannah shouted and swung at Paul clumsily, too clumsily. He stepped back, out of the arc of her sword and jumped to a wall a full fifty feet distant. Once there he took a sword from off the wall and saluted her.

The Broken began to act with purpose once again. Some started moving toward Sophie and her father. Others targeted Kieran, his uncle, and Jean.

I was mostly being ignored. I used the opportunity this granted me and snatched my sword and Chamblais' from two of the Broken.

I tossed the second blade under-hand to Sophie, who saw my intention and caught the blade. Her eyes flashed in thanks. She made an absent-minded cut at her father's unprotected back but he moved with preternatural speed and gave her a surprisingly tender look of disapproval. The man was insane. But, faced with the press of the Broken, Sophie gave up any hostile intentions to her father and concentrated on the greater threat.

Jean Chamblais used the same finger-strikes as Kieran to fell a pair of Broken. He jumped over a third, without the unnatural grace of Shatterfield or

Savannah, but with athleticism that belied his age. He landed in a roll and struck it down too.

"Don't think our business is concluded," he said in passing, but made no more hostile moves toward me.

I hazarded a look over my shoulder. Savannah was still engaging the doctor, swords flashing, incorporating movements from the Form of Limitless Cunning into her swordplay as well as those of her own. She and Kieran must have traded some of their secrets. It made me so furious that they'd done with ease what Sophie and I had so desperately sought out, but I set aside those thoughts and focused on the greater threat.

I managed to turn so that I could keep a closer eye on the fight against Paul Shatterfield. A dozen times Savannah seemed to have him on the ropes, only for him to escape at last minute by catching the blade or parrying with his forearms.

There was a tiny bit of blood on his forearms, but I'd seen Savannah fight before, he should have been missing both of his arms.

I guess he was more robust.

The last of the Broken fell beneath the blade of Sophie's father. We all turned to the fight between Savannah and Paul.

She had lost the edge, lost momentum. He was wearing her down. He threw a blow at Savannah's side with his sword and I didn't think she'd be able to block it.

She brought her huge sword down on his blade and cut it in half. I'd never seen anything like it!

Kieran took the opportunity to jump to Savannah's side, but Paul Shatterfield did not take the destruction of his weapon lying down. He dodged Kieran, caught Savannah's arm with both of his meaty hands, and threw her, tearing the sword from her grasp. It spun lazily through the air and embedded itself in the floor, sinking a foot into concrete before coming to a stop upright. Some sword.

Disarmed, Savannah showed some of the same strength and endurance that Saul and Paul had both demonstrated, but it wasn't enough. She was going to fall just as Saul had.

Kieran came to her aid again, and attacked the doctor from an oblique angle.

The two of them managed to gain the upper hand, pushing Paul back, lashing out with hand, foot and sword in a flurry of coordinated attacks.

I revised my earlier assessment. It was a pity that Kieran and Savannah both were fated to be my enemies. Together they were marvellous. I glanced across the room at the other parties.

Kieran's uncle and Chamblais had gone to the doors. They'd barred them from the inside to prevent more Broken from getting in but were far from the action. Bereft of other enemies, Sophie was lashing out at her father. He appeared to be in no danger from her, avoiding her attacks as if they had never happened, but he was distracted from the battle against Doctor Shatterfield for the moment.

And still the implacable mad doctor pressed them back, raining deadly punches down on both of them, parrying wildly with the half a sword that remained in his hands.

As quickly as they had gained the upper hand they'd lost it again. Paul was fighting them both and winning. But he wasn't paying enough attention to his feet.

The fight passed by Saul. He'd been lying still, I thought him dead, but he opened his eyes just a crack as the stomping feet of the fighters came nearer to his head. When Paul stepped close enough, Saul grabbed his ankle and clung on desperately.

It gave Kieran and Savannah the moment they needed.

They came at Paul from opposite directions, Kieran thrusting with his sword, Savannah attacking with a powerful spear-hand.

The blows struck Paul at the exact same moment. I'm not sure which wounded him more.

"You can't," he wheezed. "I'd already won." I could barely hear him. Savannah stepped away from him, her hands covered in his blood. He tried to step toward her. He slid off Kieran's blade.

Saul hadn't let go of his legs. Gushing blood, he tripped over his brother's arms and collapsed on top of Saul. He tried to speak again but no words came. He looked at his brother, drew a streak of blood down the centre of Saul's face and then his hand went limp.

Outside I heard the screams of the Broken, released from their bondage with the death of their master. The Broken within the chamber were all dead. I thought that was probably a good thing.

"Come on," said Jean from the doorway. "We have to get out of here while there is still time."

"Not yet," said Sophie. "I'll never be free of him," she pointed at her father with her sword, "until those two give up the secret of the Triumvirate sword art. And I'd rather die than go back with him to a soft, perfumed prison."

Outside, the intensity of the screams grew louder.

CHAPTER 58

Kieran

THE LUDICROUSNESS OF SOPHIE'S statement struck me so hard that I couldn't stop myself from speaking. "Seriously?" I couldn't help it. I couldn't actually believe she was serious about having it out over the damn sword manual right here, right now.

Here we stood over the still warm remains of a madman who tried to conquer the Confederation with an army of slaves bound to his will, and still all the bitch could think of was getting our damn sword techniques.

"Daughter, what have I done to wrong you so?" the Wizard said.

"You kept me like a caged bird. You never let me inherit what was rightfully mine! Why, for a promise to a dead woman?"

His face hardened. "I loved your mother."

"She's dead!" Sophie said, gesturing wildly at her father and stamping her foot. "I still live! It should be my birthright!"

"No."

"Then I challenge them to a duel."

"No, I forbid it," the Wizard said and his green eyes flashed angrily. He grabbed his daughter by the arms and looked like he was about to carry her bodily from the room.

"You can't, it's my right!" Sophie shot back petulantly, shaking off her father's grasp.

"It is her right," Kyle said, "but two against one isn't fair. I also challenge those two." His jaw was set in a look of determination that I almost respected, except that it was from Kyle MacMillan, who I could not respect.

"No, I don't recognize your customs."

"You promised me a favour," Savannah said.

"I also told you I would not act against my family," the Wizard replied.

"If you don't let her fight us here she will never let this go. I am not asking you to fight your daughter, but we are all ultimately your students. Please, step aside and let us settle this."

"I will not allow her to die."

"We've all had a belly-full of killing," I said. "The second she surrenders, we will stop." I meant it too. I was exhausted from the fight with Paul Shatterfield. I didn't relish the idea of fighting Sophie and Kyle now. Savannah nodded.

"Fine, I will stand aside," the Wizard said angrily. "But there is to be no killing."

I noticed neither Kyle nor Sophie said anything. I expected they would try to kill us. I'd spare them if I could, but we had friends here, the Wizard was running low on them. I'd rather take my chances with him than spare Kyle MacMillan and meet my death at those familiar hands.

"Arm yourself," Sophie said to Savannah.

Savannah walked over to her sword and drew it from the concrete floor. She walked over to Old Saul, who had managed to dislodge his brother's corpse, but not to rise, and crouched, whispered in his ear. "Are you alright?"

"I can't," Saul said. "I don't. I couldn't..." He was alive, but it seemed like whatever strength had given him the force of will to confront his brother was exhausted. Savannah helped him to his feet and walked him over to Dave Boyd.

"Whatever happens to me," she said, "look after him."

Boyd nodded his head tersely but said nothing. His eyes were flinty. Savannah returned to my side.

We saluted, and then the four of us were locked in battle once more.

I felt a rush of adrenaline as our swords met Kyle's and Sophie's. I could see the wild flush in Savannah's cheeks too. We fought side by side and it was as if we were one unit. I was still more comfortable with the Form of Limitless Cunning, Savannah with the Form of Limitless Aggression. We'd had very little time to practice before we'd been distracted by Paul Shatterfield, but being able to change from one form to the other gave us an edge, and a clear one.

This time we were not weaker.

The battle was in our favour. Sophie stabbed ferociously, Kyle used every ounce of malicious cunning he possessed but we all knew it wouldn't be enough. Even tired from our battle with the doctor, we were still faster than them, more coordinated, a better team.

Sophie took a cut across the cheek and her green eyes flashed. She brought her hand to her face and felt the blood there, tasted it, wiped it on her brow, and flew into a rage.

She was savage and coldly beautiful, and nearly as inhuman as her father, though lacking his restraint.

When Savannah ran her through I wasn't even surprised.

But she was. "Not again," Sophie hissed.

She dropped to her knees, grabbing at the sword that impaled her, still trying to fight.

"Sophie!" screamed the Wizard. He charged into the fray. "You've won, you've won! Let me save her!"

Savannah stepped back, pulled the sword out of her stricken foe. Sophie dropped onto her side on the ground. The Wizard dropped to his knees and produced a packet from within his robes, a paper one full of some sort of white powder. He poured it into the wound and began massaging it. Slowly the bleeding stopped.

Now I knew why he was called a wizard, for this was miraculous healing if I'd ever seen it.

Savannah stepped back, dropped her sword on the ground. "I didn't want to kill her but she went crazy," she said, but nobody was listening.

I caught the flicker of movement out of the corner of my eye. Kyle MacMillan had used the distraction caused by the Wizard tending to his daughter's wounds to sneak around behind us. He was attacking Savannah from behind. Her back was exposed, she didn't see him.

I jumped. I remembered the way Savannah had jumped when she saved me from the camp and I tried to do the same. It wasn't one of her Kite-Stepping leaps, but it carried me across the six feet between us fast enough for me to bring my sword down on MacMillan's arm.

The sword fell with his hand still gripping it and he cried in pain. He fell back from Savannah, landing roughly on his back. I advanced toward him with my bloodied sword at the ready. He scrambled back from me. "I surrender," he said in a panic. "You win."

"I don't accept your surrender," I said.

I felt a hand on my wrist. I turned to look in to Savannah's face. "Not this time," she said. "There's been enough death for one day."

And I remembered the promises I'd made: to Brutus to end the cycle of vengeance, to the Wizard in Green to abstain from killing. I looked at MacMillan, bleeding on the ground, and then at Savannah. The pain was intolerable. I had a chance to make the world a cleaner place, a better place. A single sword stroke would be enough.

"He's done so much cruelty," I said, poised between broken oaths and a better world.

"Was he in the torture cells at the garrison?" Savannah asked.

"No, but—" I began.

"If you kill him, you aren't cutting the head off the snake. Some other bastard in Fredericton will take his place and go back to doing the exact same thing. Don't become what you hate. Let him live. He's beaten."

I dropped my sword.

The Wizard had his daughter up in his arms. His face was grey and drawn. "I will return to the west with my daughter. I don't expect you will try to stop us."

From the ground MacMillan said, "No, don't take her, I love her."

"With you, she almost died of violence twice." The Wizard spat on MacMillan and walked away, dignified to the end.

I noticed he didn't provide Kyle with anything to stop the bleeding from his stump.

"If you want to live," Savannah said to MacMillan, "you should see to that wound. I hope we never meet again."

She took my hand. "Come on, let's get our friends out of here." I nodded my head and we walked away, joining Boyd and Saul, uncle Stephen and Mr. Chamblais, and we left Kyle alone, bleeding, surrounded by the dead and the dying.

CHAPTER 59

Savannah

THE FLIGHT FROM THE university remains confused in my memory. I remember the Broken lurching out of the shadows of the night. Some were screaming, staggering around, grabbing their heads between their hands.

Others tore into their peers with savage violence; most ignored us. Those few who did not met Kieran's sword, or Mr. Chamblais'.

There was no sign of the Wizard in Green. Few men I'd ever seen moved faster than him, and I doubted his daughter would slow him down much. I supposed it was for the best. He was brilliant, and powerful, and entirely untrustworthy. Though he'd ultimately helped us more than he'd harmed us I was still a little glad to see the back of him. I couldn't help but feel a little uncomfortable leaving even somebody as cruel as Sophie to his questionable mercies.

"Let's get back to Kensington," Kieran said. Nobody argued with him, even Dave Boyd had a look of newfound respect in his eyes for Kieran.

I felt Paul Shatterfield's blood drying on my hands. It was sticky and the pressure under my fingernails was uncomfortable. I'd killed before to protect myself, because I had no choice, in the heat of the moment, but I'd never deliberately set out to remove somebody from the world before.

I felt shame.

Paul had been an evil man, and in his way had been so much madder than poor Old Saul. Still, he'd been Old Saul's brother, and, in a strange way, that made him feel like family to me. I knew I wouldn't sleep well tonight.

I spared a glance at Kieran, and thought about whether I'd go to him. I didn't want to sacrifice my freedom for any man, not even the handsome man with the serious eyes and grave way of speaking who Kieran had become.

I looked over at Dave Boyd, noble and powerful, a king twice fallen, a man who routinely cheated death. I could go back. Be his spy again. He might have promised to give up his throne, but after what had happened in this city, what he'd seen, he would still be a powerful man, if there were any powerful men after the Black Trillium finished freeing the city.

I wasn't Kieran's, I'd never really be, because a part of me would always be the Scorpion Girl, sharp-tongued and reckless in the face of threats. And when I thought about it I wasn't entirely the same anymore either. I'd been changed by Saul Shatterfield, and I'd killed. I'd killed too much and I wasn't entirely sure how to square that with myself.

I still wanted the open sky, the open road beckoned. I wanted to leave Trana.

We fought our way out of the university as the army of the Broken tore itself apart. Some of the men we saw fighting and fleeing fought in organized groups, not unlike our little cluster. Some of them had swords and spears.

It looked like Kyle MacMillan and Mr. Chamblais were not the only prisoners taken by the Broken army at the second Battle of Trana.

At least a remnant remained of the Confederation army. A few Black Trillium members had survived as well, from the looks of things. Neither side was particularly concerned with fighting each other anymore, not with the Broken rampaging around the university.

A few Black Trillium members rallied around us when they saw Kieran, his uncle Stephen and Mr. Chamblais in our group. By the time we left the university we were at the center of an honour guard of fifty men and women.

We wouldn't all fit in Kieran's yard.

So we went to the Kensington Square instead.

I remembered the place. It was where I'd met Kieran the first time, more than a year ago, a spoiled merchant boy celebrating his first taste of adulthood. Of course I'd been a refugee girl running from everything, hiding at the roof of the world, back then. It was a wonder, the difference a year made.

"My friends," Kieran's uncle shouted to the assembled masses. "We have overcome a terrible threat today, but the fight is not over."

The square fell silent. Fifty Black Trillium members, many apparently strangers to the others, crowded into the concrete bowl of the now-empty pond that sat in the middle of the park. They all wanted to crane their necks, to look at the people who'd shattered the army of the Broken.

"Kyle MacMillan is a ruined man and his army is scattered," uncle Stephen continued, "but Fredericton remains.

"For now Trana is free, but that freedom came at a heavy price. The Black

Trillium cannot advance into the east yet, not until we have rebuilt our own city, fortified it, galvanized the people for the next invasion.

"Do not doubt that an invasion is coming.

"Furthermore, the Broken are still a threat. They are multitudinous and they are no longer bound. Expect Broken attacks to become an increasing concern."

"But there's a cure," I said. "Couldn't we..."

Old Saul wasn't doing well at all. It had been all he could manage to muster the courage to come for us. Confronting his brother would have been bad enough, even without the beating he sustained on top of it. Any lesser man would have died from the wounds he sustained fighting Paul.

Still he managed to hiss out, "It won't work that way." I dropped the subject.

"We can try to find a cure," uncle Stephen said. "But that is a long-term goal. In the meantime we have to be prepared."

The meeting fell into logistical issues from there and I glazed over, too tired to pay any attention.

In the end I did go to Kieran's bed, but we just slept.

The next morning, we woke up, and I went to attend to Old Saul. He had survived the night and was out of the worst of the danger physically, but he was still far from well. The guilt he felt, the pain, I could barely imagine how it would have felt, and it was nearly more than I could bear.

As I dressed his wounds, I asked him, "Why won't the Five Venoms toxin work on the Broken? Why can't we cure them?"

Old Saul closed his eyes and sighed. "I've wished it were otherwise for so long. But it won't work. The dose Saul Shatterfield took, before the fire took him, was almost a lethal one, and he'd not become Defiled yet. The drug that makes the Defiled takes time to work. During that first time the damage is easier to fix.

"No, Saul Shatterfield's research was clear. Any dose of Five Venoms toxin strong enough to cure one of the Defiled would kill them as surely as a sword."

"Couldn't you..." I wanted to ask him to continue the research, but he shook his head.

"Saul Shatterfield died in that fire, you know I can never be him again. I'm just Old Saul, just a broken old man. But, thanks to you, maybe a little less broken than I was."

I couldn't help but cry a little then.

Kieran came in, and saw the tears running down my cheek. "Hey, is everything alright?"

"Yes." I wiped at my eyes with the back of my hand. "We're alright."

"I just wanted to tell you," Kieran said. "You got a letter." He was holding an envelope of beautiful emerald green paper between his fingers. He passed it to me and I opened it.

Savannah,

As I write these lines I am sitting in the place where the Confederation army once camped. It appears that Kyle MacMillan was not fool enough to cross me. He has left your city.

I am sorry to say that my daughter bears no love for you. I know you could have killed her, I know you spared her because I asked it, as a friend, and as a friend you complied, but she sees things differently.

I am taking her back to Seattle, and I don't believe she will ever bother you again, but I wanted to send you this letter, as a sign of good faith and an indication of the friendship which continues between us.

I told you once that your sword was one of two I crafted. This is true. I also told you that the second was mine, and this is also true. But there was a third sword.

After watching how you comported yourself in the university, how you responded to the truth of the Broken, I have decided to entrust you with a secret.

I hid two swords at the edges of this world. The sword you carry was hidden in the far north, the other in the far south, in the lands now called the Yucatan.

The second sword ended up in the possession of a wandering hero named Miguel Jesus Arroyo y Lopez, and he died in Quebec City. I believe he taught Monsieur Chamblais in the days before the city fell. The sword was lost when the city fell. It would be wise for you to seek the other sword. It is a test, and an opportunity.

Do not come to Seattle, I suspect you would not receive a warm welcome, but I do hope our paths cross again in the future.

D of S

I passed the letter to Kieran, who said, "Lopez was Mr. Chamblais' first master. He was killed by the MacMillans during the raid on Quebec City."

"I want to go there," I said. "The Wizard in Green wouldn't have sent this to me if he didn't want me to look for it."

"What if it's a trap? You did almost kill his daughter."

"I still need to go."

"Then I'm coming with you," Kieran said, strong jaw set, serious blue eyes sharp.

"What about leading Trana against the Broken, rebuilding the city?"

"Don't you remember? The Black Trillium are anarchists." Kieran grinned, a hint of a joke around the edges of something serious. "Our elders might make an attempt to lead, but I have no taste for ruling others. I never wanted that."

I supposed that would do. I nodded my head and thought that maybe freedom wouldn't be so bad shared with another.

CHAPTER 60

Kyle

MY HAND HURT. I didn't know how that could be possible. It was gone, dead flesh rotting on the floor of that stinking university in Trana. My soldiers found me trying to escape the grounds. I was sick from pain, unable to fight. The sword felt uncomfortable in my off hand. I'd found my crown. It was resting on that bastard's throne.

I wanted revenge.

My army was devastated. Of the two thousand men my father and I brought to Trana, more than a quarter were dead. Another quarter deserted, and a quarter were too wounded to fight, or even to travel quickly.

My army of two thousand had become an army of five hundred, protecting five hundred injured men. I'd also lost more than half my horses.

I couldn't stay in Trana.

I didn't know how much of the Black Trillium survived. I never did discover their numbers, but I did know that the city was infested with the Broken.

Now that Paul Shatterfield was dead, hopefully the whole damn place would be overrun by them. It would be a fitting fate for Trana to fall to the savage beasts, having forsaken the civilizing influence of the Confederation.

I was still monarch. I had the crown, and if my army was reduced, I still had it. They understood how rule passed in the MacMillan family; I faced two assassination attempts from minor cousins in the first two nights. I made examples of both, crucified them. Even wounded, there wasn't a man in the army who was my match.

My father had always clung to power. He'd not lightly given command to my brothers or to me. After that my army settled down. The thousand men who remained in Fredericton were loyal to the crown. They'd follow me, even if I returned with a broken army.

I could always blame my father. After all, he had taken personal command quite publicly before his untimely demise. The wise officers who remained would know to follow my lead. They would, or the crows would feast.

I thought of everything I'd lost, everything that had been cut away from me. Oswald, Marc, Brutus, Sophie, even my own sword hand. All my weakness, all my uncertainty, all my need to depend on others had been cut away with it.

I had been a raw blade, put through the forge of loss, and tempered into a keen weapon. Kieran and Savannah, the names burned like a beacon in my mind; my enemies, my makers. These two had taken everything from me.

Revenge would be sweet. But it wouldn't be today.

"Majesty," said Colonel MacPherson. I'd thought the wild-man Jean had killed him, however he'd survived. He lost an eye, and half of his nose, to the blade of the Trillium master, but he'd had the good sense to play dead until the battle passed. When he was safe he'd shown the even better sense to organize the survivors, to make their way back to the camp at the Scar. "We are coming up on Quebec City, do you want to camp here?"

"No. If I could I'd put the whole place to the torch a second time, though I doubt there is enough wood left to burn."

"Do you know what you will do when you return to Fredericton, sire?"

I nodded.

My father was too fearful of the Southlanders. He'd stalled our western advance in his haste to guard Fredericton. I would change that policy. We would retake Trana someday. But first we would capture 'Toba and the Western Heartland. Once, the Confederation had stretched from the Atlantic to the Pacific. It had been one of the largest nations in the world before the Great Collapse.

I swore, by the fire I felt in my missing hand, by the pain and loss and grief in my heart, that I would rebuild it. I felt the drumbeat of armies marching, heard the screams of the dying. I felt the glory of the conqueror flowing through my veins and knew that it was good.

I would become the greatest monarch of the MacMillan line. I would be the heir my grandfather, the conqueror, deserved.

And then I would have my vengeance on all those who had wronged me.

"We will take command of the army. We will rein in my brothers, and then, Colonel MacPherson, the Confederation will go to war."

"What of the Southlanders, Majesty?" MacPherson asked.

"My father may have jumped at shadows in the south, but I am made of sterner stuff. The greatest threat to the Confederation lies to the west, and we will not be able to face it from behind the walls of Fredericton."

MacPherson's one eye was fixed in a look of determination. "What of Trana?"

"Trana will fall in time," I said. "Let the Black Trillium be taxed fighting the Broken. When they have exhausted themselves we will retake that city as easily as holding out our hands."

Yes, Trana would fall in time.

"Let's ride on," I said. "I am anxious to return to Fredericton."

MacPherson saluted.

I kicked my horse's flanks and smiled to myself. The sun was rising over my home, and as inevitable as the sun I would rise.

About the Author

   Simon McNeil is an author and online marketing communications specialist with a major educational institution. He is a life-long martial artist, has published several articles in *Kung Fu Magazine* and he's probably a little bit too fond of kung-fu movies. He lives in Toronto, Canada with his wife, daughter and their fierce protector Oliver the shih-poo. His wife has happily laid out rules to prevent the sword-through-glass-lampshade incident from ever happening again. *The Black Trillium* is his first novel.